Burning Nostalgia

M J Freegard

Pen Press

First published in Great Britain by Pen Press

All paper used in the printing of this book has been made from wood grown in managed, sustainable forests.

ISBN13: 978-1-906710-56-9

Printed and bound in the UK
Pen Press is an imprint of Indepenpress Publishing Limited
25 Eastern Place
Brighton
BN2 1GJ

A catalogue record of this book is available from the British Library

Cover design by Jacqueline Abromeit

Acknowledgements

I would like to thank everyone at Indepenpress for their constant help and patience. Especially Linda Clarke for her perceptive and invaluable contribution at the editing process.

I would also like to thank Lynn Ashman for her insightful help and experience in the publishing world.

And of course, not forgetting Lucy and her red pen.

About the Author

M J Freegard lives with his partner Lucy and works in Oxfordshire. Having worked in the print and graphic design industry for the past twenty-years, redundancy has led him to pursue his ambition to publish his first novel, Burning Nostalgia. In his spare time he enjoys watching films, reading and trips to the south coast, where he can kick-back, people-watch and find inspiration.

For Lucy;
you're my beginning and my end,
and every wonder inbetween.

1

The muffled sounds of Mr and Mrs Dobbs making love come from the ceiling above. In the dull light of the room Philip Morgan lies captivated in a double bed. The tips of his fingers slip through his thinning hair breaking beads of sweat. His breathing is heavy and deep. He touches his mouth and the scent of tobacco drifts to his lungs.

He fidgets, trampling his trousers to his ankles. Slowly his hand moves from his mouth, trekking over his chin and sinking under the duvet, taking in the shallow dips and curves of his thin figure. It then climbs up his swollen stomach, his fingers sliding between his belly and the duvet. The landlords at The Royal Oak and The Ship Inn have been his trainers, his life gurus. Always in his corner with an ever-ready ping from the cash till, helping him to maintain his inflated beer-belly and pickling him to keep up a youthful appearance. The ceiling fades and Mrs Dobbs greets him, her pale naked body bearing down on him. A breath lodges in his throat. 'Lydia …' he whispers her name, it hangs in the air, enchanting and powerful.

He wants to understand how things are connected. To make sense of how he fits into the world. That's why he finds comfort in fate, all worked out, set in stone, written in black and white. He can't deny it, this is how it's supposed to be. It has to be. He holds the idea tight, things don't happen by chance. There's something that binds people, no matter the distance or how much time has passed. If life is predetermined then he has a purpose and he can be free, free from himself. Tears blur his view. He can sense the person he once was and the alarming distance he now stands from him.

Every nerve ending drops to its knees, pleading to be caressed by her. Her eyes are closed, mouth erotically open, cropped hair hiding part of her face. She sets free an encouraging noise dipped in animal pleasure. Helplessly he lies beneath her, wanting to be released from being alone. To be connected in the after glow of lovemaking. Letting himself be emotionally laid bare, surrendering to the need to become lost in someone else's eyes.

Voices and footsteps outside his door break into the illusion. The emptiness of the ceiling stares back unimpressed. He snatches the duvet and pulls it tight to him. The fire door retracts and the voices fade along with the footsteps. The chest of drawers standing by the wardrobe, the kettle and the two cups on the tray, the blank screen of the TV held on a wall bracket, are all waiting for their purpose, a duty to be filled. Philip shuts his eyes, yearning to be somewhere else away from the guesthouse, away from every baited memory. He lets out a sigh. Even if he could go he'd always have to take himself. He shudders at the thought.

A few guests drift into the dining room, happily heading towards their designated tables. The room's colour scheme is blue and yellow, provoking images of sun-kissed sand and warm seas. Part of the room is divided into a communal lounge, a large three-piece sofa marking out its territory. Tucked in the corner is a small bar with bottles of spirits hanging drained, sapped of their charms. The focal point of the lounge is a large wide-screen TV. Sky news is in full throttle, images and text passing each other in a media spaghetti junction, the volume turned down to a stifled murmur. Paintings and photographs of Salmouth Bay and its nearby harbour are scattered over the walls, alongside a few old family pictures shaping a homely feel.

Another, "Good morning" breaks the surface of tapping cutlery. A young couple are at the cereal bar. On a side cabinet pushed up against the back of the sofa, an arrangement of cereals from Bran Flakes to Coco Pops line up in a world of miniature. The girl playfully jabs her boyfriend in the ribs breaking the flow of Corn Flakes to his bowl.

'Cheeky,' he says.

She cuddles in tight excluding everyone in the room.

'But you love me,' she says, leaning across the cereal bar tormenting him with a sexy wiggle of her bottom.

'Emma!' he says embarrassed. Nobody notices but his blush takes time to drain.

She enjoys his response and squeezes his hand. A few of the guests are coming to the finishing line, chasing and soaking up egg yoke and the odd bean from around their plates, armed with a piece of toast or fried bread.

The Bay View's head waitress, in fact their only waitress, Ellie Morrel, weaves in between the tables holding a pile of used plates. She's wearing a uniform two sizes too small for her and is the only one in the room who can't see this. Mr and Mrs Dobbs are at table 5 near the bay window. It looks out onto a narrow pavement, cars parked bumper to bumper in every parking space on the far side, while people stroll along the esplanade that runs along the bay to the harbour.

A couple of joggers pass by, competitive spirit on their faces. A middle-aged couple in his and hers matching raincoats sit with a Jack Russell on a bright blue and white Victorian style bench, staring past the white wooden changing huts, past the pebbled beach to the alluring sea held and calmed by the bay. A fishing boat heads to the harbour pursued by a flock of opportunistic seagulls. The weather's uncertain, it could be mid-afternoon by the time it makes up its mind what to do.

Mrs Dobbs watches her husband dissecting and eating his breakfast as if they were in a top class restaurant.

'Do you want that?' Mr Dobbs asks, pointing his knife at a half-eaten sausage and the remains of a rasher of bacon.

'No, be my guest,' she replies, pushing her plate towards him.

He harpoons them both and offloads them onto his plate. The restaurant facade fades.

She rolls her eyes at him and at the now regular conversation from table 1. "Have you been to …", "What you need to do is …" She notices the new guests opposite them on table 4 have become Mr Sutton's latest victims.

'… the battle of Portland Bill, Spanish Armada,' he says, mouth half-full of cereal, trying to get their full attention.

'George!' his wife says.

It's no use.

'First seen near Lizard Point. Hundred and twenty ships,' he says. 'Can you imagine that! One of the greatest invasion fleets in British history.'

The middle-aged couple look at one another, finding comfort in facing him together.

'They attacked Howard,' he says. 'Fiercest gun battle you can imagine.'

They look puzzled.

'Cousin to Queen Elizabeth!' he says, unimpressed but at the same time pleased at them not knowing.

Ellie walks by Mr Dobbs holding an order for table 7. Mrs Dobbs watches her husband looking at her. Ellie leans forward placing the two full English breakfasts on table 7, the seams of her skirt stretching to maximum capacity. A guest on table 3 flags her down as she retreats.

'Excuse me,' the woman says. 'The bacon, it still doesn't taste right.'

Her husband is long past caring, too occupied in scooping the last remains of tomato ketchup from his plate. Ellie reluctantly takes the plate from her and heads for the door.

'Like that do you?' Mrs Dobbs asks.

'Sorry?'

'I saw you looking.'

Mr Dobbs fidgets uncomfortably in his chair. 'Don't be so stupid.'

'You can tell me. Do you?'

'You should know me by now.'

'No surprises!' Mrs Dobbs says.

He shakes his head at her and pours himself a cup of coffee.

'Well?'

'Lydia, don't.'

'I was just having a bit of fun. You take me too seriously.'

Suddenly her mood changes. Gazing past her husband a look of unease casts a shadow across her face.

'Are you alright?' he asks. He turns around to see the owner of the Bay View guesthouse, Philip Morgan, approaching their table. Mr Dobbs nods, acknowledging him. Philip smiles timidly.

'I'm – er, sorry for the inconvenience,' Philip says, holding a tray displaying a carefully arranged breakfast.

'Don't worry,' Mr Dobbs says. 'Just one of those things. Is it sorted now?'

'Yes, well I've booked a plumber to come out,' Philip says, feeling Mrs Dobbs staring at him. 'Is the new room satisfactory?'

'Fine,' Mr Dobbs says.

'Good, good.' Philip nods, reversing away from them.

Mrs Dobbs shakes her head.

'Don't do that,' Mr Dobbs says.

'Do what?' she asks.

Philip approaches the cereal bar breaking the young couple's play; they move out of his way. Carefully he balances the tray on the cabinet. Everything on it has been cooked to perfection, the sausages succulent, flavour ready to burst out. The bacon wafts its seductive charms, eggs scrambled to just the right consistency, tomatoes sliced and cooked but still tender and firm, hash browns golden and crisp. It all fits in perfect harmony, optimising every inch of space. A rack of toast, a pot of butter, a cup of coffee and a newspaper wedged between the sugar bowl and the milk jug. He pours some Bran Flakes into a bowl, now it's complete.

Philip retraces his steps but veers off slightly to get as close as he can to Mrs Dobbs. Her body stiffens hearing him breathing behind her, feeling his eyes slipping through her clothes. She wants to hide, to sink into the fabric of the chair. She waits for Philip to pass, wishing he would hurry up.

'Teenagers,' Philip whispers. 'You were right, it couldn't last.'

The smell of his breath along with his words cling to her shoulder.

Casually he walks past her and out of the dining room.

Mrs Dobbs glares at her husband. 'Did you hear that?' she hisses, louder than she had intended.

The noise of the dining room is silenced, apart from Mr Sutton who is now telling the couple on table 4 that he can trace his ancestors right back to a chamber maid in Charles Howard's service. Everyone else is homing in on her outburst.

'Come on,' Mr Dobbs replies.

'Come on what?'

He looks around uneasily, unhooking the stares in his direction. 'He probably overheard what you were saying, that's all,' he says, his voice sinking to a murmur.

Mrs Dobbs shakes her head. 'Well I don't like him. He gives me the creeps.'

'Shhh,' Mr Dobbs says. Even table 1 is quiet now. 'What's the matter? He's just being friendly.'

'You're pathetic!' Mrs Dobbs says.

'What? Not used to my sort are you?'

'What's that supposed to mean?'

He turns away, realising he has overstepped the mark.

'That's it, do nothing,' Mrs Dobbs says. 'Typical, shouldn't expect anything else.' She lets out a deep sigh and turns away.

A plate slams down next to Ian Garret, nearly sending the sausages toppling to the floor instead of onto the two waiting plates.

'Christ, do you have to!'

Ellie ignores him. She puts a stack of finished plates down.

'That bitch is never satisfied. "*It's not cooked right. It doesn't taste right,*"' Ellie says, mimicking her. 'For fuck's sake, you're going to have to do them again.' She gives the plate a scornful glare.

'Alright,' Ian sighs. He puts the frying pan back on the cooker. 'I'll finish these off for table 6 first.'

'He won't do anything, will he?' Ellie says. 'God, this place!' She takes the stack of plates and drops them in the sink, letting them scrape and squeal against the contents of the overflowing bowl until they come to a halt.

'How are you supposed to dry up?' Ellie says, menacingly eyeing a large bouquet of flowers laid smothering a bunch of chrysanthemums on the draining board.

'Don't worry,' Ian says. 'I'll sort it.'

Ellie goes to move them.

'Ellie, please.'

'What is he doing? We're not a bloody florists!'

'They're for his wife.'

'Why?' Ellie asks. 'What do you mean?'

'It's the anniversary Friday.'

Still she looks confused.

'When she died.'

'Why has he got them now? They'll be half-dead by the end of the week.'

'I don't know.'

'Isn't anything straightforward with him?' Ellie takes another scrutinizing look. 'Why has he got two lots?'

'Don't ask me,' Ian replies.

She lifts the bouquet of flowers wrapped in plastic and held together by a big red ribbon to get a better view of the bunch underneath. 'I bet he got her these first, tight bastard,' Ellie says, looking at the chrysanthemums. She lets the bouquet drop. 'Had a bit of a guilt trip I bet.'

'I don't know, Frances always liked chrysanthemums. She liked her flowers, but would have preferred them in the garden.'

'I bet we don't see much of him for the rest of the week.'

'Hey come on, leave him,' Ian says, throwing her a look.

'You've changed your tune. You're the one who's usually slagging him off.' She opens the cutlery drawer. 'I don't think I'll last the rest of the summer ...' She pauses. 'Oh, one English and a vegetarian. The young couple are down, she looks like she had a good time last night. Definite case of shagging hair!' She grins but then realises she doesn't want to be rummaging in the cutlery drawer. 'See, my mind's going.' She shuts the drawer and flicks on the kettle. 'I need lectures, some thought stimulation. It's no good for me here.'

'Yes, yes, Ellie.'

'What would you know?'

'Hey, there's no need for that. I've done my bit at college.'

'Sorry, I didn't mean to say it like that.'

He shakes his head and opens the freezer. 'What's up?'

She doesn't respond.

'Well?'

Again he's met by a wall of silence as he strolls back to the cooker.

'Come on. You can tell me, you know that.'

Ellie slumps against the worktop. 'I'm fed up. I can't stand another summer here.'

'September's not that far away ...' He pauses, seeing if he can anticipate her mood. It could go either way but it doesn't matter, especially how he's been feeling lately. He takes aim and fires. 'No man trouble?'

'No.' She cuts him dead with a scathing look, turns her back and opens a cupboard door.

'Hey, come on. What's got into you?'

'Nothing.' She crouches and takes another stainless steel teapot and a milk jug out of the cupboard.

'I was only mucking about.' He hadn't realised he had become so out of practice.

She places the teapot and milk jug on the worktop without acknowledging him.

'Sorry Ellie,' Ian says, unsure at what he's apologising for, but he doesn't know what else to say.

He turns on the gas, back left ring. There's not much choice, only two work properly and the ignition button is deteriorating. He told Philip but he worked around it, so it wasn't a problem any more, like everything else in the guesthouse, ran from day to day. But it's all falling apart, worn out and neglected. They'd only recently had a close call with a health inspector. How did Philip get away with it? What is he thinking, he knows exactly how he got away with it, it fell to him to spend the entire night cleaning the kitchen up. Let Ian do it, it'll be fine. He hears the gas hiss and plunges his finger hard against the button; it lets out feeble electric crackles.

9

'Come on you bloody thing!' A gush of flames grapple the air and the gas ignites under the frying pan. 'This thing can't last much longer.' He turns to Ellie for sympathy.

She blanks him.

He pours some oil in and watches it coating the pan. The bacon is almost done in the other frying pan. He drops in the veggie sausages, they sizzle and spit.

'What are you sorry for? Ellie asks.

'Whatever is upsetting you,' Ian replies.

The kettle roars in a gush of steam. Ellie pulls the lid off the tea jar, competing against the boiling kettle. She's too quick. She takes a few tea bags out and hovers over the teapots dropping them in just before the kettle clicks off and begins to subside.

'If you don't want to talk about it –' Ian says.

She pours the boiling water into the pots and places the stainless steel gang on the tray.

'I'm fine.'

Ian escorts the bacon onto the waiting plates and finishes off the order for table 1.

'Don't forget the sausages for table 9,' she says, and leaves the kitchen.

Ian watches the kitchen door close behind her, he rewinds their conversation wishing he knew what he said to upset her.

The fire door closes behind Philip, blocking the view of the dimly lit landing. In front of him in the small cul-de-sac are three doors leading to guestrooms. He approaches room 8 holding the breakfast tray rigid between one arm and his chest and takes out a key. He hesitates, concentrating on his thoughts, then opens the door and walks in.

He squints as sunlight glares at him. It ricochets turning the colour contrast up on the yellow walls and the blue duvet set on the double bed. The focal point of the room is a large open window letting the sun pour in, hand in hand with voices from the esplanade. Its glimmering white framework cascades to the floor hidden by a small round table and two chairs. Magnified ripples from the sea shuffle on the far wall and scatter over the ceiling.

Philip walks around the unmade bed, past the entrance to the en-suite. A TV peers from a corner aided by a wall bracket. The standard chest of drawers and a wardrobe with a full-length mirror are lined up against the far wall. He places the contents of the tray on the sunlit table; using the tray's layout as a guide, ritually he sets out the breakfast. He glances around expecting to see someone but the room is empty. A few minor adjustments to the cutlery then he flattens the newspaper some more, taking the spring out of it. He sits down on the opposite chair as if he's in a doctor's waiting room expecting his name to be called.

Dust floats in the strong light, the side of his face is heating up. He leans back in his chair, finding some shelter in the shadow of the flimsy blue curtains. The dust particles rise and fall. The waves gently break hypnotically in the bay soothing him, reaching out and whispering to him. A thin strain of smoke appears becoming thicker and thicker.

'Philip,' a man's voice says, breaking like a wave from outside.

It startles him.

From the other side of the table the features of Mr Cole appear from out of the smoke. He's a short stocky man, grey hair encasing a thick leathery tan. He may be in his sixties but the strength and self-belief in his eyes contradicts his age. He rolls up his sweatshirt sleeves and pulls his chair closer to the table, shuffling on the carpet in a pair of tartan slippers.

'Are you alright?' Mr Cole asks out of politeness, not really wanting an answer.

'Oh, sorry.' Philip rubs his hands over his face attempting to wake himself up.

Mr Cole ignores him, surveying the mouth-watering breakfast.

'I got you some Bran Flakes this time,' Philip says. 'I nearly forgot.'

'Wonderful, wonderful.' Mr Cole looks up at him. 'And the tomatoes, you didn't even forget them.' He takes the knife and fork. 'Can't let this go cold.'

Mr Cole attacks the breakfast with the appetite of a man on the brink of starvation.

'I'm fine. It's just …' Philip says. 'Well, this time of year …' He pauses. 'It's always a bit difficult, you know.'

'Now that was good.' Mr Cole wipes a hand across his mouth.

Philip stares in disbelief at the empty plate.

Mr Cole belches and pats his stomach as if it were his pet dog. 'Pardon me. That's better.'

The strong sunlight is abruptly sucked out of the room, replaced by an unsettling gloom as if the sun has been smothered.

Philip scans the bowls and plates, letting out a stunned shiver at the speed in which they were cleared and by the drop in temperature. Everything is gone, stripped down to the last morsel. Mr Cole stoops out of sight and conjures-up half a bottle of Martini; he places it on the table. Philip watches his every move. He merrily rummages in his jogging bottoms that have never seen the outside world let alone a training track, and pulls out a case of Café Crème cigars and a battered green plastic lighter. He swigs the remaining grapefruit juice, clearing the way for a good measure of Martini.

'I don't have to ask,' Mr Cole chuckles. 'Do I?'

'No thank you, not for me.'

'Of course not, Philip.'

'On the Martini now?'

Mr Cole laughs. 'Supplies are running low on the vodka.'

He swirls the Martini in the glass and downs the measure in one.

'Bit quiet today.' Philip nods over to the portable CD player with a stack of discs that look as if they're about to topple off the bedside table.

'Trouble is, they make me think,' Mr Cole says. 'And I don't want to.'

Philip doesn't know what to say.

'When Harry James or Glenn Miller's playing, as only they can, I think about the old days, the good old days. Well, I was young so they're going to be good for me.'

'You know, reminds me of –'

'Yes, your old man, same generation …' Mr Cole pauses. 'It's nice to get away from the here and now. Don't have to deal with anything. Memories, they don't leave you.' He leans forward. 'But why should they, why would you want them to?'

Philip feels uncomfortable.

Mr Cole lets out a sigh. 'That big band sound, you can't beat it,' he says. 'So what did you really want to say?'

'Nothing, it's just usually you have …'

Mr Cole gives him a knowing stare.

'I'm alright.'

'Sure, of course. You made me rush my breakfast for that!'

He opens the case of Café Crémes, its lid plastered in a government health warning, takes one of the cigars out and lovingly rolls it between his fingers.

'I forgot the ashtray.'

'I'll manage, as I said, things on your mind?'

'Well, er …' Philip feels himself wanting to explode, he's enraged and intimidated at how easily his thoughts can be read. 'Maybe I've got it all wrong.'

'See, no point in hiding anything.' Mr Cole leans back in his chair, lights the cigar and inhales deeply filling up his lungs.

'Don't start that again.'

Mr Cole blows out a puff of smoke and watches it hover as sunlight reclaims the room. 'What if it's not? This could be your second chance,' he says, grinning at him.

'You can't say that.'

'Don't play the innocent with me Philip. I know where you've been. You wanted to feel close to her, slipped into her bed.'

'No, no you're confusing me.'

'You know she's always wanted you, as soon as she came here.'

'Please, I've told you. How could she want me, she's married.'

'Just like old times.' Mr Cole's eyes are like surgical implements slicing him open butcher style, no anaesthetic. 'What are you doing Philip?' He taps the cigar on the edge of the cereal bowl.

Philip shifts in his chair.

'Philip?' Mr Cole's eyes narrow, boring deeper into him.

'Don't.'

'The flowers, I told you to leave it.'

'I know, I know,' Philip says, 'but –'

'We've been through this. See it for what it really was. Let it go, for Christ's sake Philip, let it go. Have you any idea what you are doing?'

Philip feels trapped, mouth dry, fingernails clenching the wooden chair.

Defeated, Mr Cole looks sombrely out onto the bay. 'Don't be like me.' He squints against the light then slowly turns back to him.

Philip has never seen him looking so old and fragile before, to the point where he can imagine him drying out and being taken by a single gust of wind. It makes him feel vulnerable to his very core.

'Regrets, if you're not careful they'll get you in the end.' Mr Cole sighs. 'They hide away waiting for the moment you're least expecting it. Can't hide from them, no matter what you do.'

'You couldn't have done any more.'

'People forget, they move on …' Mr Cole pauses. 'I'm not just talking about Judith.'

'I didn't think you were.'

'Look at me. Don't I go on.' Mr Cole smirks, knowing he's teetering on the edge of wanting to cry or smash everything in his reach, finding comfort in how many pieces it can be broken into.

The waves of the bay caress the respectful silence between them. The smoke from Mr Cole's cigar loses its erratic tremor. His breathing calms, linking to the sea's rhythm.

'Room 7 were arguing again,' he says. 'You should have heard him. Likes the sound of his own voice, that one. She's just as bad, slamming about, no respect for anybody else.' He inhales deep on his cigar and then deflates, releasing an exodus of smoke. 'His neighbours must be having a holiday. Bloody typical. Wretched kid too, but what do you expect with parents like that.'

'It's never easy,' Philip says.

'Who said it should be?' Mr Cole knocks a length of ash into the cereal bowl.

'Well at least they're together.'

'I don't think the kid would agree with you, eh Philip?' Mr Cole stares at him as if he has switched a flashlight onto his soul.

2

'Come on Ellie, this isn't like you,' Ian says.

'That's rich coming from you!' Ellie stretches on the bench digging deep to evict the tiredness from her body.

'What do you mean? I'm fine.'

'You sure?' she asks, turning away to the back garden of the guesthouse. Her eyes drift to the edge of the cracked patio, where four plastic flower tubs sit empty and worn by the weather, their white paint stained and blistered. Nature is claiming back the garden; weeds have come together in an uprising to overthrow the flowerbeds and lawn. Standing in the middle of all this forgotten neglect is a laburnum tree, all but a few of its delicate yellow flowers discarded to the floor and replaced by dried-out seedpods. Its branches stretch out wildly, obscuring part of a swing's rusty chains, swaying in a cool sea breeze.

'There's nothing the matter with me,' Ian says.

'Yeah right.'

Even the bench has got a little colder to his touch. 'Well...' he pauses.

'At last, we're getting somewhere.' Ellie takes a deep breath to calm herself or to at least take the edge off her shivering. 'You're the one who's always complaining about what little he does and how he's running this place into the ground. He never does anything, he's always upstairs with that, whatever his name is. Never even seen the bloke, keeps saying he'll, "Introduce us to him" but that he's going through a rough time of it at the moment. God, what a pair! I don't care if I don't meet him, no doubt he's as weird as he is.'

'I know,' Ian sighs.

'It's not right, making him his *special* breakfast, running errands for him. What about the rest of the guests? Hardly says anything to make them feel welcome or help them out. It's pathetic, he even runs away when the phone rings. What is his problem?' She turns to Ian waiting for him to respond.

'At least the big band music has quietened down a bit.' He half smiles as his mind wanders back through the years he has been at the Bay View. It never used to be like this, but Philip was hardly ever around then. He had his own business and left the running of the guesthouse to Frances; with her at the helm it ran like clockwork. He knew where he was, if anything went wrong he knew who to turn to.

He feels used up by the frustrating absurdity of the place. How did it get to this? Is it his fault, his personality? He's not like his dad, well maybe he is and that's why they always ended up arguing. But his dad wouldn't have got himself into this sort of predicament. He often wonders what it would have been like if he had become a mechanic like his dad and his older brother. The family garage is on the outskirts of Salmouth, a corrugated hut that rattles at the slightest breeze and feels like below freezing during the winter and a makeshift oven in the summer, but he was going to be different, he was determined to break the mould.

He'd enjoyed the catering course at the local technical college. He didn't complete it but not many did; not much of an excuse but one he's still standing by. Then job after job, from shelf-stacking to jewellery making and a side list of warehouse work. He'd temped too, it had suited him at the time. There were a few times when he could have given up and worked for the family business, but the thought of being there all day with his dad and living with him as well didn't bear thinking about.

If only he was like his brother. He's convinced that's what his father thought too. Married, two kids and a three-bedroom semi in Warnby miles from anywhere; one shop, a post office and that's your lot. And what is he doing, still suck up in his bedroom. That's it, nearly thirty and nothing to show for it apart from the accumulating junk in his room. Well come on, the entire DVD collection of *Buffy the Vampire Slayer*, *Star Trek* the original series and *Voyager* are hardly junk, but not much really to show for thirty years.

'He always finds it difficult this time of year,' Ian says with forced compassion. 'You know the anniversary of when she died is today.'

'Yes I know, you keep telling me, but that was three years ago! Don't you think it's about time he got over it?'

'You don't just *get over* something like that, Ellie!' Ian's taken aback by the venom in his voice.

'Alright, alright!' She slips off the bench onto the rectangular paving slabs of the patio. Most of them sit unevenly, stained by moss and cracked with battle scars from the weather as they join to the garden path leading to the back gate.

'He's better than he was,' Ian says.

'God, I dread to think what he was like before. No wonder what's-her-name left.' She kicks at the corner of a corroded paving slab seeing if she can get rid of some of her aggression.

'Katie,' Ian says, watching her.

'If it carries on like this I'll join her.' The corner breaks.

'Ellie, do you have to?'

She doesn't answer him but continues to brush the broken pieces of concrete to one side with her shoe; opening it up like a wound gives her some comfort.

'Suppose I better get on.' She sighs but persists to break up the corner of the slab.

The doorbell rings echoing through the hallway, piercing the soft hypnotic rhythms of the sea. It rings out again longer, with more determination; this time the kitchen door swings open and Ellie comes strutting out. Mrs Fuller stares impatiently through one of the dimpled glass panels of the day door. The guesthouse's front door is open throughout the day letting the public wander into its hallway, tiled with colourful seahorses and starfish creating a border between the striped blue wallpaper and the crisp white tiles. Behind her a large suitcase and its offspring clog up the entrance hall while Mr Fuller ponders and re-inspects the price list. He notices the leaflets in a plastic dispenser on the wall and takes one.

Ellie opens the inner door and smiles painfully.

'Mr and Mrs Fuller, I rang last Friday.' The words fire out of the woman's mouth.

Ellie nods, giving herself time to fathom out what Mrs Fuller has said.

'I have the letter,' Mrs Fuller says, 'the confirmation.'

'Yes, I'll get you your keys.' Ellie disappears back into the kitchen faster than she came out.

Mrs Fuller reaches for the large cumbersome suitcase but Mr Fuller intervenes.

'No, Mike,' she says. 'You know what the doctor told you.'

'Stop fussing!' He lifts the suitcase forcing his body between her and it and swaggers into the hallway.

'No I won't!' Disapprovingly she follows behind with the two smaller cases.

'Don't be silly,' Mr Fuller says, coming to a halt near the bottom of the stairs where the reception is.

'I was worried, that's all. Doctor Roberts said –'

'Yes, yes.'

Mr Fuller takes in the hallway while Mrs Fuller rummages in her shoulder bag for the confirmation of their booking. Opposite is a telephone attached to the wall, below it on a small side table are leaflets scattered haphazardly advertising places of interest, a selection of museums exhibiting everything from Egyptian mummies to dinosaurs to teddy bears. He hopes the weather will sort itself out so they can opt for sightseeing. He remembers visiting the museums last year, the disappointment is still with him, but what did he expect, the real thing? Tutenkhamun's real death mask, the official preserved artefacts from the depths of Egypt's most famous tombs? The Valley of the Kings shipped over to finally rest here in Dorset, so that there's something to do when it rains. You have to be amazed at what you can do with papier-mâché these days. As for the teddy bears, that was too surreal, a childhood nightmare. Mr Fuller's attention moves to Mrs Dobbs who's coming down the stairs. She's wearing a dress that's cut to accentuate her figure with Mr Dobbs trailing behind her. Mr Fuller turns back to the leaflets sensing his wife's sobering stare.

As if on cue Philip enters the hallway from the dining room. Mrs Dobbs stops, her body becoming rigid as her muscles involuntarily tense. She glares at Philip, taking in his every movement. He stops and smiles, ignoring Mr and Mrs Fuller.

Mr Dobbs places a hand on his wife's shoulder. 'Lydia!' he says, jolting her out of her trance state. 'Are you alright?'

Disregarding his concern she pulls her shoulder bag close; it offers her no protection but she finds more reassurance from it than from her husband. She knows he loves her but it isn't the sort of love she's used to. He dotes on her.

It's difficult, she isn't used to holding the reigns in a relationship. Maybe that's it, it's all too easy and that's one thing her previous relationships have never been, but she always felt safe and protected, she never felt alone, fighting by herself. It seemed absurd; was she more free when she was in a cage?

Philip loiters at the bottom of the stairs waiting for them to come down. She can't believe it. What does he want? It's no good, she'll have to pass him. There are only half a dozen steps but they appear to be more. She acknowledges Mrs Fuller with a brief smile and focuses on the day door, blocking out Philip, erasing him from the equation.

As she walks past him the smell of stale alcohol and perspiration sedated by a cheap cologne violate her nose.

'Everything alright?' Philip asks.

She turns around but to her surprise he's standing next to Mr Dobbs at the bottom of the stairs.

'Going to have a look at the Durdle Door,' Mr Dobbs replies.

'They said it's going to be nice today,' Philip says.

'If you like the drizzle.'

Philip ignores him.

'Is it all fixed now?' Mr Dobbs asks.

'Sorry?'

'The plumbing.'

Philip hesitates; he can feel somebody behind him listening in on his every word.

'Here you are,' Ellie says, bursting into life, handing Mrs Fuller the keys.

'Thank you,' Mrs Fuller says. 'Do you want the letter?'

Ellie smiles blankly.

'Is it all fixed now?' Mr Dobbs asks again.

Mrs Fuller waits poised for Ellie to answer her but she's too occupied waiting on Philip's reply.

'Yes, all fixed,' Philip says hastily. 'Nothing to worry about.'

Ellie gives him a disapproving look.

'The letter, dear,' Mrs Fuller says.

Ellie doesn't notice the letter she's waving in front of her like a bottle of smelling salts.

'Oh, sorry.' Ellie takes it from her.

Mr Dobbs smiles over to his wife but she turns her back on him. He breaks the small talk with Philip and wanders over to her. She yanks open the door and hurries along the barrel of the entrance hall and out into the fresh air. Mr Dobbs follows, wishing he could fathom out what's the matter with her.

Mr Fuller surveys the rising staircase then looks back to their luggage. Philip slips ninja-like back into the dining room leaving Ellie to cope. Mr Fuller turns to Ellie; she knows in an instant Philip has disappeared. How can he just leave her here, she shouldn't be surprised, what else does she expect? Her growing contempt for him circulates through her veins making her feel uneasy in her own skin. She never thought she could have so much anger for another human being.

'Would you mind, love?' Mrs Fuller asks, nodding in the direction of her husband. 'Could you give him a hand? He's on tablets from the doctor, though he won't admit to it.'

Reluctantly Ellie takes hold of the large suitcase, letting out a defeated sigh.

'What room is it?' Mrs Fuller asks, gathering the small suitcases to her.

'Room 9.'

'How far is that?' Mr Fuller asks dispiritedly.

'Third floor,' Ellie replies, scornfully glancing at the dining room door as it slowly closes.

The telephone springs to life. Philip peers out of the dining room and up the stairs; he can hear Ellie with Mr and Mrs Fuller struggling as they mount the second flight. He walks over to the telephone, a strange fear grows in the bowels of his stomach. He lets it ring, waiting for the appropriate moment to pick it up.

Mr and Mrs Weston make their way down the stairs, their faces determined to defy the British weather. They are grappling two inadequate hessian bags packed tight to the brim. Brightly coloured beach towels and strange shapes protrude in every conceivable direction; the bag's lifespan could come to an end at any moment. The weather girl had said, "heavy showers" but what does she know, what do any of them know?

'Morning,' Mr Weston says.

Philip ignores him and continues to stare at the phone like a frog eyeing a fly. He strikes at the receiver. Mrs Weston walks unevenly carrying her bag to the door; she glances unimpressed at Philip.

'Bay View guesthouse,' Philip says, 'how –'

'Dad?' Michelle says. The word shoots out of the telephone and cuts into his mini-repertoire.

Mr Weston slips a few leaflets of local interest into the pocket of his shorts, giving him a comfortable back-up plan.

'Yes,' Philip says, turning his back on Mr Weston. His voice sinks in volume, not wanting anyone to pry.

'I can't make it today,' Michelle says. 'It'll have to be tomorrow. I'm so sorry.'

He feels dizzy, he had dreaded her not coming, she has to be here. He repeats the sentence over and over in his mind.

'It's Adrian,' Michelle says. 'He's got the flu, you know how you men get.'

He doesn't say anything but looks at the receiver blankly, hearing the day door click shut behind him.

'Dad,' Michelle says, 'are you still there?'

'Please.' Philip clenches the receiver tight, pushing it hard against the side of his face. 'You promised, Michelle, you promised. We'll take the flowers, that's what you said.'

'I know, I'm sorry. If it's not work it always seems to be something else. I'll be there tomorrow.'

'Tomorrow!'

Feebly he puts the receiver back, hearing his daughter's voice become more and more distant and then silent as the receiver snaps back into place.

Philip wanders over to the kitchen sink and stares at the pile of plates. He needs Michelle here where she belongs. He wishes she'd never met Adrian. Why did she have to go away with him? He never liked him, always had an answer for everything. All talk. He knew the type – big ideas, has to be better than anybody else. Run his own business, who's he kidding? He'll never leave that firm. He's supposed to do the accounts for the guesthouse but he always manages to come up with an excuse not to. He knows the real reason, not enough money in it for him.

Philip lifts the bouquet off the flattened bunch of chrysanthemums. He stares at them on the draining board, hearing the plastic wrapping of the bouquet crinkling in his grip. He touches them, their delicate white petals stroke and caress his fingertips. He takes a large vase from the cupboard, fills it with water and places them both in it. They sit uncomfortable next to one another, the chrysanthemums' pure beauty lost to the over-pout of the bouquet. He looks out into the garden. The rusty frame of the swing creaks; the breeze disturbs the laburnum tree shaking the last remaining blossom to the floor. The clouds are rinsing out a shower but the sun still manages to shine. Suddenly the back door opens, Ian bursts in and shakes himself down.

'Didn't expect that,' he says.

Philip smiles and turns back to the view of the garden.

The sound of the vacuum cleaner moving sluggishly under one of the dining room tables competes against Sky News. Dramatic scenes of a captured British journalist in Iraq held by an extremist group fill the screen. The video footage shows the man on his knees, a cloth bag over his head. Philip sits watching the TV on a dining room chair, propelling the vacuum cleaner back and forth. Ellie is giving the knives and forks the once over and placing them back on the tables, constantly throwing him evil glares. He switches the vacuum cleaner off and slumps back on the chair as if exhausted by all his effort. Ellie shakes her head and looks intensely at Ian, who is refilling the optics in the bar. Annoyed at her frustration, she picks up her duster and walks out, releasing some of her aggression by slamming the door as hard as she can behind her. Philip jolts up, dragged out of his daydream.

'What was that?'

'Ellie,' Ian replies. He quizzes himself for the right definition but fails. 'She's a bit stressed out.' He gives up the search for more vodka and wanders from the bar.

'Oh, seems fine to me. Do you think I should talk to her?'

Ian pulls up a chair and sits down. 'I should leave it.'

'You sure?'

'She's a bit on edge at the moment.'

'Not that Dean again.' Philip shakes his head. 'Is that his name? I don't know, can't keep up with her.'

'You don't have to tell me. Always something or someone,' Ian mutters; suddenly he feels ashamed at saying it. But what else can he say?

He can't tell him, *She hates you. She loathes you being here, loathes every wasted breath you summon up, your sheer gutless incompetence and complete lack of responsibility. How can she have any respect for you, for this place when even you don't?* How can he come out and say that to him. In his mind he can, but sitting right next to him, seeing him looking so vulnerable, a mere shadow of his former self, it would be like kicking a wounded dog.

The memories of how he used to be now seem as if they are attached to someone else. They don't fit to Philip any more, no matter how hard he tries. So where is he? Where is the man who had a cheeky glint in his eye that always shone strongest when encouraged by a drink or two. He'd always had the knack of making Ian smile. The stories he would come out with, most of then revolving around buying and selling porn videos. He had it set up in his darkroom where his small business produced film for making lithographic plates for the print industry. Or his other favourite topic of conversation, the women he had known before Frances and the odd mistake or two during, and that slush fund he had accumulated from gambling on the horses.

He had a theory on gambling; he had it all worked out. You could never lose, that's what he told him. The only problem was it required betting large amounts of money. Ian had never quite worked it out but it was on the lines of putting money on every horse, or something like that, but what he did remember is the warm glow he had when Philip was telling him all this. They would either sit at the kitchen table or out on the patio in the back garden on one of those long summer evenings. A couple of bottles of wine, the cheapest they could find, it became a bit of a competition. He didn't know how he did it, but Philip always had a habit of winning. He'd drive miles to find the cheapest bottle, some of it barely drinkable, but that was all part of the fun. They would kick back and revel in their friendship, them against the world. Opening up issues in politics, history, music, the subjects fed into one another then simmered as they put solutions to all life's problems, until they dissolved into the wine along with the evening.

There were so many times he'd stayed overnight at the guesthouse. He always liked it when one of the top rooms were vacant and he could lay there listening out for Michelle to come back from a night on the town. Hearing her giggling drunkenly up the stairs, the sliding of drawers, the squeak of bed springs, her muttering to herself. Then that beautiful silence as the night came back and she fell asleep. So near and yet so far. Other times he would sit with Michelle, Philip would have done one of his disappearing tricks to The Ship, the off-licence or who knows where. Some things never change. They would just talk. He can't remember what they ever did talk about, it didn't matter, he just loved being there with her, listening to the tone of her voice, pretending they were the only two people in the world.

Those days were gone. Michelle's now living with Adrian and Frances had died of breast cancer. It was strange but he could still sense Frances' presence sometimes, it was a nice, comforting feeling. And as for him, he couldn't help hating himself for still being there. He looks at Philip, his body language is in complete contrast to his old self. He's scrunched up, cagey like he hasn't slept for days. Ian feels uneasy, he hates to admit it but all he can do is view him with a frustrated disdain.

'Too many choices,' Philip says. 'Always feel like you're missing out on something.'

'I miss our chats,' Ian says, not knowing how to respond to Philip's random remark.

'Yeah?' he says, taken aback.

'We haven't just talked since …' He feels uncomfortable saying Frances, he's unsure how he'll react to her name, '… you know.' He looks around the room sucking in memories. 'Had some great times here. Remember the parties she used to throw, and what about the *doctor*?'

Philip's face lights up as if he's coming back to life. 'God, like yesterday. She certainly loved her parties, any excuse to get all the guesthouse owners together. She always put on a good spread.' He grins even deeper. 'And the doctor.' He shakes his head. 'You don't think I could forget about him, do you?'

'You wouldn't have believed it,' Ian says.

'They're a strange breed.' The glimmer of a glint is back in Philip's eyes.

'The Scots?'

'Oh no, I was going to say doctors. But now you mention it!' Philip laughs.

'I would have loved to have seen Frances' face.' Her name slips from Ian's lips and flies around the room. He looks at Philip, hoping he hasn't broken the illusion.

'It took a long time for her to see the funny side of it,' Philip says. 'But then she was the one who cleaned most of it up. Should have seen the state of the room.'

'Was the wedding the next day?' Ian knows it wasn't, he knows the story inside out but he's determined not to lose the old Philip. The thoughts of those evenings come back to him; he had forgotten how much he missed his company.

'No, no,' Philip says with a wink. 'They were down here for the stag do. He paid up, Frances sent him the bill for the damages and he added a little bit extra. The mess in that room goes without saying.'

'I think his stomach must have packed up,' Ian says.

'That's it, that's what happened. Along with his arse!'

They both burst into laughter.

'Oh, God,' Ian says. 'What a mixture!'

'He must have shat himself in the night.' Philip's eyes are watering. 'Got up still drunk and wandered around trying to find the light switch. That would make sense of all the smear marks on the walls.'

'And then he puked,' Ian says. 'Jesus, did he puke. I shouldn't laugh – poor bloke. What a state to get yourself into. How did he explain that one?'

'He didn't, but he apologised for the mess of the room and handed Frances his telephone number and an address for us to send him the bill.' They giggle like school children connecting as the moment slips away.

Ian gathers his thoughts, he doesn't want to but he has to break the mood.

'Philip,' he says, 'I know it's difficult for you at the moment.'

'Sorry?' Philip says. 'I, er —'

'Frances …' Ian says. 'You know, today.'

'Yes, well.' The glint in his eye fades out of sight. He shifts, troubled in his chair.

'Are you going to be alright? I know how you suffered last year.'

'Of course I am.' Philip turns away, embarrassed. 'Bit lost that's all.' He forces a smile but it quickly withers away. 'Still can't get rid of her belongings.'

'Takes time, some things you need to hold on to.'

'You sound like Michelle; I should throw everything out, start afresh.' He stands up, avoiding Ian's concern. 'I need to get some air.'

'Sure.' Ian's shocked by Philip's abruptness as he scurries out of the dining room.

Philip walks out of the Bay View; it sits in a row of Edwardian terraces all converted into guesthouses. It appears a little weary, worn around the edges compared to the others. The outside could do with a fresh coat of paint, the canopy's faded to a light blue, you can just make out *Bay View* in yellow scripture. Internal rot is blistering the paintwork of the window frames, slates are missing off the roof, grinning like a set of neglected teeth. Colourful hanging baskets sway along the length of the terraces to a chilly sea breeze. He stops momentarily, surprised at the change in the weather. Typical! He plants his hands firmly in his pockets, determined not to return to the guesthouse for a jacket.

The esplanade runs along the front of Salmouth then curves round into the mouth of the harbour. Its centrepiece is the maritime memorial, a modern sculpture created to remember all those who would not return to their loved ones. A seagull perches on an anchor, wings outstretched, ready to carry their souls to heaven. The rest of the front has a strong Edwardian style; it's everything you'd expect from an English seaside town. Postcard paint selections of blue and white paid for by the local council to spruce it up and cover over its inadequate funding, striving to hold on to its glorious past, but like most seaside towns, beneath its surface it's already sliding into decline.

On the pebble beach heading for the harbour, yellow pedalos huddle waiting for the sun to come out. Famous names are painted on them from TV and film from *Alcatraz* to *Zebedee*. Colourful lights run along the esplanade linking up the old converted gaslights. The overwhelming smell of seaweed drifts in the air, seagulls are scattered everywhere ready to swoop down on anything edible like the council's very own litter police, while some have opted for the more natural diet on the shore's edge, racing in and out to the rhythm of the tide.

Philip passes a defiant sun-kissed couple lying on the beach; they won't be dictated to by the weather in their matching black swimwear. He takes the underpass before the memorial. The faint smell of beer lingers in the tunnel, footsteps echo, people's voices become louder until he emerges out onto the other side. He walks past a row of souvenir shops, their goods sprawling out onto the pavement. Spinning racks of cheap sunglasses and all manner of amusing hats, postcards of Dorset's attractions; the Durdle Door, Portland Bill lighthouse, Lulworth Cove. They're all spectacular, captured in a way he's never seen them before and never will. And, of course, there are the classic cartoons dipped in innuendo, if he squints hard enough he can see the cast of the *Carry On* films, Sid James and Barbara Windsor at their finest.

30

He walks on. The bright flashing lights and the pumping bass of the amusement arcades catch the senses of anyone who passes by. A couple of youngsters encourage their dad to win a cuddly toy. The claw has it in its grip, dragging it to the top of the sealed transparent box. It jolts, moving across to drop it down the chute but it falls away agonisingly close. They look helpless at one another until Dad puts his hand back in his pocket and finds some more change. Next to the amusement arcade is the friendly but dishevelled Crown Tearooms, Philip slips into its open doorway and sighs with relief, one of the tables next to the window is free.

Mesmerised, Philip watches holidaymakers bumbling along the esplanade, their eyes always glancing upwards, willing the sun to break free now the cloud has thinned out. He's uncertain how long he's been sat there; it could be five minutes, maybe ten. What does it matter? He stirs his tea, a half-eaten slice of carrot cake lays broken and mauled on a plate. It's so different when the sun shines. The town breathes differently, connecting in time to the mood of the bay. With the sky mirrored in the sea it can unhook the rush of travelling from A to B, people hold up time and appreciate it more.

He loves sitting watching people, seeing how they react to one another. It's like a puzzle that can never be completed. Have they been arguing? Is he hiding something from her, her from him? Are they in love? Will it last, or has it through some traumatic experience? He loves looking at families, there's something so enchanting at how they respond to one another. Guessing how the mum and dad had met. When they first kissed, the first time they touched each other. How did it make them feel? When they made love and held each other, could they see themselves where they are now?

It's all different now; well, he presumes so. Terrestrial and satellite TV told him and the newspapers blurted it out, it even contaminates some of the broad sheets. Sex, it's all about sex. How much are you getting? Are you getting enough? Haven't you done this; missionary, doggy, spit roast. It's all detached, marooned and afraid of feeling something, anything. Is this how it's supposed to be? Is this progress? No emotions, no way of getting hurt.

He would rather put his own storyline to their relationships. Romantic fairytale meetings where everything falls into place, music all around them to heighten the mood, lit by the moon in all its splendour. It makes him smile and brightens his day. Or perhaps a dramatic crusade, he's always liked them. Battling the elements, to reach their true love, down cliff faces and over mountains, crossing obstacles of wonder and danger and at the end of it all capturing her love and seeing a future full of happiness together, a family.

A murmur places him back in the cafe.

'…What's her face again. I'll swing for her,' Mr Cole says. 'It's ridiculous.' He stares despondently into his coffee.

'June Whitfield again?' Philip asks.

'No, no,' Mr Cole replies. 'None of them have got any manners …' He pauses. 'Mind you, needs must. Always know where you are with a prostitute, hey?'

Philip glares at him. 'Stop that!'

'Whitfield, is that what you said?'

Philip nods, his anger subsiding.

'Bloody fear mongers, all of them, daytime TV, I don't know. It's this bloody country, they've got to try and get you every step of the way.' He jabs the air with his spoon. 'Bleed every last drop from you. You can't win, bureaucrats the lot of them.'

'You are cranky today.'

'Sometimes.' He shakes his head. 'How did I get here, to this! Sorry, you're the last person I have to tell it to.' A smile holds on his face but quickly disappears. 'Everything changes, can't do anything about it. Powerless, when you lose people you love. It haunts you the most, the helplessness, you wouldn't have thought that.' He wearily places the spoon into the cup and stirs.

Philip doesn't notice a young waitress hovering by his table.

'Sorry – erm …' she says to Philip, and then to the empty seat.

Her eyes travel back along his extended arm stirring the coffee.

'Would you like anything else?' she asks, trying to comprehend what she's seeing.

It's only her third day at work, she has listened to the gossip about him but she didn't know what to expect. "He's harmless enough. Just a bit odd – who isn't? We get them all in here." Their voices repeat like a soothing Eastern chant.

'I'm fed up of this,' Mr Cole says. 'You've completely ignored me twice now.'

His voice increases in volume. The whispers of private conversations and the clattering of cutlery on plates drops a decibel. She senses people looking in her direction, but she's hypnotised by Philip, the contortion of his face caught in the dazzle of an optical illusion. She feels giddy. Is this for real or is it a trick, some sort of joke? Should she applaud or hold out for a punch line?

'What have I got to do to get your attention?' Mr Cole asks, the tone of his voice pumped in menace. 'If I was *fit* or some half-baked celebrity you'd be chewing on your knickers by now.'

Philip's features change again, swinging to the other extreme.

'He's a bit cranky today,' Philip says, 'ignore him.' The polite unassuming man she served before returns.

Whispers ricochet off the walls. The waitress backs away from the table, each step carefully placed. Her instincts are telling her something is about to happen and she needs to get out of the line of fire. He's going to ignite and she doesn't need this shit, she's not paid enough to deal with nutters. She steps back to a safe distance and then escapes behind the counter.

'There's no need for that,' Philip says.

Mr Cole slams the spoon onto the saucer. 'Yes there is. I don't like being ignored, that's all, there's no need for it!'

'She's probably nervous, I think she's new.' Philip sees her at the back of the tearoom, flanked by the two other waitresses. He smiles and to her bewilderment, she smiles back.

'Ellie was the same when she first started,' Philip continues.

'She's not a great example.' Mr Cole sneers.

'Alright, I didn't have much choice. Everyone else turned down the money.' He withdraws his arm and takes a sip of his tea.

'The only reason she took the job was to please her parents so they would help her out at university.' Mr Cole argues.

'OK, it wasn't a very good example.'

'No good for anything, that one. They'll fill her head full of ideas. Leisure and business studies, what the hell's that all about?'

Philip shrugs.

'How many jobs will there be if everyone's got a degree? What then? Back on another bloody course! Aspirations, if you get too close they can have a nasty habit of burning you.'

'What is it with you today?' Philip asks.

'Everything. I wish I'd never come back here. Sick of it all, sick of being old, sick of not belonging. What happened? Hey, is this really England? It wasn't like this when I left.' He leans forward. 'You know who I wanted to be like when I was a boy?'

Philip's uneasy at what he is about to say. 'I – er …'

'I wanted to be like my old man. That's all, sounds corny but I really did.'

34

A young acne-riddled duty manager stressfully weaves through the tables towards Philip. People in the tearoom are weighing up the situation, sipping at the thrill of it all as if it's a soap opera showdown. He stops at the table, making sure he's out of arm's reach. He attempts to visualise himself as a prize-fighter but it's difficult to hold the image against his own neglected chubby frame.

'I'm – well – erm …' he stutters, 'going to have to ask you to leave – sir.' His voice has a quiver to it and he's annoyed at how weak it makes him sound.

'A misunderstanding, that's all,' Philip says. 'I'm sure there's no need –'

The young manager cuts Philip dead, tapping into a growing confidence.

'Come on, please,' he says. 'I want you to leave.'

'I don't think that's necessary,' Philip says. 'I've been coming here for years. I run the –'

'I suppose,' Mr Cole says, 'you're the manager.'

The words ring in the young man's head, it's worse than Sarah had told him. His voice, his body language, the way the warm light in his eyes dies and is replaced by a cold piercing stare.

'I remember when that meant something,' Mr Cole says. 'Now? Underpaid salary slaves, that's all.'

'Hey, alright. Come on, I think you'd better go.'

'Ever stood up for something more than a stupid little job title?' Mr Cole asks.

'I'm sorry about this,' Philip says. 'You'll have to excuse my friend.'

Philip stands up, frail and thin, his bloated beer-belly catches on his shirt. He subserviently walks past the manager.

'You were lucky.' Mr Cole snarls. The manager is face-to-face with Philip, staring helplessly into those deep vacuous eyes. Philip has a hold of his shirt; it strains against his chubby torso, pinching him hard under his arms. His powerful grip contrasting against his fragile frame. 'If you knew what I could do to you …' he whispers.

'Let – let go, I'll …' the manager whines. 'I'll call – call the police. Do you hear me?'

'You're not worth the aggravation,' Mr Cole says. 'You mean that little to me.' He releases his hold, pushing him backwards.

'I'm so sorry,' Philip says. His apologetic smile melts the cold bitterness of his expression.

Philip steps back, everybody looks away, caught out by their prying stares and now uncertain of what to do. He sheepishly heads to the door, leaving the manager standing with his shirt pulled and creased.

3

Ellie rushes through the hall to the dining room and back again serving the guests. Everything looks the same – all served up with a portion of chips, but at least it's quick, straight from the freezer with nothing like preparation to get in the way. She keeps drifting into a dream scenario picturing herself on a candid camera show. None of this is real, it's all a very cleverly thought out prank. She's being tested, a huge stack of money waiting for her at the end. She's sure she is doing well, all her family and friends watching, cheering her on in a studio somewhere in TV land. No, they're next door on the edge of their seats, that's it. It's all going to be over at any moment, then from out of nowhere Davina McCall will appear all hyper and beautiful. She'll give her a girlie hug and say the programme's magic words to her to break the spell and rescue her from this mad world she has found herself in. *We've caught you out. It's a set-up* or *What's it like to look this stupid!* Yes something like that, and then she'll hand her a cheque for a thousand pounds. It might be more, it should be more. She grins, placing the two plates of chicken and chips on table 4. So much more.

Mrs Miller coughs into her clenched fist, wishing she could shoot a poison dart at Ellie to get a response from her. She rolls her eyes at her husband, who nods in agreement. Ellie stops hovering by their table and jolts back into the reality of the room; she looks at the remains of a lamb chop and chips and the gored crust of a steak and kidney pie. She sighs, collects the plates and leaves the dining room.

Ellie scrapes the remains into the pedal bin and slams the plates on the kitchen worktop.

'Do you have to keep doing that!' Ian says, jumping.

'This is beyond a joke.' She ignores him, nothing is going to stand in the way of her fury. 'It can't go on like this. I'm not a skivvy you know!'

Ian takes the plates and watches them sink into the mound of bubbles.

'I thought you were going to talk to him?'

'Sorry?' He knows exactly what she said but doesn't want to acknowledge it.

'Nothing,' she sighs, slumping against the kitchen units. 'He's not the only one with problems.'

'Here we go,' Ian mutters, returning to the safety of washing up.

'What did you say?'

He doesn't respond; if only he had a buffer zone in his mouth to let him think before he speaks.

'You don't know what's been happening to me.'

'Your boyfriend's been putting his foot down again in one of his jealous rages, or maybe your parents are giving you a hard time, or –'

'Fuck off. What do you know?'

'More than you'd like me to.'

'What do you mean by that?'

'You have a habit of contradicting yourself, Ellie.'

'Me? Contradict myself. Charming, it's probably working in this place.' She takes a deep breath to stop herself from hitting him. Then her tone changes. 'Is something wrong with the plumbing?' she asks casually.

Ian looks at her strangely. He'd expected a playful whack from her, he likes it when she does that. Or maybe a scornful glare followed by a great arrangement of abusive words firing at him as if they had been loaded into a sub-machine gun. But of all the things he thought she might say or do, this isn't one of them.

'What?'

'You heard me. Ask him about the plumbing in room 2, I bet he didn't mention that in your cosy little chat. He's been sleeping in that room as well. What is he up to?'

She struts off to the small utility room that's been transformed into a makeshift office. Ian follows her, wiping his hands on his apron.

'What are you talking about?'

She unhooks her coat and folds it over her arm.

'Hey, what are you doing?'

'I've worked through my lunch break for the past two days. I'm going and I'll be in late tomorrow.'

It's rare to see Ian perplexed and she savours the pleasure it gives her.

'You can't –'

'Just watch me.'

'What about the evening meals? I can't finish them on my own.'

'Only desserts left for table 4: two apple pies with ice cream. I'm sure you'll manage.' She smirks as she walks past him and out of the back door, slamming it hard.

In the light of the television screen a hand picks up the remote control from a coffee table, aims and fires. The television hurtles through the channels. It's the advert break and Adrian Butler is giving his thumb an aerobic workout. Michelle looks at him sprawled next to her on the sofa. It's taken him three days and a mere sniff of a cold, well, a man's cold, to turn him from a prestigious accountant to a vagrant who's reluctant to move off the sofa and find a park bench.

Fine stubble has set in and his hair glistens in grease even in this dim light. She adjusts herself swinging her legs from the sofa. He's slouched in his favourite pyjama bottoms and that awful faded festival T-shirt he refuses to throw out. She can't remember what festival it's from, the lettering has almost worn away. She's certain his pyjamas haven't seen the inside of the washing machine for at least a week and to go commando really doesn't help matters. She sniffs the air, certain she can smell a faint whiff of urine coming from them. Rolling her eyes she leans in and sniffs again, she really doesn't want to be right.

How can she say anything, what would be the use? Their constant arguing is becoming the norm. She has given up so much to be with him – her life in Salmouth, her support assistant's job at the local primary school, the guesthouse, her mum … She tried to get to the hospice in time but had been too late. "I didn't want to worry you," she can still hear her dad saying. The anniversary has re-opened old wounds, suppressed emotions are running free as fresh and vigorous as the day they were born. She knows she should be with her dad but she can't help feel resentment towards him; she hadn't realised how much it had built up over the years. It's an awful thing to admit to.

She remembers when her mum was ill. She hadn't noticed at the time but Philip loved all the attention, he wallowed in it. Mr and Mrs Gardener from next door would pop around to see if she was alright, but they had enough trouble of their own with their youngest, Steve. Mrs Gardener said the police had picked him up for playing around the back of the garages, but once she was out of earshot Mr Gardener put another slant on the story – caught sniffing aerosols was the police version. He shook his head in despair; he was a nice man but had the look of someone who carried the weight of the world on his shoulders. Maybe they both cared too much, wanting their well-ordered and immaculate guesthouse to reflect their family life. The harder they tried the more they failed.

They tolerated Philip but always seemed uncomfortable at him being around, throwing him disapproving looks at his constant drunken state. The cancer gave him all the excuses he needed, cranking his drama-queen act up another level to rake in the sympathy votes. They would come in, guilt carved on their faces. She knew they'd been talking to Philip out the front. Yet Frances was always so matter-a-fact about it all. She tolerated it in the beginning and accepted it at the end. Nobody else did.

The loathsome feeling hits Michelle again, making her feel vulnerable and uneasy. She looks at her watch, why hasn't he rung her back? Whenever they argue it's always him who builds the bridges and makes the peace. Maybe something's happened. She pushes the notion from her mind, angry at falling for it all again. She knows what he's like. He could play her like a one-armed bandit, an emotional payout every time. Why did her mum stay with him? She plumps up a cushion and wedges an elbow in for stability. She often wondered was it because she thought she was too old? Her mother's previous marriage to Ted had broken down, he'd seemed like a nice enough man though.

She's seen the photographs of their wedding, the holiday snaps of their honeymoon on the Isle of White. Frances never said a bad word against him, but then again she'd never said a bad word against Philip, considering how much they used to argue. There was quite an age gap between her and Philip. Married before and then in a relationship with a nineteen-year-old, "Got herself a toyboy," people would say. But the way they spoke to each other sometimes, it wasn't right. The mocking, the constant jabs at one another. Michelle wished she

41

could remember a time when they hadn't been like that but she couldn't. It would have made things a little easier – perhaps.

'He'll be alright.' Adrian places the remote on the coffee table and leans back into the moulded cast he's made in the sofa.

'How can you say that?'

'Hey, come on, he's been alright 'til now, hasn't he?'

'What about Christmas? You probably liked him like that.' Michelle adjusts her elbow in the cushion.

'What?'

'Look at the way your mum and dad are.'

'Don't compare them to how he carries on.' He crosses his arms and dramatically puts his feet on the coffee table. 'The way he treated your mum.'

'Don't you dare. It's got nothing to do with you.' She turns away from him.

'Hey, come on, I –'

'He's the only family I've got.'

'I'm sorry.' He moves his body towards her, feeling her loosen at his approach. 'You must admit he was a bit strange, he hardly said a word.'

'I'm not surprised, all I heard was you talking about your-self.'

'Come on, that's not fair.'

She edges her body away from him. He retreats, annoyed at himself.

He has to push it, it's like a game to him. Why does he have to? It's only a couple of days ago they'd had a blazing row. She'd accused him of having an affair and not for the first time. He tries to defuse the situation, not wanting it to blow up into a full-blown argument.

'Anyway, mine are hardly normal,' he sighs. 'Dad just can't move on.'

'Let's hope you're not like your mother.'

42

'Now I really don't feel very well.' He shudders at the thought.

'I'm going to have to go first thing tomorrow morning,' she says, without looking at him.

Adrian leans forward and picks up the remote control again. He doesn't respond, he can only stare at the TV screen finding a reassuring solace in flicking through the channels.

The evening puts in a reminder that it's still summer; the sun's broken from cover and coated everything in an orange-red tint. The dreary afternoon is a distant memory, holiday mode is quickly resumed. Couples appear as if by magic, strolling along the beach, scanning the sea-washed shoreline for any polished shells or unusual trinkets the ocean has discarded. Tables and chairs from cafés and pubs have come out onto the esplanade. People sit having evening meals, sipping drinks on provided benches; others have congregated to the window seats, all joined in taking in and savouring the view of the bay.

Philip and Mr Cole sit on the pebbled beach underneath the Old Pier, its heyday a distant memory. The refurbishment cost is reflected in how it inadequately juts out and falls short of the sea. They can hear the sound of slot machines, screams of arcade guns being fired and hitting their shrieking enemies, all wrapped up in retro chart music resonating from the back wall of the amusement arcade. Above them on the concrete stilts a Chinese restaurant is in full swing. The clanging of stainless steel and brief shouts from the Chinese staff float down to them.

Philip pours the last remains of a bottle of red wine into a plastic cup. He squints, the alcohol kicking in hard. Mr Cole whistles merrily, rummaging in an off-licence bag. He stops. Philip holds his breath. He's at that dreaded stage where the body has put in its assessment report warning him that if he proceeds it'll blow a fuse. Dizziness, vomiting, no bladder control, memory loss, they're all queuing up to be on the list of evening events. To Philip's dismay Mr Cole triumphantly pulls out a bottle of white wine.

'I was getting worried,' Mr Cole says, proudly examining the bottle. In a precise and forceful twist of his wrist, as if breaking the neck of a small animal, he de-corks the bottle and sniffs. 'Should be alright, not as good as the New Continent wines, can't go wrong with them.' He eagerly pours some into his cup; it takes on a pinkish complexion as it swirls into the dregs of the remaining red. 'Prefer red but they had a special on, too good to resist.'

Philip looks on helpless.

'Three for two. French.' Mr Cole curls his face up. 'Trouble is, they export all the shit – typical. And the bloody Germans are as bad.' He takes a swig and swallows, his face twisting as he wrestles down its bitter aftertaste. 'Takes a bit of getting used to, but you can't complain at the price. You pay through the nose at The Ship.'

'I didn't know you went there.'

'Oh yes, old haunt that place.' He looks up, annoyed at the piercing shrieks of people rushing about in the kitchen. 'They're all the same, just like that lot in Korea. Always shouting and rushing about ...' He pauses and smirks. 'Like the way I ran the hotel, used to get Judith's back up. If you're going to do something, do it properly, no half-measures.' He raises his arm. 'Here's to them.'

Philip awkwardly lifts his plastic cup and smiles.

'Come on, Philip, she's got her own life, she's not a young-ster any more. You'll be fine.'

'It's strange her not being here, it doesn't feel right,' Philip says. 'I should have gone to the grave by myself but –' He concentrates on his oil-like reflection flickering in the wine. 'Got her favourites, chrysanthemums.'

'Get rid of the other flowers Philip,' Mr Cole mutters. 'What's Michelle going to think of you taking her to visit Helen at the cemetery as well, on Frances' anniversary of all days –' He shakes his head in pure frustration. 'Sort yourself out. You're out of your depth there, you hear me?'

'Sorry.'

Above them a tray hits the floor sounding like a miss-timed cymbal. Voices rise up again.

'I got deployed to one of their camps in Korea. Bloody MacArthur's fault, should have eased back and they might not have entered into the war.' His memories unhinge. 'No sense of humour that lot. You know, we organised a table tennis tournament for them.' His grin reappears. 'All got together. We started off playing table tennis, like this.' He giggles, making the motion as if he is holding a bat and hitting the ball.

Philip smirks.

'They just stood there watching us, completely baffled at what we were doing. We didn't have tables or bats or even a bloody ping-pong ball! But we kept on playing the game. Must have thought we were stark raving mad.' He releases a belly laugh.

Mr Cole extends his arm, the wine bottle hangs at a precarious angle. He nods, encouraging Philip, who reluctantly places his cup under the bottle.

'They're a nosey lot as well, I can tell you. Me and Hirst used to fold up pieces of paper, always making sure we were being watched, and bury them. Then we'd watch them dig them up.'

'What for?'

'So when they dug up the pieces of paper, they'd read them. We wrote, *Stop being so bloody nosey. This has nothing to do with you!*'

Philip's uncertain how to react.

'It sounds stupid but you had to do something.' He rests the bottle between his legs hearing the glass scrape on the pebbles. He takes a swig then glances down into the pink mixture. 'This is the one thing that has never left me, good old alcohol. A true pal.'

Philip looks on sombrely.

'My father never touched the stuff … but then my fathers changed like the wind, from one foster home to the next,' Mr Cole continues.

'I know.' Philip turns back to the cup, it's full to the brim. His stomach turns over, wanting to back away at the thought of drinking another drop. 'There's been so many times when I've needed them,' he mumbles to himself.

Mr Cole looks out at the sea. 'Goodnight, my loves,' he says, 'I'll see you soon.' He drunkenly takes to his feet and sways like an inspired crab trying to walk in a straight line for the first time. Philip discreetly empties the cup, watching its contents drain away through the pebbles; he gets to his feet and follows.

A refreshing breeze caresses Mr Cole. His eyes close, savouring the wind's attention. Philip walks over to him, his gaze latched onto the horizon. The tranquillity of the bay hits him, his body aches, all of a sudden the stars are shining through the dusk sky as if he has jumped forward in time. He's always loved watching them, letting them provoke him to wonder what infinity could possibly be like. What is at the end of all this? Are we held suspended in something? Does nothing really matter or does every single thing we do make a difference?

There's so many questions that don't line up to a definitive answer. The feeling of insignificance is a bitter-sweet pill, it's the same when he looks out at the vast ocean. But that feels different. It has the ability to draw him into a state of mediation, to show him a glimmer of peace. Even the alcohol loosens its grip, his breathing coupling to the rhythm of the sea.

'Does it help being here?' Philip asks.

Mr Cole opens his eyes. 'I thought it would. I thought if I left Spain, came back here to happier times, before it all went wrong. I didn't mean that,' he sighs. 'They say things come in threes.' He tries to make a joke out of it but it isn't working.

'I don't know how you coped,' says Philip, his stare lost out at sea.

Mr Cole turns to him, warmly smiling. 'That's something, coming from you.' He glances back to the horizon. 'You have to cope. What else do you do?'

'I know. I don't know what to make of it all.' Philip shrugs his shoulders in complete dismay.

'What do you mean?'

'Everything.' Philip, feels the vastness of the sea drowning him.

'Maybe you're not supposed to.'

'Do you really think so?' he asks.

'What can you do?' Mr Cole's voice has a slight tremor to it. 'You make a choice. That's all there is. It might be the wrong choice with hindsight, but as long as you think it's the right choice at that moment in time, that's all you can ever do. When Becky was involved in that hit and run. Day after day, traipsing to the hospital. Medical staff with the same smiles of false hope. Seeing her lying there, hearing the beeps and the sounds of the machines, the only contact to your daughter. So what do you do, let her become a vegetable with no quality of life? You watch them grow up, want them to do so much better than you did. There's always going to be setbacks, but you don't …' He swallows hard, '…or you give them the nod and let her go, let them switch off the machine.' His voice trembles. 'Then Judith …' He pauses, making sure he can go on. 'From the sheer stress of it all.' He clenches his fist, his fingernails embedding into his palm.

47

'Don't, please don't,' Philip says.

Mr Cole's strong sturdy frame is tense and coiled. 'Choices. That's all there is.' He sniffs hard as starlight shimmers in the film of tears, but he refuses to let them go. He's cried enough, no more.

Philip can only stare at the shoreline, anxious at seeing Mr Cole like this.

Laughter comes from outside the front door of the guesthouse. A metallic jabbing sound echoes in the hall followed by the lock turning on the outer door. Mr Cole swaggers in and comes face-to-face with the glass panels of the day door. Philip falls against the wall, his body and mind exhausted from steering them both to the guesthouse. He slides down the cold tiles landing in a heap on the floor. Mr Cole examines the two keys in his hands.

'Which one do I use?' he asks with a slur.

'It's – erm blue.' Philip chuckles. 'It's the big blue one. All blue for that door.' He pushes the front door shut with the sole of his foot.

Mr Cole holds the keys up, catching the orange glow of the street lamp.

'Bloody hell.' He squints. 'Shit!'

Philip breaks into a fit of uncontrollable laughter.

'It's not fucking funny!' Mr Cole throws the keys onto the floor, helpless to the warm sensation of urine swelling the fibres of his Marks and Spencer's Y fronts. 'Waste of bloody time now.' Defeated, he waddles over to Philip.

'Good job we didn't get lucky tonight.' Philip points at Mr Cole's baggie trousers now with a wet patch spreading from his groin.

'I think they all had a lucky escape.' He lifts his saturated trousers from his crotch. 'It would have been a night to re-member for them.' He winks at Philip. 'I would have certainly got 'em wet.'

48

Philip places a finger on his lips, remembering where he is. His feet are bathed in a pool of streetlight. Suddenly his head wobbles, the taste of stinging sick fizzles on his tongue.

'You alright?' Mr Cole's voice distorts and dissolves.

Philip coughs, his brain is on sick-reaction alert; all it needs is a sudden jolt and he'll be at the mercy of a tremendous volume of vomit. The rigging of his neck muscles unshackle, letting his head roll free. He holds fast, his brain like a bedspread in a washing machine. His head slumps backwards scooping up the heavy weight of his eyes, then he jerks forward and falls haphazardly. The floor slaps him on the side of his face but the stinging sensation quickly disappears. His arms sprawled, he knows nothing is going to stop him from being sick.

'Philip!' a woman's voice snaps.

Mr Cole's footsteps echo in his head but they're coated in perfume. It forces its way into his nostrils, spreading into his body, creasing him, making him curl up and be submissive to its powerful presence. It doesn't make sense, he tries to push the thought from his mind. How can this be?

'Your father's going to have to see to you,' his mother's voice says.

It hits him deep and hard and at such ferocity he's finding it difficult to breathe. He sees a pair of women's shoes come to a halt in front of him. He can't look up to his mother, he knows he's about to be sick.

'I haven't got time for this,' his mother says. 'Do you hear me? Stop whining, Philip! If there's one thing I can't stand it's that whining voice of yours.'

She moves closer to him, a surge of vomit pushes forward but he manages to suppress it. He focuses on his mother's shoes, the immaculate black and white pattern glares back at him. They're poised, waiting desperately to go out. His eyes journey up her legs, nylon clinging to her youthful calves. Anger swells his body, he wants to grab hold of her and shake her, show her the pain in his eyes. To make her shut up, make her stop constantly moaning. Always something wrong no matter how hard he or his dad tried, there always had to be something. Another surge pushes ahead this time making his airways feel fresh and vibrant.

He needs to face her to look her straight in the eye, see her reaction to his outburst. Maybe she'll realise she was wrong, that it's all a mistake and plead for forgiveness, telling him she regretted every single hour, every minute from that moment when she left them. And once and for all wipe away those false smiles in the photographs he has of her, always making him question how he should see her, teasing him with doubt. But the anticipation is all too much. His heart misses a beat and he blacks out before his head hits the floor.

4

Ellie puts her coat on the last available hook in the small office. The room is caught up in an identity crisis. What am I, a utility room or an office? Schedules are pinned all over the walls showing when guests are due to arrive and when they'll be leaving. Lost in amongst all this are two racks of room keys and a local Indian restaurant calendar with various dates ringed with a red marker, and some crossed out with striking exclamation marks. Above the freezer is a work rota, neglected and peeling off the wall at one of its corners. According to the rota, last October hasn't even started yet. Past the fridge there's a tumble dryer against the far wall next to a desk, trays line up stuffed with unpaid bills. A computer sits in the midst of the mayhem, covered in post-it notes as if it's got a tropical rash.

'Turned up then,' Ian says, startling Ellie.

'Shit!' She gets her breath back and adds, 'Bastard!'

He grins, savouring her reaction. 'In a better mood today?' He looks at his watch. 'Well it's –'

'So I'm late, sack me, see if I care.' Ellie playfully barks at him and pushes past, making a point of lingering a little too long. 'I'm sure I can get another job like this. Not that I'd want it.'

'Calm down, I'm only joking.'

'There was a queue for the bathroom,' Ellie says. 'I can't work through today, I'm meeting mum for a coffee. Making it a regular thing so you'll have to find another skivvy. Nobody ever appreciates it so why should I bother.'

Ian smiles, shaking his head.

'They've opened up a new coffee bar on Broad Street.' Ellie ignores him.

His grin doesn't flinch. 'Alright, you've made your point.'

She rolls her eyes. 'Sorry, it's this place, it really gets to me sometimes. If it wasn't for you being here ...'

'You're not going to go all gooey on me, are you.'

She fondly hits him. 'Sod off!'

'Hey, come on, you know I like it like that!' Ian playfully rubs his arm.

'Fuck off.' The words purr on her lips.

'I love it when you talk dirty to me.'

'What do you think Maxine would say?'

'I was only mucking about.'

'You never know where it might lead.' She raises an eyebrow suggestively.

'Yeah right.' He laughs, suddenly feeling uneasy at being in her company and moves over to the kitchen worktop, slipping into the safe gear of work mode.

'So how is he today?' Ellie asks.

'Oh yeah, you won't believe this.'

She sighs. 'What's he done now? Or just the usual nothing.'

Ian's expression lights up, savouring what he knows.

'He hasn't wound up any more of the guests, has he?'

His face glows.

'The way it's going we'll need another complaints book.' She examines his face for any clues. 'He's left?'

'No!'

'No idea then.' She shrugs her shoulders at her wishful thinking.

'Come on, I'll show you.'

Ian leads her out of the kitchen and along the hall. The smell of fried food hovers in the air. He stands by the dining room door and finally his imbedded grin slithers away. His mannerisms change, taking on the role-play of a magician about to reveal the grand finale to his show-stopping act. He pushes the door open and curiosity beckons to Ellie. She peers in and can't believe what she sees.

It doesn't make sense. She turns back to Ian, whose grin is back with a vengeance. The dining room is spotless, guests are at their tables happily talking and tucking into their breakfasts. In the middle of all this is Philip, who's about to take tables 6's plates. He swoops in, strikes and elegantly glides up on the thermals of happiness that ooze from everyone. Ellie watches as he powers towards her. She's frozen to the spot, not knowing how to react. He's not going to stop, he's going to collide into her. But at the last possible moment he sidesteps her, smiles and glides past. All she can do is catch her breath and watch him whistling merrily along the hall until he disappears into the kitchen.

'I think I preferred it when he was just plain weird,' Ellie mutters to herself, not wanting to look at Ian's grin any more than she has to.

Michelle packs her clothes into a small suitcase. It bobs gently on a lake of restless wriggles spreading out from Adrian's body beneath the duvet. There's a pile of short-sleeved tops and knickers next to the case but only a small space is left inside. It's a close call but she's determined everything is going to fit. She takes the pile and force-feeds the suitcase. Adrian spies her every move.

'How long are you going for?' He sits up, the duvet slides away revealing his thin but gym-maintained body.

'I'll be back Thursday.'

'Thursday!'

She holds down the lid with her arm and zips up the case.

'I thought you were staying for a couple of days.'

Michelle ignores him, pulling the case off the bed and letting it drop hard onto the floor. 'I need some time by myself.'

'Don't give me that crap!' Adrian's legs jettison from under the duvet, his feet landing just inches from his boxer shorts.

'I'm sure you will keep yourself amused.'

'And what the hell does that mean?' He pulls the boxer shorts on and paces over to her.

'I'm fed up with this!' She turns away, determined not to cry this time.

'Look, we just need to talk.' Adrian places a hand on top of the suitcase, attempting to defuse the tension between them.

'Talk!' Michelle says in pure despair.

He's using his usual charm tactic, making everything swing round so it looks like it's her fault. She's in the wrong and he's the innocent party. His mannerisms soften, the tone in his voice unthreatening with a measured amount of vulnerability. It's in total contrast to how he was last night; he hardly spoke to her, crumbs of a conversation making sure he kept her there but at a distance.

'Please Michelle.'

'You pick your moments.'

She had laid in bed with her back to him feeling her frustration turning to anger. Was she programmed to repeat the relationship of her mum and dad at the mercy of some sort of perverse fate? She needed to end this; her body shook, the notion stared at her cold and unsympathetic. Was she finally facing what she really wanted? What was the matter with her? Their relationship had to work – it represented so much. Her mother didn't really like him, she never said it but it was blatantly clear in the way she was with him. The disapproving glances, the snide remarks that pivoted between sarcasm and distaste. But she was hardly a great judge of character, or maybe she was, maybe all those years with Philip had made her evolve a sensory gland, a dickhead detector to sort out the men from the idiots.

She used to imagine Philip wasn't her father. That she was really the sister, not the best friend of Kerry Meadows. If he could have only been like Kerry's father, Gordon – he was sedate compared to Philip. A family man moulded to just the right shape and consistency, nothing seemed to worry him. A man marooned in a house full of women, the territory of his crumbling empire marked out around his armchair. There was Anne – his wife – the other half of the perfect domestic set-up, along with Kerry's two younger sisters. He was definitely out numbered. But he was happy and she could tell he wouldn't have it any other way.

They'd been as thick as thieves when they were growing up, each one taking it in turn being the shadow. Academically they were different and the rot set in when they went to secondary school. She had heard Kerry had graduated from Southampton University and was now working in logistics for Oxfam. She knew she would never stay in the area, she was one of those people who were secure enough in themselves to live anywhere. Not like her though, Salmouth kept drawing her back no matter how hard she tried to escape.

'I'm not going to be gone for long,' Michelle says.

There's a control in her voice that startles Adrian.

'I get worried, I can't bear it when you're not here.' He wraps his arms around her, holding her tight.

She wants to hold him and believe things will get better but something inside of her has stopped working, or at least the batteries are flat. She doesn't know how she ever got into this state or more importantly how she will ever get out of it. Maybe some time away will make her see things more clearly, step back and see the whole picture for what it really is, not for what she thinks it is. She says she will be back on Thursday, but there's no rush, no rush whatsoever.

The morning weather hangs heavy and dull with no sign of shifting. Philip is at the kitchen table delicately folding the morning newspaper. The breakfast tray is fit to burst. He wedges the newspaper in between the pot of tea and the sugar bowl. He steps back, viewing the breakfast as if it's a work of art placed in a gallery to muse over. The breaking of an egg disturbs his concentration. Ian is at the cooker working through an order, the egg slips popping and spluttering into the frying pan.

'Perfect,' Philip says, his attention back with the tray. 'Just the way he likes it.'

Ellie sorts out her dusters and estimates how much polish she has left in the can by giving it a good shake. She's knelt by a cupboard door, her blue plastic cleaning tray by her side. She keeps glancing over to Philip, viewing him with an uncompromising suspicion. Philip proudly takes the tray and leaves the room, whistling a Harry James big band tune, up-tempo and happy.

'I don't know what to make of him.' Ellie takes a new duster from the back of the cupboard but decides to put it back.

'It's nice to see him happy,' Ian says, flicking oil over the spitting egg.

'It won't last.' She looks at her tray, all ready to go, and is amazed at how long she has been kneeling there. 'He'll soon be back to his old ways.'

'You never know. Maybe it'll be different, he might be coming to terms with it all.' He tilts the frying pan.

'What is it with you?'

'Sorry?'

'Why aren't you complaining about him the way you usually do?'

He moves the spatula in again, disregarding what she has said.

'Well?'

'Well what?' He keeps his back to her. 'Leave it, will you.'

Ellie flares up, desperately wanting him to share in her frustration, to back her up and make her not feel like she's acting like an overgrown child. That's what her mother always said about her. She slams the plastic container on the kitchen table for added effect and struts over to him.

'No!' Ellie says, arms folded, brimming with attitude.

'What's the point?' Ian turns to her. 'If you really want to know, I'm just fed up of it. Fed up of this!' He looks back into the pan. 'If you don't like it, Ellie, you can always go. It's as simple as that. Why let it eat you up.'

Her aggression instantly defuses, she feels disorientated.

She knows she has managed to glimpse his true thoughts. Is he really thinking of leaving? They used to talk, have a laugh at any opportunity. He isn't the sort of bloke she would ever think she could be attracted to. He looks like he has more oestrogen than testosterone in him, but he has grown on her. Now, for the first time, the reality of their relationship has finally slapped her across the face. They have drifted apart and she's to blame, it's all her fault.

She'd wanted him to make the first move. How long was she supposed to wait? She couldn't help it, it's in her nature to be impatient, even jealousy never worked. She thought mentioning Dean would have provoked him. She lied, exaggerating how bad Dean is, if only he could be that exciting! God how sad is she? That desperate she wanted him to want her out of sympathy. And then he starts dating that Maxine. What could she do? She couldn't stop the feelings she had for him, turn them off like a light switch to save on her emotional energy.

She steps towards him, her nerve ends tingling. She wants to reach out and touch him, to feel his breath on her skin, the caress of his hands clambering over her body. She has to stop herself. Anxiety moves in, it would only make matters worse. But she knows there's something between them and it has never been as powerful as it is right now.

Philip makes his way up the narrow flight of stairs trying not to unbalance the equilibrium of Mr Cole's breakfast tray. Mrs Dobbs rushes out of the fire door into the claustrophobic landing, narrowly avoiding a head-on collision. He manages to steer himself out of her way. The atmosphere locks tense between them; he looks sheepishly at the tray finding a soothing comfort in the way everything has found stability and is still in its rightful place.

Nervously she manoeuvres past him but all he can do is stand there. He's going to have to say something to her, he can't throw this opportunity away. He hears her begin to descend the stairs. He turns, half blurting her name out to catch her before she disappears but to his surprise she is standing in front of him. She reaches out and touches his arm. His body tingles at her touch.

'I can't talk now,' Mrs Dobbs whispers, tucking a slither of paper into his clenched hand.

He can't take his eyes from her; her slender lips, the magical playful freckles under her foundation. It's strange but he can hear footsteps moving hastily down the stairs. A faint tremor takes hold of the tray. He catches his breath and it subsides. The sound of the day door opening and slamming shut echoes in his head.

Philip looks behind him, guests are coming down the stairs. He turns to see Mr Miller from room 4, impersonating a human pack-horse laden down with every weather eventuality, covering Sahara-proof beach wear to full-on Arctic survival kit.

Mr Miller nods half-heartedly at Philip, his thoughts busy, painstakingly mapping out the journey ahead, calculating how far he has to carry all this and if it's worth risking a heart attack for. The bags are already cutting into his hands and he isn't even out of the guesthouse yet. His petite wife comes into view following close behind.

Philip turns back to Mrs Dobbs but she has gone. The couple pass him on the landing, Mrs Miller so engrossed in rechecking the contents of her shoulder bag that she doesn't even see him. He stands there baffled for a moment then continues on his journey to Mr Cole, but this time expecting, hoping Mrs Dobbs will appear along the way.

Mr Cole attacks his breakfast, his slurping and munching broken by constant concerned glances at Philip.

'You look pleased with yourself.' Mr Cole gives him a knowing look.

'Yeah, well …'

'Feel alright about today?' Mr Cole asks. 'You're still going?'

'Yes, of course I am.'

'You're playing a dangerous game,' Mr Cole says, trying not to choke on his food. 'You know that, don't you?'

'Sorry?'

'Feeling a bit lucky?' Mr Cole nods to the newspaper.

'I don't know what you are getting at?'

A thin strip of newspaper has been torn off along the bottom edge.

Philip looks despairingly.

'If it worked before, why try and fix it.'

Philip lets out a shudder. 'Don't, please,' he says.

'It's all there.' Mr Cole taps a finger on the side of his head. 'All living and breathing, memories, it's just a matter of how you want to see them. So how do you want to see them, Philip?

Think about it. As for Helen, she was just too immature, out of her depth. Of course she'd have taken the easy way out. Sign on the dotted line and that's it, hand your kid over, let somebody else look after it, same as your dad did with you. That's what they were like, Philip, and make sure you don't forget it …' He pauses. 'Sorry I'm only teasing, ignore me, a bit groggy today.' He puts his knife and fork down and winds himself with a couple of pats to his stomach, belching loudly.

Philip's fingernails sink into his palms.

'It's that Mrs Dobbs.' Mr Cole looks at him.

Philip jerks back as if he had taken a swipe at him.

'A married woman.' Mr Cole chuckles. 'You like them like that. Like them a lot younger as well, old stomping ground. You must feel dizzy. You don't learn, do you? Round and round like a merry-go-round.'

'Stop it,' Philip says. 'I thought you were –'

'Of course I am,' Mr Cole says. 'But you don't help yourself, do you. You know what happened last time. Separate them, Philip. Whatever you do, see people for who they were.' He shakes his head. 'Frances and Helen, they were two different people, two very different people.'

Philip shifts uncomfortably in his chair.

'You're not helping matters.' Mr Cole sighs. 'You are your own worst enemy.'

'What do you mean?'

'Got your head in the clouds, haven't you. Romance!' Mr Cole's mood lightens. 'That's what you think, isn't it? Always elaborating on what really happened. Stop being soft, Philip.' He leans forward. 'If a woman wants you, there's nothing more to it.' He takes his fork and digs it into the last remains of a sausage. Philip watches it sliding helplessly, picking up egg yolk from around the plate. 'It's not up to us, got no say in the matter.' Mr Cole grins but it unexpectedly disappears.

'Is everything alright?' Philip asks.

'Oh, don't mind me, I can't help but think of Judith.' Mr Cole rests the fork on the plate. 'All this talk of romance, you know. I can remember when a load of us went down to The Royal Oak. Come to think of it, it wasn't that long after that I was shipped off. Hadn't long finished my National Service. It's all different when somebody's taking a pot shot at you.' He ponders over his last remark. 'Anyway, had some good swing bands playing there. None of this thud thud thud rubbish, no fancy food and alco-bloody-pops to encourage kids to drink either.' He slumps back into his chair getting comfortable with his memories. 'As soon as I saw her ... listen to me, it sounds corny but it's true. Kept thinking if only I could get close to her. Kiss her. Just one kiss ...' He pauses, letting in her smile. 'Never thought anything past that. Different now.' He slips a hand into his pocket to realign his testicles on the cut of his trousers. 'Ah, that's better.'

Philip's uneasy at sharing the experience.

'When you're in a barrack block there's no privacy.'

Philip nods half-heartedly.

'Then before I knew it I was engaged, then married and about to be a father. I wasn't even twenty-one.'

'I know, yeah,' Philip says, traipsing over familiar ground.

Mr Cole is disappointed at his reaction.

'She wants you, Philip, is that what you want to hear?' he asks. 'But make sure it's her, Philip. Whatever you do, make sure it's her. People are who they are, not who you want them to be.'

Philip quietly closes the door of room 5 behind him. He takes a deep breath, his heart pumping adrenaline through his veins at a rapid rate. No one is there. The morning light seeps through the partially open curtains. The room is in a peculiar turmoil, cupboards and drawers have been frantically opened, clothes sprawled out of them as if they have been examined and discarded.

'Philip,' a woman says. 'Is that you, Philip?'

The voice makes his whole body tremble. To his surprise he feels the soft texture of underwear rapidly sieving through his fingers. He feels dizzy memories of the guesthouse are bearing down on him. The voice came from the direction of the bed but he's afraid to look. He swallows hard and gradually turns his head. He has to blink.

He can't understand what he is seeing. Spiralled provocatively on the bed is Mrs Dobbs, sexy underwear accentuating the beautiful curves of her body. Nervously he looks to the carpet but her seductive figure is etched on his thoughts – every dip, every arch held and cherished. His libido has been disconnected but it's waiting anxiously in the wings for him to get over the shock. He hears her move from the bed. His body's frozen, his breathing sporadic. She approaches, her stockings rubbing against each other, creating a sexual friction.

She touches him and his whole being melts, hitting the floor. She moves up close cupping and aligning his face in her warm delicate hands until their eyes meet. Her gaze drinks him, her perfume sedates his breathing as she pushes her sensuous body against his.

'I can't help myself,' Mrs Dobbs says. 'I can't, Philip.' Her breath caresses the side of his face. 'Why does it have to be like this?'

She rubs her silk panties on his leg, letting out a suppressed groan. He touches the flesh of her exposed thigh, it provokes a cue to his libido to come out on to the stage and entertain.

'I didn't want to let you down.' Philip bites hard on his lip. He can't help himself, he knows he shouldn't. The voice in his head shouts out not to go any further but it feels so right, so true. 'I wanted to marry you. I did. Believe me Helen.' There, he's said it.

'You didn't hate me, did you Philip?' Mrs Dobbs asks. Her breath snaps cold, sending a shiver down his spine.

'No, please,' Philip replies. 'Don't say that. It's not true. No.'

'I can't help it. I wish I could, but I can't help but want you. Do you understand me?'

She takes hold of the waistband of his trousers and leads him to the bed.

They fall, coiling in an animalistic embrace, tongues dancing and frolicking with one another. She stradles him, he lies submissive, panting vulnerably, taking in her pale complexion and savouring every movement of her limbs that cry out for him. She forces his trousers down, licking her lips as she manages to unhook his pants as well. He closes his eyes, his head rolling back. The cool air of the room strokes at his skin, tingling his testicles though not diminishing his erection.

He looks to his crotch but it's lost in the blonde mound of Mrs Dobbs head. The sensation hits him, smacking him straight between the eyes. His body goes limp; the pillow cradles his head. He reaches out and thankfully touches her head. Strains of her hair fall through his fingertips while her head bobs up and down. She calms her enthusiastic rhythm and looks up to him.

Pleasure turns to confusion. He stares at her, uncertain of what to make of her expression. It's a concoction of bewilderment and dread. 'No time for me, did you?' she shouts. 'Don't love Helen, please, you can't. She's just a kid, I'm your wife for God's sake!'

The words echo in his head.

He's stunned. Not knowing how to react.

'What the hell are you doing!' Mrs Dobbs says. Her voice has taken on a deep and menacing quality, breaking through to another gender.

He pulls himself away from her, protectively pulling up his pants and trousers. She mouths the words but he's certain they come from somewhere else in the room.

But nobody is there.

'Please, calm down,' Ian's voice says.

But where is he?

Philip turns back to the bed. Mrs Dobbs has gone. Just her underwear remains, laid out in perfect proportions.

Frantically he looks around the room, this time finding Ian attempting to be referee between Mr and Mrs Dobbs. What's happening? How did they get here?

'Is that it!' Mrs Dobbs says with utter contempt to her husband.

'This is not getting anybody anywhere,' Mr Dobbs says, trying to calm his wife.

'Do something!' Mrs Dobbs screams. 'For once just do something!'

Ian gives Philip a disapproving look then beckons him to make his way to the door.

'What do you want me to do?' Mr Dobbs asks. 'Hit him?' He shrugs his shoulders in desperation.

Philip stops in his tracks. Reluctantly, Ian protectively stands in front of him wishing he could anticipate how this is going to pan out.

'That's it, isn't it?' Mr Dobbs continues. 'That's what you really want from me. Violence, it's what you're used to.'

'What do you know about what I really want?' Mrs Dobbs says. For the first time she feels like she is getting through to him.

Ian ushers Philip out of the room.

'With your track record with men, what should I expect?' Mr Dobbs looks at her.

They hear the door shut and turn to see Ian standing there awkwardly.

Philip rushes down the stairs; he can hear Ian battling against an avalanche of questions from Mr and Mrs Dobbs. It was his chance at happiness, his chance at starting again and getting it right. Even though it was a disaster, he feels overcome by a strange sense of freedom, leaving him the alluring possibility that if he reaches far enough he'll be able to take hold of his true desires. Mr Cole was wrong, but how could he tell him? He descends the second flight of stairs, pulling his belt tight, seeing the hall leading to the front door.

He runs along the hallway, his breathing heavy and full of emotional pain, fumbling with the buttons on his shirt. He tries to open the day door but it's jammed. Someone's coming down the stairs. He tries the handle again, twisting and pulling at it.

He doesn't want to explain what has happened, how can he rationalise something he is only just beginning to understand himself.

'Alright Philip?' Mr Cole asks.

Mr Cole's standing by his side but Philip doesn't want to face him. Not now, definitely not now.

'I heard what's been going on. Think the boy's sorting it out.'

Philip gives him a stern look. 'Please,' he says. 'I need to get some air.'

The door handle springs back into place and he gives in.

'It takes time. You want it all at once, that's your trouble.' He pats him gently on the back. 'Michelle will be here soon.'

Philip stares thought one of the glass panels of the day door out onto the esplanade, to the sprawling view of the sea.

'This isn't about Frances,' Philip says. 'Do you hear me? I know that now.'

'I've told you,' Mr Cole says. 'We've gone through all that.' He places a hand on Philip's shoulder. 'You can't go

65

there. Helen's got nothing to do with this. You've got to listen to me, Philip.'

'It's different for you. You and your family, your career. You went to Spain and ran the hotel, you did it. You fought and you got what you wanted.' His lip trembles. 'I didn't even try. Do you know how that makes me feel? Have you any idea?' He watches the waves break in the bay.

'Come on, Philip.' Mr Cole attempts to guide him away from the door but Philip pulls away.

'No! I didn't even try.'

The door handle glides down, clicks and unlocks. Philip watches as the door independently swings open. He steps back then slips through into the outside world.

The door clicks shuts and the waves are the only sound that can be heard in the hall.

Philip drunkenly stares at Helen Yates' grave. He has been mulling over her death more and more, ever since Frances died. There are so many *ifs* and *buts* about Helen to contend with. It is as though they have all been waiting for him, poised for the right moment to pounce, pin him down without an ounce of mercy, until that fateful moment when he can't deny them any more, when he's forced to deal with Frances' death. He's always known they were there, lingering in the background, wedged in the subtext of his daily life. But he had no idea of the power they possessed, devouring his thoughts like an unstoppable virus.

Why has it all gone wrong? Is it all his fault? He's convinced himself it is. This isn't the way it was supposed to be. They didn't have a chance. The white marble cross stares back at him, stained by sprawling patches of moss. All he's left with is the heavy burden of hindsight to pinpoint where it went wrong. Where he's convinced it all went wrong. It was at the funfair on the beach when he met up with Helen.

Frances had found out Helen was pregnant and that she had left the guesthouse. Helen loved him, she wanted to be with him. They could have been a family. His mind pictures them both, that night on the Ferris wheel where his new life could have begun. His body tremors with emotion. But no, he had to do the right thing and save his marriage. Listening to what his head was telling him rather than his heart. But the truth was, he did it because he was too scared, too weak. So he sacrificed the one thing that had given his life meaning.

He's sombrely drawn to the grooves of Helen's name clogged by dirt and cracked by the weather. The other gravestones have inscriptions of, *Beloved grandmother. Devoted grandfather. Husband. Wife. Adored. Missed. Eighty-seven. Seventy-three. Sixty-eight.*

And hers.

She should have had so much more time. He wonders if any of those others had appreciated it. Should they have? Could it all come down to what life dealt you? The way you saw good luck and bad luck? Did they even need to appreciate it or was it all about getting on with it, being happy with your lot? He only has to look at himself. Who is he to judge them, what has he really done with the time he has been given?

It was his first funeral – what a one to start with. He can still feel the weight of his trauma pushing down on him, making his knees almost give way when he saw the black hearse pull up outside. They had all congregated at the front of the guesthouse but for some reason he hadn't expected the hearse to be there displaying the coffin. He didn't know why. He had probably been told what would happen but nothing had sunk in. He was just there, a shell of his former-self, everything stripped away faced with the sinking predicament of nothing having any meaning for him.

He couldn't hear the waves breaking in the bay, holidaymakers were silenced, even the calls of the seagulls had been erased. There was just an unearthly stillness that no one wanted to break. Mesmerised by the coffin, he kept attempting to visualise her, placing her in there at rest with the world, but she'd spring back, hair saturated in sweat, crying out in frustration and pushing with all her might. And after, he remembers the way Frances held Michelle, gently rocking her. Her mothering instincts had kicked in, it was strange to see her like that, he never had her down as a dot-ing mother before.

Michelle was a beautiful baby but the older she got the more she began to reveal traits that reminded him of Helen. Espe-cially over the last four or five years when he had to contend with her looking more like her as well. It put a strain on their relationship; he couldn't help it, it let in a constant mocking at how weak he had been. He shakes his head, wanting to throw off his memories and the cool air. Helen never even saw her own daughter's face, she died giving birth to Michelle. You accept death when it's someone old; after all, it is one of the few things you can rely on. A year later, his grandmother had passed away.

He had traced her through some of his dad's belongings that the adoption agency had sent him. He always loved to visit her, let her reel off stories about his dad. It made him feel closer to him. The times he sat with her were priceless. He knew he could never put all the pieces of his dad's past together, but to see an overall impression lifted his heart. She wasn't all there in the end, conversations would become caught up in loops. By the time they had moved her into the residential home on Berry Street she had unwittingly terrorised the neighbour-hood. The final straw came when she woke up Mr and Mrs Rodhouse – her next-door neighbours – standing at the end of their bed viciously pointing at Mrs Rodhouse to get out of her house and leave her husband alone. She didn't have a stitch on, which took the edge off her anger and made the situation more bizarre than threatening. If only they had asked for the spare key back after she had looked after the cats.

The whole neighbourhood ended up having some grievance with her. He kept on having visions of them gathering in an angry mob and burning her at the stake like a medieval witch. They had even put a petition together and filed it with the local council, but nothing could detract from how he felt about her. It only made him smile that one old lady could cause so much grief.

Bread and butter puddings, the smell of the cool pantry. She never lived in the front room, it was preserved like a section of a museum, *The way we lived in the forties*. Always in the backroom sat in front of the open fire. The council eventually put in an electric one but she never quite got the hang of it. She'd switch on the light, not putting the bars on and would be heated, psychologically by the fake flames.

It's funny what you remember. He swills the can around in his hand, estimating how much is left. He looks to the grave again, wanting something to provoke him, but he's face-to-face with an unmoving nothingness. The urge had been as intense as ever to come here, the place where he could propose the question *what if?* Its power is seductive but it's wrapped in guilt. He had let Helen down and now he's caught in a conundrum that inevitably keeps leading him back to that conclusion.

He looks across to the pathway, through the trunks of the conifer trees. He can visualise the rest of the cemetery. His mind travels down one of the small pathways from the main path. He can picture himself back at Frances' grave. Guilt swells in him, twisting his insides. He couldn't bring himself to look at Frances' headstone, to see the inscription of *Beloved Wife, Cherished Mother,* as he pulled the dead flowers out of the container and put them into his off-licence carrier bag. The flowers he'd brought were still back at the guesthouse propped up in the vase by the kitchen sink.

He shudders, breaking the illusion. He tips his head back and tastes the last drops of lager slipping effortlessly down his throat. He discards the empty can into the bag and takes out another, drags the ring back to a hiss and takes a hearty swig. He belches, the fizz hitting his nostrils. Then he reaches back into the bag and pulls out the flowers. Their lifeless bodies are drained and brittle; he kisses them and holds them close to his chest. With some effort he clambers to his feet, preferring to fall over than to drop them. He stares at Helen's grave, cradling the flowers tightly.

Oncoming headlights pierce the darkness inside the car, jolting Philip back from his drunken state. The rotting chrysanthemums lay on the passenger seat, their shadows race around encircling him.

'It wasn't like that!' Philip says defensively, harpooning the flowers with his stare.

An empty lager can rolls out from beneath the seat. The steering wheel slips from his hands, making the car gyrate over the road's white lines. A car's horn screams past him then sinks in to the darkness. He steadies the car, tightening his hold on the wheel, but his attention is drawn back to the passenger seat.

From nowhere a foot crunches down hard on the rolling can, a hand picks it up and gives it a shake.

'Charming,' Mr Cole says. 'Not a drop left for your old mate.'

He sits in the passenger seat, face screwed up, rubbing his backside onto the flowers as if he's about to defecate at any moment. Disappointed, he drops the can on the floor.

He sighs deeply, giving the can a kick. 'Is this supposed to make you feel better?'

'This has got nothing to do with you,' Philip says.

'Don't kid yourself, Philip, you can't fool me of all people.'

Philip turns away in disgust.

'Does it hurt, Philip?'

He holds the steering wheel tighter.

'Come on, Philip. Frances was always there for you, you can't deny that. She stood by you every step of the way and how did you treat her? Like this! How could you? Isn't it about time you faced facts instead of trying to blame everyone else.'

Philip's whole body shakes, wedged solid between anxiety and anger. His foot pushes harder onto the accelerator. He changes gear, making the gearbox squeal as the car speeds along the twisting road.

'Deny it, Philip, go on... I mean, why not. You're still using her to get what you want.'

'No! You don't understand,' Philip says.

Mr Cole pulls out a handful of chrysanthemums from beneath him. Some of the flowers crumble and fall from his hand. In a defiant denial he squeezes them, until they bleed a filthy grey liquid. 'Don't dismiss this!' He rubs his hands together, watching them fall to the floor. 'Always wanting Frances' approval no matter what you do, couldn't do anything without it. You can't see it, you're still trying to convince yourself this is all to do with Helen. You're going to have to face it all sometime.'

Philip watches the petals cascade, his foot pins the accelerator to the floor. He hears a car swerving, another horn shrieks out in desperation at him from the outside world.

Mr Cole watches the petals fall to the floor.

The car jerks uncontrollably, the scraping of metal groans all around them. They leave the road and hurtle against an ill-prepared hedgerow. Everything slows down, working in a different time zone. Philip is oblivious to what is happening, he smiles at the chrysanthemums on the floor. Petals gracefully float and tumble, their dishevelled appearance has gone, showing off the vibrant colours of their pollen-filled youth.

The car slides down into a ditch and is propelled into a violent rolling momentum. The roof buckles, smashing the windscreen and sending glass in every direction. In amongst all this chaos Philip calmly reaches out to Mr Cole, who screams in pure desperation at him. He touches Mr Cole, watching him break up, turning into a wash of petals.

'Got to have Frances to deny me. Can't make a decision by yourself,' Mr Cole says, until only his eyes are left, pleading to him.

The car comes to an almighty halt, mangled and defeated. Philip looks at his blood-covered hands, he can taste it in his mouth but he feels safe. His nerve endings sting from a multitude of flesh wounds but their agonising pain is subsiding. A smile eclipses his face, enchanted by the sight of beautifully formed petals eagerly coming to his aid. They frantically suckle at his cuts, cleaning them and taking away the pain. He can feel them nibbling around his ears, a dense mass have congregated on his cheek making him feel ticklish. He rotates his hands. They flee, hovering cautiously, but can't resist the urge to come back and nurse him again.

He passes out.

The petals drop, dishevelled and lifeless to the floor, cuts reappear over Philip's face and hands.

5

Echoing footsteps and the smell of disinfectant flicker at Philip like a Morse code SOS. Time has folded into itself; it has no linear line any more, no narrative to recognise. He can sense people lingering by his bedside, their concern hanging over him, not wanting to spill a drop. Voices entangle, he tries to see who they belong to but their features are smudged against the white glare of the hospital ward.

From this concoction the hazy figure of a young girl reaches out and takes hold of his hand. He's startled but her touch lets a soothing calmness into his body. Suddenly bright lights dance playfully around him as if he's at a funfair, carrying the beat of a bass line that pushes hard on his chest. No matter how hard he tries he can't make out the spinning rides or hear the melody of the music. The spectacle rapidly disperses, leaving him and the girl alone. He doesn't understand what she is saying to him, but the tone of her voice is strangely mature. A woman kisses his cheek, her perfume is familiar but he can't recollect to whom it belongs.

The girl disappears and now he can just make out the woman at the bottom of his bed. She waves to him as she leaves. Philip's head spins, he feels like he's drunk. His mind injects snapshots from an evening he tries desperately to remember. He's in his car, is that Mr Cole? The flowers, he can't see anything but a blanket of white petals, beautiful white petals surrounding him, holding him, making him feel safe.

The figure of a man walks awkwardly towards him and sits on the edge of his bed. Philip tries to decipher what he is saying but it's no use. He's left with tones of the hypnotic voice that soothingly swings between masculine and feminine until he passes out.

There's no accountability to the amount of times he has come surging to the stodgy surface of reality, only to sink like a stone back into his illusions, and to the healing arms of sleep. But now he is finally coming coughing and spluttering into the hospital ward and nothing is going to stop him. Its whiteness glares at him, the smell of people's body odours sits lingering in amongst the heightened clean aroma of the ward. Michelle puts her *Take a Break* magazine onto the plastic chair and rushes to his side. She wants to say something to him, give him words of encouragement, hold his hand but all she can do is stand there and stare at him.

The staff nurse notified the police once Philip had regained consciousness. At quarter past three Sergeant Wilson and PC Collinson stand at the bottom of Philip's bed. Sergeant Wilson has a well-maintained middle-age spread. His hair is immaculate, not one strand out of place. Philip's unsure how he manages it; it isn't gel, maybe a heavy-duty hairspray. He is also showcasing a moustache that any cop from a seventies police series would be envious of. The other, PC Collinson, is obviously gay. His sexuality is so powerful it radiates through his uniform, from his stance to the blonde highlights in his hair.

Philip had been told they were coming, the anticipation kept him restless. The staff nurse had explained to him that he'd been here for a week, a whole week gone, all that time lost to this bed. His mouth is dry and coarse, a drip feeds cool into his arm. He has lost plenty of Friday evenings before, Saturdays and Sundays as well, maybe a few others in the week but he didn't want to be too honest with himself. All alcohol induced, of course, however an entire week is something else.

To his surprise he had to stop himself from laughing at the police when they first turned up, but now he looks troubled at them, his head slumps back groggy while his body feels tender to the touch.

'Mr Morgan,' Sergeant Wilson says. 'Just a few moments of your time if you don't mind.'

He pulls a notebook from his breast pocket and walks over to Philip's side followed closely by PC Collinson.

Michelle stands protectively by his bedside.

'We need you to make a statement about the accident,' Sergeant Wilson says, obscuring PC Collinson's view with the bulk of his body.

'Can't this wait?' Michelle asks.

'Sorry, you are …?' Sergeant Wilson replies, homing in on his notepad.

'I'm his daughter, Michelle Morgan.'

Sergeant Wilson places his cap on a vacant chair and proceeds to jot her name down, taking time to weigh her up. 'Well, Miss Morgan, I'm afraid we need to investigate your father's accident.'

'But do you have to do it now?' Michelle asks. 'Look at him!'

'We also need to follow up the incident which happened on …' Sergeant Wilson glances over his notes, ' …the sixteenth of July. Concerning a Mrs Lydia Dobbs and a Mr Martin Dobbs.'

The names knock Michelle off balance. She remembers the distress on Ian's face when he told her what had happened. She had been shocked at what he told her and at how frank he had been. It wasn't like him. She usually had to follow a trail to get anything out of him, wear him down with her feminine charms and scoop out what was really going on. But not this time. This time he wanted to tell her, wanted to be free from it. This was her problem and he didn't want to share it.

'He's not ready for this,' Michelle says. 'Please.' It makes her feel weak, shaving the aggression off her anger but she has to stand up for him, he's her father. He's the only family she has.

'I can understand what you are saying, Miss Morgan,' Sergeant Wilson says, his voice void of any sincerity. He's moving through the motions heading straight to where he wants to go. 'But we need to establish the facts.'

Michelle steps forward, standing defiantly just inches from him.

PC Collinson pipes up from behind the sergeant. 'I have to warn you that it is a criminal offence to obstruct a police officer, this can be –' His tone is professional and contradicts how Michelle and Philip presumed he would have spoken. It's not quite the stereotypical camp performer they expected it to be.

'Quiet!' Sergeant Wilson says, cutting PC Collinson in mid flow. He turns to Michelle. His anger instantly washes away, slipping back to a professional manner. 'Michelle. Can I call you Michelle?'

She nods, startled at his outburst.

'Please, come over here,' he says, pushing past PC Collinson and escorting her away from the bed.

Collinson follows, not wanting to be left out but Wilson glares back at him almost letting slip a growl. He stops dead in his tracks.

'Look after Mr Morgan,' Sergeant Wilson says to him. 'I'm sure that's in the procedures manual.'

He takes Michelle out of earshot.

'Basic training,' Sergeant Wilson says, throwing back a look of contempt at PC Collinson. 'Michelle, I know you're upset, but you have to realise the consequences of both of these offences; this could have been very serious indeed.' He places his notepad in his top pocket. 'His blood test shows he was three times over the legal limit. He could have died and taken a few others with him.'

She has to face it, in the back of her mind she always thought something like this would happen, a matter of *when* not *if*. Seeing his car parked at strange angles at the rear of the guesthouse when she was off to school, Frances constantly making excuses for him or brushing it off as the norm. She knew though. It didn't take long for her to weigh it all up and compare her life to other people's. But she thought that was all in the past, well she had convinced herself it was. And the other thing with Mrs Dobbs, what was he doing? Her own father. It makes her spine tingle. She could see it on Sergeant Wilson's face. She wants to look away from him, to try and somehow distance herself from what he is about to say.

'I presume this is linked to the incident with Mr and Mrs Dobbs,' he says.

'I – erm … I don't know.' She looks helplessly at him. 'I'm still getting my head round it all. I don't know, I just don't know what to do. God, what is the matter with him! If it's not one thing, it's another.'

'Is there something else we should know?'

She sighs. 'I thought he was doing alright.'

He looks puzzled.

'The alcohol, I thought that was all over.' Michelle doesn't want to say anything about the incident with Mr and Mrs Dobbs. She doesn't want to make it real to herself.

'Yes, well, it's not your fault.' He smiles.

She's taken aback at how warm and genuine he now speaks to her.

'It never is, you remember that,' he adds.

Her lips quiver, the emotion of the week's events bare down on her. The crash, the strain it's putting on her relationship with

Adrian, the anniversary of her mother's death. It's up to her, she's the one who has to be strong, to hold it together. But she doesn't want to any more. She's tired of it all.

'He needs plenty of rest,' Michelle says. 'You'll just have to wait.'

'Look, we'll get the basics down so I can file a report and I'll follow this up at a later date. There's a discrepancy over Mr and Mrs Dobbs' statements at the moment. It's not what you call straightforward, but what is when people are involved?'

'Yeah.'

'Domestic friction shall we say. We need to go back and take another statement from them, so as I said we'll get the basics down for now.'

'Alright,' Michelle says, relieved. 'Do you mind, I could do with a glass of water.'

'No problem.'

Sombrely she walks back to Philip's bedside, where a solitary *get well soon* card from her partly obscures a jug of water and a couple of plastic cups.

Collinson snatches the opportunity and hurries over to Sergeant Wilson who watches his approach with a brooding loathing.

'What is it with you?' Collinson asks.

'What?' Wilson replies.

'Don't come the naive with me. They told me about you.'

'What do you mean?'

'The family man,' he mocks. 'Who you trying to kid, yourself?'

Sergeant Wilson's whole body recoils. 'Look, gay boy, if you push me …'

'That's it, hit a nerve have I? And you'll do what?'

Sergeant Wilson turns away from him and walks off, his anger in a tight headlock.

Michelle slams the car door and locks it. She stares at her reflection in the window. It's been another long and emotional day and it isn't even five o'clock yet. She feels old, worn down at the edges. Her body hangs heavy on her like a drenched winter coat. She's hardly eaten, a constant flow of instant coffee from the hospital café and a mini packet of chocolate cookies, she couldn't face anything else. And to top it all she hasn't slept properly for days. Her pillow should induce sleep but it is as if she is plugging herself into an enormous battery night after night. Charged memories play out in her mind, she only catches hold of them briefly in the morning, then they're gone, only to return the next night.

She slouches against the car door and looks up at the row of guesthouses, their backs shabby and neglected compared to their public facades. The Bay View's narrow car park leads to a concrete wall where the garden's wooden fence protrudes haphazardly. The gate is open swaying to the breeze. She can't get the accident out of her head, seeing him lying there wired up to a machine. Its constant beeps comforting her through the hours she spent there as if she too was attached to it, a reassuring link from her world to his.

It brought home to her how much they have drifted apart. What if he had died? There's so much she wants to tell him but they never really talked. He was always there, but so was the furniture along with every other inanimate object. She can't remember the last time they actually sat down and had a conversation or felt a bond between them. And now he was lying there so near and yet so far away. She'd held his hand and it all poured out of her, she couldn't stop herself. She talked about her mother at first, how Frances religiously cleaned the guesthouse, the saucy comments she would come out with. The guests always warmed to her, nothing was ever too much trouble. It all came out of her in no particular order, plucking memories from bygone years up to when Frances was at the hospice. She'd see her every weekend; her mother didn't change, nothing seemed to dampen her spirit. She never thought about herself – always too pre-occupied with everyone else, fussing over Philip, asking how he was doing, if the guesthouse was still standing. Whenever Michelle had asked if Philip had visited her, she'd always changed the subject.

She'd had no idea how desperately she wanted to talk. Adrian had helped her through Frances' funeral and the months after, but there's only so much sympathy someone can give. And besides, she wasn't ready to grieve then, that reared its head a good year later. Everyone else seemed to have moved on by then. She had suppressed her emotions the best she knew how but they wouldn't leave her. Deep down this is what she had been craving to do. She wanted to share Frances' memories, open them up to someone close to her so they could add to them, fill in the missing pieces or spin them off into different routes through her life. It would of course have been better if he had been conscious but at least it gave her some comfort.

Philip always avoided mentioning Frances as if purposely erasing her from his life. She couldn't believe he had thrown out all of her belongings, all her clothes were gone. He just did it, never asked her, never talked about it. She knew grief could twist people around in so many directions, revealing sides of them you didn't know were there. It's a humbling experience, taking the taste out of life, but it was getting through it that mattered. She keeps telling herself that.

The accident comes back to her again, followed by Mr and Mrs Dobbs. What was he thinking? She can't be responsible for him – he's a grown man. She'd convinced herself everything was fine but she was seeing what she wanted to see. The drinking had stopped, the depression neatly boxed away and at last he was putting his life together, facing each day as it came.

She shivers, guilt can have an alarmingly low temperature. She feels drained by everything. The looks he'd give her had the ability to peel away and expose her vulnerable concern for him. The rehearsals had gone well in her head, pin-pointing exactly what she wanted to say to him, until she had to face him fully awake. Him staring back at her, slurping with a dry mouth. She hardly said anything to him.

She prises herself off her car and walks to the gate. The prospect of Adrian being at the guesthouse for the weekend is another complication she doesn't want. It feels like she's in an emotional tug of war. She can't be in two places at once, if there was a way she would. Adrian has a way of making her feel guilty. He seems to have a direct link to her maternal instincts. The little lost boy routine never fails, he'd played the same role when her mum was ill but this time it's different.

Michelle strolls wearily through the gate and into the garden. She spots Ian having a smoke on the dilapidated wooden bench against the back of the guesthouse. He notices her and nods. She wanders along the uneven path. The garden looks different, overgrown and left to nature. She smiles to herself. It was all so different when Mum was alive, her pride and joy, her sanctuary when she needed time for herself. We all need that. How we all need that.

She follows the path as it feeds into the patio area. Ian watches her approach. Before she knows it she's standing in front of him. He drops his half-smoked cigarette.

'Must cost you a fortune,' Michelle says.

'Yeah, they do.'

'I thought you were giving them up,' she says, sitting down next to him.

'Got an appointment at the surgery,' Ian replies. 'I've tried doing it by myself … just can't.' He grinds his foot onto the cigarette.

'I've heard about that.'

'It's easier when you're being motivated. I think that's half my trouble ...' He pauses. 'How is he?'

'Alright.' She turns to the garden. 'We had the police turn up.'

'Yeah.' Ian nods, not knowing how to gauge his reaction.

'It looks like they could be pressing charges.' If she squints hard enough she can just about see the way the garden used to be, all those bedding plants. "You can never have too many flowers," her mum would say.

'Sorry. I knew this was going to happen.' He shakes his head.

'Thanks for telling me straight away.'

'You needed to know.' Ian joins her gaze on the garden. 'I've carried the can for him a few times, but this ... I can't keep doing it. Besides, I'm thinking of –'

'Don't feel bad, you can only do so much.' Michelle stops him and lets out a heavy sigh. Reluctantly she tears herself away from the distorted memories of the garden. 'What a mess, I'm so glad you're here, Ian.'

She places her hand on his but she can feel him wanting to pull away.

'Ian, are you alright?'

Michelle's propped up in bed, eyes so tired she can hardly focus. She puts her magazine down on the bedside cabinet. She looks at her alarm clock and wonders what is taking Adrian so long in the bathroom.

It's a peculiar feeling being in her parents' bed, it's as if she is trespassing on sacred ground. The dull white wardrobe and cabinet stare back at her. They're losing their shape like the way a spine does when it compensates for an agonising pain in the body. She looks over to the dresser. A stack of un-opened envelopes, a pile of change and an array of screwed-up receipts impose on the few reminders of Frances.

It used to be so neat and tidy. A couple of old photographs of her and her mother are still there along with several she's forgotten all about. Where did he get them from? She hasn't seen them for years. She thought he'd banished them from sight with Frances' other possessions. She looks so young, barely ten-years-old. There weren't many of her after that age, probably her own fault. She's always had a habit of ruthlessly vetting photographs of herself, she hates having her picture taken. There's a nice one of Frances in the back garden, she'll have to get a copy. In front of Frances' jewellery box is a small picture of Gabby. Michelle can't help but smile. The picture draws her in. How she misses that cat. It's as if she's staring out of the photograph with a mystical knowing frown as only she could, never had a care in the world. She remembers seeing her sat in the middle of the road outside the guesthouse, leg cocked in the air, cleaning her private parts, oblivious to the oncoming cars. She doesn't think she has ever run so fast in her entire life before or since, scooping her up and returning to the safety of the back garden, to continue with her intimate grooming! She blinks, through the thin film of a tear.

Whenever they visited before she'd have her old bedroom. Adrian would get out the brightly coloured lilo from the wardrobe. She'd watch him from her single bed struggling for a good half an hour blowing it up; it didn't take long before he got himself a foot pump.

Everything is the same in her old room with a building layer of dust. It didn't feel right. She'd even catch herself lying there in the early hours staring up at the illuminating stars and planets still stuck on the ceiling, expecting to hear Frances' voice, smell her distinctive scent of cigarettes and perfume. She always loved *Coriandre* by *Couturier*. Philip bought it for her at Christmas. Well, just about every Christmas she can remember. She'd loved the smell of jasmine.

She expects to hear her race up and down the stairs, snapping at Philip to organise himself for the breakfast shift. She'd eventually get fed up and carry on without him, leaving him to sleep off one of his hangovers. The amount of times Frances told him she was going to leave. It became so common, an almost everyday remark.

Adrian walks in from the bathroom. She's annoyed at him, convinced it's taking him longer and longer to get ready for bed. It's bad enough when he's getting ready for work. She glances back at the clock on the bedside table, wondering what he gets up to in there, it's been nearly an hour! He's only down for the weekend and already the bathroom is cluttered with face creams, body lotions, and an assortment of hair gels. She can't help but smile to herself, he's not going to grow old gracefully. She has noticed a few flecks of grey at his temples but she doesn't have the heart to tell him – it'll be the dye next.

He slides in bed next to her, his cold feet making her jolt away. He smirks and starts to double-check his mouth with his tongue for any pieces of food the toothbrush has missed.

'I thought you cleaned them,' Michelle says.

'I did.'

She rolls her eyes and sinks into the bed.

'I still can't believe it.'

'What?' Michelle asks. Even that single word feels like too much encouragement.

'Ian, he never changes.'

'It's been difficult for him.'

'It's difficult for most people.' Adrian's tongue finds something on the back of one of his molars.

'Life's never that simple,' Michelle says.

'No it's about taking control. He works all those hours here for what? What has he got to show for it? How old is he? Must be thirty and still living at home.' He shakes his head, wriggles out of his boxer shorts and drops them onto the floor.

'None of us stand still.'

'Well, he's the same as ever. Never goes out, never does anything. Hardly had a drink when he'd finished.'

'Don't worry yourself, you made up for him.' Michelle turns her back to him and fluffs up her pillow.

He discards her last remark. 'At least Ellie can have a bit of fun.'

'You don't have to tell me that.' She pulls the duvet closer to her.

'Don't start that again. I was just trying to be sociable.'

She turns to him. 'Talking about yourself and ignoring everybody else. Great.'

'What is it with you and Ian?' he asks, his tongue slipping back on to his molar to get more leverage.

'Takes a while but we eventually get there, don't we?' Michelle replies. 'If you had let him talk you might have found out something.'

'What do you mean?'

'But no, as usual everyone else has to listen to you,' she sighs. It's too late for her to toy with him, if only she had the energy.

'What are you going on about?'

'He's in love. All ready to move in with her, so I suggest you put that over-active mind away.'

Adrian's taken aback. 'I just get a bit. You know – jealous.'

'I know. It's no excuse though.' She turns away from him.

'It won't happen again.'

'Of course it won't.' She squeezes the pillow tight, as his hands touch her back.

'Switch the light off.' She bounces on the mattress springs as he leaves the bed and snuggles deeper into the covers along with her thoughts.

Coughs and splutters pierce the darkness of the ward. Mr Cole slaps Philip's bed, waking him from his drifting sleep.

'Hard as nails,' Mr Cole says. 'Not built for comfort.' He's perched on the bed, legs swaying, unable to touch the floor.

'What?' Philip murmurs.

Mr Cole leans closer to him. 'God, you look awful.'

'Thanks.'

'One drug after another, what a way to go on. You'll be dead from the side effects, it's like Russian roulette. And them antibiotics are no good for you.' He lifts his left leg up for comfort. 'I hate these places.' He looks suspiciously around the ward. 'Doctors … bunch of glorified pharmaceutical reps. There was a time when you had respect for them. You wouldn't want to come in here looking untidy, shirt and tie affair. But now, if you don't question them, they'll run amuck.' He grins. 'Takes more to train a vet.'

'Hey, come on,' Philip says.

'It's just …' Mr Cole stares at him. 'I don't have to tell you, do I?' He pauses. 'I should have done more.'

'Why do you say that?' He tries to prop himself up but feels light-headed.

'Steady on.'

Philip slumps back onto the comfortable territory of the bed. 'You were always there for her, having to watch your wife deteriorate like that. It's not right.'

'I'm sure it was all brought on because of Becky. ME can be triggered by stress, I read that. I don't know …' Mr Cole shakes his head. 'She never got over it, it's not natural to bury your own child. Listen to me, she could put on a brave face, but I knew.' He looks at Philip. 'You should have seen Judith's face when she died, so peaceful. Maybe she found a place where she could see everything for what it truly was,' he smiles. 'They could argue them two, go at each other like cat and dog.'

'What do you mean?' Philip asks.

'Sorry?'

'About a place, you said she found a place.'

'Put your house in order. You know, before you die. So you can rest in peace.'

'Do you really think so?'

'Of course, why not? I certainly hope so. You lose people around you, some less fortunate than others. The ones that are close, you know they'll stay close. You can feel them, catch them near you sometimes when you least expect it. They don't leave you, they never leave. And the others, yeah they have a habit of slipping and flying away from you but when it's time they'll be back, they all come back. That's when it's time to put everything in order, to make sense of your lot. We spend half of our lives reflecting over things, it seems only right that's what we do before we die.'

'What about when they're only young?' Philip asks. 'How can they – ?'

'Why should they? The good go first, the rest of us ...' He turns away from him. 'The rest of us just follow with all our mistakes.'

'Shut it, will ya!' a man's voice cuts across the ward. 'I'm trying to get some kip.'

'What did you say?' Mr Cole's head spins to the direction of the voice.

Philip takes a hold of his arm, seeing the aggression twist over his face. 'Shhh, not so loud, hey. He didn't mean anything by it.'

'Alright, alright.' Mr Cole's face relaxes but the tone of his voice stays the same.

'Please,' Philip says quietly.

'Sure.' Mr Cole adjusts the volume. 'I'm sorry, it's these places, they wind me up.' His clenched fist opens up.

'You couldn't have done any more. You must know that.' Philip tries to soothe him.

'There's always something more.'

Philip can only watch him sit there peeling off the memories.

Suddenly his mood dramatically changes, shaking off his yesterdays. 'There's a lot of foreign doctors and nurses here. Nothing against them – do the job, get paid for it. I just pity their own hospitals.' He leans in on Philip. 'Some of them Filipino women, well, so small. I could be like a young boy with a toy with one of them.' He winks at him. 'You know what I mean?'

Philip gives him a disapproving frown.

'Don't look at me like that, no harm in window shopping,' Mr Cole sniggers. 'Besides, needs must. Sometimes you've just got to put your hand in your pocket and pay them, eh Philip?'

'Don't say that!' The dizziness comes back at him making his vision blur.

'Don't be such a prude, Philip.'

'I don't want to know.'

'Accept the way it is.' He shakes his head in frustration. 'I'm not getting through to you, am I? You know what we said about Helen but still you –'

'I need to get some rest. I'm tired.' Philip butts in. 'You'd better leave.'

'Come on, there's no need to be like that.'

'Please.'

'It's just …' Mr Cole pauses. 'Yes, maybe I should go. As you said it is late, you've got to get plenty of rest.' He pats him on the shoulder. Philip doesn't want to react like this but the mocking realisation of how uneasy Michelle seems to be around him is becoming blatantly clear.

Her life has become separate from his in every conceivable way. She's hardly phoned him since Frances died. He only sees her at Christmas, birthdays and anniversaries or when she's struck with guilt and thinks she'd better pay him a visit.

'Can't let it defeat you.' Mr Cole places his hand firmly on Philip's shoulder. 'You don't know how these things are going to turn out.'

'But what about – ?'

'Don't think about it. You know what the doctor said.'

'What, that over-qualified rep?'

Mr Cole chuckles. 'Don't listen to me.'

Philip shuts his eyes tight, making colours burst. 'What am I going to do?'

'What are *we* going to do?' Mr Cole replies. 'I think that's what you mean.' He squeezes Philip's shoulder tight.

Philip looks surprised at him. 'I thought you were going back to Spain.'

'There's no rush. Spain can wait, not quite sure if the golf swing can though. Priorities change, you should know that by now.'

6

Ellie stands behind Adrian who is comparing a batch of cheques against the business account's software, on the office's inadequate PC.

'What an absolute mess,' he says, shaking his head.

She leans in close to him, bored at all the attention the computer is getting.

'Where are the …?' Adrian says. Ellie's breath warms his earlobe. He turns away from the monitor, his train of thought derails with the sight of Ellie's blouse clinging to her breasts. He retreats back to the confusion of the monitor.

'… er, the receipts for the VAT?' He sniffs in her perfume and enjoys how it accentuates her youthful body odour.

She points to a box wedged in amongst what looks like a small open landfill site. 'There.'

He catches sight of the box and carefully pulls it out, narrowly avoiding a landslide.

'How long did you study for?' Ellie asks. She comes into view and leans against the desk.

Adrian nestles the box on his lap. 'An eternity. Well it seemed that long.'

'Maths was never my thing. I bet it's good money though?'

'Yeah, well – I do alright …' He pauses. 'I'm thinking about starting my own business.'

'Really?'

'I'd be better off. There's nowhere for me to go. Palmer's the head accountant and he isn't going to move. He's only two years older than me, martyr to the job.'

'You've been there a long time.'

'Yeah, it's been good though, plenty of perks.' He leans back in his chair. 'It's amazing how much money you can save yourself, if you know what you're doing.'

'And you don't have to put up with this sort of rubbish,' Ellie sighs, looking despairingly around the room.

'I was lucky, qualified through the firm so no debts hanging over me.' He sieves through the box optimistically, trying to find some sort of logic to the way the contents have been put there.

'Sometimes I wonder if it's really worth it.'

'What?' Adrian asks.

'Getting a degree.'

'If you get the job you're after, of course it is.'

'That's a mighty big *if*.'

'You can't think like that.' Adrian scrolls down, seeing if he can tally up a cheque from a Mr and Mrs Knight, but there's no sign of it.

'My boyfriend will probably end up earning more than me.'

'It's not all about money.' His eyes run up and down the monitor. 'It's about expanding your outlook on life as well.'

Ellie giggles. 'You sound like a quote from a prospectus.'

He wants to smile but it's difficult with the VAT riddle constantly mocking him. She places a hand on his chair. He's flattered at all the attention but there's no mystery about El-lie. What you see is what you get, no luring chase, nothing to make his stomach go queasy, to torture him with a hopeless want. And he can't help but think if he did make a move, she would either boil over, unleashing some sex-starved predator, or slap him abruptly across the face and accuse him of sexual harassment. Flirtatious roulette is something he doesn't have time for.

'Ellie, has everything been done?' Michelle's voice ricochets around the office and settles, breathing heavy on Ellie's shoulder.

Ellie freezes, her eyes roll up and sluggishly she turns around.

'Just helping out.'

'So there's nothing left to do?' Michelle asks, walking towards them.

Adrian plunges deeper into the box wanting to keep out of Michelle's firing range.

'I've done most of the rooms.'

'We're only half full!' Michelle says.

'It won't take five minutes to do room 7.' Ellie stands up straight and glances at room 7's key hanging on the wall. 'It just needs the once over.'

'Aren't you forgetting something?'

'They're not arriving until one o'clock.' Ellie shrugs her shoulders and looks to Adrian for support, but he's too wrapped up in tutting and shaking his head at the box of receipts and then the computer screen.

'What about room 8?'

'Sorry?'

'We've got a guest who's been here for over a month and since I've been back you haven't mentioned cleaning his room. He's due to go in a few days. What are you going to do, leave it until then?'

'Philip deals with him, I'm not allowed in the room.'

Michelle's stunned by Ellie's statement.

'It's that Mr Dole or Mole, something like that. Never seen the bloke.' Ellie turns away from her. 'And he's been here longer than that,' she mutters under her breath.

Michelle ignores her and focuses on the room keys displayed on the wall, dismissing the graphs and market strategy she had painstakingly put together.

'Have you got the room key?' Michelle asks.

'No.'

'Well, where is it then?'

'I said, Philip takes care of it.'

'Ellie just finish room 7.' Michelle's frustration bubbles at the surface.

'It won't take me —'

'Just do it!' Michelle cuts her dead, the sound of Ellie still protesting fills her with venom.

Ellie storms out the room.

'That was a bit harsh.' Adrian looks up appearing punch drunk from the pile of paper work.

'I know, I know. I didn't mean to be like that with her,' Michelle says. 'Is everything alright?'

'No, I can't make any sense of this.'

'Why couldn't you have helped him out?'

'Hey come on, Michelle, that's not fair.'

'You said you would.'

'You know what work's been like recently. Besides you can't blame me for this!'

'I'm sorry. Can you sort it?'

'If I could fathom out what's going on.'

'What do you mean?'

'It seems to have got worse over the last three months, I'm hoping the last tax year isn't anything like this.' He turns back to the monitor. 'Hardly anything's been accounted for, apart from a Mr Cole. According to this data sheet the guesthouse has only had one guest for the last two months. That's it! No taxable earnings because nothing's been entered on the system. On the plus side it does look like most of the records are in this box. And you know what? I can't find any deposit from this Mr Cole.'

'What nothing?'

He shakes his head.

Michelle doesn't know whether to let her anger erupt or stand there and laugh.

Adrian knows she's about to crumble at any moment. He gets to his feet and holds her. Her body moulds to his as he feels her tension subside. He's ashamed but it makes him feel good.

'Look Michelle there's probably a perfectly good explanation for all of this.'

She nods. A brief smile floods her face but departs as quickly as it arrived. He kisses her tenderly on the cheek.

'Fancy a cuppa?'

'Sure.' She doesn't move, wanting everything he has said to somehow sink in and come to rest without any protest.

Ellie has her back to Ian, taking her aggression out on the oversized vacuum cleaner. He sits precariously on a chair taking a mid-morning break, engrossed in the reader's letters in *The Sun*.

'What a mess.' Adrian places the box of receipts on the kitchen table and scratches under his arm as if it might somehow magically spark inspiration.

Ian peers over his newspaper and shrugs his shoulders in a visual *I don't know*. 'Baffling as our *Dear Deirdre*,' he smirks.

Adrian stops scratching.

'Should she sleep with her boyfriend's dad or – wait for it …' Ian turns to Ellie but doesn't get a response, 'carry on the affair with her recently discovered bisexual step-sister?' He shrugs again. 'Hey, what's a girl to do?'

Adrian grins at him and walks over to the kettle.

'It does happen, it's here in back and white.' Ian points at the page.

'Yes, alright.' Adrian takes a couple of cups from the rack. 'Does anybody want one?'

Ian looks over the bunker of his newspaper. 'I'm fine.' He nods to his half-full cup on the table.

Ellie grunts, could be a yes but it needs to be clarified.

'You know I had the same trouble,' Ian says. 'Well I'm sure it was going that way.' He giggles to himself and the chair lets out a strained groan as he tilts it further back.

'I'm sure you did,' Adrian says. 'You probably thought you had. Probably a misunderstanding, yeah?'

Ian places the chair back on all fours. 'You never know.' He insists, his smile still fixed and glowing.

Adrian turns to Ellie. 'Ellie, cuppa?'

Ellie notices Michelle at the doorway. 'Better not, too much to do.'

Michelle wishes she could defuse the tension between them, but knows her mere presence is intimidating Ellie.

'A misunderstanding, like the Dobbs,' Ellie says. 'Of course that's what it was.'

They all look at her, not knowing what to say.

Ellie seizes the moment. 'Don't know what went on but I bet they had to be paid off.'

Ian sits upright in his chair, taken aback by the comment. 'It wasn't like that.'

'Plumbing that bad! It's like musical-bloody-rooms this place.' Ellie snatches the vacuum cleaner and her cleaning tray. Adrian and Michelle look puzzled at one another.

Ellie avoids eye contact with everyone and strops out of the kitchen.

'Plumbing?' Adrian says.

Ian tries to ease himself back into *Dear Deirdre* but knows there's no sanctuary left for him.

A commotion is in full swing behind the distorted glass of the day door. A key is inserted, Michelle opens the door and steps in, holding it to its furthest point. The opening frames Philip in his wheelchair with Adrian at the helm. What a morning! She's convinced it would have been so much easier without Adrian. But what could she have done? The doctors gave Philip the all-clear and the hospital phoned to arrange for him to be picked up. It had been one snide remark after another, she felt like a referee at a boxing match, no remarks below the belt please.

'Easy. Baby in a pushchair coming through.' Adrian pushes Philip into the hall. A wheel catches the doorframe and spins it on a collision course with the wall.

'Adrian, careful!' Michelle's voice is strained.

'Christ's sake.' Philip looks like he's about to burst out of his chair and take a swipe at him.

The chair comes to an abrupt halt against the wall, nearly embedding Philip's foot into the plaster.

'Mind what you're doing!' Michelle guides the chair from the front.

'Don't worry, it's alright,' Adrian says.

'Prick,' Philip mutters under his breath.

'It was just a bit of a bump, that's all.' Adrian surveys the crinkled graze on the wallpaper.

'Another so-called bump,' Michelle says, exchanging a knowing look with Philip.

'What do you mean by that?' Adrian asks.

'It's not his fault is it. Shock can do funny things to the body,' Michelle says angrily.

Philip sighs. 'If I'm that much trouble ...'

'Don't,' Michelle says to Philip.

'Stop being so dramatic.' Adrian pushes the wheelchair nearer the stairs. 'Wasn't that bad, was it?'

Philip is unimpressed. Adrian's voice has this annoying way of shooting up in volume ever since he's been in the wheelchair. He suspiciously watches Adrian assess the stairs and then look back to him with an impatient frown.

Ian enters the hall, nods and walks over to them, hands firmly in his pockets.

'How about that for timing?' Adrian grins.

'Sorry?' Ian's confused, eager to find a clue to what he's walked into.

'Got to get him up these stairs,' Adrian says.

Michelle crouches next to Philip. 'How are you feeling? We've got room 1 ready for you, it'll be easier.'

'He's fine, stop fussing over him.' Adrian beckons Ian to him. 'Yes, right ...' He pauses, trying to fathom out the best approach to the dilemma. 'If you come around this side, I'll ...' He points, using a strange type of crude sign language instructing Ian to help him get Philip out of the wheelchair.

'Wait a minute, will you.' Michelle gets to her feet.

Ian stops, waiting to see who's going to win the leadership battle.

'What are you rushing about at? We can move him later.'

'Later? We should get this sorted now.'

'What for? Because you want to! The doctors said it could be weeks 'til he's back on his feet, he can't be stuck upstairs all that time.'

Ian catches Philip's gaze nestled in between them. Philip smiles at him. It's a smile he hasn't seen in such a long time. He seems unusually at ease with himself, not the sort of thing he thought he would say about Philip. Maybe this whole incident has been a blessing for him, a wake-up call. Their relationship had taken on so many different disguises; employer, friend, mentor, even a bit of a father figure, or maybe a father he would have liked to exchange for his own once in a while, not afraid to take him down the pub and have a few drinks with his mates.

Ian winks and smiles back.

'All I'm saying is, once he's upstairs at least he'll be settled,' Adrian says.

'Maybe he doesn't want to be settled. Maybe he wants to sit outside and get some air.'

Adrian rolls his eyes.

'They had a garden at the hospital,' Philip says.

Michelle and Adrian look at him, weighing up what he had said to play to their advantage.

'See,' Adrian says. 'What did I tell you. He's not bothered.'

'Well, pots really, but I liked sitting there,' Philip continues.

Michelle grins and throws Adrian a defiant look.

'Alright, alright.' Adrian grabs the handles of the wheelchair and reluctantly pushes him in the direction of the back door.

Adrian increases the volume of the CD player and simultaneously pours himself another glass of red wine.

'Not so loud,' Michelle says. She's tired. It feels like she's always disagreeing with him, nagging at him at every given opportunity.

'There's hardly any guests here.' Adrian pours too steeply, the wine engulfs his glass and spills onto the worktop. 'Shit!'

Ellie giggles.

'Typical.' Michelle tears off a piece of kitchen towel, rerouting and soaking up the pool of wine before it finds the floor.

Adrian steps back and smiles to Ellie, who's gently sipping her wine at the kitchen table.

'Can't do two things at once,' Adrian slurs. 'Don't know how you women do it.' He raises his brimming glass and toasts them both. 'Here's to …' He pauses. 'To women and their many wonderful attributes.'

'You're beyond embarrassment.' Michelle wipes the bottle and puts it back next to him.

'Thank you,' Adrian says. 'Thank you very much.' He takes a hearty gulp of wine.

Michelle sits back at the table next to Ian.

'Is he alright?' Ian asks, not wanting to shout but needing to carry his voice over the noise.

Michelle stares at Adrian who's being enticed by another bottle in the wine rack. 'He gets depressed,' she replies.

'About what?' Ian asks.

'No reason. Just the way he is, I suppose.'

Ellie is sat at the other end of the table wishing Adrian would sit back down and put some distance between her and Philip. Philip's examining Michelle's mobile phone, frustration is starting to get the better of him. He's come to the point where if he doesn't put it down he's liable to smash it on the floor. What does he have to do to find the guesthouse phone number? There's so much trivial rubbish he has to wade through. He puts the phone on the table. Ellie watches his every move, a pained expression on her face.

Philip looks annoyed at the CD player. 'Not my sort of music, nothing like a good tune. Fifties and sixties that's my era. Nothing's really topped it since,' he shouts to Ellie who stares blankly back at him. He deflates back into the arms of his wheelchair. 'Funny things these mobile phones, nice of Michelle to lend it me though.'

Ellie wriggles nervously in her seat. She can hardly hear him over the music and the thought of getting in earshot of him makes her feel apprehensive.

'I need a top-up, do you want another?' Ellie raises her voice.

'Oh, not for me.' Philip puts his hand over the top of the glass. 'Thanks.'

She downs her drink in one and wanders over to Adrian, leaving Philip wondering whether to have another attempt at getting to grips with the phone.

'Does he take anything for it?' Ian asks. He tries to distract Michelle's gaze away from Adrian but fails miserably.

She watches Adrian, seeing him lap up the amateur attention Ellie is displaying him. She isn't even a woman, just a stupid little teenager – her blatant eagerness turns Michelle's stomach.

'I'm going to get some fresh air.' She stands and walks unnoticed by Adrian out into the garden.

Ian is baffled, uncertain of if he's said the wrong thing. He looks over to Philip. 'You alright?' he asks. 'I said, are you alright?' Ian raises his voice a little louder pitching it over the music.

'No.' Philip puts his hand back over the top of the glass. 'No thanks,' he nods and smiles at him. Ian nods back, knowing it's a good time to leave the table unless he wants to play charades with Philip all night.

He follows Michelle and slips outside into the garden.

Ian shuts the back door and the music is compressed into an incoherent muffle. The evening's grinding down to a dusky light. Michelle sits on the bench peering into her glass, scattered white plastic patio chairs encircle her. He sits down besides her.

'Strong stuff,' Ian says. 'Not much of a wine drinker anymore.' He looks back to his glass. 'Are you OK?'

'Just ignore me.'

He takes a gulp of wine. 'That's a hard thing for me to do.'

She looks at him, he's not sure if it's the wine or his remark that makes her skin look like she's blushing.

'Michelle, can I talk to you?'

'Erm – yes, sounds a bit grim.' She looks worried, unsure where he's going to lead her. 'What is it?'

'I'm leaving.' A weight is lifted from him. The pure sense of relief it gives him is liberating, hearing it roam free, not caged up inside of him begging for his attention.

'Leaving!' Michelle's surprise quickly flips to disappointment.

'Yeah,' Ian says, savouring the moment, not wanting it to be broken.

'But –'

'I've got a job at The Regal.'

'How did you – ?'

'Craig,' he says, expecting an instant recognition from her but her expression remains blank. 'You know, when we've been out. You met him at The Ship a few times. Tubby, short hair, always grinning, Sci-fi nut.' Still nothing.

'I – erm …' Michelle says. 'I'm not quite sure.'

'Well he works there.' Ian breathes out deeply, his body giving way to complete peacefulness at telling her. 'It's about time. I need to make some changes in my life.' He laughs. 'I'm starting to sound like my old man. I'm sorry, I need something more than this.'

'Pick your moments, don't you?' She takes a sip of wine. 'But I don't blame you.'

The stifled music tunes in as Adrian steps out into the garden.

'This is nice and cosy,' he says, swaggering over to them.

Michelle doesn't acknowledge him.

'Hey!' Adrian takes a gulp of wine and struggles to control a belch.

Michelle continues to ignore him, making Ian feel even more uncomfortable.

Adrian stands in front of her trying to be intimidating. 'What – What's going on eh?' He sways. 'What do you take me for?' He stares at Michelle, desperate for a reaction from her, any reaction. 'Do you hear me! Michelle, do you?'

'Come on.' Ian stands and faces him.

'Good old Ian, always there when you need him. Come to save the day have we? Fuck-head!'

'Adrian, you've had enough,' Michelle says quietly. She swirls her glass, watching the wine spin round and around.

'Come on just leave it,' Ian says.

'Ian, please.' Michelle takes another sip and looks Adrian straight in the eye. 'You'd better sit down Adrian.'

The tone of her voice instantly sobers him. Obediently he sits on one of the chairs.

7

Philip is taking a nap in the mid-morning sun, dressed for protection. Baseball cap, sunglasses, trousers and a long sleeve shirt, with any remaining exposed skin plastered in high-protection sun cream. Ian sits next to Michelle who is laid on a blue and green chequered blanket on the lawn, her skirt hitched up, legs glistening, freshly shaved. Her top is tucked under her bra exposing her slender pale torso. He can't help himself, his eyes instinctively run up and down her body, constantly being drawn back to any exposed flesh. Every twitch or flinch makes him turn away, holding up a mirror to how creepy he must look.

'I don't think he's going to have any sunburn worries,' Ian says.

Michelle hasn't moved a muscle for at least five minutes and he knows he has spent far too long admiring her. He feels he's betraying Maxine but he can't help himself, he's got to snap out of it.

'He's in his element,' Michelle says.

The bitterness in her voice smacks him hard across the face.

'Yeah.'

She wipes the sweat from her neck. His breathing stops as her hand travels over the top half of her breasts, destroying the beads of perspiration.

'He's got everyone running around after him.' Michelle's damp hand glides through her hair. 'That's all Mum ever did for him.'

'You never know, he could be up and about at any time.'

Michelle sighs. 'It had to happen now.'

'What?'

'Work.'

'I thought the school was fine with it all.' Ian tries not to but his eyes keep wandering back over her skin.

'Don't get me wrong, they've been great.' Michelle cups her hands, shielding her eyes from the sun's glare. 'It looks bad, I really want this job. It's different, you feel you're really helping.'

'I couldn't do it, bad enough with normal kids.' Ian feels uneasy at his last remark and isn't sure if she's seen him staring at her breasts. 'Sorry, didn't mean that.'

'I know.'

'Are any permanent jobs going to be available?'

'There seems to be two in the pipeline.' Michelle pulls herself up onto her elbows. 'The more time I have off, you know, it doesn't look good.'

'What are you going to do?'

'That's what I've got to decide.'

Ian hears a door slamming; he squints in the sunlight and sees Adrian stepping out the back door. He slumps against the back of the guesthouse and stares at him. Ian feels anxious. He wonders how long he's been watching him, maybe from the kitchen window or one of the empty rooms upstairs. He turns to the lush green of the lawn wanting to shrink and run into its jungle undergrowth.

'Will you close it down?'

Michelle doesn't respond.

Ian looks up, sunlight cuts part of his vision of the guesthouse. 'It would be a shame.'

'Ellie's got to change her attitude.'

'Don't be too hard on her.'

Michelle turns over onto her side, her breasts bunch together elevating their cup size. 'I just want her to do her job, especially now you're leaving.'

'Don't, I feel bad enough as it is.'

She brushes a hand through her hair, looping as many awkward strands as she can, and tucks them behind her ear. 'It's not your fault.' Michelle props her head up on her other hand.

'I know. I feel guilty, that's all.'

'Well don't.' She looks at her watch. 'I can't believe the time.'

'You've only been out here for ten minutes! You've got to take it easy.'

'I can't sit still, never could. Shit, I've forgotten to pay in the cheque from the Fullers. What am I like, head like a sieve.' She giggles. 'Getting old.'

'Old! Don't be stupid.'

'Stupid as well am I?'

'You know I didn't mean it like that.'

She collapses on the blanket, her body submitting to the power of the sun.

'Damn, there's the cash and carry as well. I forgot all about that.'

He watches her close her eyes, the fine hairs of her exposed body beckon him to touch her.

'I can take care of that for you.'

'You're your own worst enemy.'

Ian shrugs his shoulders. 'Just want to help out.'

'I know. You've been too good to him.'

He looks at her, not knowing what else to say, feeling Adrian's eyes boring into his back, but this time it only heightens his excitement.

'And of course we need a new cook,' Michelle says. 'That's if we can afford one.' She breathes in deep, sucking the sun's rays into her pores.

There's a prolonged silence.

'Yeah, well – er …' Ian looks over to Adrian wanting to change the subject. 'So how long is Adrian staying for?'

'Work's letting him have a few days holiday. He's got to go back next week …' She pauses. 'I always wanted you two to get along.'

She looks to him but he is still staring at Adrian.

Adrian wanders over to Philip, who's stirring from his nap. He keeps one eye firmly fixed on Ian and Michelle.

'Didn't expect that,' Adrian says, leaning back against the wall.

'What?' Philip asks, annoyed at being disturbed.

'Ian, leaving.' He digs a heel into the wall. 'Still getting over the shock of him having a girlfriend, let alone moving in with it.'

'I'll miss him.'

'Thought he'd be at his parents forever.' Adrian forces a laugh out. 'Anyway once you get yourself together you won't need a cook.' He shakes his head. 'By the state of the books you're going to be struggling to keep your head above water. You could always sell up.'

Philip looks at him with a sinister contempt.

'I'm just saying, that's all. You could get over the odds for this place, or re-mortgage.'

'I'm not interested.'

'Yeah sure…' He pauses. 'Don't know what else you can do.'

'I'll manage.'

'I'm sure you will,' Adrian says suspiciously. 'Unless you've got some money hidden away somewhere. A slush fund? You must have got lucky on the horses at some point.'

'I've got a bit.'

'Yeah, this could be the perfect opportunity for you. Get in some temp to cover yourself until you're on your feet and then get rid. We've got a month to sort it out before he goes.' Adrian sits on the bench and drags over one of the chairs to put his feet on. 'Let's face it, you had a good business there for a while and this place as well. You must have a fair bit tucked away.'

'It's not a great deal of money, keep a temp for a couple of months I suppose. Been over ten years since the business collapsed. Bloody computers, ticking over nicely, making film for the local printers. Half-tones were sometimes a pain in the arse mind you. All done for you now, couple of clicks and that's it.'

'Hey come on, you weren't to know how things would change, none of us ever do. You went through a lot … the business, Frances. It couldn't have been easy for you …' He pauses. 'For you or Michelle.'

'One minute they're young kids playing merrily, and then the next they're off. All grown up.' Philip looks vulnerable. 'Does she ever say anything?'

'About Frances?'

'Yes.'

'No.'

Philip shakes his head and manoeuvres the wheelchair around with a burst of frustrated energy, which takes Adrian by surprise.

'I'm not sure, what you mean,' he adds, afraid he's said the wrong thing.

'It doesn't matter,' he snaps. 'It doesn't matter.'

Philip aggressively propels the wheelchair towards him. Adrian has never seen him like this; he's more stunned than frightened. He retracts his legs from the chair just in time as Philip barges it out of his way.

Philip stares at the broken egg on the kitchen floor. Ellie glances over to him, loathing on every muscle of her face. She doesn't want to feel like this towards him. She tries to focus on the wheelchair, to attempt to provoke at least a little sympathy. It's no use though, she's banging her head against an emotional brick wall. She can't get around or over it. She just sees him. That pathetic lingering smile of his, the odd snippet of a conversation that never finds a common ground between them. The place ran better without him. Whenever he got involved she knew something was going to go wrong. What if they don't replace Ian? She can't imagine herself working with Philip, it would be a disaster. She isn't like Ian, he's always been too soft, too considerate. Philip's never appreciated what Ian does. He's the one who runs the guesthouse. There's only one conclusion, the outbreak of a full-scale war between them.

She can't believe how much she hates him. It's a side of herself she never knew existed to this extent. She watches as Michelle comes to his aid with a piece of kitchen towel. His body aching with appreciation. She turns away. The desire to hit him and wipe that stupid grin from his face is starting to get the better of her. She slots back into the safe haven of the morning routine, and waits for Ian to finish the last breakfast order for table 2.

'Are you alright?' Michelle crouches, wiping up the last remains of egg.

'It slipped, I'm so –'

'Don't worry.' She folds the kitchen towel up, making sure none of the egg can escape.

'I can't even do a simple thing like …' He turns away helplessly, biting on his lip.

She rests a hand on the arm of the wheelchair. 'Come on, it's just an egg.'

'Thanks,' Philip says softly.

'Don't worry.'

He reaches out to her hand but she pulls it away.

'I don't deserve you.'

Michelle stands up. 'Look …' She pauses, gathering all her strength. 'I can stay another week but …'

He throws her a vulnerable look. It's exaggerated by her viewpoint of staring down at him cradled in the wheelchair.

'I'll need to go back and sort some things out.' She wants to tell him about the carer's job at the special needs school. Make him understand she can't keep taking time off, putting her life on hold. She has a life without him, without being here, but he has the ability to conjure-up the same lost expression as Adrian. She'd seen it yet again when Adrian had left on the Sunday.

'It's only a temporary job, isn't it?'

A burning rage rushes through her, but she knows she's being watched. She glances to Ian and Ellie, taking control before it erupts and scolds him.

'There you go, Ellie,' Ian says.

Ellie doesn't respond, she's too absorbed in the frustrated aggression that is consuming Michelle.

'Ellie!' His tone sharpens.

'What!' Ellie looks at the two waiting breakfasts in her hands. 'Oh, yeah.' Unwillingly she saunters to the kitchen door.

Michelle turns back to Philip. 'I need the money.' She feels uneasy, her voice resonated too much of her bitterness. 'If I don't work I don't get paid.'

'You're working here, the amount of hours you've put in. Take what you want.'

'They've been good to me.' Michelle scrunches the kitchen towel in her fist, feeling the coldness of the raw egg.

'It isn't your problem, if we have to close, we have to close.'

'Don't.' Michelle walks over to the pedal bin.

'What?'

'Don't do that to me.' She presses down hard on the pedal, stops and turns to the kitchen door. Ellie is standing there; she springs back to life like a wound-up toy that's been placed in the right direction, and leaves the kitchen.

109

Ellie yanks the cord from the back of the vacuum cleaner and plugs it in, all the time playing the conversation over and over. She stamps on the switch and it roars into life as it's dragged groaning to the kitchen door. Were they going to have to close? What would she do? She'd got used to the extra money. Did it really matter? She would cope, Dad would help her out. She places an ear against the kitchen door, dampening the sound of her pushing the vacuum backwards and forwards.

No doubt Ian knows what's going on. Didn't tell her though. He's got secretive since he has been seeing Maxine. It took him long enough to tell her he was seeing someone. The telephone ringing stops her heart dead. The sound of footsteps comes from the kitchen. She lets go of the vacuum cleaner, letting it fall clumsily to the floor, and dashes over to the phone, almost taking it off the wall.

'Bay View guesthouse,' Ellie says. 'How may I help you?' She steadies her breathing, wondering why she panicked at answering the phone. Why didn't she carry on vacuuming? At least it's more natural.

She looks to the floor, hearing the vacuum cleaner switch off.

Michelle enters the hall.

'Yeah,' Ellie says. 'Oh really, is that true?' A grin spreads across her face. 'Oh yeah. You cheeky git!' Her body re-adjusts itself, caressed by the caller's voice. 'Yes, you did say that.'

Michelle stands unimpressed, eyes smouldering into the back of her head. Ellie smirks so wide she could unhinge the top of her head. 'I bet you say that to all the girls.' She giggles like a girl half her age, coiling her fingers haphazardly around the telephone cord.

'Ellie, this is not the time or place for personal calls.'

She slowly turns around, uncoupling her fingers from the cord.

'I'm sorry, I've got to go. Things to do.' She holds the receiver to Michelle as if it's a dirty rag. 'It's for you.'

'For me?'

'It's Adrian.'

Michelle looks dumbfounded at the receiver then snatches it out of Ellie's hand.

'Yes!' she snaps, squeezing it tight.

Ellie struts along the hall back to the vacuum cleaner and steps on the switch making it jump back to life. She picks up its elongated neck and half-heartedly vacuums the carpet.

Michelle turns her back on her, wanting to hold her composure.

'You're going to have to speak up.'

Ellie makes her way along the hall towards Michelle, feeling the tension between them building, and enjoying every precious moment of it.

'Hold on.' Michelle turns to Ellie. 'Can you just wait a minute.'

Ellie carries on vacuuming, looking like she hasn't a care in the world.

Michelle lets the receiver dangle, strides over to the vacuum cleaner and with one hard stamp kills it dead.

'Ellie, please. For God's sake do something else!' She shakes her head and returns to the phone.

Triumphantly Ellie walks past her and into the dining room. Michelle turns away, winding her conversation down to a whisper.

Ian looks over at Ellie dusting down table 4's placemats.

'You're pleased with yourself,' he says.

She glances to the only remaining guests on table 2. They were the last down every morning. Ellie had noticed the back of the girl's hair was scrunched up, back-combed by the pillow.

'Why shouldn't I be?' Ellie pulls a cloth from her apron and starts wiping the cutlery. 'How are you?'

'Yeah, alright, thought you could do with a hand, that's all.'

'That's good of you.' She lifts up one of the placemats. 'I think someone's had a bit of a spillage here.'

Ian looks over.

'Spilt their tea. Why don't people just say something rather than putting a placemat over it.' She sighs. 'I'll have to put this in the wash.'

'Don't worry I'll do it. You can carry on with the rooms.'

'Thanks.'

She smiles to the couple on table 2. They timidly nod and carry on eating their breakfasts. She stops next to Ian.

'So when were you going to tell me?'

'I had to tell Michelle.'

'So it's her guesthouse?'

'No, but – you know she's calling the shots now.'

She gives him a knowing look. 'What is it with you two?'

'What do you mean by that?'

'Getting a bit defensive are we?' Ellie tucks her cloth back into her apron.

'Anyway what do you care?'

'Don't be so flippant.' She stares at him. 'I don't get you sometimes.'

He's put off guard. He has never seen her look so vulnerable.

'What does it matter?' She turns away.

He feels ashamed but he has to break the illusion, bring back that playfulness of their relationship. 'I'm sure they'll get in a fit young bloke you can drool after.'

'Don't be like that,' Ellie says.

'Or girl!'

'What do you think I am?'

She leaves the room, frustrated, not even wanting to look at him.

8

It's been almost a month since the accident, she can't believe how quickly the time has gone. Michelle flips the wheelchair's brake down hard. She's exhausted, more mentally than physically. If only she could split herself in two and please everybody, so as not to be riddled with this clinging guilt all the time. She sits down on a bench next to Philip, looking at him snuggled comfortably in his wheelchair. He smiles his usual helpless smile and then takes in the sights and sounds of the harbour.

He does nothing to help himself and it's starting to grate on her. She can't help it, it chips away at her, grinding away her compassion for him. It's a strange thing to admit to, but every time she looks at him she's convinced he's wallowing in self-pity. He's cancelled his physio twice. She only found out when Mrs Wiles, the physiotherapist, rang to confirm another appointment. She explained that part of the hospital is being refurbished and the physiotherapy section has been closed until further notice. This time she'll have to come to him. Unbelievable, she's coming to him and still he doesn't want to make the effort! What is the matter with him? He's not wasting that poor woman's time again. Michelle seized the first available slot and to her delight and Philip's horror it's this afternoon. She still can't believe his reaction when she told him. She clenches her teeth hard subduing her brooding anger. He looked like he was about to burst into tears when she said Mrs Wiles was coming at two.

He can be pathetic sometimes. She turns away from him, looking out onto the harbour, sensing her fury rising. It feels like she's being groomed to run the guesthouse, broken down to except her fate, taking the reins from Ian like the true heiress to the kingdom. But she doesn't want this, this isn't her life. It isn't the way it's supposed to be. She feels like she's becoming her mother. She swallows hard, her throat surprisingly dry. She doesn't want to go there, she hasn't the strength to risk it, to carry its heavy emotional load, knowing it has the power to break her. She shudders at the thought.

At the mouth of the harbour two rowing boats are carrying people from one side to the other. She watches the line of people depleting on the far side, nine to a boat. The oarsman stands like a surfer, hand out to guide them into his swaggering boat. She has phoned up the Robert Wise School and spoken to the head, explaining the situation to him. He stopped listening once she mentioned she wouldn't be back for at least another week, her excuses and his pity were running out. A nauseating feeling hit her when she put the receiver down and it still lingers.

The rowing boats pass each other in the middle of the harbour. The breeze is cool but offers little respite for the oarsmen, rowing back and forth across the harbour's yawning mouth. Priorities line up for Michelle's attention, with the looming prospect of Ian leaving at the end of the week the main concern. She'll go to the cash and carry after Philip's seen Mrs Wiles. She's going to make sure he goes through with it, even if it means her being with him every step of the way. It's no good, she's going to have to be stern with him, no more caving in and running around after him. Things have to change, she can't just sit back and believe they will on their own.

It's her who has to get him up in the mornings; he never offers or wants to help out. He just relies on her to do everything for him, and they're fully booked. She doesn't expect him to be running up and down the stairs but she doesn't want him to just sit there fishing for sympathy, making her feel as if she doesn't care. He has a pair of arms, for God's sake! It's winding everybody up. He has his usual nap in the back garden in the afternoon or sometimes in the kitchen, depending on the weather, then has to be carried up the stairs to watch the six o'clock news. At least the big band music has stopped.

And that Mr Cole, what's going on there? He's never talked about him before to her and every time she mentions his name he clams up. The only thing she's managed to prise out of him is that he's staying on for at least another month before he returns to Spain. She still hasn't met him, never known anybody so elusive, she always manages to just miss him. Apparently he's paying his bill at the end of his stay in one lump sum. Something's not right. She's worried he's one of Philip's dodgy mates, he has a habit of meeting people down the pub and being taken advantage of. But is it really her problem? He's a grown man, isn't he?

She looks at Philip and smiles to herself. She was determined to tell him today. But she couldn't. What's the matter with her? One of the rowing boats reaches the far side, the oars spring up and the boat drifts to the metal steps that cling tight to the harbour wall. Adrian will be on at her tonight, she's dreading phoning him – the tutting, the sighs, his mood draining out of the receiver. The trouble is, how can she try to reason with him when she knows he's right? The more help she gives Philip the more dependent he becomes on her.

'We're going to have to make a move,' she says.

Philip doesn't respond. His attention is firmly fixed on the leisure boats bobbing on the calm waters of the harbour.

'Dad.'

He shuffles in his wheelchair, his thigh has gone to sleep. 'I'm not sure if I'm ready for the physio today.' He rubs his

116

stomach, blowing hard. 'I think I've eaten something that doesn't agree with me.'

'I'm sure you have.'

He ignores her as she takes to her feet.

'Could you give Mrs Wiles a ring? It'll be alright, arrange it for another time.'

She unclamps the brake and forcefully swings the wheel-chair around.

'Michelle, what are you doing?' Philip gasps in astonishment.

He looks up at her but her expression is set in determination.

'Now, Mr Morgan. I'm going to slowly bend your leg towards you.' Janice Wiles, a stocky black woman with a warm smile and no-nonsense attitude looks disappointed at him as he grimaces dramatically. 'Have you been doing any of the exercises on the leaflet they gave you?' Her stare intensifies, exaggerated by her braids pulled tight into a ponytail.

Philip lies on a dark blue sponge mat, wearing tracksuit bottoms and a faded brown T-shirt, staring up at the ceiling of room 1. Next to the mat a pair of fluffy tartan slippers wait for him. 'Er ...' Philip tries to find an excuse, hoping to pluck one out of the air.

'I'll take that as a *no* then.'

'Well ...' He knows he's up against it but he has to try. 'I've –'

Mrs Wiles cuts him dead. She has heard it all before, been in the job long enough to hear all the excuses they can come up with. You can only do so much, it's up to the individual in the end. She winks to Michelle. 'Yes, well you're not going to be back on your feet with that sort of attitude. Let's face facts. You haven't been doing any of the exercises, have you?'

Philip turns away.

'Mr Morgan.' Mrs Wiles scorns him like a troublesome adolescent, she isn't going to let it go.

'You see –'

'Mr Morgan. Please, you're only lying to yourself.'

'No – I – I'm sorry.' He gives up, why prolong the inevitable?

'At last. You're going to ache, but don't blame me.' She laughs, folding his leg into itself.

Philip lets out a whimper of a cry.

'That's a good sign, we've got some response from down there. If you'd have done what you were supposed to it wouldn't be so painful.'

She repositions herself, giving Philip a full view of her generous backside.

'Let's have a look at your foot.' Mrs Wile's hands grapple around his ankle. 'You sure got a beautiful daughter there.'

Michelle blushes.

'Got two myself, never had a son. Been many a time I wish I had, mind you.' She shakes her head. 'Must be less hassle.' She twists Philip's foot, he bites his lip against the pain. 'Eldest is Denise.' She smiles at Michelle. 'How old are you?'

'Twenty-four,' Michelle answers.

'Few years older than you. Married, got a son Joshua. Lovely boy, but, well, I would say that. Wonderful family, nothing's ever too much trouble. That's what it's all about in the end.'

'What about your other daughter?' Michelle asks.

'Oh, don't get me started.' She twists Philip's foot the other way. 'I don't know what to do with that girl. Don't know where she is half the time, and the other half ...' Her thoughts jump up for attention. 'Breaks my heart it does.' She places a hand over her mouth, flustered. 'Look at me! You don't want to hear my problems.' She moves on to Philip's other leg. 'Let's hope we can get some results from this one.'

He groans as he sinks exhausted onto his back.

Philip lies on his bed, his body gently throbbing. It's late afternoon, a good couple of hours since Mrs Wiles left. The sensation of her twisting his body, contorting it in an array of bizarre directions, still lingers. He opens his eyes, the heat of the day on his face. Sunlight is bursting through the window, the curtains breathe peacefully pumping in a fresh sedating sea breeze. From the powerful light, Mr Cole paces into view.

'Thought she'd never go. Bloody woman. Didn't she go on!' He stops, making sure he has Philip's full attention. 'Don't think she even drew a breath. Good lot of meat on her though.'

Philip lifts himself up. 'You don't have to tell me.' He slowly swings his legs onto the floor.

'Stiff are you?'

'You could say that.' Philip stands, wincing at the effort.

'You want to get out a bit more, no point in being here all cooped up. Fresh air, you can't beat it.'

Philip walks past his wheelchair and into the en-suite. Mr Cole watches him disapprovingly and follows closely.

Philip lifts up the toilet lid, sensing Mr Cole behind him. He wants to tell him to leave but he hasn't the strength.

The mirror distracts Mr Cole. 'Are you going to tell them about your miracle recovery?'

'How can I?' Philip groans as the urine drains from his body bringing chaos to the calm blue water of the toilet.

Mr Cole looks at his reflection. He pushes up his nose with a finger to inspect his nostrils for untamed hairs.

'It's a right mess.' Mr Cole lets go of his nose and it flicks back into place.

'It's a family business, that's what it should be. Once Ian goes –'

'What do you think will happen? She'll stay? Leave you to your afternoon naps? Don't kid yourself.' Mr Cole brings his face closer to the mirror for an examination of any ripe blackheads on his nose.

Philip tightens his bladder, wringing out every last drop as he attempts to keep it away from the toilet seat but fails.

'She doesn't want to be at the guesthouse. Face it, Philip, she never has.' Mr Cole snarls, staring at his teeth, then pulls at his lips for a more probing investigation. 'And she certainly doesn't want to play nursemaid to you.' He sticks out his tongue as far as it will go.

Philip pulls up his tracksuit bottoms and turns to face him. His reflection enters the mirror. Mr Cole stares at him, their expressions swirl in a mixture of confusion and unreasoning stubbornness.

'You'd better check out your options.' Mr Cole looks him up and down, then straight into his face. 'Family. Is that what you think, Philip?'

Philip stares back at him. Mr Cole's eyes have turned from brown to blue, shining just like his mother's used to. Is he wearing mascara? Yes he is, he's sure he is.

Ian has his forearms submerged in the brown foamy water of the kitchen sink. The draining board can hardly be seen. Chrome saucepans lean precariously against one another, suds lumber off small stacks of plates, cutlery is haphazardly scattered on any available space. He catches hold of something under the water and pulls it out for a closer look. Ellie hovers behind him. He glances at the soggy piece of hash brown between his fingers.

Ellie grins. 'Nice.'

He squeezes, its white insides ooze out.

'That's revolting.'

He drops it back into the water and turns, grinning to Ellie. His hands covered in a mass of foam, he claps, sending the suds into the air.

She giggles, backing away. 'Just a big kid, that's all you are!'

Ian playfully flicks suds at her. 'No point growing up, it's over-rated.'

'Piss off, I'll be glad to see the back of you.'

'You don't mean that.'

'Might do.'

'Yeah, I bet you will be glad to see the back of me,' Ian says, snapping the playful mood in two. 'You know, to tell you the truth, I don't really feel anything.'

'What do you mean?'

The remaining suds slip from his hands and dissolve on the floor.

'About leaving, about this place. I thought I would ...' He pauses. 'But I feel nothing.'

What's the matter with him? It's as if he's a ghost caught between the real world and the spirit world, not knowing where he belongs. All that frustration has gone. He's on the last stretch, having nearly worked this month's notice. It doesn't seem possible, he can't believe it's virtually a month ago when he told Michelle that evening in the garden. He expected her to act differently. He didn't know how he thought she would react but not like that. She's become cautiously distant from him, but what did he expect? She was worn down at being back at the guesthouse, dealing with Philip on a day-to-day basis with no escape from him. Her relationship with Adrian is taking a battering, snapping at one another on the phone, the bleep of text messages stopping altogether, when Adrian realised Philip was reading them before passing them to her, and in the midst of it all is Philip. The last time he saw him this happy was a good six or seven years ago, when he got lucky with an outsider on the Grand National.

Ian came to the Bay View on work experience, part of his college course. Philip's repro business was ticking over on the old Grimsby industrial estate. The guesthouse was always fully booked back then. Frances, pushing herself way too hard, had to be involved in every aspect. She would never delegate like Philip. Ian had just fitted right in; it felt comfortable, steady but not too busy. Michelle was only fourteen. He can't imagine her being *that* young any more, but it's all leaving him now, memories being carefully filed away somewhere in the back of his mind.

A month's notice had been way too long. He wanted to start his new job to see how it fitted him, mark his territory out and become established as soon as possible. He's said he'll come back and visit but he knows it wouldn't feel right. He's disorientated, everything has somehow slowed down, the routine of coming here day after day is nearly over, it's all going to be different.

'Will you miss me?' Ellie looks sheepishly at him.

'Of course I will,' Ian says, drying his hands. 'All them tales of sexual depravity. I'll only have *Dear Deirdre* to rely on. Never as good as the real thing.'

'Thanks!' Ellie leans against the cupboards.

'Sorry, I didn't mean it like that.' Ian's failing to judge the situation yet again, he really has lost his knack. 'Are you still coming out at the weekend for a celebratory drink?'

'Yeah,' Ellie replies. 'So how many nights out have you had so far?'

'Not that many, a general run-up to the weekend.'

'It's only Tuesday!' Ellie says. 'Sunday should be fine for me.'

'You can always come out tonight or tomorrow or –'

'Sunday's probably better. Your mates should have run out of steam by then. Only so much of them idiots I can take,' she says, rolling her eyes at him.

'They're not that bad,' Ian says, but he's bombarded by flashbacks of them leering drunkenly at anything passing as female. Egging each other on with cheers and caged monkey noises to drink as many pints and chasers as they could. And of course the nightclub, piling into Metros, mugged at the door by extortionate prices. Followed by all of them ending up at the Peking House for a takeaway, or any one of the nearby fish and chip shops – depending on the cash flow. Bunched together, telling each other about how fit all the women were, and then what they'd do next time. It'll be different. They'll go somewhere else, do something different for a change. It didn't happen though. They just did it all over again.

Ian finds some redeeming inspiration. 'It's karaoke tonight at The Dog.'

'You must be desperate to go to that place.'

'It's not that bad.'

'Of course not. I've got you something.'

'Yeah?' Ian glows like a small child. 'Well, where is it?'

'You're not having it just yet. I'll give it to you on Friday.'

'Is that right? I don't think that would go down very well with Maxine, but hey, I don't blame you for trying.'

'You cheeky bas –'

A cough erupts from behind them, simultaneously they turn to see Philip sitting smugly in his wheelchair. He moves closer, not picking up on Ellie's hostility towards him.

'How did you get down here?' She fires at him.

'The stairs,' Philip says. 'How else do you think I got here?' He chuckles but no one else sees the funny side.

'But –' Ian tries to understand the effort it must have taken, but it doesn't match the calm and composed Philip sat grinning at them. It doesn't make sense.

Philip leans back, quietly taking in their questioning expressions.

'You could have hurt yourself,' Ian says.

'Stop fussing. I didn't, so it doesn't matter.'

'Michelle got you your own mobile, all you had to do is ring.'

'Hey, come on.' Philip relishes his concern.

'You can't crawl up and down the stairs with guests about.'

'Alright, alright. I just wanted to try, no harm done. Anyway, Mr Cole helped with the wheelchair.'

'I can't see Michelle being pleased.'

The playfulness drains from Philip's face. 'There's no need to tell her just yet.'

'Why not?' Ian asks.

For the first time he acknowledges Ellie. 'Are all the rooms done, Ellie?'

She pulls herself up from supporting the kitchen worktop and lumbers unwillingly to her cleaning tray. She deciphers the coded message straight away, cryptic for go away, get lost. Or is it leave now? It all leads to the same conclusion.

Patiently Philip sits in silence until she has left the room. Then he reaches out and takes hold of Ian's hand. Ian's taken aback, too shocked to pull away.

'I owe you.' Philip's stare intensifies. 'I'm sorry for the way I've been behaving recently.' He stretches out his other hand and places it firmly on top. 'You know what I mean. Frances thought so much of you. You know that, don't you?'

'Yeah.' Ian nods uneasily. 'I – I miss her.'

Philip releases his grip, his hand sinks into his trouser pocket and produces an envelope. He places it in Ian's open hand and holds it there. 'A bit extra to spend.' Philip smiles.

'You've paid me a couple of extra weeks' money already.'

'Please, take it.' Philip recoils back into his wheelchair to enjoy Ian's reaction on opening up the envelope.

Ian's stunned, there's at least a dozen twenty pound notes staring back at him. 'I don't know what to say.'

'It should be more, a lot more.' Philip smiles.

'I wasn't expecting this.' Ian folds the envelope up and stuffs it in his pocket.

'Go on then.'

'Sorry?'

'Take the rest of the day off.'

'But what about the evening meals?'

'Don't worry, we'll be alright. I hear you're making a marathon of it, going out every night.'

'Yeah, well it has to be done. What about Michelle?'

'She'll be a couple of hours yet, at the cash and carry.'

'Can you tell her to meet us at The Ship at half-eight, if she can. She said she might pop out tonight.'

'Sure I'll tell her. No need waiting around for her.' Philip turns away. 'You've done plenty of that already,' he mutters.

'Sorry?'

'Give yourself time to get ready.'

'What are you trying to say?' Ian comically attempts to smarten up.

'Go on, on your way.' Philip gestures for him to leave.

Michelle sneaks into the kitchen; she's supposed to be weighed down with carrier bags from the cash and carry, having done her usual trick of taking too many from the car, and then dropping them in a large heap on the kitchen floor. Her head is spinning, what is she like? She's driven all the way to the cash and carry and forgotten her purse. She's getting worse, has senile dementia set in already? No, let's be honest, it's her attitude. The auto-pilot switch has been engaged helping her hold onto the idea that if she doesn't think about it she might be able to get through this. It has to end, like waking from a bad dream; if she stops she'll have to face what she's doing, acknowledge her life before the accident.

How can she assess her feelings for Adrian? She'd wanted to step back but not like this. Distance is now part of their relationship. They have settled into a weekend routine. He turns up sometime on Saturday afternoon – a small night bag and a DVD rental. The evening either turns out to be forced petty chit-chat or a full-blown argument. What's happening to her! She's hardly asking for the world – normality, that's all, a good clean slice of it. She smiles but it springs back to a frown.

She expects to see Philip having his usual afternoon nap, soothing away that drained expression he acquires after his exercises. At least it should give him more of a routine if he manages a small session each day. Instead of the one where he's slumped pretending to be a fat cat napping, with the one concern of making sure he can hear the fridge door being opened. She grins, remembering when Mrs Wiles first came round and put him through his paces. That's what he really needs, a kick up the backside, not pampering to his every whim.

She thought he would have been out on the patio. Although the sun isn't out, it's still warm, but he's nowhere to be seen. Maybe he's been adventurous and is sat out at the front of the guesthouse; it's a wonderful view of the bay. She'd be surprised, though, he's always felt uncomfortable out there. It's like a little village community along the row of terraces, Frances loved it. Taking small breaks throughout the day, soaking in the view, having a chat, a cup of tea and a cigarette, no wonder she had wrinkles and a leathery complexion, but they all did. It was like part of the guesthouse owners' uniform.

But for Philip there's always been some excuse. Either there are too many people staring at him, it's getting too hot or the breeze has too much of a chill. Or even accusing the neighbours of prying when they're just being friendly. He never could see it like that – *"poking their noses in"* is how he's always put it. He never got on with the likes of the Walkers who were a few doors up, or his new neighbours, the McKee's, who replaced the Gardeners. They hadn't long moved into the property. It was their first season here, came down from Lewisham – a nice enough family. Their son mopes around lost, must be still in his teens, constantly going back to Lewisham for the weekends to stay with his mates. But now, of course, Philip's favourite excuse is that he needs someone to help him back in with the wheelchair, he didn't want to be in the way. She wanted to kick herself sometimes, she has only added to his stubbornness, just for a quieter life.

She walks through the hall and opens the day door. The sound of the sea hits her. She carries on through the tiled entrance out through the open front door. Her hand shelters her eyes from the glare of the sun as it escapes through a gap in the clouds. A couple of plastic chairs are still stacked up where she sat out with Ian only a few evenings ago. She breathes in the sea air, the sun feels good on her face charging up her energy supplies. This is what she missed. Her hand comes away from her face, the sun disappears behind a cloud that stretches to the horizon. She takes in the motion of the bay. The view, the invigorating fresh salty smell, the constant flow of people along the esplanade. A seagull cries out up above, she looks down the street hearing the arcade games in full swing coming from the Old Pier.

They're embedded in her, making the day more palatable. She sighs and smiles. *Purse,* she thinks, shaking her head. It might have been worse. Could have trudged around the cash and carry, trolley bursting and found out she'd forgotten it at the checkout. Now that really would have been humiliating.

127

He must have got Ian to help him back upstairs, she reasons to herself. But where is everybody? She turns her back on the bay and disappears into the dim light of the hall.

Climbing the stairs she reads over and over the shopping list in her hand, trying to think of anything else she needs to turn this set back to her advantage. She stops on the landing. Can't think of anything else they need. It's no good, she'll have to bring back a box of chocolate biscuits rather than the plain ones, a little treat for her troubles.

She opens the fire door and faces the small cul-de-sac of guest rooms. Somebody moving about in one of the rooms catches her attention. She thinks it's coming from room 2 but it's hard to tell in these old terraced houses. She notices Philip's door is ajar. She steps closer. The fire door retracts behind her to a cushioned click.

'Dad,' Michelle calls.

No reply.

Slowly she pushes the door open, walks into the room and stops suddenly. Her body goes ridged, frozen to the spot trying to comprehend what's in front of her. Philip's empty wheelchair stares back at her like a discarded shell. Questions bombard her. She draws a deep breath, knowing there must be some reasonable explanation, there has to be. She looks around the room but he isn't there. Even peering into the en-suite, she doesn't expect him to be there but she has to look. She approaches the chair. Why is it empty? Where is he? Where is everybody? The wheelchair stares back cold and still, mocking all her unanswerable suspicions.

She rushes out of the room, hitting the fire door with a thud. She mounts the stairs, desperate to find Ian or Ellie, stopping on the second landing to catch her breath. What if he's been taken to the hospital? He isn't that ill, is he? Oh God, what if he really is. A wave of guilt makes her dizzy, she holds on to the banister. The fire door opens, cutting off her thoughts. It's Ellie; she never thought she'd be so relieved to see her.

'Ellie,' she says, panting.

'I've done them.'

'Done what?'

'The rooms.' Ellie folds her arms on the defensive. 'I'm taking my break now.' She looks at her watch.

'Yes – sure – whatever.' Michelle shakes her head. 'Where is he?'

'He's gone.'

Michelle's shocked. 'What do you mean, he's gone?'

'He let him go. That's it, he's finished for the day, lucky git. He'll be in town propping up a bar.' Ellie grins. 'Good luck to him.'

'Sorry, who are you talking about?'

'Ian.'

'No – Philip, where is he?'

'In his room.'

'I've been in his room, he's not there.'

'He must be with Mr Cole then.'

'With Mr Cole?' Michelle looks up the stairs. 'How can he have got up there?'

'Mr Cole probably helped him.'

Michelle ignores her, still staring confused up the stairs.

'I've got to go, Mum texted, she's already there. I'm late as it is!'

'Alright, alright Ellie. But –'

Ellie looks annoyed at Michelle and emphasises it with a sigh.

Michelle's patience crumbles. 'Oh just go,' she says. 'Go.'

Ellie struts defiantly past her to deny her authority. She stops and turns but to her dismay Michelle is climbing the flight of stairs oblivious to her efforts.

Michelle steps onto the landing. Nothing feels right. She glances back, wanting to see Ellie there but she's nowhere to be seen. Even with her hostility at least it gave her a familiar reassurance. She can trace this unsettling feeling all the way back to when she stepped into the kitchen. She'd dismissed it at first but it has lingered by her side, growing, feeding on her tension. She slowly pushes the fire door open. What is she doing creeping about the guesthouse? This was her home. But she has to, she knows she has to, it's as though she is seeing the guesthouse at a completely different angle. The sound of voices stop her in her tracks. Her other senses turn down letting her hearing become dominant. The voices are coming from room 8. She can't make out what they're saying, but she knows by the tone that one of them is Philip. She steps closer to the door and places her ear against it. To her surprise it's unlocked and she has to catch herself from tumbling into the room.

'Are you sure you can cope?' a man voice asks.

It has to be Mr Cole but there are tones in the voice that sound vaguely familiar. She crouches down and peers through the gap in the door.

'Yes, alright.'

This time it's Philip; his voice is tired and drained. She tries to catch sight of him but her view is limited to the large window and the small table and two chairs. The aftermath of a breakfast is still sprawled on the table, a trail of smoke wafting from an ashtray. A figure suddenly walks past, subduing the light. She draws back but her curiosity gets the better of her. The figure cuts into her view from the other side of the room. She gasps. It's Philip.

But he's walking. Michelle watches stunned as he walks across the room and sits at the table.

'Nice gesture,' Mr Cole says. Philip's body contorts, his features become rigid and stern. 'Knew him a long time didn't you, been through a lot together.'

He takes the thin cigar and drags on it, its mystical vapours drain from his mouth. He turns his head as if he's talking to someone behind him.

'It'll be strange without him,' Philip says.

What is he doing? Michelle's confusion is replaced by a hollow void. The lies he has told her, the guilt he has so easily provoked, come racing at her, pushed on by an uncontrollable rage. She rises to her feet and barges into the room.

'What's going on?' Michelle slams the door behind her with a violent bang to get his full attention.

Philip almost falls from his chair.

She looks around the room wanting to find an alternative answer to what she has been witnessing, reaching out for anything to explain it all with a light-hearted conclusion. But she is met by a stale stench that fills her lungs and lays heavy in her mouth. She heaves. The pattern of the carpet is almost lost to pieces of decaying food, woven and bursting in white furry mould. The room is covered in filth, its smell and neglected state almost knocks her back. Exasperated, she looks at Philip.

He rushes to her. 'Michelle!' he says, alarmed and flustered.

She pushes him away.

'Please,' Philip pleads. 'Please, Michelle.'

'Get away from me, you can walk! Why didn't you tell me? What the hell are you playing at?' She doesn't know whether to scream or cry.

He looks at her, stunned.

'You don't change, do you?' Michelle focuses, calming herself down. 'Look at this! What were you thinking?' She looks helplessly around the room. 'I can't do this any more. I thought Mrs Dobbs was –' She shakes her head. 'No, no I've had enough. It's your mess, you can sort it out.'

Philip smiles pathetically at her.

Her rage shatters the surface at his reaction. 'That's it! I want nothing to do with you. You sort this place out, do you hear me? Sort yourself out!'

'Oh no, Michelle please.'

She turns away from him.

'No, you can't say that.' Philip's tears swamp his eyes.

He lunges and grabs her by the arm.

'Let go of me!' Michelle snarls at him. She wrenches her arm out of his grip and strides towards the door.

Philip snatches hold of her arm again, this time it's forceful and determined. He spins her around with an alarming strength. She stares at him, her anger holding defiant.

'I said, let go of me!' she screeches at him.

'You can't go,' Philip says. 'Please don't, Michelle.'

'Get your hands off me!' She tugs at his clenched grip like a snared animal. 'You don't want me.' Her eyes narrow. 'You don't want anybody.'

'What do you mean by that? It's not true. No.'

'Save it. I've heard it all before.' She backs away from him. 'What?'

'You heard me,' Michelle spits with pure distaste. 'You know what I mean.' It's no use, she has to say it. Her emotions have been clogged up for too long and her anger now lubricates them, setting them free. 'The way you treated Mum.' She turns away from him. 'How could you? You should have been there for her. You never even visited her at the hospice, just couldn't be bothered. Had more important things to do at The Ship, did you? You're a waste of space.'

'Michelle, you can't say that.'

'You didn't love her. Hold you back, did she?'

'Shut up.'

'Hit a nerve, have I? That's it, isn't it? As long as you're alright, that's all you're worried about ...' She pauses. 'You're pathetic.'

His head slumps like a child who's being told off.

'It's over. I'm through with you. Through with all your stupid lies, you're not treating me like Mum.'

She tries to walk past him but he blocks her way, his gaze lifelessly fixed to the floor.

'Get out of my way.' Michelle's body shakes with animosity and pumped adrenaline. 'You make me sick.'

'She's not your mother!' Philip shouts.

Springing to life he hits her hard across the face. She tumbles back, almost falling to the floor.

She screams at him, kicking him hard in the shins. Philip shrieks in agony. Taking her chance she rushes towards the door, her whole being focusing on it, all the time hearing him charging at her, smelling his body odour becoming more and more potent. Philip throws every last ounce of his strength forwards to stop her, his hands grab at the air. She flinches, moving out of his way but his clawing fingers entangle in her hair, violently jerking her head back.

He falls clumsily. The door disappears and she stares helplessly at the ceiling. The weight of his body sends her hurtling forward. Her chin smashes against the door, the sound of bone cracking and grating echoes in his head. His body collapses on hers, sending her chin scraping down the door until it hits the floor with the breaking of her neck.

The room is filled with a suffocating silence.

Philip doesn't move. Michelle's body is warm underneath him. The muffled sound of waves breaking in the bay creeps in to the room. Bewildered, Philip carefully lifts himself off her. The side of his face and his shoulder ache from the collision and fall. A cold shiver takes hold and shakes him. He stares at Michelle, desperately wanting to latch on to any movement – the rise and fall of her lungs, a swallow to ease the dryness of her mouth, or maybe a flinch from a muscle. Anything, please anything to say she's alive. This can't be happening. She can go back to Adrian, he can cope. He'll sell up. It doesn't matter any more but please not this, anything but this. He crouches, his breathing unsteady, hands battling against uncontrollable shaking.

'She is your mum.' He reaches out and touches her hair, letting it slip through his fingers. 'You know that, don't you? You know. Please tell me you know.'

His heart pumps in pure disbelief as he stares at his daughter's lifeless body, frantically wanting to match Michelle with what is in front of him. Her smile, her stubbornness. How proud and yet envious he is of her. What has he done? She's a grown woman in her own right. He couldn't see it, only saw what he wanted to see. What does she want with running the guesthouse? She has a life of her own. He's a good dad, isn't he? He stares into himself, an uncompromising emptiness is opening up and he knows it will be impossible to ever fill. He has lost it all, only himself left to face. It's all down to him, no one else left to blame. But what about his dad? Wasn't it his fault for being weak with his mother, dying before Philip had found him. Can he blame his dad for that? He has, he still wants to. He'd blamed everybody for the demise of his business, but he didn't adapt, didn't invest. He let it all slip away from him. As for Frances, he could never see beyond the cancer that took her. Never saw her or appreciated how much she, she – His head spins, veering him away from that one-way street he doesn't want to venture down.

And there's Helen, for some reason everything was leading him back to her, dying while giving birth to Michelle. Why did she have to die? It would have all been so different, he knew it would. He'd held the event up as if inspecting a wondrous archaeological find, a link enabling a whole chain of events to make perfect sense. He only has one thing left to blame, one thing that connects everything together. Right from that moment when Helen died in the hospital leaving him and Michelle. It could have all been so different. He held the notion tight to him preparing for the impact. Fate. The word bit at his body like a sharp frost. He falls from his thoughts, facing what fate has dealt him yet again. He blinks and looks again at Michelle, making sure, hoping somehow to banish what he's seeing, never having to visit it again. But it's still there in front of him, warped in all its madness.

He swallows hard.

Her stillness provokes him more than her anger ever could. Her eyes stare up to the ceiling, mouth open, expression caught between fear and disbelief. Her head and body are at an unnatural angle to one another. Adrenaline makes the back of his eyes throb and his head hang heavy. Slowly he traces a smear of blood running down the door. He starts to hyperventilate, shaking and rocking steadily back and forth in time with the waves breaking in the bay.

9

Philip splashes water from the en-suite sink onto his face. His reflection stares back coldly from the cabinet mirror. He can't erase the image of Michelle lying against the door from his mind, her body still and lifeless. He'd crouched by her side, watching her, willing her to move. Every muscle rigid with pleading. Only his eyes moved, racing over her body, wanting to find any indication she was still alive. Relentlessly they searched until their muscles throbbed and they stumbled, tripping themselves up from fatigue. He'd played out options in his head – maybe he should shake her, slap her face or throw cold water over her. They all spun around and around like slices on a roulette wheel. But he didn't do anything, he was nailed to the spot, watching her like a bystander mesmerised by a road accident.

He'd give anything to see her face light up, her smile, her runaway laughter and that passionate driven anger of hers. He doesn't care what she thinks of him any more. It doesn't matter if she screams at him, shouts and brings the house down – he'll take it. Even if she walks away and disowns him, tells him she doesn't want to see him ever again. For the first time in his life he's able to take her rejection, but not this empty unmovable silence. Anything but this. He inspects the water racing unevenly down his face. He has no recollection of how long he was by her side, everything had stopped. The sun in the sky, the dust particles floating in its hot rays, even the curtains caught up in play by the sea breeze had all become still.

Mr Cole had eventually woken him from his trance. The room went dark and let in a sudden chill. His limbs weighed heavy, aching at being held in the same position for so long. He strikes out, wiping some of the droplets from his face, destroying them with one foul swoop. He remembers Mr Cole helping him up and insisting on putting Michelle into bed. It seemed the right thing to do. He put her to bed, all the time Mr Cole supporting him in a supervisory role the way Frances used to. The whole act, the familiarity of it calmed him. He got lost in it, allowing his thoughts to drift and find a stillness. It reminded him of when she was a little girl. His rose-tinted glasses were tightly on, blinkers and all, not letting in any creeping distortion from either side. The smell of the soft white sheets when he used to tuck her in, the click of her bedroom door after he had said goodnight to her, the warm nourishing feeling she was safe and well, it soothed him and he hung onto it tightly.

He'd slipped willingly into Michelle's old bedtime routine, but felt as if he was constantly tripping up on false memories – they felt awkward and unfamiliar. He kept glancing over to Mr Cole, wanting to catch his eye. He had stepped away from his supporting role and was sat at the table, head down. He longed for a nod of reassurance from him, a smile to pat him on the back. But Mr Cole sheepishly avoided him, his body twitching and jolting, caught by a fear as if he were on a roller coaster ride that wouldn't let him off. He kept mumbling, "She needs to sleep, she needs to sleep. That's right we'll put her to bed. Got to get her to bed." Over and over.

Philip jolts back to the present. His other hand swings into action, frantically removing any moisture from his face. He hears the comforting sound of waves breaking on the shore.

'What's the matter?' Mr Cole asks from behind him.

Philip stops, his hand rakes down his face. He takes in a deep breath and faces Mr Cole.

'Are you alright?' Mr Cole asks, taking a swig from a small bottle of vodka and belching. 'Oops, sorry. Pardon me.' He pats his chest, winding himself.

Philip shakes his head and turns back to the mirror. He opens the cabinet, revealing the different shapes and sizes of medication bottles, all in neat rows like the skyline of a minature city.

Reluctantly he turns back to Mr Cole.

'What's the matter? Are you alright?' Mr Cole takes another swig from the bottle and belches. Vodka dribbles down his chin, his mouth full. 'Oops, sorry. Pardon me.' He pats his chest again, winding himself, perfectly replicating what he had previously done. Every expression a precise carbon copy.

'Shut up!' Philip says. 'Please shut up.'

A drop of water hits the surface of the half-filled sink. He concentrates on the ripples spreading out until calmness resumes. He explores his hands and face wanting to figure out where it came from.

Mr Cole reaches across him and plucks a bottle from the cabinet.

'These aren't going to do you much good.' He brings it in close for a more scrupulous examination, squinting his eyes. 'Got a pill for everything these days ...' He pauses. 'All crutches, you can't turn your back on them once you start. That's it, they've got you, sedating you. Why fix the problem? There's no need to do that, we can all get along when we're sedated. There's a reason for pain, a defining reason, Philip.'

There's a knock at the door.

Philip seizes the rim of the sink, his legs about to give way.

'What do I do?' he asks.

'It's alright, I'll deal with them,' Mr Cole says.

He stares at Philip with a bemused look masking his face. It's as if he's at a junction and doesn't know which way to turn.

'Are you alright? Oops, sorry. Pardon me,' Mr Cole says, confused for the first time at what he's been saying. He looks at Philip sternly. 'Stop it, do you hear me, stop it!'

'Just put your weight on my shoulder,' Ian says.

Unsure, Philip slides free from the wheelchair. Ian manoeuvres him away from it but Philip's attitude is proving more of a hindrance than he'd expected.

'You sure you've got me?'

'Of course,' Ian replies.

The physiotherapist puts her bag on the dressing table and props a walking stick against it. An Eastern-style jewellery box catches her eye. It's lacquered in a deep blue-black and embedded with delicately cut shells, showing splashes and swirls of vibrant colour. Their shapes fuse together, depicting a scene of a man in a small oriental fishing boat, his wife waving to him from the shoreline.

'I brought along a walking stick for you.' Janice's attention fixes on the jewellery box. 'This is what we're aiming at. Got to know where you're heading, I think it's good to get used to the stick. Lean against it, see how it feels against you.'

She turns back to the commotion from Philip and Ian. But to her surprise Philip is out and ready to do his exercises. Ian kneels awkwardly next to the him, not knowing what to do next.

'Well now, there's an improvement,' Janice says, smiling. 'Good job I brought the walking stick. It looks like we'll be needing it sooner than I thought.' She turns back, lured by the box. 'Is this a jewellery box?' she asks, pointing a finger.

'Yes,' Philip replies, frustrated that her attention is focused on it rather than him.

'I didn't notice it here last time,' Janice says. 'May I?' Her arm is reaching out, childhood wonder ahead of her adult restraint. She stops her hand in mid-flight before it flicks open the clasp. 'Can't resist things like this. Always find me at a car boot sale rummaging around. Fascinates me.'

'It plays a tune.'

'Does it? How wonderful!' Janice's finger almost touches the latch. She stops and glances back at him, not wanting the magic to be broken. 'It still works?'

Philip nods.

She opens the box but no music greets her.

'I thought you said it still worked.'

'It does, probably needs winding up.'

She spots the key in one of the red velvet compartments.

'Sure, I've got it.' There's no stopping her, she has to wind it up.

Shall we Dance from *The King and I* clumsily chimes from the jewellery box. Ian notices Philip's body language has changed; he looks uncomfortable.

'Isn't that adorable. It's perfume bottles that I'm really into. Just trying to imagine who owned them, how they lived. Makes your head spin.' She turns and smiles. 'They can be expensive … I sound like my husband now.' She shrugs her shoulders. 'You've got to spend your money on something, but he doesn't see it like that.'

She opens the curtains and steps back, taking in the view. 'Will you look at that sea.' A perfect summer's day is framed by the window. The pebble beach is awash with holidaymakers scattered like debris. 'I could get used to seeing that every day …' She pauses. 'I suppose you're used to it. But what a sight to get used to, nothing like this in Dorchester.'

She wanders over to Philip, who's waiting for her on the mat. Ian stands up sensing the appropriate moment to leave is near. She stoops down next to Philip.

'If you need me …' Ian nods to the mobile phone on the dressing table. 'Just give us a ring.'

Janice nods, cupping her hands under Philip's leg. He lies back. She folds up his leg letting his knee hover above his shoulder.

'Where's that lovely daughter of yours?' Janice asks.

The music slowly winds down.

Ian stops.

'She's –' Philip begins.

Her words rip him out of his body and throw him next to himself. Is this really him? How did he manage to get here, to this predicament?

'She, she's home.'

'I knew it. She couldn't keep away from that man of hers.' Janice laughs.

Philip's embarrassed. What is she talking about? His Michelle? It doesn't make any sense.

'Come on, you can't blame the girl for that.' Janice feels a little uneasy at Philip's glare. She didn't have him down as a prude. 'She'll be back when she needs you, they're all the same. Know when they've got a good thing.' She winks at Philip. 'Thinks the world of you. I can tell she does.'

Ian sluggishly leaves the room.

'Young love, you don't know where you are with it,' Janice says. 'Take my man, he's not much to look at, but you get no surprises, you know what I mean?' She giggles. 'At my age the last thing I want is surprises.' She puts pressure on his leg. 'They're best when they're children, less trouble.'

'Yes, knew where you were then.' Philip smiles, distantly.

'I shudder to think what my youngest is up to.' Janice continues, 'I'm worried sick. You don't know what could happen. You hear about it, see it on the news all the time.'

'She could be mischievous.' Philip's muscles relax and the redness drains away from his face.

'It's all changed. Not like now. I mean, I had my fun there's no denying that, but it's not how it used to be,' Janice says, leaning in hard. She expects him to wince in pain, but he's serene as if he's meditating. The harder she pushes the calmer he becomes.

'She was always in the back garden, loved it out there. Bit of a tomboy really,' Philip says. 'Her own little world, away from all the guests.'

Janice looks at him but he's staring straight through her.

'She'd be out there picking up worms and snails.' A warm smile begins to grow consuming his features. 'Or she'd be making perfume from the rose petals. God that stuff stank! We had the wigwam and the paddling pool out for her in summer. She loved playing games with her friends, dressing up, doctors and nurses or hide and seek. Even when ...' He pauses. 'When me and Frances were arguing. There were times it seemed like that's all we ever did, she'd be always happily playing.' He laughs. 'If someone had to have an accident it always had to be her. Always had to be her. Just like Frances she could never throw anything away. She has to be her daughter.' He stops, mulling over what he has said. 'A mummy's girl she was.' He nods. 'That's right, I can't get away from it. No I can, no ...' His body violently trembles, anger consuming him. He turns his face away, whispering, 'Damn you, Helen, damn you.'

For the first time Janice is uneasy at being alone with him. She looks over to the door and then to the mobile phone for comfort.

Adrian searches through his side of the wardrobe, he's naked apart from a pair of navy blue socks and a wristwatch. He runs a finger over his shirts. They all look the same, a full spectrum of white. He glances at his watch and a look of displeased concern scurries across his face. He's flustered. Snippets of Ian's phone call hang mocking him. The unnerving sensation of the blood draining from his body is still with him. Michelle isn't at the guesthouse. He sent Ian to search for her, reeling off a list of things he wanted him to check. He knew by the tone of his voice that Ian was worried, dazed and not thinking straight; this was affirmed when he eagerly took the instructions. It must have been a good ten minutes before he phoned him back.

The list rolled over in his mind. Her clothes were still in the wardrobe, her suitcase wedged under the bed, her toothbrush and face creams were waiting for her in the bathroom. The relief at her car being parked at the back of the guesthouse at least soothed the sickening feeling he had in his stomach. He lost it for a brief moment, he was sure Ian had picked up on how cagey and edgy it made him sound, not the reaction of concern and compassion he wanted to show.

Where is she? Is she trying to catch him out? He always has to push his luck. Why not give up while he's winning? No, that isn't good enough for him. He has to play the game, making sure the stakes are as high as he can stack them. Loves the buzz it gives him, but he's in a place he doesn't want to be, teetering with no control on the edge of losing her. It's all going to be alright, he keeps telling himself, as long as he remains calm and doesn't lose control. He rechecks the growth of his stubble, a shave is inevitable but that would have to wait, he has too much else to consider. He turns to the bed, the covers are twisted, lounging unevenly. On the bedroom floor clothes are scattered in clusters. Someone shuffles under the duvet.

'Are you getting up?' Adrian asks.

A protesting groan comes from beneath it as the figure rolls over.

'Come on, please come on!' He climbs on the bed and tugs the duvet, revealing the short blonde hair and slender back of a woman.

'Fuck off!' she says, playfully taking hold of the duvet and trying to gather it to her, but failing miserably. Reluctantly she rolls over onto her side and faces Adrian, nuzzling her head in the pillow, her arm cradling her breasts.

'What's the matter with you?' she asks, suppressing a yawn.

'I need to get going,' Adrian replies.

'What for?'

'Come on, please.' Adrian pleads.

She smiles at his dangling penis and pulled-up socks. '*"Quality time,"* you said.' She grins, rolling onto her back exposing her nipples. 'A good bit of afternoon pumping and grinding, you dirty boy! The company's paying for this. It's their time we're using.'

Adrian perches on the bed, he feels exhausted already.

'We could have gone to a hotel.' She reaches out and strokes his small, lost island of chest hair. 'It doesn't seem right, you know, in her bed.'

He brushes her hand away. 'Come on!'

'Why? It's going to come out in the end, Melissa suspects anyway.'

'Why didn't you say?' Adrian snaps.

She ignores him and takes hold of his hand, pulling it under the duvet.

'I don't need this.' Adrian snatches his hand away. 'It's not right.'

'Not right!' Bitterness glazes over her eyes. 'You mean it doesn't seem right now!' She forcefully yanks the duvet, covering every trace of her naked body.

He holds his hands up, for protest and to suppress her outburst.

'Look I'm sorry.'

'Sorry!'

He gets off the bed and picks up his trousers from the floor.

'So is that it? This is what you call spending time together?'

'Vicky, please.'

'God, why do I bother! Claire warned me about you.' She makes a quick scan of the floor and homes in on her knickers.

'Don't be like that, I told you not to listen to her.'

He watches her lean over and scoop up the red lacy garment. The duvet falls away, revealing the sensual curve of her tanned back flowing down to her white-stencilled bottom.

Aggressively she puts her underwear on.

'I don't like being messed about.' She blows the fallen hair from her face. 'I'm not going through this again, I've told you.'

'I'll sort it, I promise you. You've got to believe me,' Adrian pleads.

She gets out of the bed, vacuums the floor with a jabbing precision, collecting the rest of her clothes, and walks over to him.

'I can't take this any more. I'm not that sort of girl. No more excuses.'

'I know, I know.' Adrian bows his head, not wanting to be ensnared in her eyes, worried she might catch a glimmer of the truth through the mirage of promises, seeing them for how flimsy and insincere they really are.

She storms off, the red lace accentuating her pert buttocks as she heads to the bathroom. He can't help himself, the closer they come to breaking up the more he wants her.

Philip isn't sure when Janice had left but the echoes of her constant chit-chat are still floating in the afternoon sunlight. He's laid on the bed not wanting to move a muscle. He tries to steady his breathing, willing a sedating peacefulness to let him think more clearly, to introduce a logical explanation, but he can't shake the phone call out of his head. Mr Cole is napping in a chair, feet up on the table. Sunlight slices through the window making segments of his body invisible.

Mr Cole flinches. 'You have to …' he mutters. 'I know, I know …' He sways from side to side answering to his dream world.

The mobile phone erupts into life playing an electronic Mozart tune. It vibrates furiously on the bedside table like a huge upturned insect trying to right itself. Mr Cole stirs, Philip stares at the phone, wanting it to stop, to splutter and die. But it doesn't. He can hear its stubbornness radiating through. It's no use, he snatches the phone from the bedside table and silences its ring with a jab of his finger. He pulls himself up from the bed and places it against his ear. His feet drop to the floor. Mr Cole slothfully slips back into his dream world and the twitching starts again.

'Hello,' Philip says softly, sitting anxiously on the edge of the bed.

No answer.

He pushes the phone harder to his ear. He can hear the faint sound of someone breathing as if they are in shock.

'Hello. Who is this?' Philip asks.

The breathing alters in tempo becoming more composed.

He switches it off and places it gently back on the bedside table, convincing himself any false move could bring it back to life. This is the third call he has received in the last half an hour. He turns to Mr Cole who's still asleep, but is trying to find a more favourable angle in the bony, wooden chair. He's going to have to wake him, this isn't right. There's something about the tone of the breathing that makes him aggravated, but at the same time it strangely sings to him, sweet with an alluring warmth. Mr Cole hardly slept the previous night, restlessly turning on the make shift bed on the floor next to him. Philip had woken in the small hours to see him standing at the window staring out at the bay. He watched him until he drifted back to sleep; it made him feel safe. But it's no good, he'll have to wake him up.

He stops. The breathing is back sending a shiver shooting up his backbone. He looks to the phone but it's lying lifelessly on the bedside table. His eyes dart to the door. The breathing seems to be coming from outside it.

His mouth dry, body shaking nervously, he shuffles over to the door. He glances back to Mr Cole, who is quivering in his sleep, as though he has become exposed to a sudden cold draught. Philip reaches out, his hand entwines around the door handle. The breathing is strong and constant. He can sense it seeping through the pores of his hand and spreading up his arm, consuming him, beckoning him to open the door. But he can't do it. He won't do it. His grip tightens on the handle, making the door shake.

The breathing stops.

A childish giggle erupts from behind him, freezing him to the spot. He can feel the presence of someone else in the room. A breath burns as it travels down his parched throat, every muscle rigid. Whoever it is they're moving towards him. The giggling echoes in his head. He has no choice, he has to face it. He's not ready though, he knows he's not. What could this do to him if he looks? Fear twists his stomach, making him want to buckle, to cower into the door. He snatches his breath in tight and turns around but to his surprise there's no one there. Instead of relief, he's strangely disappointed.

'I can't find it,' Mr Cole says. The tone of his voice is soft with a hardened layer of frustration. 'It's got to be somewhere, I've tried it but it won't open. Tell me where I go?' He turns over in his chair as if looking for something. 'Someone's coming.'

The sound of soft footsteps run away from the door and along the hall. Philip takes hold of the door handle and wrenches it open. The fire door slowly retracts. He swallows hard and deep, his mouth bone dry, hands still shaking.

Mr Riley is hovering in the hallway near the *ring for assistance* bell while Mrs Riley patiently waits, beach bags resting against her legs. He steps up to the bell. All of his heaped-up annoyance rushes through his body, channelling through to his thin hardening finger. He strikes at the electric bell, holding it down, wanting to pulverise it into the wall, teeth snarled and clenched.

'Come on, isn't there anybody here?' he moans.

Ian wanders carefree out from the kitchen, wiping his hands on a tea towel.

'Everything alright?' He tries to defuse the tense atmosphere with a smile.

'Look, I'm not one to complain, but –' Mr Riley begins.

'Isn't the breakfast, is it?' Ian asks. 'Any special requests, I'm happy to oblige.' His feeble attempt to drain some of the animosity only manages to provoke him even more.

'No, no.' Mr Riley shakes his head, raising his hands in pure desperation. 'Look, please. Can I speak to the owner? This has got to be sorted out.'

'Erm – that's a bit difficult at the moment.' He should be so lucky. Ian's barely even glimpsed Philip the last couple of days, let alone managed to talk to him.

'Excuse me?'

Mr Riley must be in his early sixties. He always says, "Hello" and "Good morning", with an incision of general chit-chat. Where they have been and of course everything comes around to predicting what the weather is going to do. He's reasonably fit for his age, but now it's as if his anger has unleashed his youth. Ian is finding it hard to read how this is going to play out.

'Look,' Ian says, 'tell me and I'll get it sorted for you.'

Mr Riley glances to his wife who nods her approval. She's eager to leave the guesthouse and enjoy some sun.

'This can't go on. This is our holiday, how are we supposed to get any sleep?' Mr Riley says.

Ian's mystified.

'What sort of place are you running here!'

Mrs Riley joins in. 'No consideration for anybody, I pity that child.'

Her husband nods, united as she continues.

'No wonder this country is in such a state. Always someone else's problem. It was never like this when we brought up our two boys, we just got on with it …' She pauses to fill her lungs and to savour how good it makes her feel. 'What's going to happen when he's older? But he'll be alright. They'll all be alright. One big welfare state this country is.'

'Sorry?' Ian's taken aback by how much rage is in Mrs Riley. 'I – I don't know what you're trying to say.'

'Room 8!' Mr Riley says abruptly. 'I want this sorted –' He points forcefully at Ian.

Mrs Riley butts in. 'The boy, he's been running amuck all night long and this isn't the first time.'

'That's right. Two nights in a row,' Mr Riley adds. 'We've had enough of it.'

'Room 8,' Ian says. 'Are you sure?'

Mr Riley rolls his eyes. 'Deal with it, I'm not putting up with this, do you hear me!'

'Sure. Sorry,' Ian says. 'I'll do it right now.'

Ian strides up the second flight of stairs. He scratches at his ear, still ringing from the abuse from Mr and Mrs Riley. He walks onto the narrow landing and pushes the fire door open to the top rooms. He has a strange feeling of *deja vu*. Here he is, doing all the donkey work for Philip again. The everyday running of the guesthouse, dealing with the guests, making sure Ellie's doing her job. He still can't believe he got roped into doing the cash and carry run, no idea how that happened. Come to think of it, he has no idea how any of it happened. The shopping was never his responsibility before.

149

It used to be something Philip loved to do. He'd vanish for most of the day, then turn up from the cash and carry with only half the items that were on the list. And then he'd be merrily out again for most of the next day fetching the rest. It had now come to the point where it was less hassle when Philip wasn't around. The only thing Ian hasn't been lumbered with is the accounts. Philip had tried, dropped hints about it, mentioning it would look good on his CV, but there's no way he was being drawn into that. It's strange but for the first time it really grates on him. He has finally stepped outside of himself but he still can't shift the guilt about the money Philip has given him; he didn't expect so much. It's as if he wants to pay at least some of it off, all the extra little jobs he's done over the years.

He needs Michelle more than ever. This last month was as if he had passed the reins over to her. He didn't realise how much he had been carrying Philip. How he has become a crutch for him, a maintenance man to all his problems. It makes him uneasy and ashamed at how he has contributed over the years to what Philip has become.

But where is she? It isn't like her to disappear, nothing makes sense. He just wants to know if she's alright. Well, if he's honest, prying is his main motivation. He's convinced it has something to do with Adrian. The way he was on the phone, catching him off guard. He didn't expect Adrian to pick up the phone, he hoped Michelle would be there. She'd said he worked strange hours, some sort of flexitime. According to him she hadn't even rang. He had been so cagey and edgy, not his usual calm, calculating self, but where was his compassion, his concern for her? Did he know where she was but didn't want to say? And when he had phoned him back, every question he answered Adrian seemed to take as some sort of threat. It had been a couple of days since he phoned but the hostility in his voice hadn't let go of him.

The fire door retracts behind him. None of this is like her at all. She's a very conscientious person, she wouldn't leave and not say anything. Is it his fault? Has his flirtation been too much? It's all just harmless fun. He shakes his head. She knows that, what is he thinking? Paranoia is creeping up, jumping on him from so many unexpected directions. And what does he get from Philip, where is his concern? He just dismissed the fact. What is going on? Is he just over-reacting? Or has the world gone completely mad?

It all has to lead back to Adrian; there's something not right between them two. But why are her clothes still here? Her suit-case under the bed and her car still parked out the back. What if something else has happened? Michelle said she would meet him at The Ship; it isn't like her to let him or anybody down. You hear about it all the time on the news; abduction, rape, murder. No, he's not going to be drawn down any of those alleyways. Everything turns over his mind again making him feel light-headed.

At first he thought he had been a little too hasty calling the police. He couldn't help himself, he needed to do something and now with hindsight he's convinced he did the right thing. Anyway what could he do? It's over and done now. It won't be long until they classify her as a missing person. The police-man sounded like he hears this sort of thing a thousand times a day. Where else does he turn? No Philip, no Adrian. He can't just sit and wait. Once he's sorted this misunderstanding out he'll ring round some of Michelle's friends; he's sure Donna's still in the area.

He stops outside room 7, back to the door to compose himself, then knocks. The Rileys must have got confused; it's the Kirkwoods who are in the family room.

Mrs Kirkwood opens the door.

'Yes?'

He hasn't prepared for this. He was expecting more of a build up. Glancing at the floor provides an opportunity to arrange his thoughts.

'Mrs Kirkwood. I – I'm afraid ...' Ian lowers the tone of his voice. 'There's been a – complaint – about erm ...'

The door opens wider revealing Mr Kirkwood's half-dressed body. How hairy can one man be?

'Good and it's about time you did something about it.' Mr Kirkwood looks at his wife knowingly. 'I told you we should have said something; we've got every right to complain. It's hardly cheap, this place.' He glares back at Ian. 'I want a full refund of our deposit. Have you got that? That's my right.' Mr Kirkwood turns his back and walks off before Ian has a chance to retaliate.

'I'm sorry about that. He gets wound up when he hasn't had a good night's sleep. Always been like it,' Mrs Kirkwood says.

'So ...' Ian says, slowly trying to fathom out what's going on. 'You've been hearing a kid running round and misbehaving?' He pauses and looks to the other two doors. 'In room ...'

'Eight!' Mrs Kirkwood says, puzzled.

'Yes.' Ian reluctantly nods to room 8. 'Of course.'

'It was worse last night, I had to stop him going over there.' Mrs Kirkwood lets out an annoyed glare at room 8's door. 'We thought the other family room was downstairs?'

'So did I,' Ian mutters.

'Sorry?'

'Rose!' Mr Kirkwood barks from inside the room.

'Look, we don't want to make a fuss,' Mrs Kirkwood whispers, constantly peering back into the room. 'He doesn't mean to be like that. He's never got used to the shifts he has to work. I don't want him round there causing a scene. It's not right though, letting a young girl run around like that all night. Scraping on the walls and banging doors.' She glances back to the door. 'She must sleep all day.'

'Girl?' Ian says.

152

'Yes, I know you expect that sort of thing more from boys. But these days, well.'

'Rose!' Mr Kirkwood shouts again.

'I'll have to go. But please, can you get this sorted?'

She shuts the door abruptly.

Ian shakes off his bewildered state. Girl, boy, what does it matter? All adds up to the same thing – annoyed guests. He approaches room 8 and hesitates. About to knock, he's certain he can hear someone talking. He leans forward. The voice stops. He can only hear the Kirkwoods arguing now. He knocks but there's no reply. He leans against the door, sieving for any response.

Knocking again, he calls, 'Hello, are you in there, Mr Cole?' Silence. 'Is there anybody there?' He hangs poised.

Ian pulls away from the door and straightens himself up. In a last desperate attempt he tries the door handle. It's locked, but what did he really expect?

'I'll have to have a word with Philip,' he mutters to himself. 'Can't remember the last time I've seen the keys.'

Ian wanders down the stairs. He's confused. He had hoped by the time he was making his way back down everything would have fallen into place and he could have resolved the problem, or at the very least be satisfied he could solve it. This place! Nothing is ever straightforward. Would working at The Regal have this level of mystery? Incompetence? This amount of fuck-ups with nobody wanting to be in charge when it mattered, side-stepping accountability and responsibility? Don't you believe it, he chuckles to himself.

He descends the last flight of stairs and to his relief Mr and Mrs Riley have dispersed from the hall. He steps into the hall and peers out the glass door. At last, a bit of summer sun and for the second day in a row. Its warmth bathes his face, he turns his back on the outside world and makes his way to the kitchen.

He's greeted by the sight of Ellie on her knees. 'So what are you going to do about this?' she asks. 'Have you told him yet?' She hurls the questions at him the moment he enters into the kitchen.

Ian vaguely acknowledges her.

Ellie throws down the dustpan and brush and folds her arms.

'I'm not cleaning any more mud off this floor.' Her tone is firm and rooted to the spot, but to her annoyance she doesn't get the desired response. She doesn't get any response. 'What's the matter with you?' she asks.

Ian slumps against the kitchen table.

'Nothing.'

'Yes there is.'

Her arms relax as she stands up and walks over to him.

He looks exhausted. 'You told me this morning that was the last time you were going to clean it up or you'd walk out.'

'Yeah and you don't seem to be listening.' Ellie views him suspiciously. 'What is it with you? Is it Maxine? It'll get worse when you start living together.' She turns away, uneasy at uncloaking herself.

'No.' Ian's surprised at how harsh he sounds.

'I'm only asking.' Ellie slouches next to him.

He grins with a playful smirk.

'Cutting back on the drinking, can't keep up the pace?' She teases.

'No.' Ian lifts a leg from the floor, arranging himself more comfortably on the table. 'Look I'm sorry, I didn't mean to take it out on you like that.'

'It doesn't matter, I'm as bad. If we can't take it out on each other, who can we take it out on?'

'Yeah, it's not right though. Me and Maxine are fine. It's this place.'

'Tell me about it.'

'I don't know what's going on. I don't know what to do any more.'

'It's not your problem. You don't have to put up with this much longer. You lucky git!' She smiles but it's under protest. 'Can't see myself staying here much longer after you leave.'

'Well, there's plenty of summer jobs out there.'

'You're right. Trouble is, I'll have to work in the real world.'

'I know it's cushy here. He just lets you get on with it. Sometimes I think it's too cushy. Makes you lazy. If he's not bothered why should you be.' Ian swings his leg.

'Can't win, can you?' Sunlight radiates through the kitchen window. 'Michelle had the best idea.'

'Don't say that.'

'Why?'

He turns away from her, agitated at what she has said.

'Do you think something bad has happened to her?'

He doesn't answer her, he can't.

'Well?' Ellie persists.

'Don't be so dramatic.'

'It's all a bit strange to me. All started when she was supposed to pop out for a drink with you.'

'Leave it, will ya. You don't know what you're talking about.'

'The police might want to talk to me.'

'What?'

'I might have been one of the last people to have spoken to her.'

'Do you have to?'

'I was only mucking about.'

'Well don't.'

He's anxious, afraid of saying something he might regret.

'She was probably worried about you,' Ellie says.

'What's that supposed to mean?'

'Were you going to get her drunk and have a bit of a fumble?' Ellie replies with a forced giggle.

'You have to bring everything down to that level?'

He launches himself off the kitchen table.

'More like your level. She's probably trying to get back at Adrian for something,' Ellie replies. 'You've seen what they're like together.'

'No, no –'

'Both as bad at each other, I bet she's with him now making up for lost time.'

'You see, you don't know. She isn't. I've phoned. She hasn't even been there.'

'Yeah?' Ellie sees her feeble theory unravel at the seams. 'I thought perhaps she was playing the insecurity card. That's odd.'

'No, it's more than that.'

He wants reassurance from her but she frowns knowingly at him.

'Ian, stay out of it, it's not your problem.'

'Maybe she's still down here. Staying at a friend's place.'

'Come on she'll be alright. She probably needed to get away from here.' She looks dispirited around the room, the kitchen just in the realm of the Food Safety regulations. 'You couldn't blame her.'

The kitchen door opens with a shudder. Philip walks into the room aided by a walking stick.

'Takes a bit of getting used to, especially the stairs,' he says.

Doubt holds their expressions tight, scrupulously examining the twist and turns of his body. It isn't the fact that he's out of his wheelchair and using his walking stick, a miraculous recovery from Janice's last visit. It's the way he carries himself, the technique his body is using. They stare at the over-dramatic struggle, full theatrical agony on his face that over-dramatises the movement of his legs. They're captivated, wedged between wanting to laugh at him, and the humiliation that he could think they are so stupid. Philip flops into a chair.

'We've had some complaints,' Ian says.

'You know what to do, put them in the book,' Philip says.

'This is different.'

'Now that wasn't too bad. What were you saying?'

'Room 8, your friend Mr Cole,' Ian says.

Philip protectively pulls his walking stick close to his chest. 'What sort of complaint?'

'Well this is it, I don't understand. Has he got a niece or nephew that's come to stay?'

'No,' Philip replies.

Ellie turns away. 'Maybe he's a kiddie fiddler,' she mumbles under her breath, raising an eyebrow at Ian.

Ian ignores her and is relieved Philip hasn't picked up on what she said.

'Well whatever it is, the Rileys in room 9 and the Kirkwood's in room 7 have been complaining. So –'

He wants Philip's help, his reassurance at dealing with the situation, but he is met by his usual, *what's it got to do with me?* expression. Philip then looks up, wanting to put the onus on him to make a decision.

'Does Michelle know?' Philip asks.

Of all the things he'd expected him to say, this isn't even in the top one hundred. 'Michelle's gone,' Ian replies, baffled.

'Did she say anything to you?'

Again his follow-up is just as mystifying. 'Sorry. What do you mean?' Ian asks.

'She's with Adrian,' Philip says.

'No, she isn't. I phoned him.'

'Why did you do that!' Philip's anger explodes out at him.

Ellie bolts upright from slouching against the kitchen table.

'Alright, alright,' Ian says.

'Ian, just go. There's nothing for you to do now.'

Ian tries to ignore his last remark, even though it's as if he has punched him hard in the stomach.

'I'm sorry, I had to,' Ian says.

Ellie is stunned. She has never seen Philip blow up with so much anger before.

Philip turns away from them. Ian isn't sure if it's to curb his rage or to re-emphasise that he wants him to leave.

'Hey come on, I'm sorry, what else can I say? I don't know where she is. It's not like her, you know what she's like.' Ian tries to explain. 'I'm worried about her. We can't do this by ourselves.'

'What do you mean by that?' Philip asks, looking at Ian intensely, his eyes and ears calibrating to grasp any cloaked reaction. He's known Ian too long, he knows he isn't good at lying. The kind of person who would desperately skirt around the issue, fumbling and tripping as he did. His affection for Michelle has been blatantly obvious over the years.

'You haven't called the police, have you?' Philip asks.

Ian doesn't want to reply but there's nowhere else for him to go. He's nailed to the spot in an instant. 'I – erm … yes,' he replies.

'Why did you do that? There was no need to get them involved. We have to wait, she'll turn up, she's not missing.'

'Not officially,' Ian says.

'What did they say?'

'They haven't started their investigation yet.' Ian makes a justified stand against him.

'Investigation!' Philip's anger surges out again.

Ellie's astonished to see Ian standing up to Philip. Her body lets out a tremor. She wants to sneak out the room but she's captivated at what's happening in front of her.

'It's normal procedure when someone is missing.' Ian's tone remains controlled and righteous.

'Ian, I appreciate your concern but this is a family matter. I didn't want to alarm you, that's all. I got that wrong. What I'm trying to say is that this hasn't got anything to do with you. It's not your problem.'

He digs his stick in the tiled floor and lifts himself up from the chair, in one effortless move.

'What do you mean, not my problem?'

'What I said,' Philip says. 'I'll do the evening meals tonight. Goodbye Ian. And good luck.'

Philip smiles at him, bows his head in an apologetic manner and hobbles energetically out of the kitchen.

Ian turns around searching for something to kick. Ellie looks nervously at him.

'I've had enough of this shit!' she shouts, half wanting Philip to hear. 'What is his problem?' A quiver resonates through her voice.

'Whatever it is, it's got nothing to do with me any more.' Ian undoes his apron and throws it onto the table.

'You can't go now!' Ellie's eyes widen.

'You heard him,' Ian says.

10

Philip battles to take control of running the kitchen. In theory his plan is flawless. He's taken anything he found difficult to cook off the menu, keeping it plain and straightforward. So what is going wrong? How has he ended up in such a mess? All his efforts are met by more and more complaints. Too cold, too hot, there isn't enough, plates are dirty; there's always something. Isn't anybody ever satisfied? Mr Riley had stormed into the kitchen, his lamb chop still frozen in the middle. To save time Philip had left the complaints book open on the kitchen table, its trusty pen poised at its side.

Ellie slams down two plates, one chop with a scoop of peas and a portion of mauled potatoes. The other untouched.

'Table 9, complaining about the potatoes.' Ellie looks at the plates disapprovingly. 'Overcooked.' She savours the frustration twisting and grinding over Philip's face.

She can't help herself, she's relishing every minute. Her contempt for him has found another gear to ease into, stoked by the way he had treated Ian. He was the stabilising influence to their working relationship, defusing tensions and soothing out grievances, but he's gone. She can still see him walking out the back door. The way his arms had felt wrapped around her, if only he was able to hold her just that little bit longer. She knew when he stepped out the door nothing would ever be the same again. The delicate kiss on her cheek lingers putting stress on her heart as it pumps a rage through her body. She isn't bothered any more. What could he do, sack her? That's what she wants anyway. She'd get a bit of grief from her parents, the majority of it from her dad, but it wouldn't last long, it never did, and anyway, after years of practice she knows exactly how to manipulate him.

'Some people!' Philip barks.

A saucepan boils over, sizzles and burns in the gas flames. Philip dramatically hobbles over to the cooker, walking stick in tow. He props the stick against the kitchen cupboard and lifts the lid of a saucepan, defusing its boiling pace but he catches his arm on another pan.

'Shit!'

Pain slashes deep at his arm, he cradles it hard against his chest. Ellie knows he can't take much more. The role call of complaints churns over in her thoughts. She has watched each one gorging, picking at his confidence and wearing him down and she loved the feeling it gave her. The power she felt when she suggested it would be easier if he put the complaints book on the kitchen table. They pumped an addictive energy into her. It's like loading each complaint into a metaphysical gun anticipating the anguish each one could cause him, her confidence soaring on a high. She has him in her sights, trapped and caged liked a bemused prisoner. There's no way he's getting up to his normal tricks of sneaking off or side-stepping his responsibility, leaving someone else to sort out his problems. She smirks at him pathetically hobbling over to the sink and rinsing his arm under the cold tap. First it's both of his legs hurting him, then the left and then the right. His walking stick stands propped lonely up against the cupboard. The only thing she knows for certain is his arm is hurting. She grins, recollecting when she encouraged Mr Riley to go and see Philip, the half-eaten meal on his plate clasped in his hands. She led him to the kitchen and let him loose at him.

The gloves are off.

'Table 3 are still waiting for their dessert.'

'Aren't any of them happy?' Philip snaps, rotating his arm under the cold tap so that the pain subsides briefly.

Her grin slithers back, figuring this would be an appropriate time to leave the room and she abruptly does so.

Philip stares out onto the garden wanting the evening to disappear, but there's still a long way to go.

In the dim light of room 8 Michelle's mobile phone rings. A hand grabs hold of it and throws it to the floor. Its case splits but the mobile keeps ringing defiantly. The heel of a shoe plunges repetitively down on it until it can't take any more.

Silence. Its screen fades.

'Bloody things!' Mr Cole crouches over it as if examining the remains of a dead animal.

Philip stands transfixed by Michelle hidden under the bed covers. He spots something clinging to the duvet, it's hard to make out what it is. He reaches out and touches it, to his surprise it's a hardened piece of mud. He pulls at it but it crumbles between his fingers. He sees another piece and then another. He starts to unravel the duvet.

Mr Cole holds up the broken phone, its components spewing out like entrails. 'Not much to them really.'

Philip drags the duvet away from the bed. He stops, stunned at what he sees.

'What?' The empty mattress confronts him, the duvet falls from his hands. 'Michelle, where are you?' Philip asks.

He hears a giggle roaming around the room; it subsides to a steady breathing, the same as before. He backs away from the bed.

'Can you hear that?' Philip asks for reassurance, but Mr Cole is still pulling the mobile phone to bits. The breathing stops. Philip turns to the bed, almost willing it to start up again. 'Did you?'

'Hear what?'

'Stop doing that. Where is she, what's going on?'

'All about gossip. Would you believe it?' Mr Cole says. 'Greatest invention of the twenty-first century!'

Philip walks over to him. 'Did you hear what I said?'

He's about to snatch the mobile from him when he hears the giggling erupt into the room again. His body tightens, he's sure it's coming from behind him this time.

Mr Cole grins. 'Come on Philip, where's your sense of humour. We've all got to live together, that's what it's all about.'

'What's that supposed to mean?'

Mr Cole drops the mobile on the bedside table.

'I told you it's going to be alright. You know what she's like.'

Philip turns away.

'Philip, look at me.' Mr Cole's voice is controlled and precise. 'You have to listen to me, come on Philip.'

Philip's baffled and afraid.

'Game's up, eh Philip; you know where she is. It's all part of the game isn't it? We like games don't we?'

'No. What are you saying, you can't …?' Philip shakes his head. 'She's —'

'Families stick together, that's what it's about. You know that, don't you?'

'Not this, don't do this,' Philip pleads, but he realises it's no use.

'You know where she is.' Mr Cole's voice lowers to a whisper. 'We can do this, you know we can. Together, it's the only way, Philip.' His eyes narrow to intense slits. 'If we don't —'

Mr Cole breaks into a fit of laughter, igniting a burst of giggles from behind him.

'Philip, you really shouldn't take life so seriously.' Mr Cole laughs, turning to a mocking tone. 'Always dwelling on the past. It's about the future, that's what this is about.'

The laughter stops. Philip turns around but there's no one there. Mr Cole wanders over to the wardrobe and knocks on its door in a theatrical manner. He winks at Philip.

'Are you going to come out now?' Mr Cole asks.

A silence hangs menacingly in the room, disbelief holding every expression on Philip's face.

'She's just playing, you know what they're like. I mean, what do you expect? It's supposed to encourage their learning ability. Maybe that's not quite true. She was bored, they all get bored.'

'Bored? Playing?'

'You have to treat it like this, as a game, it's the only way she can get through it,' Mr Cole snarls, baring his teeth.

'But –'

'It's just a game. She always liked playing hide and seek. Playing in the garden, bit of a tomboy wasn't she? Well life is sort of a game, isn't it?'

'How can it be, how can it be a game?'

Something shifts in the wardrobe.

'Maybe we took it a bit too far.' Mr Cole looks anxiously at him.

'A bit too far? What are you trying to do to me?'

'Hey, come on, you know what I said – focus. There's no other way.'

He touches the wardrobe.

Optimism surges through in his voice. 'Michelle. Come on.'

Nothing happens.

'Please Michelle,' Mr Cole says softly. 'Come out of there.' Gently he touches the wardrobe again. 'You didn't get lost again, did you? It's going to be alright.' He turns to Philip. 'Isn't it?'

Philip nods helplessly, his body trembling uncontrollably as if it's caught by a fever. He hears a scraping noise like a spurt of panicked fingernails on wood, followed by what sounds like a couple of kicks to the door.

'I – I – thought –' Philip stutters.

He can't make sense of what's happening. He feels like he has taken a wrong turning, and the more he tries to correct his mistake, the further it takes him away from where he wants to go.

'Michelle!' Mr Cole swings open the door. 'Whatever you do, don't panic. I told you we'll get through this. You like the games, don't you? You know they'll get you through this, Michelle. They always did, didn't they?'

'Stop it! Do you hear me! STOP IT, STOP IT!' Philip shouts, fingers clawing at his ears.

'Philip, you're scaring her. Calm down.'

Mr Cole pops his head into the wardrobe. He says something but it's too muffled for Philip to decipher, then he steps back and holds the wardrobe door open. Philip can hear the beat of his heart echoing through his body.

From the shadows a bare foot extends out covered in dried mud. Philip watches, mesmerised; his hands fall to his sides as it slips through Frances' skirts and dresses. The small delicate foot steps onto the floor. Cuts rupture in the famine dryness of his mouth and throat. It makes it appear as though the wardrobe is a womb giving birth to a child.

A young girl.

Her head appears, hung low, a mob of spiral hair hiding her face. She's wearing a flowery patterned dress, hints of an eighties-style around the cut of the collar. Philip can't move, his heart is pounding. She approaches him.

'Sorry Michelle. You had a bit of a fright back there.' Mr Cole soothes, 'I'm sorry, I didn't realise you couldn't get out. It can be confusing if you're not sure which way to go.'

'But –' Philip turns to him, not knowing what to say or do.

She stands in front of him, head bowed submissively.

'Well done. You nearly got lost in there, didn't you?'

She shrugs her shoulders.

'Who is – who is this?'

Mr Cole looks puzzled at Philip's question. He scratches his chin, then a crack of a grin appears; he points a knowing finger at Philip.

'You had me going there.' A smirk floods his face. 'Just for a minute, I'll give you that.'

The girl shakes her head.

'I'm not joking, who is she?'

Silently he looks down at her, seeing her spiralling curls shine, even in this lifeless light. She tilts her head to greet him and her hair falls away from her face. A growing nauseated presence rises up, bubbling acid from the pit of his stomach.

Their eyes meet.

He wants to turn away but he can't. She holds him firmly in her gaze. He can't interpret what he's seeing. His thoughts hastily collate his memory in some sort of logical order, so he can try and work out how he has reached this point in time. But they're overloading his system, falling over each other and compressing into a bottleneck. He feels dizzy, certain he's about to faint.

It's Michelle, but how? Why?

Her young complexion gleams back at him.

'You know, my daughter looked like her when she was that age. You forget how much energy they have.' Mr Cole smiles.

Philip stares, confused at him, then to Michelle. She smiles timidly at him.

'It's alright, you haven't upset him. I told you he wouldn't be mad, didn't I. Isn't that right, Philip?' Mr Cole asks with an encouraging nod.

Sergeant Wilson sits at the kitchen table, taking in and assessing the way Philip is responding to his questioning. PC

Collinson is behind him, pacing the length of the table, scribbling in frenzied bursts in his notepad. Philip jolts up, his chair squeals like a calling fox against the tiles. PC Collinson stops pacing.

'Sorry, where are my manners? How rude of me,' Philip says from across the table. 'Me being in the service sector as well.'

The sergeant and PC look bemused at each other.

'Would you like more tea?' Philip asks with a nod of enthusiasm to them both.

PC Collinson shakes his head.

'No, Mr Morgan.' A firm authority echoes through the sergeant's voice. 'No more, please.' He takes hold of his half-empty cup and brings it out of Philip's reach.

'It'll be cold by now,' Philip says. 'Nothing worse than a cold cup of tea.'

'No!' They both say, turning to each other, embarrassed at revealing so much annoyance in their voices.

'OK. Is there anything else I can get you?' His eyes jump from one to the other.

They both frown.

'Please, Mr Morgan.' Sergeant Wilson indicates him to sit down.

Philip sinks back into his chair. The sergeant rubs his eyes. He's having one of those days when no matter what he does, the job has him in a corner and is determined to wear him down. He knows it's getting to PC Collinson too. They had been at a domestic earlier, the woman's face swollen like a beach ball. An elderly neighbour had complained but the wife refused to press charges. And at the weekend, they'd been on night shift and were called into the town centre. That really had been a baptism of fire for PC Collinson. He enjoyed a few drinks, but how some people used alcohol to satisfy their own self-loathing, it was all beyond him. But the job's about dealing with the public and there's nothing straightforward when you put in the human element. People's stupidity has become the running theme of the week and Philip is the icing on the cake.

'Now, is all that clear to you?'

Philip nervously wipes his mouth. 'Erm – sorry?'

Sergeant Wilson leans forward, excluding PC Collinson. 'Is there anything bothering you, Mr Morgan?'

'I'm, I'm fine,' Philip replies.

His eyes flick from side to side hearing Mr Cole behind him. He had been pacing in time to PC Collinson but now his footsteps echo alone.

'Correct me if I'm wrong, but you seem to be getting distracted by something?'

'Sorry.'

'Mr Morgan, you don't have to keep saying sorry.'

'Erm – what –' Philip's eyes drift to the left, locking on to Mr Cole. They then leap to Sergeant Wilson's confused expression. 'What were you saying?' He edges forward on his chair.

Sergeant Wilson lets out a deep sigh. 'Mr and Mrs Dobbs have dropped the charges against you.' He stops.

Philip's eyes are on the move again.

'Mr Morgan!'

Philip's attention jolts back.

'Now, you understand that?'

He nods.

'But you will be charged with reckless driving and driving under the influence of alcohol. Yes?' He can't believe it, Philip's eyes are wandering again.

His stern silence pulls Philip back.

'Considering the circumstances I think you've come out of this very well.'

Philip doesn't say anything. His mouth nearly hits the table as Mr Cole walks into his line of view. He strolls around the table and stands next to Sergeant Wilson, who's putting his notepad in his breast pocket and leaning back in his chair. PC Collinson hovers on the other side of him.

'Indecent exposure!' Mr Cole snaps.

Sergeant Wilson jumps. 'I beg your pardon,' he says.

He looks at him but Philip doesn't acknowledge him. He's too concerned about Mr Cole, the displeasure glares out of his eyes. Sergeant Wilson follows the line of his stare, for some reason he's looking to his side, but there's nothing there. Mr Cole throws Philip a mischievous look then to his horror unzips his trousers.

'Please, no!' Philip almost chokes the words out.

Sergeant Wilson is flabbergasted. 'Now what is it?'

Mr Cole takes out his penis and places it next to Sergeant Wilson. 'There you go,' he says, beaming with pride and admiration.

Sergeant Wilson is momentarily stunned. Philip is now grinning and staring at the same spot. PC Collinson is uncertain what to do next; over the last month his confidence has taken a battering. He loved the theory side of the job, but the more he came up against the practical, the more dispirited he was becoming. He wants to be back at the station behind his desk; he doesn't want to get his hands dirty any more. Sergeant Wilson slams the palm of his hand hard on the table making him rise from his chair. Philip winces while Mr Cole tumbles backwards, penis dangling out his trousers.

'Mr Morgan,' Wilson says, suppressing his anger through his clench teeth. 'I don't want to waste anybody's time here. Alright?' He hauls himself up. 'I think that's enough for now.'

'Are you sure you don't want another cup of tea?' Philip asks.

Sergeant Wilson shakes his head. Philip's friendly manner grates deep at him, slithering under his skin and making him want to scratch it until it bleeds.

'Cup of tea?' Mr Cole leans against the kitchen table. His penis gently sways from side to side.

Philip sinks deep into the chair, his features contorting as if he's wrestling an uncompromising twitch. PC Collinson heads to the back door, he can't even summon up a goodbye, he doesn't want anything else to do with Philip. He looks like a form-filling nightmare; there's theory and then there's bureaucracy. Sergeant Wilson goes to follow PC Collinson to the back door, but stops and waits for him to step outside. He leans over the table, puncturing Philip's stare.

'You're lucky, the kind of day I've had. You act like that the next time we pay you a visit and I'll drag that sorry arse of yours in.'

He throws Philip a disapproving look and walks abruptly out the back door.

'Hold on. You call this justice?' Mr Cole follows Sergeant Wilson out into the garden.

Philip stands up and wanders over to the window. The sunlight makes him squint, vibrant colours of the garden come into focus. He hears Mr Cole aggressively shouting, he follows the garden path and catches up with him trailing behind the two policemen, raining down a storm of muffled abuse at them. A sharp chill makes him shudder, he feels strangely vulnerable. To his astonishment he sees his penis dangling out of his trousers. Ashamed, he tucks it back into his pants and zips up his trousers.

Ellie yawns, rolls her head to one side and glances over to see two policemen making their way to the back gate. The younger one opens the gate for the other. He ignores the gesture and pompously walks through. To Ellie's wonder the young policeman smiles. For a moment she thinks, what is he doing? How could he be so weak? But the more she plays the scene back the more it becomes apparent it isn't that sort of a smile. It's a knowing smile, a smile that if she caught it at the right angle, she could see its stealth and power.

She fidgets, taking the discomfort from her backside, edging it over the plastic runs. She's sprawled across two patio chairs soaking up every last drop of the sun, blouse unbuttoned to her chest with her skirt hitched up for maximum exposure. A figure breaks the sunlight. She jumps up, startled, her clothing digging in tight.

'Fuck!' She shields her eyes to decipher who the intruder is.

'You're jumpy.' Adrian lights the protruding cigarette rocking on his lip.

She squints; his voice leads his features out of the silhouette.

'Do you have to creep up on people like that?'

He ignores her. 'I see the police have been.' Adrian takes a drag from the cigarette and gestures over to the back gate. 'Got their work cut out with him.'

'What do you mean?'

He doesn't reply, just stares at the back gate and grins.

She can't believe the police visit has gone unnoticed by her. Typical. Whatever happens in this place she's always the last to find out. Annoyed, she vigorously arranges her clothes, buttoning up her top and pulling her skirt down. Adrian takes in the exposed parts of her body but avoids any eye contact.

'For that I'll have one.' Ellie nods to the packet of cigarettes he's putting back in his trouser pocket.

'Still no sign of her?' Adrian's tone is clinical with not a single sign of emotion. He opens up the lid and takes one out for her.

'No.' Ellie positions herself more comfortably and takes the cigarette from him. 'You don't seem very bothered.'

'Of course I am…' He pauses. 'Well, it's not the first time.'

'Bit of a regular thing with you two, is it?' Ellie asks, placing the cigarette in her mouth.

He pulls out his lighter and ignites the end in one precise action. He thinks it looks like an iconic movie moment, years of practice, not a bad exchange for playing Russian roulette with his health.

'You could say that,' Adrian replies.

She takes a deep drag on the cigarette and exhales. Her body relaxes, finding every curve and recess of the chair. 'Why?'

'I don't know,' Adrian replies. He can't help but think of Vicky, seeing her laughing, her body close to his, the excitement, the powerful want he has for her is intoxicating. It lures him back again and again, his guilt is too weak, always manages to put in an appearance when it's all too late, approximately five seconds after they've had sex.

She forces a laugh. 'Come on, there's got to be more to it than that.'

His defences are up. 'She wasn't at Donna's, I've been round there.' He looks around as if he's checking if anyone's listening in on their conversation. 'She hid out there last time.'

Ellie takes another drag of the cigarette and stares at him, analysing his responses. Through the swirling veil of smoke she's certain a different Adrian is standing there, the usual self-confidence drained from his face. Even his well-groomed appearance makes him look as if he's trying too hard. She doesn't know what to say next, being vulnerable isn't something she'd ever associated Adrian with.

The sun's rays clip the edge of the kitchen table. Philip sits staring dreamily into a cup of cold tea, another two cups stand abandoned. The conversation with the two policemen has broken down into fine disconnected pieces of sediment that are settling over him. He hears the back door open and the sound of footsteps approach the table. He tunes in to them but his stare doesn't waver from the cup.

'Why did you have to be like that?' Philip asks, his voice softly spoken but it doesn't hide any of his bitterness.

'Can't help it.'

Startled, he turns to Adrian, who's stood grinning.

'So.'

'So what?'

'The police.' Adrian sits down. 'What did they have to say?'

The back door opens, Philip's whole body grinds to a halt. Ellie scurries in. They both watch her. She takes out her tray and disappears out of the kitchen.

'Have they found her?' Adrian asks.

'No.'

'Shit.'

'They weren't here for Michelle,' Philip says. His expression swings from anxiety to an awareness that makes his eyes shine.

'I see.' Adrian nods, savouring the moment. 'Was it to do with – ?'

'What?'

'You know.'

'I don't know what you mean.'

'You and Mrs Dobbs.'

'Drop it, will you.' Philip glares at him.

'Alright, alright.'

A silence descends between them, broken by Adrian tapping his fingers on the table.

'So you haven't heard anything from her?' Adrian asks.

'Yes.'

The tapping stops.

'Yes?' The word echoes between them. 'Why didn't you tell me? Jesus Christ, Philip, what's the matter with you?'

173

'It's not right.'

'What do you mean?'

'None of it.'

'Shit,' Adrian mutters under his breath.

'Things have changed.'

'Hey, cut the bullshit.' Adrian leans in close. 'She knows, doesn't she?'

'Knows what?'

'Come on, she must have said something.' Adrian squirms nervously on his chair. 'I know it's going to be difficult, I'll do whatever she wants. Please, you've got to believe me. You've got to let me see her.'

'She's tired, she's had a lot to deal with.'

'Sure. I know, I understand that.' Adrian swallows hard. 'I know we don't always see eye to eye Philip but –'

'It's not going to work, Adrian.'

'Philip, you've got to help us out. Let me see her, that's all I want.'

'It's not right.' Philip shakes his head.

'Just let me talk to her.'

'Tomorrow, then you've got to go.'

'Hey, but –'

'If that's not good enough.'

'No, no, that's fine, tomorrow's fine.'

'You can sleep in one of the guest rooms.'

'Thanks, mate.' Adrian sinks into the chair.

Philip places his hands around the cup, its coldness bites deep.

11

Philip surveys the tray cradling Mr Cole's breakfast. Painstakingly he re-arranges its precise composition, not wanting to disrupt its overall layout, as he makes a space for Michelle's breakfast. Ellie walks past him channelling her contempt through her eyes, boring into his skin, wanting it to crackle and spit as it burns. But however hard she tries, it's all lost on him, she can't break into his remote little world. Dejected, she passes the kitchen table and suddenly something catches her eye from underneath it. She hasn't noticed it before, been too occupied in trying to mentally inflict some sort of sadistic pain on Philip. Her loathing has climbed up to another level; she'll only settle for his head served up on a plate now, nothing else will do.

She stoops, dodging the light, but still can't make out what it is. She kneels next to Philip's walking stick propped up against one of the chairs to get a closer look. She thought it might have been a piece of cutlery the way the light reflects off its surface.

But of all things it's a doll splattered in mud with torn pieces of paper stuck to it. The sunlight reflects off its smooth plastic exterior. She reaches out and takes hold of it, dragging it out for a closer inspection. It's a Barbie doll. Well, she thinks it is, but it's so distorted and neglected she's not sure if time has been brutal to it, or if it's fallen foul to the hands of a spiteful child, or maybe both. Instead of a cascading flow of blonde hair, vacant plug holes scatter along the temple of its hairline. Random strands cling for survival in matted clusters of mud. She also notices there are pieces of polished shell radiating out from the mud. She straightens up and looks at Philip, letting out a disapproving sigh, and slams the doll on the table.

She waits, wanting him to react, to say something about the doll, about Ian, about the mud she keeps finding everywhere from the kitchen to the hall. She needs to release the harness of her rage, she desperately wants to be free from it all. He glances at the doll and then to Ellie. Then he picks up a banana and peels and slices it over a bowl of Bran Flakes. She's about to explode. If wishes came true he'd be holding his heart in his hand right now, his legs folding, knees plummeting to the floor, crying out for her forgiveness, wishing he had appreciated her more. He drops a few grapes in the bowl and places it next to Mr Cole's full English.

Ellie looks on, exhausted and puzzled.

'You've got to eat properly.' Philip talks to himself as if she's been erased from the room. 'So many obese children these days.'

Ellie doesn't know how to react.

He takes a newspaper, folds it and wedges it under his arm. Smiling at her, he picks up the tray and hobbles unconvincingly to his walking stick.

'Philip.'

He stops in front of her but doesn't look at her. 'Yes.'

'Mrs Kirkwood has just spoken to me. They're leaving, it's the noise.'

'Right.'

'Could you sort out their bill?'

'Course I will, as soon as I've taken this upstairs.'

'I've told them to wait in reception, when they've finished packing.'

'Fine. That's good, well done, thank you.'

He turns his back on her and hobbles to the door, his walking stick hanging from under the tray.

Ellie seizes the doll from the table, small pieces of paper fall away from it. 'I found this.'

She holds it up, wanting him to stop. Her grip tightens on the doll. She wills him to turn around. Her wrath rises up again, rushing through her body, igniting her confidence. This is it, this is the moment she's been waiting for, she knows she could face up to him once and for all. But to her dismay his head drops and his stride slips up a gear as if nothing at all is wrong with his legs. He fires out the kitchen like a man being propelled out of a cannon.

Ellie puts the doll carefully back on the table. She notices that several of the pieces of torn paper are actually pieces of an old black and white photograph. Delicately she picks them up, scratching at the mud without destroying the image. Two of the pieces fit together. Ellie looks at them closely. She can just make out the features of a young man, he's wearing what looks like an army uniform. She places the pieces next to the doll and then carefully strokes its unkempt hair.

Philip doesn't know where the morning is going; the more he tries to do, the less he seems to get done. He stares anxiously at his watch. She can't be late for school, it's up to him to make sure. Mr Cole means well but he's always interfering, letting her get her own way. You can't compromise with children – you need to take control, show them where the boundaries are. Mr Cole should know this, what is the matter with him? He has to accept he can't rely on him any more, it feels strange and unsettling. Mr Cole has been his rock, the one person he's able to depend upon, knowing he'll be there in his corner whatever life throws at him, but cracks are starting to appear in their relationship. Now his loyalty is leaning more favourably to Michelle, Philip feels jealous of the relationship he has with her but he doesn't want to admit it. He shakes the notion from his thoughts. It's petty – she's his daughter, his responsibility, nothing can ever change that. But it's the same as when she had been with Frances.

Mr Cole exaggerates a stretch, soaking up its comfort. He leans back from the yolk-stained plate, leaving the remains of two rashers of bacon and the smear of tomato ketchup on its once-white surface. The rim of the plate frames it like a piece of abstract art. Unbuttoning the top of his trousers, his belly spews out to a relieved sigh as he takes in the view from the window.

'What a wonderful day.' Mr Cole gently rubs the trench across his stomach where his trousers have been digging in.

Philip sits opposite him with Michelle perched precariously on his knee. She's dressed in her school uniform; it bulges, revealing the immense struggle it took to make her wear it. Her hair is morning-wild, needing a comb to tame her curls, her face screwed in a defiant glare at the bowl of cereal still waiting to be eaten.

'Come on Michelle, it's better for you,' Philip says.

He taps the spoon on the side of the bowl and brings it up to her mouth but Michelle scrunches up her face even more reluctantly. He takes the spoon away.

'They don't taste right.'

'So you keep telling me.'

'It's a shock for her,' Mr Cole says.

'Don't start that again. You'll only encourage her.'

'Stop fussing over her.'

Philip gives him a stern look but Mr Cole is too occupied in soothing his stomach.

'She can't be *that* ill, running around the guesthouse and the back garden all night. What were you thinking?' Philip shakes his head at him. 'As soon as she's eaten her breakfast she's off to school, and that's final.'

'She's been through a lot,' Mr Cole says.

'She's got you wrapped round her little finger.'

'It's all new to her.'

Philip pushes the spoon at her again, ignoring Mr Cole's last remark. 'Come on Michelle, I'm not going through this every day.' His tone pleads for her to give in.

'No.'

'I'm not putting up with this.'

He hopes Mr Cole will redeem himself and back him up but he stares dreamily out of the window, soaking up the satisfaction of being fed and at the alluring peacefulness of the bay.

'I don't want to.' Michelle rubs her head. 'It hurts.'

Philip tugs her arm away and holds it tight. 'Stop this! There's nothing wrong with you.'

'I don't want to go.'

'You know how much you like school really.'

'I – I …' She pauses, wrestling with her thoughts. 'Yes – I don't know.'

'You were doing so well.'

'Yes, but –' Confused, she cradles her stomach. 'It hurts, it does.' She then touches her neck for no apparent reason and to her surprise her body judders.

'Don't do this, you're not getting around me young lady. Not after what you've put me through.' Philip's lip trembles as he watches her.

'She's a mummy's girl.' Mr Cole winks at her. 'That's what's wrong with her.'

Michelle slips off Philip's leg, almost sending the spoonful of cereal flying.

'What did you say that for?' Philip asks, the question sieving through his clenched teeth, not wanting Michelle to hear.

Mr Cole turns back to the sea.

'Michelle!' Philip slams the spoon hard on the table irritated with them both. 'Come back here. You don't just leave the table.'

Michelle sits on the edge of the bed. She touches her neck again. She looks helplessly at Philip and then suddenly remembers to rub her head and cradle her stomach.

'Come on, she's just a kid. She's a bit tired,' Mr Cole says. 'That's all.'

The sunlight bathes his face and for a brief moment Philip notices the light makes it almost transparent. Michelle climbs on the bed and curls up as if she wants to disappear.

'I told you not to have her up half the night again,' Philip says.

'Don't exaggerate, we've been over this.'

'She's got her own room. She shouldn't be downstairs with you.'

'She wanted some attention, that's all.'

'This has nothing to do with you. She's my daughter.'

Mr Cole shakes his head, letting his anger fall from him like autumn leaves. 'Hey, come on, there's no need for that.'

'Sorry I didn't mean to …' He pauses. 'A routine, that's what she needs.' He glances over to her, dropping the volume of his voice. 'She needs to be in bed at a decent hour, eat proper meals. It can't carry on like this, can't you see she's playing us off each other.'

'I never saw her before.' Mr Cole's voice suddenly changes.

Philip's line of conscious thought dissolves in an instant. He doesn't understand what he's hearing. The tone and texture of Mr Cole's voice is identical to that of his mother's.

Philip's gaze swoops down to the table, avoiding any eye contact. His mother's presence seeps into his pores, slipping and crawling with a domineering force.

'I know.' Philip's unsure of why he said the words, but they make him feel better.

Mr Cole's hand rests on the table. Its hard, bulky roughness becomes slender and smooth. Nails grow, maintained and youthful, manual work has never troubled them. He concentrates on the faint band of white where a wedding ring once was. The reception bell rings out but then gently fades away.

Again Ellie rings the bell, hoping to see Philip coming down the stairs. There's no way she's taking the whole brunt from Mr Kirkwood. Why should she? She's not like Ian. He was way too soft and look where that got him. She's totally different and he'll have to get used to it; she won't even compromise. If there's one thing that gets her back up it's when somebody takes advantage of her. That's what happened to Ian. He did more and more until there was no definition of what his job was and what he was just doing to help out, his goodwill lost to the norm. The guesthouse ticked over and who cared who was carrying most of the load? Philip certainly didn't.

She glances back up the stairs, Philip should be here by now. What is he doing up there?

She goes back to the bell, knowing Mr Kirkwood will be there at any moment. 'Come on, where are you?'

She hears a pair of footsteps sluggishly descending the stairs. Expectation lifts her heart, but it's Mr Kirkwood who appears, swaggering, loaded with suitcases. She smiles at him as he steps into the hall, strained at struggling with the luggage and looking as if he has bit into something sour. She stands awkwardly, wanting to make a quick exit, then a glimmer of hope – she hadn't realised Mr Kirkwood's son is there holding onto his sleeve. Mr Kirkwood's expression changes, the sour bitterness becomes more dominant. He comes to a halt inches away from her and drops the two large suitcases, making the ground tremor.

'Right, I want my money back.'

She doesn't know what's worse – his blunt attitude or his bad breath.

'There'll be someone along in a minute.' Ellie optimistically peers over his shoulder to the stairs. Who's she trying to kid? But at least it gives her an ounce of comfort.

'We've complained but nothing's been done about it,' Mr Kirkwood says. 'Three nights in a row.' He holds up his fingers. 'Three nights!'

'I know, I know.' Ellie takes a step back wishing the wall wasn't so close.

If only she can defuse the situation, say a magic word to subdue him or even better make him disappear. She looks him straight in the eye and faces the inevitable truth, there's no way she can ever reason with him.

'You're not fobbing me off, you hear me?' Mr Kirkwood says. 'I want my money!'

'He – he won't be long. He's –'

'Pete, please.' Mrs Kirkwood appears. She nods to their son, who's becoming distressed. 'Do you have to?'

The young boy has both hands gripping his father's sleeve, as if he's holding the lead to a rottweiler desperately wanting to keep it under control.

Mr Kirkwood unwillingly picks up the suitcases.

'I'll get this lot to the car,' he says, turning to Ellie. 'When I come back it'd better be sorted.'

Adrian comes down the stairs. Mr Kirkwood views him suspiciously and leads his family out the door, leaving Ellie wheel-clamped to the spot.

'What was all that about?' Adrian's attention flicks back and forth from Ellie's distressed appearance to the Kirkwoods disappearing out the front door.

'Have you seen Philip?' Ellie's anger almost bursts out of her skin.

'Are you alright?'

She lets out a deep wounded sigh. 'He always manages to avoid everything, that wanker! Always gets by, by the skin of his teeth.' She shakes her head. 'Not this time, he can deal with it.'

'Hey, calm down Ellie.'

'No, no I don't want to. He can stuff his job. You can tell him. I quit!'

'Ellie, there's no need for that.'

She turns to storm off but he takes hold of her arm.

'Come on, you know what he's like –'

'Don't you start sticking up for him.'

'I'm not. He can be a bit freaky but he's harmless enough.' He smiles. 'I mean it's a bit sad really, he must be lonely. If the only pleasure he gets is copping off with Mrs ...' His voice peters off.

'He was what?'

'You don't know, do you?'

'Know what?' Ellie fires at him.

'I just thought –'

'What did he do?'

'He – erm – he was caught ...' He pauses. 'It was nothing.'

'Is that why the police were here, over nothing?'

'It was about the accident, that's all. I shouldn't have said anything.'

'I'm not stupid, it's about Mrs Dobbs as well, isn't it. Ian wouldn't tell me. I want to know.'

'It's difficult, it's –'

'I have a right to know or I'll walk out the door right now!'

'Alright, alright,' Adrian sighs. 'He was caught – sort of – you know – like playing with himself with Mrs Dobbs' underwear.' He turns away, uneasy at what he has said.

'Shit, you're joking!' A hand rests on her open mouth. 'Dirty bastard!' Her body shakes as she wrestles with the idea. 'Dirty, filthy bastard.'

'Come on Ellie, maybe –'

She snatches her arm away from him.

'Get off me! That's it. I've had enough, I'm out of here.' She snarls, baring her teeth. 'He's a fucking weirdo!'

Ellie turns her back on him and heads for the kitchen, leaving Adrian standing wondering what he has contributed to.

Mrs Briston drags her suitcase out of her room and uses it to prop open the fire door. She can hear her husband muttering with interludes of slamming drawers and doors. He has to go through every single one. Not just once, oh no, it has to be a good three or four times. It isn't as if he'd scattered his belongings to the four corners of the room, he'd used the small bedside cabinet and a slither of the wardrobe. What is he fretting about? If anybody is going to forget something, it's going to be her and she's already rechecked everything twice.

Her suitcase moves forward and stops, resting against her leg, pushed by the unrelenting surge of the fire door. She can't stand being in the same room when he's in one of his flaps, she has to just leave him to it. He won't rest until everything is in order, only then can he move onto the next stage. According to his schedule, they'd be gone by about eight-thirty and she knows full well that he meant eight-thirty on the dot. He could stifle the very air she breathed, making her want to slap him across the face and shake him until he stopped. She liked to think she'd do it some day, it made her feel better.

But how could she? She loves him, even with all his little ways – they accumulate together to make him what he is. So she'll stick to getting out the way, take five and re-introduce herself back to her sanity. The suitcase pushes harder into her leg but she doesn't want to move. Another drawer slams or maybe it's a cupboard, it sounds as if it's come from the en-suite. She has to stay out of his way a bit longer than usual. This holiday has to come to an end, and it should have been sooner rather than later – she can't put up with it any longer. She badly wants to salvage the rest of the week, stop off somewhere on the way back home or get the deck chairs out and relax in the back garden. Someone distracts her, ambling down the stairs. She turns and sees Philip, walking stick in hand. He smiles at her but she can't respond.

'I didn't realise you were leaving today, Mrs Briston,' Philip says.

'We think it's for the best.' She smiles at him but it doesn't last.

Abruptly she turns away, defusing any chance of a conversation between them. Another set of footsteps approach, this time coming up the stairs. She seizes the opportunity and pulls the suitcase away from the door, letting the fire door retract, and slips back into the room to witness her husband rechecking the wardrobe for the fifth time.

Adrian comes into view. He nods to Philip, coinciding with Mr Miller descending the stairs, wrestling a couple of swollen suitcases. He stops on the landing giving them both a disapproving frown.

'Mr Miller,' Philip says. 'Is everything alright?'

'Too late for that,' Mr Miller replies, putting the luggage down.

'Didn't see you at breakfast,' Philip says.

Mr Miller shoves a hand into his pocket, pulls out a cheque and puts it in Philip's hand.

'That takes care of us.' Mr Miller sighs. '*Is everything alright!*' he mutters, picking up his suitcases. He carries them down the stairs almost knocking Adrian out of the way.

'I'm sorry to hear you're leaving,' Philip calls after him. Mr Miller stops on the stairs, shakes his head and then stomps the rest of the way.

'At this rate there'll be no guests left by the end of the day!' Adrian smirks.

'That isn't funny.'

'It wasn't supposed to be, I've just had an ear-bashing from Mr Kirkwood.'

'Yes – Mr Kirkwood, I was just on my way to sort that out.'

'Don't worry. It's all been taken care of.'

'What do you mean?'

'We came to a compromise.' Adrian shrugs his shoulders. 'There's no petty cash left.'

'What? Never mind.' Philip attempts to walk away from Adrian.

'Philip.' Adrian stops him. 'Hey, I didn't know what else to do.'

Philip tries to side-step him but he blocks his way.

'I'm sorry.' Adrian looks around in case someone is eaves-dropping on their conversation. 'Is it still alright?' He tries to make eye contact, wanting to judge Philip's mood but fails. 'I know you said about seeing her today …' He pauses. 'It's just I need to see her. I've been so worried.'

'She'll be leaving for school soon.'

'For school, you're joking!' He rubs the palm of his hand on his forehead, wanting to soothe his thoughts. 'Shit, she hasn't got her old job back?' He leans on the banister feeling off balance, taking onboard that it might be too late. He may have already lost her. 'This is the end for us, isn't it?'

'What are you talking about?' Philip asks with a distaste-ful stare.

'This is what you want, isn't it?'

'Adrian, please. What's got into you?'

'I know what you think about me. Don't even try to deny it.'

Philip ignores him and heads to the stairs.

Adrian steps out in front of him. 'I've got to see her, please Philip!'

Philip tries to get past him but fails again.

'She's been a right little madam. I think it's her mother, they were always so close ...' He pauses, sinking into his thoughts. 'I know she didn't want to leave her, it wasn't her fault, maybe –' He grinds to a halt.

'Please Philip, if this is where she wants to be, then fair enough. I just want to talk to her. Let me see her before she goes.'

Philip doesn't move, his expression cast in stone.

'Are you alright, Philip?'

Life flickers back on Philip's face like a monitor after its computer has been rebooted. 'Had a bit of a funny turn there. Haven't got used to being up and about.' He smiles. 'Did the evening meal shift last night, I think it's taken a lot out of me.' He breathes in slowly.

'You'll wear yourself out, Michelle must have taken some of the pressure away from you?'

'I'm not sure about that. She hasn't been very well.'

'Not well? She's alright, isn't she?'

'Don't worry, she's fine, I think half of it was attention seeking.'

Adrian looks puzzled.

'It's hard to bring them up by yourself. It isn't right,' he continues.

'She did take it bad.' Adrian's confused at what Philip said but puts it down to him being tired. 'She felt guilty not being there as much as she would have liked to have been.'

An awkwardness settles on Philip's face. He brushes it off. 'Come on then,' he says. 'Before she goes to school, you've got to be quick though.'

Adrian smiles as relief washes through him. Philip hobbles over to the stairs and plants his stick firmly onto the first step.

He turns to Adrian. 'Going up is always the difficult bit.'

Adrian reaches out to help him but Philip declines the offer. He grabs hold of the banister for support and pulls himself up onto the step.

Adrian follows, not noticing the inconsistencies Philip makes as he clambers up the stairs. He's imagining himself with Michelle, talking to her, trying to reason with her. It's all going to be different. He can change, he has to, but Vicky pops up in his thoughts, his guilt wrapped around her, wanting to drag her away. The alluring smell of her body calls to him, the intensity of their relationship purring in his ears. He manages to push her away. No, it's not right. He can't go on like this. What's the matter with him? He's going to have to show Michelle commitment, show her he's deadly serious. If Salmouth is where she wants to be, he'll join her. There's no way he's going to lose her. He'll sell the house if he has to, change his job – it doesn't matter, whatever it takes. The greater he hypothesises the more he raises the stakes to keep her.

Philip reaches the top landing and glances back. 'I don't want you upsetting her. I don't want her being late today. I still haven't made up her lunch box.'

Adrian looks at him – what a weird thing for him to say.

Philip hobbles through the fire door leading to the guest rooms, while Adrian hesitates for a moment on the landing. He had presumed Michelle was in her old room, through the door marked *private* and up the small flight of stairs. He shrugs his shoulders and slips through the fire door to see Philip hovering outside room 8.

'She's here?' Adrian glances behind him. 'Not upstairs?'

Philip nods. 'They get along. I'm glad really.' His tone contradicts what he has said.

Adrian lingers nervously behind Philip, pulling and brushing at his shirt and trousers, making sure he's at his presentable best. To his surprise Philip takes a set of keys out of his pocket and unlocks the door. It seems a strange thing for him to do. Why didn't he just knock? The door opens and Adrian's attention immediately focuses on more important issues, like patting down any stray hairs that are on the loose and not restrained by a controlling slick of gel.

'I didn't realise, she never told me. Who is it?'

Philip doesn't answer him.

'Yes, they get on very well.' The jealousy in his voice sprays Adrian.

Philip's a mystifying individual, but what can he do? He's Michelle's father and he has to accept that. Families … you can't choose them, as long as he doesn't have to live with him. That's one scenario he's always backed away from, the bench-mark. If he has to step over this one he would be on dodgy ground – if that was his only option of them being together. He shoves the idea from his thoughts. He can't deal with that now. He follows Philip into the room, checking his breath and making any last adjustment to his appearance whilst lining up the different scenarios to combat her grievances.

He walks past Philip. The room is dimly lit. He squints, trying to make out where everybody is. A stale smell punches his lungs as he hears Philip closing the door behind him. For some reason the curtains are drawn and there's a peculiar smell in the air. The door locks behind him. He's about to turn around and ask what Philip is doing when he notices the figure of a woman on a chair by the window. Is it Michelle? He turns back to Philip, who nods and smiles at him, encouraging him to walk on. Then instantly his expression changes, suspicion moulds his features, it's as if he's looking straight through him. As though somehow Adrian has been erased from the room. Adrian looks nervously back to the woman in the chair and steps closer.

'Michelle?' Adrian calls her name but he doesn't expect her to answer him. Nothing seems right, he feels giddy. His eyes are adjusting to the room's dim light. What is the matter with her? Is she sprawled asleep or drunk? And what is she wearing? He battles to understand what he's seeing but it keeps leading him back to a place where he doesn't want to go. He coughs. The room's stale stench scrapes down his throat, flipping over his stomach. Why is Michelle dressed in a mini skirt and tight fitting top? This isn't the way she dresses. It's very rare you ever see her in a skirt; it's her ankles, she hates her ankles, always complaining they're too fat.

'Michelle?'

She doesn't move. Cautiously he steps closer. Something squelches under his foot. In the fragmenting light he can make out pieces of food scattered over the floor.

'Shit.'

'Come on Michelle! You're going to be late.' Philip tuts behind him.

Adrian wants to throw an annoyed glare at Philip for making him jump, but the closer he moves to Michelle the more he is unwilling to take his eyes away from her. His stomach bubbles. Why doesn't she move? He tries to reach out to her with his mind, to somehow will her to react, to wake her up from the trance-like state she's trapped in. And what *is* she wearing? The question comes back to him again, but deep down he already knows. He doesn't want to acknowledge it; somehow hoping he can manoeuvre around it.

'It's no good moping around. You're going to school and that's final. Do you understand me?'

Adrian's fascination breaks away from her. He swings around as Philip wearily rolls his eyes. He turns back, hoping for a response from her – any response. But he doesn't rouse a single twitch. He can feel any reasonable explanation slipping through his fingers. Feebly he takes another step closer but his will is dragging him down. He can't even hide behind the dull cloak of the room any more, his eyes have adjusted to it.

The reality of what he is seeing hits him with its full force no longer skirting around the back of his mind.

It is Michelle and she is dressed in a school uniform. Its stressed seams gorge into her skin, almost bursting at accommodating her body.

'Mr Cole, I don't suppose you've seen her maths homework have you?'

Bewildered, Adrian looks around the room. Who is he talking to?

'Nothing to do with me,' Mr Cole says. 'The things they have to do these days. I'm staying well clear of that.'

Adrian homes in on the voice. He turns to see Philip sieving through the chest of drawers. He pulls out another drawer, sending his walking stick tumbling to the floor.

'Philip what's going on?'

Philip ignores him.

Adrian turns back to Michelle. 'Michelle, Michelle!' His voice stumbles.

'Sorry, I don't think we have met before,' Mr Cole says, walking towards Adrian, his arm outstretched to shake his hand.

'What are you doing?' Adrian asks.

'I don't feel well,' Michelle says.

Adrian watches Philip approach, his arm still outstretched, his expressions taking on an appearance of innocence. He backs away from him and almost falls into Michelle, but manages to steady himself on her exposed shoulder. He notices her hands are caked in dried mud, her fingernails embedded with dirt. Her cold, damp touch startles his hand, he snatches it back making her head roll unnaturally. Momentarily he sees her face, channels of dried blood seeping from her nose and mouth. Then it disappears to the swirls of unkempt hair. She slips off the chair and slumps to the floor.

Philip seizes his arm.

'What the hell are you playing at!' Mr Cole says. 'Did you see that Philip?'

'What the fuck are you going on about!' Adrian screams. 'What have you done to her?'

'Don't you dare use that sort of language in front of a young girl,' Mr Cole spits. 'What is your problem?'

Philip looks down at Michelle lying sprawled on the floor.

'What the bloody hell did you do that for?' Mr Cole asks.

'What – What are you talking about?' Adrian says. He's lost in an ocean of emotional abandonment.

'Is he blind as well as stupid?' Mr Cole asks.

Philip shakes his head in utter despair.

'Adrian, what are you doing, what's going on?'

'What have you done to her?' Adrian says again, looking in horror.

Philip looks baffled at Michelle.

Adrian crouches by her side and gently touches her hand. 'No, please Michelle, please no. It would have been different this time, I swear to you.' Her cold skin snaps at his fingertips.

'What's the matter with him?' Mr Cole asks.

'He's my boyfriend,' Michelle says.

Philip's eyes narrow.

'What did you say?'

'That's enough of that sort of nonsense, Michelle. I've told you to get ready for school. You have a lot to catch up on, the children need your help –' He comes to a grinding halt, confused by what he has said.

Adrian watches Philip's features swirl in a concoction of confusion.

'Come on, Adrian,' Philip says. 'Sort yourself out. You're going to make her late. I knew this was a bad idea, but you had to come here, didn't you?' He looks anxious and ashamed at the same time. The volume of his voice turns down, conscious of anybody overhearing. 'It can't go on the way it has been. It's not right.'

'I hurt my head,' Michelle says. 'I don't like the pain, it frightens me.'

Philip rubs his head then starts to sniffle.

'Did you say boyfriend?' Mr Cole asks.

'You only bumped it.' Philip gets more impatient with her. 'Will you sort yourself out!' He stoops down and grabs her hand. 'I've told you to clean them, they're filthy. It's all going to change from now on – no more late nights for you young lady. Bedtime will be seven o'clock on the dot. I'm fed up of your excuses.'

'They're not excuses,' Michelle says. 'It's Mr Cole's idea. He gets scared. That's why we play games. Stops him thinking about what's been going on.'

'Stop blaming other people,' Philip snaps.

'My God, you disgust me,' Mr Cole snarls at Adrian.

'No, please Mr Cole,' Philip says.

'Don't you dare stand up for him,' Mr Cole says. 'He thinks he's her boyfriend!' He grabs hold of Adrian's arm.

'He is –' Michelle says, with another attention-seeking sniffle. She looks at her clothes. 'I'm sure – that's right, isn't it?'

Adrian snatches his arm away. 'Get your fucking hands off me!' he spits.

His captured state has been broken, his heart racing, bewilderment morphing into rage. 'What the fuck's going on!' Adrian shouts.

'What sort of a man are you?' Mr Cole asks. 'You haven't touched her, have you? I can't even think about it, not that.'

'Alright, alright,' Philip says, pleading. 'It's all different, it's all different now.' He shakes his head. 'You've got to understand, Michelle needs her family. You've disrupted her too much, taking her away from here.' His bottom lip quivers. 'Living with her …' He pauses. 'I suppose you'll want to marry her eventually.'

'MARRY!' Mr Cole screams out in desperation. 'Marry you!'

Adrian turns away from Michelle and his fury bursts out. He shoves past Philip, making him topple over and strides towards the door.

'You're finished,' Adrian shouts, tears rolling down his cheeks. 'You hear me, you fucking nutcase! They'll lock you up and throw away the fucking key.'

From nowhere Mr Cole surges at him, spinning him round and thumping him hard in the stomach.

'I've had enough of you,' Mr Cole snarls. 'You make my skin crawl. You think it's normal do you? Is that what you think – to carry on like that?'

Adrian cradles his stomach, summoning his breath to come back.

Mr Cole snatches a clump of Adrian's hair and yanks his head back. 'Marry you. Is this what this country has come to. You make me puke. Bloody liberals, let in all the scum like you. Don't want to take away any of your rights. Oh no, we don't want to do that. You people don't deserve any.'

Adrian is shocked by the immense power of Philip's hold, feeling his breath on his face, smelling the alcohol and contempt seeping through his pores.

'Too many do-gooders in this country,' Mr Cole says. 'If I had my way, I'd stamp out the lot of you. Not worth the taxes to keep you locked up.'

Mr Cole flings Adrian to the floor.

'Fuck off.' Adrian splutters. 'You mad fucker!'

He tries to scramble to his feet but is kicked hard in the face. Adrian groans, a mixture of saliva and blood smears his nose and mouth. He holds his face as it throbs, pumping hard under his hand.

'You're finished, you here me,' Adrian says. 'It's all over, you're finished.'

Philip paces up and down in front of him.

'Get her out of here,' Mr Cole says.

'No, Mr Cole,' Philip says. 'Please don't do this. I'm begging you.'

'You heard me, Philip, I want you to go, take Michelle and get out of the room. This is going to end here, it's the only way. Put the family first, it's not going to be destroyed this time. Not by some little sick shit like this.'

'But –'

'Do it!' Mr Cole shouts.

Philip stoops and cowardly shuffles over to Michelle. He takes hold of one of her arms and drags her into the en-suite. The door slams shut and an eerie silence takes hold of the room. Adrian pulls himself up, his arms shaking out of control. He looks to the door. Muffled voices come from the en-suite. He turns back to the door, determination pumping through his veins giving him a surging strength. He supports himself on his arms and brings up a leg for leverage. As he reaches out towards the door, the en-suite door bursts opens and Philip strides out – his stern stride carries him over to the chest of drawers. He crouches down, ignoring Adrian.

Adrian laughs at him, a reaction that astonishes them both. 'Family, what the fuck do you know about family?' His body shakes uncontrollably. 'Michelle told me all about you.'

Philip turns around and walks over to him. Adrian notices he's gripping his walking stick.

'It's a little late for that, don't you think?' Adrian's body defrosts and slumps on the floor. 'What are you going to do, convince me you can't walk now?' He tries to suppress his laughter but it splutters out.

Philip stands over him.

'You took her away from me once,' Philip says. 'When I needed her most.'

His body stands sturdy and menacing.

'People like you destroy families,' Mr Cole says. 'I had to watch it gnaw at Judith day after day. She didn't get over Becky's death. I had to watch it destroy her.'

Adrian looks up at him, feeling his repulsion weighing down on him.

'What the hell are you talking about? Who's Becky?'

'Seeing her deteriorate like that.'

Philip lifts the walking stick from his side like an ancient solider drawing a sword in battle. He raises it over his head.

Adrian holds up his arm to protect himself. He shuts his eyes, wanting to disappear.

'Nothing I could do. Nothing I could do,' Mr Cole repeats.

Pain erupts and spreads along Adrian's arm. It bursts again and again as the walking stick pounds at him at an unstoppable pace.

'Never been so helpless, nothing I could say or do!' Philip splutters.

Adrian's arms crumble at the onslaught.

'Do you know how that feels? Do you?'

The agonising pain then transfers to his head. The unrelenting blows merge into a deep echoing drone until his skull collapses with a final sickening thud.

12

Philip places pieces of processed chicken on a slice of buttered wholemeal bread. He slices a tomato and perches it on top; its juice quenches the dried blood clinging in the crevices of his fingernails, smudging the whiteness of the chicken. He takes another slice from the bread bin and sits it on top, pressing it down firmly. By the side of the chopping board is an old plastic sandwich box waiting to be loaded up. It's faded to a washed-out yellow and pink, looking like a forgotten Liquorice Allsort, its fixed yellow handle chipped with stress marks of white. A muffled voice comes from behind him but he ignores it. Taking a knife from its wooden block he cuts the sandwich in two. The reception bell rings. He hesitates for a moment, his grip tightening around the knife. He controls his breathing and places the knife down on the chopping board.

Philip opens a drawer, pulls out a roll of sandwich bags and rips one free. Carefully he takes hold of the sandwich and brings it up to meet the bag, but part of its crust catches the opening and it falls apart. The reception bell rings again, but all he can do is watch as the sliced tomato and chicken make an exodus from the sandwich and land haphazardly on the work surface. As he steps back the heel of his shoe sinks in to a pile of blood-stained blankets heaped on the floor. Faded smears run along the kitchen tiles stopping abruptly at the door of the office. Philip pivots on his heel and heads to the hall.

Mr Riley lingers next to the reception bell. He rings it again, this time holding it down even longer. The kitchen door swings open. Philip approaches him at a rapid speed. 'Do you mind!' Philip's frail frame is pumped.

Mr Riley is taken aback by Philip's attitude but he won't be intimidated – this isn't right, there's only so much he can take. Besides, it's different now, the second-hand American influence *customer's always right* mentality has invaded our shores. The whole work place has become one big service sector.

'Yes, I do mind!' Mr Riley snaps.

Philip doesn't expect so much defiance to come out of such an unassuming man clothed in his Marks and Spencer range, a baseball cap hiding his grey, thinning hair. The only time he's seen him without it is when he's with his wife at breakfast. She's a large woman but he had hardly noticed her either.

'I'm fed up of the constant screaming and shouting at night, children running around,' Mr Riley says. 'What sort of place is this?'

Philip walks forward. 'I need to make some sandwiches.'

Mr Riley's baffled. 'Sandwiches? I'm making a complaint here and …' He pauses, his thoughts lost, tripping over what he has said. 'And all you're worried about is sandwiches!'

Philip nods at him. 'Sorry, yes you're right.'

Mr Riley presumes he's making some headway, a glimmering light at the end of this communication tunnel. But to his astonishment Philip turns around and wanders back to the kitchen. Mr Riley watches as the kitchen door slams shut.

'Hold on a minute!' Mr Riley shouts. 'What are you doing?'

He stands there in the hall wanting to find some way of venting his fury. The leaflets stare at him, mocking him with all their promises of good times. You're on holiday, you have to enjoy yourself, you've paid your money, it's your right. He turns to the reception bell, but finds no relief. It's no good, what else can he do? His finger hits the bell with a mighty force – any harder, he's sure it would break it in two.

To his amazement Philip returns promptly and unimpressed.

'Mr Riley!' Philip gestures to his finger still welded to the bell. 'Do you mind?'

'Oh, yes,' Mr Riley says, removing his finger. 'Sorry.'

'Right.' Philip pulls out the complaints book from under his arm and opens it.

Mr Riley sighs, his foot tapping as if on a bass drum. Philip runs his finger down the page and locates several complaints already from him.

'I'm not logging in another complaint.' Mr Riley folds his arms. 'What's the point? How many times do I have to keep going over the same thing again and again?'

Philip's puzzled.

'I want to cancel the rest of my stay.' Mr Riley takes a hold of his fury, hearing his tone wavering in places.

Philip nods and takes a pen to the complaints book.

'And I want a refund of my deposit.' Mr Riley extends a finger to emphasise the point. 'I'm going upstairs to pack and I'll be back here in half an hour – I want you to have this sorted for me. Is that clear?'

Philip is too pre-occupied writing in his complaint.

'I said, is that clear?' Mr Riley raises his voice.

'Yes.' Philip looks up at him but his eyes hastily plummet back to the safety of the book.

The list of complaints stare back at him one after another. He can hear their voices filtering through the fibres of the page, ridiculing him. He has nowhere to run to, nowhere to hide. It feels like the very building could fall down around him at any given moment and there's nothing he can do about it. He slams the book shut and looks up but Mr Riley has gone. His muscles let out a groaning ache. He has this strange feeling he's been standing examining the lists of complaints for a long time. He takes a step back, wanting to be detached from the notion. The book is snatched from his hands. Mr Cole opens it and scornfully scans over the pages.

'Not another one, that's all some people want to do. So petty minded.' Mr Cole shakes his head disapprovingly. 'Dirty soap, cracked mirror, only one towel, can't get channel five, why haven't you got Sky, no Playstation for the kids, need more sachets of coffee, people running around at night – mud on –'

He quickly moves on, flicking over to another page and randomly takes in the core of the complaints, scattered with, Would you mind, Could you just please or Everything is fine but …' Mr Cole gives Philip an adamant look and turns to another page.

'It's time we sorted this place out,' Mr Cole says. 'Complaints are always a two-way street.' He shuts the book and holds it to his chest. 'That's the trouble, when it's all geared up for the consumer, you're always having to cower to them. If someone is always right they're always going to be fallible.' Mr Cole grins to Philip. It's a grin that fills him with optimism, but it lets in something so sinister and foreboding he can feel its pure menacing presence flaring up his skin in goose-pimples.

'Not any more,' Mr Cole says, with a precise and condoning conviction. He glances behind him. 'Right then, we'll lock the front door and deal with these complaints from the bottom to the top. Time for a bit of re-education, you saw what it did for Adrian.'

Philip feels uneasy.

'He's just settling in, that's all. We got off on the wrong foot,' Mr Cole says. 'A misunderstanding. I can see it all working out just fine.'

Philip wants to turn away from him but something's making him dizzy.

'Michelle. I need to make her sandwiches,' Philip says, holding a pleading frown.

'School can wait another day, we need to sort this mess out,' Mr Cole says. 'Besides it's nearly the weekend. She's a good kid, she can come along, it'll be a learning curve for her as well.'

'But –' Philip's palms are covered in sweat.

'It's about time she learned how to deal with customers and more importantly how to stick up for herself. One day she'll have to run this place by herself.'

'Do you think she will?' Philip asks.

'This is what you want, Philip, don't expect it to be given to you on a plate. Nothing ever comes to those who are worthy, not in this world. Do you understand me?'

Philip nods.

'You can't wait for it to just happen,' Mr Cole says. 'You know, what I'm trying to say is –' Annoyed he shakes his head.

'Are you alright?' Philip asks.

'Stop it, stop it now, Philip,' Mr Cole says. 'Pull yourself together. It'll be the way you always wanted it to be. You've got to be strong for all of us.'

He tucks the complaints book firmly under his arm and walks over to the front door. Philip can only stand there as if he's connecting to some unseen future misfortune. He can't work it out but the sheer scale of it engulfs him. From somewhere inside of him a small faint voice tries to reach out, screaming at Mr Cole to stop.

'We're in this together. You helped me, Philip, it's time for me to do the same. That's what it's all about.' Mr Cole stops. 'Did you say something?'

Philip stands there, the faint voice inside of him becoming more and more dishevelled until it's poised on the verge of extinction.

'Sorry, I thought you said something,' Mr Cole says, standing at the front door looking back at Philip.

'No, nothing,' Philip answers as the voice fades away as quickly as it appeared.

Philip and Michelle are standing outside the fire door leading to room 2, waiting for Mr Cole to arrive. Philip stares helplessly at the fire door, not wanting his eyes to wander away from its boundaries. Perspiration makes his clothes cling heavy to his skin. He hears Michelle by his side battling with Mr Cole's portable CD player. A clammy foreboding sensation rolls in his stomach. He longs for that inner voice to somehow ignite back into life, to find a momentous strength to clamber out of its suppressed prison and rise up like a righteous army that would roar from his mouth. To enable him to stand defiant against Mr Cole, or at least give him enough strength to turn around and run; run down the stairs along the hall and out of the guesthouse into the outside world. To let it carry him along through the ambling crowds on the esplanade, around the mouth of the harbour, past The Ship and over the Town Bridge. Giving him the strength to keep going until his muscles set on fire and his bones give way, buckling and breaking. But he knows he'd have to run so much further to escape from this. To his dismay nothing happens. He stands abandoned as guests' voices resonate through the door, making his body shiver.

'Now who do we have here?' Mr Cole asks from behind Philip.

Mr Cole's changed, looking very smart in a dark grey suit with all the trimmings – gold cufflinks, a silk blue tie and a shimmering crimson waistcoat. Philip notices his walking stick is leant against him, luring him, radiating a seductive charm, but it's all spun with a threatening peril.

'Can you just hold this for me?' Mr Cole places the walking stick in Philip's hand and opens the complaints book. 'Right, Mr and Mrs Reynolds.'

'It won't work, I tell you.' Michelle sits next to the portable CD player, its lead lying lifelessly on the floor.

Philip wants to let go of the walking stick, let it drop to the floor. But his grip holds it tighter and tighter, squeezing it, wanting to siphon off every morsel of its menacing presence.

Mr Cole takes in the list of complaints.

'Typical, never happy these two. Always got something to complain about.'

Michelle smirks at him. He reverts back to the book.

'The food, the view, the towels. Want more channels. Want something for nothing. Parasites!' Mr Cole nods to Philip. 'Philip.' He gestures to the fire door. 'Remember what I said, it's all in the attitude and the way you present yourself. If we stick to what we've discussed then it'll go smoothly.'

Philip hesitates, feeling his clenched hand on the walking stick.

Mr Cole cups his arm. 'This is what you want.' He gives him the full visual once over. 'You could at least have taken an iron to your shirt.'

Philip looks around the landing, not wanting to be drawn into Mr Cole's stare. But he can't deny him or the addictive adrenalin that's pumping through his veins.

'I'm doing this for you.' Mr Cole seizes Philip's arm.

'How can you say that?' Philip asks.

'Don't be ignorant of what you really want.' He glances down at Michelle then looks at Philip intently. 'This is the only way to make this work and it will work, it really will.'

Mr Cole guides Philip's arm to his pocket. He takes out a bunch of keys.

Michelle stands up and kicks the CD player.

'Michelle!' Mr Cole says. 'I hope you haven't broken it.'
She views the CD player with contempt.

Mr Cole smiles at Philip. 'Please, if you wouldn't mind.' He gestures to the door. 'It's just about reaffirming your relationship with people. It's for the good of the majority in the end, that's how it all works, that's how government works.' He winks at him. 'Even if the people don't know it.'

Philip pushes the fire door open. The sweat on his fingertips smears the door. Mr Cole follows him with Michelle dragging the CD player behind her. They gather outside room 2. Philip flanks the door while Mr Cole stands directly in line to it, psyching himself up as if he's about to step into the realm of TV land. He inspects his suit and plucks a small piece of fluff, discarding it with pure distaste. Michelle lets go of the CD player's lead; it hits the floor with a bang.

'Michelle!' Philip hisses, aggravated by her attention seeking.

'Alright, alright, don't worry, it's all in the timing.' Mr Cole stoops down and presses the eject button on the CD player. 'You make it special.' He grins, making her blush.

Before the lid of the player has time to open fully he slams it back down and selects play. The restless drums of Harry James' *Crazy Rhythm* start to play. Michelle claps her hands in excitement and picks up the CD player, gathering it protectively to her stomach.

Mr Cole approaches the door and stops by Philip; his attention falls on the walking stick. 'I'd better take that. Nothing like a big band to stop you thinking about the here and now, eh Philip?' Mr Cole looks as if every drop of humanity has somehow been drained from him.

Philip holds out the walking stick to him, his arm trembling, fingers pale.

'Please Philip.' Mr Cole's tone is calm and at a pitch that jumps over a whisper.

Philip lets go, feeling it slip through his sweaty fingers. Unlocking the door, he steps out of the way as Mr Cole strides into the room, complaints book against his chest, walking stick nestled under his arm like a brigadier's baton.

A woman shrieks.

'What's going on?' Mr Reynolds' voice snaps. 'This is an invasion of privacy. Get out!'

'You heard him,' Mrs Reynolds shrieks hysterically.

Philip and Michelle peer through the doorway, the angle of the room obscuring Mr and Mrs Reynolds.

Mr Cole calmly takes in the list of complaints as if he's on stage and they're watching him from the wings. The big band drums erratically tumble in a restless spirit.

'Now let's sort this little lot out shall we? First let me reintroduce the owner of the Bay View and his daughter.' Mr Cole gestures to Philip and Michelle to enter the room. Philip sheepishly walks in escorting Michelle who's cradling the CD player. He sees Mrs Reynolds sitting upright in bed, the duvet gathered around her for protection. She looks in confused horror at Philip. Mr Reynolds is on the other side of the bed frantically zipping up his trousers, his shirt clumsily thrown on with half his face covered in shaving foam.

Mrs Reynolds looks to Michelle, a scream lodges firmly in her throat. The swirling rhythm of the drums surrenders to a big band swing.

'Let me see, not enough clean towels complaint on the 15th – erm … not enough hot water, not enough coffee and tea.' Mr Cole glances up from the book with a knowing frown. 'A lot of *not enough* here.' He reads on. 'Noise, TV remote, etc, etc.'

'What the hell are you talking about – look at her for Christ's sake!' Mr Reynolds points dumbfound at Michelle, the words dribble from his mouth.

Michelle lunges forward, leg coiled to take a kick at one of Mr Reynolds' shins but Philip pulls her back. Mr Cole lashes out with the walking stick, striking hard at his kneecaps, making him shriek out in pain. He strikes again hard and precise across the back of his head. Mr Reynolds crumbles, cowering to the floor.

'You see it's never their fault,' Mr Cole says, 'always have to point the blame to someone else.'

The scream lodged in Mrs Reynolds' throat explodes into the room. The Harry James' band lifts up the rhythm of the swing catching hold of the scream.

Philip puts his hands over Michelle's eyes, she protests but he won't let go of his grip. Mr Reynolds crouches whimpering on the floor wanting to wake up from this inflating nightmare. Mr Cole elegantly takes off his jacket, letting it fold into its creases and then his waistcoat, placing them at Michelle's feet. Ashamed, Philip turns away. Mrs Reynolds looks at him, her head shaking, desperate to say so much but it's all coming out at once in an incoherent jumble. He continues to undo his cufflinks, tucking them away in his pocket, rolls up his sleeves and returns to Mr Reynolds. He stares unmercifully down at him, his frail body pleading. Mr Cole spits on his hands and wraps them around the walking stick. He strikes the stick hard down on Mr Reynolds' curved back making him cry out. Michelle tries to pull Philip's hands away but his clasp is too strong. Mr Cole strikes again, this time in sync with the music. Michelle sighs in defeat. Above them a seagull lands on the guesthouse roof. The music finds and rides high on its swinging beat in time with Mr Cole. The seagull screeches, calling out for another gull.

'They leave the room in a filthy mess,' Mr Cole says. 'No respect, no appreciation.'

Mrs Reynolds flings herself at Mr Cole, clawing at him but she can't stop the rhythm of his swing. Eventually he stops. Mrs Reynolds falls, exhausted, hitting the floor in a clumsy mess. Through her tears she sees her husband sprawled face down, faint murmurs drift from the bloodied heap and then a stillness rushes at her shaking her to her very soul.

The music stops.

Mr Cole turns to Mrs Reynolds, his white shirt covered in splashes of blood – crimson freckles cover his face and arms. He raises the walking stick and looks directly at Philip. Another gull lands on top of the guesthouse and screeches piercingly. Philip is captivated, staring helplessly into Mr Cole's eyes. His hand tightens on Michelle but she still wriggles desperately, wanting to look at what's unfolding.

'Let me, it's not fair. You look …' Michelle pauses. 'You still don't get it, do you?' She stomps her foot hard on the floor.

The two gulls stare inquisitively at each other. One nervously approaches the other and rubs its beak against its white plumage. For a moment their beaks touch.

Michelle pushes Philip's hands away; he tries to close his eyes but it's no use. He lets out a faint sob, his knees give way, and he falls to the floor. Mr Cole delicately places the bloodied walking stick against the bed next to Mrs Reynolds who lies sprawled on the floor next to her husband. Michelle hears the sobs from Philip behind her but it just makes her grin. Mr Cole lets out a sigh and wipes a hand across his face, smearing the splattered blood.

'I think that's aired out our grievances with you both.' He snorts back the mucus in his nostrils.

A gurgling sound echoes in the room.

Mr Cole stands, steadying his breath.

'Yes it has,' Mr Reynolds says, 'and I thank you. It shouldn't have come to this.'

Mr Cole strolls over to the curtains and draws them tight, shutting out the dull day.

'They said it was going to be a nice day today,' Mrs Reynolds says, 'little overcast in the morning, lots of sunny symbols over us for the afternoon though.'

Philip follows the source of the voice to the window. Mr and Mrs Reynolds are standing hand-in-hand, they simultaneously smile. Sunlight breaks through the clouds, the sea ripples as if applauding its appearance.

Michelle inquisitively wanders over to Mr and Mrs Reynolds. Philip looks up and is surprised to see Mr Cole standing towering over him.

'They're quite charming once you get to know them.' A knowing grin sneaks across his face.

Philip clambers to his feet, ignoring him, his attention turns to what Michelle is doing but Mr Cole blocks his view second-guessing his every move.

'See, you just have to meet people half-way,' Mr Cole says. 'Break down the barriers so to speak.'

'Are we going to the swannery today Mike?' Mrs Reynolds asks.

'Yeah,' Mr Reynolds says. 'If it stays like this.'

Philip glimpses over Mr Cole's shoulder. Michelle is stood next to Mrs Reynolds. She touches her arm but she doesn't respond. Mr Cole blocks his view but with a quick and decisive move Philip out manoeuvres him. Sunlight races into the room. Michelle sinks a single finger into Mrs Reynolds' skin. Briefly she moans in pain.

'We could get a little picnic from the mini-market,' Mrs Reynolds says. 'They do a good selection there, all nice and healthy.'

'You and your picnics,' Mr Reynolds says.

He tenderly kisses her on her forehead, a gasping bubbling noise makes Philip shudder to his core.

Mr Cole cups his face. 'I don't want any of that, you hear me? It's sorted now. Get a grip, Philip.' Mr Cole throws an arm around him, swinging Philip around to face the door. He glances back to Michelle. 'Michelle, come on!' he says sternly.

Mr Cole massages Philip's shoulder. 'It's all going to be different now,' he says with a seductive soothing tone. 'It's the start we always craved for.' He looks over his shoulder. 'Michelle!'

Philip hears her walking over to them. But the sickening feeling is moving closer and closer as he hears Michelle approach, dragging the walking stick with her.

'But —' Philip says.

'No, Philip,' Mr Cole says.

'Goodbye Mr Morgan,' Mr Reynolds says. 'And sorry about the crossed wires. These things do happen sometimes. They shouldn't but they do.'

'Yes, we're very sorry,' Mrs Reynolds says.

'That's it, Philip,' Mr Cole whispers to him. 'You've got it. I knew you could. I just knew it. You're doing well, I'm proud of you.'

He pats him on the back.

'Bye,' Michelle says from behind him.

They spill out on to the landing. Mr Cole smartens up Philip the way any mother would when she wants to show her child off to the world.

'It wasn't as bad as all that,' Mr Cole says. 'Was it?'

'The Pritchards are in,' Michelle says.

They look over to her. She has her ear against the door of room 3, CD player under one arm with the walking stick propped up against the door.

Mr Cole turns back to Philip and stares down to the master keys he's holding.

'It's all a walk in the park now,' Mr Cole says.

Two more seagulls land on the guesthouse roof. Philip walks over to room 3 and inserts the key, listening to the door's mechanism unfastening. He opens the door. Mr Cole strides past him, complaints book open and this time closely followed by Michelle, dragging his walking stick behind her, still holding the CD player.

The two seagulls silently watch as the new arrivals call and scream, stressfully fluffing out their feathers. Philip reluctantly follows, shutting the door behind him. Harry James' big band begins to play again.

The gulls' tormented cries come to an abrupt halt. A while later the curtains of room 3 are drawn. The racing music climbs up through the guesthouse, echoing through its corridors until all the curtains of the remaining occupied rooms are closed.

Eight seagulls stand silently looking at each other. They waddle over to the edge of the roof and stare sombrely out over the bay. Even in the dull overcast day the sea is alluring with its soothing rhythm. Suddenly one of them lets out a tremendous cry and simultaneously they all take to the air, swooping down from the guesthouse, over the streams of people walking along the esplanade. They beat down their wings and glide up, soaring over the white changing huts protruding like teeth from the gums of the esplanade. They fly past small pockets of people scattered on the pebbled shoreline and then hit the vast expansion of the sea. Sunlight cracks through the dense clouds; they alter their flight path and head straight for the growing beautiful light.

13

It's mid-morning. The clouds are rinsing out a dense drizzle, dashing any hope of seeing an appearance by the sun. The early morning presented itself with so much promise – blue sky and the sun exposed in all its splendour. Now the taunted holidaymakers' expectations have faded, the day wanting to be crossed off and forgotten. Some are out. Determinedly they wander along the esplanade semi shell-shocked by the turn in the weather. Others sit defiantly, wrapped in waterproofs on the pebbled beach, taking in the sombre mood of the rapidly changing sea. Time hangs sprawled out in front of them.

The weather forecast didn't predict this last night in the main news or in the regional. But when do they ever get it right? It was going to be a straightforward day, lounging on the beach soaking up the sun, watching the day unfold and letting it effortlessly put itself away. It's not often people have the chance to just watch and wallow in doing nothing. It's a skill all on its own. But that was out of the question now, everything's wet and the sea stares back with a brooding restlessness. The alternative pastime is looking more and more to one of those Dorchester museums, the swannery or maybe the sea life centre, but they all come with a cost not budgeted for.

The small terrace of guesthouses are a hive of activity. People dashing out to their cars mentally squeezing themselves through the rain, faces despondently peering out of the windows. In amongst all of this the Bay View guesthouse stands silent and motionless. The curtains are all closed keeping it distant from the rest of the lively esplanade, as if it has somehow stepped back into the shadows. Subdued sounds of car doors slamming and people calling out names from the outside world, seep and roam around in the silence of the guesthouse. Philip is curled up in a foetal position in bed, willing himself to sleep. Michelle is under the covers fidgeting in her sleep, sandwiched between Philip and Mr Cole, who's snoring rhythmically. He's dressed in a sweatshirt and jogging bottoms with one slipper hanging precariously on his foot. Flickering shadows from the silent TV cut onto them, day-time chat shows in full commotion, hypothesising as they take events and lead them to even more dramatic conclusions. The shadows merge. Philip rolls over and faces Mr Cole, his eyes are tightly shut, anxious that he can sense someone else in the room.

The coloured shadows of the TV form into a strange human figure. He can feel it hanging over him, his body twitches in a nervous spasm. He doesn't know what to do, too scared to open his eyes. His paranoia has cut his nerves to pieces, he doesn't know if he can take any more. In desperation he shuffles closer to Mr Cole but Michelle lets out a disapproving squeal that jolts him back. A hand touches him on his forehead, its cool touch makes his body let out an uncontrollable tremor. Slowly opening his eyes, the notion of someone standing over him dissolves, as to his astonishment it's Mr Cole's hand on his forehead. His outstretched arms push Philip away, reacting independently to the rest of his sleeping body. Philip sits up. The TV images blare at him as he clambers exhausted out of the bed and staggers to the en-suite, wearing a vest and pyjama bottoms. Michelle turns over under the covers with a deep hopeless sigh, Mr Cole's arm cuddles her, instantly sedating her impatience.

Philip hangs over the sink with the cold tap on full blast. He cups the water feeling it numbing his hands and swills it over his face. He pulls the cord of the light above the mirror and stares at himself; it's an odd sensation but he doesn't expect to see his own reflection staring back. Turning his hands over, he sees they're covered in large blisters and sores. The cold water subdues their sting. He's groggy as if he's been deprived of sleep for weeks on end, caught up in some sadistic, torturous regime. Desperately he wants to lull back into his pillow, let it caress his achingly tired body, sedate his mind and enable him to find peace in sleep.

'Philip!' Mr Cole startles him, manfully slapping him hard on his backside. 'Come on, look at the state of you.'

Philip groans, backing away from him. 'Do you mind!' he snaps.

Mr Cole's dressed again in his dark grey suit with all its trimmings. His white shirt is whiter than white, but this time he's kept his tartan slippers on and discarded his waistcoat.

'Get yourself together. We've got a busy day in front of us.' Mr Cole opens his mouth wide and examines his teeth in the mirror. 'Not bad, not bad.'

Philip puts his hands back under the tap and slumps against the basin, hoping his pain will wash down the plughole.

Mr Cole's unimpressed. He shakes his head and emphasises it with a sigh. Opening the mirrored cupboard, he takes out a bottle of perfume and sprays it on his neck.

'Mmm smells nice. Got to present yourself in this game.' He puts it back in the cupboard.

Philip doesn't respond. Mr Cole takes a hold of Philip's arms, making sure his suit doesn't get wet, and pulls them out from beneath the tap, turning them over, palms up. The pain drains away, the biting sores and leaking blisters retreat back into his skin. Mr Cole lets go of his hands and looks back at himself in the mirror. Philip stares at him, a building bitterness shifts in him, resenting how he makes him feel weak and dependent. He tries to work out what's really happening but he keeps coming up against an uncompromising mental block. There's no way in, but when he concentrates he senses the power of its foreboding secrets, hidden enticingly close as if they're just around the next corner. But he doesn't want to go any further, he knows he mustn't go any further.

The connection to the walking stick, the hostility Michelle has for him, and now Mr Cole standing there carefree, trivialising over his tie. What can he do? Deep down he knows that if he faces it all he'll be enslaved to its ferocious mercy. Is it connected to Mr Cole? Where is he leading him? Is this really what he wants?

'Come on then,' Mr Cole says. 'I'll sort out Michelle.'

'Why did you say that?'

Mr Cole ignores him and strolls out of the en-suite. Philip wrings and rubs his hands roughly, wanting the pain of the blisters to return.

Philip thunders down the stairs, the hall rapidly getting closer. He feels dazed in his frantic rush. His clothes are half flung on, shirt buttoned out of line and spilling untidily out of the back of his trousers. He holds onto the banister wanting to shake the resentment for Mr Cole from himself. He breathes in and the air soothes his lungs, invigorating him. He steps into the hall and follows the sounds of the sea's tranquil rhythms calling to him from outside the front door.

He can hear conversations and bursts of laughter from holidaymakers outside the guesthouse. Sunlight shines into the hall, its warmth bathes his face. He touches the door wanting to push it open and reach out to them but it's cold to the touch. The sound of a plate smashing comes from the kitchen; he steps away from the door and unwillingly heads down the hall to see what has happened.

Michelle's at the kitchen table, taking sheets of paper from a large collapsed pile and drawing on them. Philip approaches her, noticing some have been ripped up or half-heartedly screwed into balls and have spilt from the table to the floor. He picks up one she has discarded. There's a drawing of a house and a young girl by it holding hands with someone. He isn't sure if the person is male or female.

'Is this you, Michelle?' Philip points to the picture of the girl, his finger quivering.

'Yes,' Michelle says, with an air of suspicion.

'And the –' Suddenly he notices the drawing is on the back of one of the guesthouse schedules. 'Michelle, what are you doing?' he shouts.

She ignores him and carries on drawing.

He picks up one of the pieces of paper from the floor and unravels it. It's part of the booking graph for the season. Frantically he snatches another, this time it's part of the cash and carry rota. A bang comes from the office.

'Stop this, Michelle!' Philip shouts, reaching out for her crayons.

'No!' Michelle gathers them from the table and holds them to her. 'I need to do my work.'

'What work?'

'Practice my case studies for the students.' Michelle's expression reflects his own puzzlement, but she sounds comfortable at saying the words to him. 'It's different there, not what I'm used to. They all have problems.'

'What are you talking about, Michelle?'

She looks at him with more questions than he has.

Mr Cole emerges from the office ripping up more pieces of paper. Philip rushes over to him.

'Stop it, please!'

'Schedules. Won't let you think, is that it?' He flings the pieces of torn paper into the air and watches them fall to the floor. Michelle claps her hands, applauding him.

Philip frantically tries to catch them.

'What's the matter with you, remind you of better times? You've already let them go. You hardly kept them up to date.' Mr Cole smirks.

Michelle holds up a torn timetable, a crayon drawing of a young girl with boxes stacked on her head.

'This is what they want, I think I can do the assessments,' Michelle says proudly. 'Was Adrian in my class?' She pauses. 'No, he couldn't have been. We're not together any more.'

Philip snatches the picture out of her hand. She curls up her face at him.

'What have you done?' Philip thrusts the drawing at Mr Cole. 'I thought you were going to sort things out!'

Mr Cole gestures over to the office door. It slowly closes, the handle pulling down. It clicks shut. Philip pushes Mr Cole out of the way, and tries to open the door but it won't budge.

Michelle shakes her head and carries on drawing.

'Come away from there.' Mr Cole takes hold of Philip's arm, pulling his locked grip from the door. 'We don't need any of this, it's all being taken care of. The way it should have been from the start.'

Philip hears the hum of a computer being switched on in the office.

'Well, what about Michelle?' he asks.

Michelle's head tilts, adjusting for maximum reception, but she never takes her eyes away from her drawing.

'What about her?' Mr Cole replies.

Philip squares up to him. He knows deep in his heart he shouldn't. That whatever happens he's going to be on the losing side, but he couldn't live with himself if he doesn't at least try.

'She's supposed to be at school,' Philip says. 'And she's going on about –'

'She can start afresh Monday,' Mr Cole says.

'She's going today.'

'She can't.' Mr Cole's voice barely stretches above a whisper but it doesn't conceal any of the menace it has.

Philip stares into Mr Cole's eyes. A line has been drawn between them. He wants to deny his authority but he has no passion for what he's fighting for. Mr Cole's right, it's the end of the week, it won't do any harm starting back on Monday. Yet he's compelled to stand up to him, if only to see the consequences if he steps over that line. His mental block stands firm only letting him see an unlinking patchwork of the past.

Michelle peers over to them, not wanting to break the illusion of being absorbed in creating a picture.

Mr Cole holds out another schedule and gestures to Philip to rip it in two.

'Alright, alright,' Philip says. 'We'll do it your way, but please stop this.'

He looks defeated at the torn paper lying on the floor. Mr Cole winks to Michelle. She smiles back and carries on drawing with a beaming excitement, legs swinging under the table.

'Next week she's going, and that's final.' Philip snatches the piece of paper away from Mr Cole.

'Look at the state of you. They're meaningless, you know they are.' Mr Cole circles Philip. 'They were half completed, half-heartedly used. We're in this together. There's no point going against me, you're only denying yourself. As I said, it's all been taken care of now.' Mr Cole leans in close. 'You know that, don't you?'

He picks up a glass fruit bowl from the worktop, tipping the apples and oranges out. They stay unnaturally clumped together. He turns and faces Philip, waving the glass bowl under his noise.

'It will break,' Mr Cole says, 'yes, if I drop it?'

He turns to Michelle. She stops drawing and nods a *yes* back at him.

'Because …' Mr Cole says with a dramatic pause, 'that's what happens. Yeah. Of course that's what happens.'

'Put it down and stop mucking about,' Philip says.

'Suppose I drop it?'

'Yes!' Michelle eagerly claps her hands.

'I said stop it, will you!'

Mr Cole lets go of the bowl. It falls then stops millimetres from the floor. 'Don't hide it all, Philip. You have to know, it's for your benefit.'

Philip stares at the hovering glass bowl. Michelle puts her crayons down and joins them. Mr Cole knocks over everything that isn't glued down on the worktop. Pans, plates, knives and cups all come to an abrupt halt and hover over the floor. Carefully he steps through them towards Philip and Michelle.

'Tell me what you want? Please, I need to know.' Mr Cole looks nervously at him. 'Look, we can make anything happen. You have to believe me.'

Philip's taken aback, it's unusual to see him like this.

'It's time to tell us,' Mr Cole says.

His voice has others wrapped weaving through it. He can hear his mother and father reaching out to him.

'I –' Philip says.

'No Philip, be truthful please. It's better in the long run.'

'I need to –'

'Philip don't.'

An unexpected sound of smashing plates and cutlery startles him. He looks around him but everything is still hovering above the floor. He turns to Mr Cole and Michelle, their expressions haven't changed.

Philip's face is flushed red, veins straining in pain. He stares up at the ceiling, a focus point for all his efforts.

'Push, damn you!' Mr Cole barks in his ear. 'It's no good slacking. You know the routine by now.'

Philip's outstretched arms meet above him, gripping two dumb-bells. They connect, ringing out like wine glasses.

'Yes!' Philip screams out in triumph.

'Now do it again.' Mr Cole's face comes into view peering down at him. 'Four more and –' He looks away from him.

'Ten!' Michelle shouts.

'Yes, you'll get to ten,' Mr Cole says.

Philip parts his arms, teeth clenched, battling against the dragging weight of the dumb-bells. They hit the floor to an uncontrolled bang, he breathes out a sigh of relief.

'Come on, again,' Mr Cole says. 'Then rest. You can do it.'

Veins pumped, Philip shrieks out, bursting in perspiration, the dumb-bells come into view again and collide to a ring – jackpot!

'That's it, that's it! You know you can do this.' Mr Cole's hand curls into a fist, encouraging him.

Philip begins to work out at a more vigorous pace, the colliding ring of the dumb-bells spur him on until he lies exhausted on the floor, crucifixion fashion. He had found them tucked away in the loft that's become an Aladdin's cave full of memories. He had cleared away everything that reminded him of Frances but he couldn't throw any of it away; it all had to be close and safe but only on his terms. But now, piece by piece, they were finding their way back, bringing her presence with them, making the guesthouse breathe to her charms again. There's still a rail of Frances' clothes waiting for her to bring them to life. He was embarrassed at the way they felt when he touched the material and to his shock he found small strips had been cut from them. There were also stacked boxes packed with photo albums, and Frances' magazines and books. A few were piled with shoes and her gardening tools or filled with ornamental reminders that took him right back, like a looking glass through time. Some of the boxes had been ransacked, scrunched newspaper scattered around them as if a small explosion had gone off. He can't remember the amount of times he had taped up the boxes, constantly trying to take control of Frances' things escaping from them.

The last time he had used the dumb-bells Helen was at the guesthouse. He'd become concerned at the way he looked. She had the ability to make him feel older than he really was. The instruction sheet that came with the weights depicted a straightforward step-by-step guide to achieve an alluring physique. He smiles, his intentions are true even though his commitment is as weak as ever. The workout makes him feel as if he's back there, back with his youth, hand-in-hand with all those strong aspirations.

Mr Cole steps over him. 'Are you alright?'

'Fine.' Philip catches his breath.

'What were you thinking about?' Mr Cole's eyes narrow in a probing manner.

'What is this, twenty questions?'

'Oh, nothing …' He pauses. 'Usually I know what you are thinking. I thought maybe you were … no. That would be stupid, very stupid.'

'What would?'

'Just me being a bit paranoid.' Mr Cole shakes his head. 'Never mind.'

Philip looks at him suspiciously.

Mr Cole holds out his hand. 'I knew you could do it.'

Philip's breathing finds normality. He releases one of the dumb-bells, his fingers moulded to a hook. Mr Cole effortlessly pulls him to his feet and ushers him to the wardrobe mirror.

'Now, you take a look at all your hard work.'

Mr Cole helps him take off his T-shirt. Philip stares at the mirror in disbelief. His plump expectant mother stomach has gone. His body doesn't hang any more, skin draped like clothes on a washing line. He turns to Mr Cole but he looks away as if he is hiding something from him. He turns back to the mirror's reflection trying to take in the crafted definition of his torso, even his face is more youthful, skin radiant as if he's had a face lift. What has happened to him? Why isn't he out of breath? A moment ago he's on the floor gasping for air, his face throbbing and glowing, T-shirt hugging his sweat covered body, but the mirror tells a completely different story. His eyes ricochet from his reflection to his physical presence, trying to catch out the illusion. He runs an index finger over his arm and torso to make sure it's real, and then touches his face.

'Not bad for a first attempt.' Mr Cole warmly pats his shoulder.

'First!' Philip says. 'We've being training more than that, haven't we?'

Mr Cole ignores him.

'I used to look like that.' Mr Cole nods at Philip's reflection and pats his stomach. 'Mind you, it's a few years ago now.'

Philip notices Michelle is kneeling on the floor rummaging through the bottom drawer of the chest of drawers.

'Michelle, what are you up to?'

Immediately she moves away, hoping to look like she's doing something completely different. Mr Cole rubs his hand on Philip's shoulder, staring at his reflection.

'Leave her be. You shouldn't stifle a curious mind.'

'Michelle, come away from there.'

'Come on, Philip, look at what you have achieved.'

Philip looks back at the mirror. He still can't make the connection between himself and the reflection but a growing feeling of well-being is filling his body, a feeling he had long forgotten.

'It all has a knock-on effect. When you feel good about yourself, you feel good about everything else and everything else feels good about you. It can be wonderful.'

Philip smiles at Mr Cole but is unnerved to see Michelle taking something out of the drawer and scurrying from the room.

Philip shakes a can of polish and aims it at the duster. Michelle clambers onto one of the dining room chairs to see what all the fuss is about.

'Do you want to help tidy up the tables, Michelle?' Philip asks.

Michelle stares at him. He smiles awkwardly, wishing he could dodge her glare as she scrutinises his every move.

'Pack it in, Michelle.'

'What?'

'It's not a game,' Philip says. 'You'll be going next week.'

'I'm not, it hurts.'

'Michelle!' Philip says, exasperated.

'Mr Cole listens to me,' Michelle says. 'That's why I like playing games with him, it stops us hurting. It makes me feel good and it stops him feeling alone …' She pauses. 'He told me what happened to his family.' She reaches out and touches Philip's hand but shows him no compassion.

He doesn't know what to say to her.

She turns away from him. 'Did you hear that?'

He shakes his head, focusing all his energy on polishing the table.

'Are you sure?'

She goes to slide off the chair. 'Don't you dare move,' Philip says, not looking up from his cleaning.

Michelle moulds herself back in the chair, crosses her legs like a young virile woman and blanks him.

Mr Cole strides into the room. 'You haven't got time for that!' He snatches the polish and duster from Philip and places them on another table. 'We've got to get this place ready.'

'That's what I was doing. We've got no Ellie.'

'Ellie!' Mr Cole says, bewildered.

'Maybe I should phone her, she hasn't been in since –'

'I've told you we don't need her. Money down the drain. She's gone, walked out. I don't know where and I don't care. Good riddance, that's what I say.'

'Walked out! Why? She wasn't that bad.'

Mr Cole shakes his head, annoyed at going over the same conversation. He gestures for Philip and Michelle to move away from the table, wanting Philip to take his opinions of Ellie with him.

'Got to get ready for what?' Michelle leans back in her chair.

Philip shuffles back.

'What do you think we do here?' Mr Cole smirks at her. 'Come on, you're in the way there.' He lifts Michelle off the chair and places her next to Philip.

Mr Cole faces the tables; he breathes in but gets caught up in a coughing fit. Michelle is about to come to his aid but he raises a hand to stop her.

'I'm alright, not to worry.' He pats himself on the chest. 'Wow, they are filthy!'

He straightens himself up and breathes more easily; a defiant cough slips out but doesn't break his determination.

Mr Cole takes in a deep breath as if he's sucking all the air from the room. Then he blows at the surface of the table creating a high gush of wind at table 5. The table mats, cutlery and salt and pepper rise up and hang in the air. Michelle steps forward, eagerly blowing, wanting to join in as dust from the table swirls up and up. Mr Cole moves from table to table stripping everything of dust and sending it soaring high up into the air. Michelle lingers behind him mimicking his every move.

'That will do nicely,' Mr Cole says.

He puts a finger on Michelle's pursed lips to curb her enthusiasm.

The dust travels along the ceiling and then falls as if it's being channelled down an invisible funnel. They all watch as the dust begins to form into a translucent body. Michelle looks on curiously at it as it raises a hand to itself and lets out a shocked squeal, making her shudder.

The dust figure runs to the door.

'Mostly dead skin you know,' Mr Cole says, watching it leave.

'Yuck!' Michelle screws up her face.

'Got to look after these hands, it's amazing what can happen to them if you're not careful.' He holds up Philip's hands and ruthlessly inspects them.

The dust figure trips and falls in the hall, disintegrating to a puff of dust on the carpet.

'Shit!' Mr Cole turns to Philip. 'That sort of just moved the problem – never mind.'

'I'll get the vacuum cleaner,' Philip says.

'Practical but efficient.' Mr Cole smiles.

It takes Philip a while to clean up the dust in the hall, all the time he's becoming more and more inquisitive about what Mr Cole and Michelle are up to in the kitchen. They've walked past him a few times up and down the stairs. He asked what was going on but was met with a grin and a knowing wink. Michelle didn't even acknowledge him. His curiosity has got the better of him and besides he's cleaned the mess up. He pulls the plug from the wall and drags the vacuum cleaner to the kitchen. It's time to investigate.

Michelle's sitting on the kitchen table. There are three small mounds placed by her, and a stack of glass mixing bowls to her right accompanied by half a bottle of red wine.

'Ah, just in time.' Mr Cole hands her a piece of paper. 'Drop it down over there.'

Philip lets the vacuum cleaner fall and approaches the table.

Michelle doesn't look up from scrupulously examining the piece of paper. Philip looks closer at the mounds; they look like small islands of food on an ocean of wood. From left to right, the first consists of one small onion, a shrivelled melon, the stems of a ravaged bunch of grapes and a small plastic tray of stale fruit. The middle one has a pitiful piece of chicken breast, the leftover fat from a lamb chop, one carrot and a pea. Philip hovers by the kitchen table, fingers lightly dancing on its surface. He's confused, no further in knowing what they're up to. He takes in the last mound. It's made up of a whole egg, a slither of butter and a chunk of chocolate. Michelle fidgets, trying to find a patch of comfort on the hard wooden table. She pushes herself back, consciously trying to avoid the stack of glass bowls, but misjudges the distance between her and the wine bottle, knocking it over.

Mr Cole leans forward and catches it.

'Mind how you go, we don't want to be losing this.' He brings it safely to him, giving Philip a knowing nod. 'Do we?'

He takes a swig and wipes his mouth, offering the bottle to Philip.

'No, not for me.'

'Not for me!' Mr Cole giggles, sitting the bottle back on the table.

'Now then.' He strides up and down the length of the table. 'We're going to prepare eight organic evening meals.'

'Organic?' Philip's amazed by being able to do anything with what's on the table, let alone something healthy. Michelle hangs on Mr Cole's every word.

'That's the trouble with people today.' Mr Cole ignores Philip's last remark. 'Never had a good meal inside them, too fussy and too lazy.' Mr Cole looks at his watch. 'Ten minutes and counting.' He rubs his hands together, nodding to Philip.

'We don't do evening meals any more.' Philip says.

'Well that's what they want,' Mr Cole says. 'Don't they, Michelle?'

She nods.

'Michelle's listed the guests' requests,' Mr Cole says. 'We're in the service industry. We've got to mould the business to what they demand of us, simple business practice.'

'Yeah, but you said, "It's not a one way street".'

'I know, I know,' Mr Cole says. 'We've ironed out our grievances and it's now time to move on, onwards and up-wards. While you've been cleaning we've been talking to the guests – finding out what they want, with limitations of course.'

Michelle nods, unsure if she should agree.

'You've got to communicate with the customer. That's the key to our success. They'll tell you what they want, not directly, but you'll know if you listen hard enough.'

'Yeah, but –'

'No buts,' Mr Cole says. 'Think positive, it'll make us money. Why run a business if it's not for the money?'

A tapping sound comes from the office as if on cue.

'See, I told you.' A deep sinister grin cuts across Mr Cole's face.

Philip shifts curiously to the office door.

'All the ingredients accounted for.' Mr Cole pulls at Philip's arm, turning his attention back to the table. 'You have to get involved at all levels to make your business work.' He beams proudly. 'Now, food preparation, it can make life so much sim-pler. It's the same with everything, all in the preparation.'

Philip takes in the orders clenched in Michelle's hand, men-tally comparing them to the ingredients on the kitchen table.

226

'Apply the correct discipline,' Mr Cole says, 'and it's amazing what you can achieve.'

He leans over, plucks out a pinch of flour from the top glass bowl, and mischievously flicks it at Michelle.

She giggles, waving it away.

'I thought you said "*Discipline*".' Philip frowns.

'Loosen up, Philip! You don't want to lose your sense of fun.'

Michelle scoops a handful of flour and throws it at Mr Cole.

'Michelle!' Philip shouts. 'See what you've done. Do you have to encourage her like that?'

She dusts the flour from her hands.

'Alright, alright,' Mr Cole says, turning to the list, giving her a wink of camaraderie.

'*Coquilles St Jacques Meuniere*,' he reads.

Michelle looks puzzled at Philip.

'Scallops in butter, basically,' Philip says. 'Far too complicated. Think of the other guests.'

'You see, that's right!'

Philip's surprised.

'Wasted on them, that's what you mean. You're right, absolutely right. We're in the cheap and cheerful end of the market; it will have to be as I've prepared.' He smiles at the first pile of food, the onion and shrivelled melon. 'So we can start with the Bay View soup of the day or fruit salad.' He turns to Philip for his seal of approval.

Philip nods, uncertain of what he's letting himself in for.

'See,' Mr Cole says. 'Once the basics are down we'll be almost there.'

Philip scans the list. 'Has anybody ordered a starter?'

'No,' Mr Cole and Michelle reply together.

'So why are we doing starters?' Philip emphasises his confusion by the shrug of his shoulders.

'We're pre-empting the situation. This is what they want. They don't know it yet, but I assure you they will. I didn't run a successful hotel on the Costa Blanca and not learn a thing or two. A good three-course meal is money in the bank.'

A burst of tapping noises comes from the office again, as though fingers are flurrying over a keyboard.

'They'll go for it.' Mr Cole leans over to him. 'I've got a feeling they'll be staying a lot longer than usual.'

The tapping starts up again, this time even faster.

'So we've introduced a flat rate for a week. The longer they stay the cheaper it is.'

'I know that!' Philip says. 'It's just simple –'

Mr Cole ignores him. 'Money in the bank.'

The tapping escalates.

'That's what we want. We should start making a good profit.'

Once again the tapping increases in volume and then comes to a halt.

Philip turns to the office door.

'Come on then!' Mr Cole says.

Philip snaps out of his hypnotic state.

'Right, all this here, Philip, I want you to place in the mixing bowl.'

Mr Cole selects one of the bowls and hands it to Philip. He takes it and sweeps the small amount of ingredients into it, glancing up for reassurance.

'What is this?' Philip asks.

'Starters. Haven't you been listening.'

'But out of this!'

'Don't you see. We take something completely worthless, change it to what the customer thinks they want and make a tidy profit on it …' He pauses, releasing an antagonising grin. 'Capitalism at its very best.'

228

'But nobody's going to want this.'

'They will, they always do.' Mr Cole chuckles.

Philip doesn't know what to say as Mr Cole continues.

'So much of everything, well, of basically the same thing. I mean, do you know how many different types of chips you can buy? It's a fucking potato, it's so simple, but oh no we can't appreciate its simplicity. Always thinking something new is better, mainly to increase the profit margin or to iron out previous mistakes. You've got to muck about with it to own it, that's how this world goes around.' Mr Cole shakes his head in dismay. 'Shall I tell you what they don't sell you, what we all really need?'

Philip shrugs his shoulders.

'Time,' Mr Cole says, 'and a half-decent plumber! And what we could all do with is a BOGOF in manners. A bit of polite consideration makes everybody's life that more tolerable.'

Philip's transfixed.

'BOGOF.' Mr Cole explains. 'Buy one get one free. Stir, come on give it a stir.'

Philip frantically stirs while Mr Cole lingers as appointed supervisor.

'Good, good, as long as it looks like what it's supposed to look like – that's the secret. Never think about the taste, it was all so different when I was abroad. In this country it all comes down to ignorance and what you're prepared to pay.'

Philip looks at the concoction.

Mr Cole dips his finger in and samples it. 'Mmm, coming along nicely.'

'Are you sure?' Philip looks at the mess cowering at the bottom of the bowl.

'Main course,' Mr Cole mumbles. 'Michelle.' He points behind her. 'Pass me the other bowls.'

Michelle shoots into action, eager to please, lining the bowls along the edge of the table.

'Put that one down please.' Mr Cole gestures to Philip.

Philip lines it up with the others.

'That's it, in a line. Right, what have we got? Starter, main course and …' He points at the bowls, pauses, and grins to Michelle. 'And of course, for those who have a sweet tooth …'

She blushes, legs swinging into action.

'Afters. Must admit …' Mr Cole licks his lips. 'My favourite part of a meal. Now, main course, that bowl.'

'Yeah, alright.' Philip's annoyed at his condescending manner.

He picks up the small piece of chicken breast, the ravaged lamb chop, along with the solitary pea and carrot. Then he reverts back to the list Michelle is holding, while Mr Cole places three saucepans on the gas rings.

'What have we got for table 2, Michelle?' Mr Cole asks.

Michelle holds the list rigid, knowing the look he gave the guests when they ordered. Mr Cole snatches the list away from her. A dispirited frown descends on him again.

'I still think it's far too plain, no imagination. Let's add a bit of flavour.'

'What about cheap and cheerful?' Philip asks.

'You've got to evolve, can't stay still,' Mr Cole says. 'Always have to keep redefining.'

He takes a couple of spice jars from the rack, next to the cooker, and sprinkles a couple of pinches into the middle bowl, then adds a scoop of flour to the mixture. He hands Michelle the empty water jug.

'Fill this for me, Michelle.'

Michelle's face cuts a frown, saying *why me* at him.

Mr Cole places his hand on her shoulder. 'It all hinges on this.'

Baffled, but anxious to please, she jumps off the edge of the table and scoots over to the sink, jug swinging precariously in her hand.

'It's all about the sauce. If you can get that right, you're laughing.'

Philip looks at him, not quite sure what to say.

Michelle returns the jug half-full, puddles splattered on the floor behind her.

'That's my girl.' Mr Cole crouches down. 'Just the right amount as well. As I've said, this can make or break a dish.'

Michelle beams proudly, holding out the jug for him.

'Hold on, just a moment,' Mr Cole says.

He takes the bowls over to the cooker and pours the contents of each one into the waiting saucepans. Michelle pursues him with the jug. He then scoops any remainder onto a baking tray and pops it in the oven.

'Plates, Philip! We need plates, soup bowls and don't forget the dessert bowls.'

Mr Cole slams the oven door shut, mule-kicking it with the back of his heel. Michelle offers him the jug again. It shakes under her weakening grip. This time he accepts. Ruffling her hair, he takes the jug as she laps up his appreciation. He carries it over to the cooker and sporadically adds the water to the saucepans. Within moments the strange concoctions are bubbling and spitting.

Philip takes a pile of plates and bowls from the cupboard next to the sink and puts them on the kitchen table, then returns for the dessert bowls, leaving them stacked. His curiosity getting the better of him, he walks over to Mr Cole and Michelle.

Mr Cole steps back from the cooker, almost bumping into him. 'Oops! Sorry about that,' he laughs.

Philip peers over his shoulder to see what is happening. Michelle pushes between them, wanting to be part of what's going on.

'How's it going?' Philip asks.

He bends to pick Michelle up to enable her to get a better look but she backs away. To his annoyance, Mr Cole intervenes and lifts her up, cradling her under his arm, her long legs dangling down his body.

'Wonderful, it's looking wonderful,' Mr Cole replies. 'Even if I do say so myself.'

They all move closer, peering down into the saucepans. Philip sneaks a glance to Michelle, wishing she were in his arms.

'Still looks a mess to me,' he says.

Mr Cole and Michelle look angrily at him.

The simmering mess springs into life, bubbling furiously, rising to the rim of the saucepans.

'Looking good, I told you.' Mr Cole adjusts the heat.

He stoops down to the window of the oven. Philip and Michelle follow his lead. From the splattered chaos on the baking trays, the delicate crusts of pies are being born.

Mr Cole inhales. 'Blackberry and apple with just the right amount of cinnamon. Lovely. You can't beat home-made.'

He returns to the kitchen table to arrange the bowls and plates ready for the food. Michelle takes on his shadow, always there to help him at any given opportunity.

The clanging of plates and bowls being unstacked fades away from Philip. He stands upright, stretching his back to lean a little bit closer, amazed at the miracles the cooker is creating. Mr Cole breaks his wonderment as he snatches up a saucepan and wanders back to the table. Philip follows as if on a lead, trying not to stumble over Michelle. Mr Cole eyes up the plates and with a flick of his wrist evenly disperses the simmering mess onto them.

'You have to judge this bit,' Mr Cole says. 'Don't want too much.'

Shapes start to rise from the coagulated substance. A succulent lamb chop emerges, faultlessly cooked, roast potatoes done to perfection, then a cluster of glistening tender peas all rise from what has become an elegant velvet sauce.

Philip and Michelle gasp.

'It – it's perfect.' The words are sweet on the back of Philip's throat.

'Good, I haven't lost it. The hotel was renowned in Spain for its food.' Mr Cole turns to Philip. 'Now it's your turn.'

'My turn?' Philip asks.

'Of course. You can't rely on me all the time.'

'I thought –'

'Come on, Philip, have a bit of faith in yourself for once.'

Mr Cole hands him the saucepan.

'Erm – What's next?' Philip nervously asks Michelle.

Michelle scrolls down the orders, never once looking him in the eye.

'Table 3, chicken and chips with peas and carrots.' She reads it out with not a flicker of emotion.

Mr Cole slides the perfectly cooked meals out of Philip's way and steps back, basking in his glory. Philip carefully holds the saucepan over a waiting plate. Chicken and chips with peas and carrots; he says it over and over again as if conjuring-up a spell. He's about to let the bubbling substance drip onto the first plate when Mr Cole intervenes.

'No, not like that. It requires a whip of a pour,' he says, pushing his body against Philip, moulding to his framework. 'It's a knack,' Mr Cole whispers in his ear. 'You get it right and it'll be perfect, if you don't …' He pauses. 'No half measures.'

Michelle turns away and strokes the list of orders. Philip flicks his wrist, guided by Mr Cole sending an even amount onto the plate.

'Now that looks good,' Mr Cole says. They both watch the liquid spread over the plate. 'Hey, that's it. You've got it!'

From the simmering mixture emerges a chicken breast, its skin crisp and stained in a sensuous spicy sauce. The chips are crisp and lightly seasoned. By their side sits a cluster of peas and carrots, their freshness radiating. Philip clenches the saucepan handle, trying to recapture and absorb exactly how Mr Cole had mentored him.

Mr Cole flings a towel over his arm. 'Better start serving, don't want it spoiling.'

Michelle dips her finger into the sauce. Her body shudders, at it's cold and lumpy texture. She tastes its bitter acidic flavour as it gnaws at her mouth.

Excitement fills Philip's head. He's being lifted up, floating on a high that carries no definition of time. He can't decipher the day or pin-point exactly what he has been doing but it doesn't matter. The serene scene of the dining room smiles back at him. He watches the guests joyfully tucking into their starters. They're not fully booked yet, but to see the guests happy and savouring how wonderful everything tastes, their voices consuming the room, incoherent but full of enjoyment swells Philips chest. Each spoonful of soup, each slice of melon coated in honey activates moans of delightful pleasures. Other guests have mournfully finished and eagerly wait, plates and soup bowls scraped bare. Philip holds two main courses in his hands. Lamb chops with a mound of roast potatoes and lush green peas, all wrapped up in a luxurious gravy. The guests stare at him, eager expectation in their eyes, each one wanting to lure him over to their table.

Philip happily nods to the wide-eyed, pleading guests. He stops at table 5. Mr and Mrs Sullivan solidify, not wanting to tempt fate. He gracefully places the meals on their place mats; their eyes drop to the feast before them, marvelling at how much expertise has gone in to creating such a meal. Everyone else lets out a disappointed sigh – they can hardly bare it, their mouths wound up in a salivating frenzy.

It takes no time for all the guests to consume every last morsel of their starters and main courses, scraping and clawing at their bowls and plates. Some look at the smears of sauce giving in to the enticement of scooping up every last drop with a rigid finger or two. The dining room door swings open. Once again the claustrophobic want sharply turns to heightened desire as Philip wheels in a trolley heaving with seductive desserts. There's chocolate mousse, sponge cakes, cheesecakes and a collection of freshly cooked, still steaming, hot fruit pies. Behind him Michelle struts in precariously holding an oversized home-made Black Forest gateau, created to a dazzling perfection.

'My word, Mr Morgan!' Mrs Riley makes the sound of a woman quivering at the threshold of an orgasm.

Philip comes to a halt in the middle of the dining room enabling everybody to get a clear view of this spectacular bounty of sweet-laced wonders. Michelle struggles behind him, the weight of the gateau bearing down on her arms, Philip tries to help her but to his dismay she spurns him. No matter how hard he tries, he's met by the same animosity.

'No!' Michelle snaps.

Philip smirks uneasily at everyone, embarrassed at the public rejection.

'I'd just like to say …' a man's voice says.

Philip turns around and is confronted by Mr Sullivan, who is stood up at his table.

'I don't usually do this kind of thing,' he says, clearing his throat. 'So bear with me.' He surveys the other guests, encouraged by their smiles and approving nods.

'I think I – I speak for everyone here,' Mr Sullivan says. 'When I say that the meal and the service has been absolutely fantastic …' He pauses. 'Sorry, I feel like the father of the bride. Last time I did anything like this, I was!'

Laughter ripples across the room.

Philip sheepishly turns away, shielding himself from everyone's dazzling stares. He spots Mr Cole standing at the doorway beaming at him, arms folded, leaning back against the doorframe in a *told you so* slouch.

'You know, so would I,' Mrs Pritchard says.

She stands up and begins to clap, gesturing for unity from the other guests, but they need no motivation as it builds into a round of applause. Philip stands there as the whole room takes to its feet.

Voices hurl at him. 'Yes, well done,' a woman says.

'I've got friends who would love it here,' another woman says.

'You can say that again.' A man agrees.

Mr Cole walks towards him, clapping in a steady rhythmic beat. Its robust sound cuts through everybody else's burst of admiration.

'That's right.' Mr Cole nods, in a calm, regal manner to everyone. 'Tell your friends. Tell everyone.'

He stands proudly by Philip's side soaking up the esteemed affection.

'We should have a drink to celebrate,' Mr Cole says.

'Dessert and then a couple of drinks,' Mrs Sullivan says mischievously to Mr Sullivan.

'Are we having a party?' Michelle asks, battling with the weight of the cake.

'What an excellent idea,' Mr Cole replies.

Everyone cheers.

'I didn't realise you liked parties,' Philip says.

'Come on, Philip, there's always an excuse to have a party. Have a get-together with friends old and new, breaks down barriers, brings people together.'

'I don't think this is a good idea,' Philip says.

Mr Cole gives Mrs Pritchard a seductive look. His eyebrow raises, lips curl back. She playfully turns away.

'Yes!' Michelle shrieks.

Part of the Black Forest gateau breaks off and slides from the plate; Michelle watches in horror as it tumbles and hits the floor but nobody else notices except Philip. She stands in its way trying to obscure the mess from his view. He's caught in her stare. She always looks away from him as if she's annoyed or ashamed at a secret she is hiding, but now he's caught in her gaze, mesmerised by her.

'I could dress up,' Michelle says. 'Couldn't I?'

He wants to hold her, protect her, but he doesn't know what from. All he can do is stare helplessly, knowing there's nowhere else to turn.

'Isn't there someone missing?' a voice asks.

The question brings an eerie silence to the room.

'Who said that?' Mr Cole asks, pushing past Philip, his anger lit.

'Oh no!' Philip's fingertips touch his face.

Mr Cole glances back at him. 'Shut it, Philip! I don't want any of that.'

'This isn't right.' Philip leans against one of the dining room tables for support, feeling suddenly disorientated.

'Do you want some cake?' Michelle asks.

'No Philip. Pull yourself together.' Mr Cole rushes to his side.

'She needs to be here,' Philip whispers. 'Isn't that right, Michelle?'

'You don't want any then?' Michelle lets the rest of the gateau drop onto the floor.

She looks nervously at the mess.

'We never had a chance. Don't you see?' Philip says, hopelessly to Mr Cole. 'You can't deny that, you can't.'

Michelle sinks to her knees frantically crawling at the gateau, trying to scrape it out of the carpet and rebuild it on the plate, but the harder she tries the worse it gets.

237

Guests whisper suspiciously to one another.

Mr Cole takes hold of him. 'No, don't you dare. I should have realised that's what you were trying to hide.' He shakes his head. 'It isn't what this is all about, you hear me? It's not about the past Philip, it's about a new start.'

'What about Michelle?' Philip asks.

'You're confusing it all. I let you latch on to happier times to get you through it. Don't you see? I thought I was going to lose you.' He bares his teeth in a snarl. 'Don't push me away Philip, if you do you won't survive, believe me. You've got to believe me!'

'It's her isn't it?' Philip's caught in some sort of trance. 'I can do it, I can do it. I can change the past, make it right. The way it should have been.'

'No, listen to me, for God's sake,' Mr Cole says. 'If you do as you please then so will I.' His voice resonates with the tone of his mother, her carefree attitude dancing in his eyes.

'No.' Philip snaps back to life. 'Not this time, nobody's going to ruin it, least of all you!'

He pushes Mr Cole's hands away from him, wrestles off his wedding ring and shoves it in his pocket.

'Please, Philip,' Mr Cole says, back in the driving seat.

'I have to go to her,' Philip says.

'Where do you think she is Philip? Tell me that.'

'She's still there, isn't she?' Philip replies. His breath reveals itself as if the room's temperature has dropped below zero. The memory of the winters night when he went to see Helen at the hospital attaches itself to him.

Mr Cole's voice trembles and breaks. He pleads, nuzzling his face into Philip's chest, battling not to cry as Philip calmly pats the back of his head.

'It's alright,' Philip says. 'This time it's going to be alright.'

He smiles at the guests and their concerned expressions spring back into laughter.

14

Philip wipes the condensation from the windscreen; the heater is at full blast. He stares out at the dreariness of the afternoon aided by the car's sidelights. A chill bites hard at his hands as they cling to the steering wheel. His breath swirls, exposed to the cold even though it's mid-summer outside. But nothing matters. He's never been so focused. He wants to be with Helen more than he has ever wanted anyone or anything in his entire life. He's not taking the easy option any more; he'll go straight to the hospital – no relying on alcohol to support him, to give him strength and shelter him so that he doesn't have to deal with what life has dealt him. Another driver hurries past Michelle's car, arrogantly denying the dreadful weather conditions, leaving a ringing sensation in his ears. Is this the hospital? He's sure he must be there by now. He grapples with the steering wheel, veering it away from the curb. He's confused, put off balance, his train of thought is on a different route. All he knows for certain is that the further away he journeys from the guesthouse, the more the weather turns on him.

All of a sudden the radio clicks on by itself, lighting up another part of the dashboard. His blood goes cold as the tuning dial rotates and snippets of different musical tastes and voices leap from a wall of white noise. The dial comes to rest on Buddy Holly and the Crickets' *Everyday*. He tries to focus on the road but the song fills his head, surging uncontrollably through his body.

Its familiarity reaches out, desperate to connect with him. He hears someone move on the back seat; frantically he looks over his shoulder but is confronted with emptiness. He focuses on the road, channelling his determination. Nothing is going to get in his way. He tries to switch the radio off but it's no good, the dial won't move. Another scuffle comes from the back seat. His gaze latches onto the rear view mirror but still he can't see anything. Desperately he swerves onto the side of the road, slams hard on the brakes and comes to a sudden halt. He feels the presence of someone leaning towards him; his body locks, a breath lingering in his throat. The stale smell of cigarettes and the familiar scent of sandalwood and jasmine punctures the air. It's *Coriandre*, he's sure it is. The radio turns itself off and the silence releases him from its pinned embrace. He glances behind him hoping once again to catch the intruder, but still there's nobody there. Feeling unnerved he continues on his way.

Eventually the car turns into a small, pot-holed road running alongside a red brick wall, which leads to the back entrance of Salmouth's main cemetery. The car slowly comes to a halt outside its gate. He flicks the sidelights off. Daylight has suffered a premature death, with the murky grey of the afternoon rapidly fading to black. Turning off the engine the wiper blades stop in mid-flow and fine drizzle descends on the windscreen, distorting his view. The cemetery gate hangs broken on its hinges. The walls either side have become faded showcases for aspiring graffiti artists. Wearily he steps out of the car and zips up his jacket, gaining at least some protection from the relentless drizzle.

Clicking open the boot of the car, Philip ignores a six-pack of Tennents Extra and takes out a spade, its handle wrapped in a dirty plastic film with half a dozen dried flowers bound together by a big red bow. He rests it on the rim of the bumper and slams the boot shut, sending the spade sliding onto the broken gravel. He's about to turn around when something catches his eye on the back windscreen. He leans forward. It gleams at him as he reaches out and plucks it from the windscreen, bringing it to him for a closer inspection. Its delicate splendour amazes him; he drops it in the palm of his hand, taking in the exquisite white petal of a chrysanthemum. Another falls onto the window then another and another. The overcast day is being replaced by a brilliant whiteness that is coating everything around him. He looks up, the grey clouds have turned into a magical blanket of winter-white as it snows perfectly sculpted petals. A surge of blissful happiness erupts through him. The shapes and contours of everything around him are being distorted, merging into a white oneness. Insects and birds rush and take shelter, dodging the downfall. The entrance of the churchyard appears so different, all clinical and clean. He picks up the spade, hearing the plastic wrap crinkle in his hand and walks towards the gate.

He makes his way along the cemetery's main path but it's being lost to the downpour of petals. Wiping them from his face, they feel strangely wet and slimy to the touch. He walks deeper into the graveyard, which is now completely covered by an enchanting white veil. He can see people everywhere, laying down snuggled under blankets of petals, graves; like row upon row of hospital beds. Young and old, some silently breathing while others are caught in gentle snores, but all have the way life has treated them etched upon their faces. He shivers as a light wind rustles past him parting the petals and uncovering a yellow pathway. Crouching down, he touches its bumpy texture, releasing faint swirls of pollen covered in a potent fragrance. It makes his head dizzy; he senses a belch but intervenes and covers his mouth.

In a dreamy haze he follows the yellow path. It bursts at every step he makes, soothing and enticing him to go further into the cemetery, making his nose bubble to a warm fizz. The pathway veers off, leading him through a narrow entrance. As he walks along he knocks clumps of petals from the bushes standing either side of the path; they fall like lumps of snow revealing the lush green summer vegetation beneath, yet hit the ground with a strange hollow clattering like cutlery hitting a floor. He turns away, wanting to distance himself. He can see the path come to a halt at a bed but he can't see Helen.

'Hey, hold on,' a man's voice calls.

A middle-aged man wearing a porter's uniform appears out of nowhere and stands in front of him, smelling of alcohol.

'Please, out of my way!' Philip's hand tightens around the spade making the plastic wrapping crunch.

The man's head is swaying, his eyes trying to focus.

'You can't come in here, not like that.'

'Please, I have to.' Philip holds up the wrapped spade like an invitation.

He can smell the stench of sick rising from his stomach, he's so close to her. This can't be happening. The weight of his emotions bear down on his legs; they're about to give way at any moment.

'I'm going to have to ask you to leave,' the man says, turning away. 'Sister, go and get Dan, we'll have to get him out of the ward.'

The man's voice swims around in his head.

'No!' Philip shouts.

He drops to his knees as everything goes silent, holding the spade close. The birds stop singing, the sound of the wind darting through the trees disappears, even the petals stop falling.

Opening his eyes he sees a pair of shoes walking away from him, making tracks in the petals and then vanishing. Turning back to the path, a tension snaps inside of him. He focuses on Helen, expectation robbing his mouth of saliva.

Philip reaches the end of the path. He places the spade down and kneels next to a raised mound of petals. Carefully he brushes them away but to his frustration he can't find her and the mound hardly moves. Two elderly people lay either side of her, a bitterness turns over in him. He tries again scraping at the petals. They lodge deep under his fingernails but it's no use – he's not getting anywhere. Frustrated, he clambers to his feet, takes hold of the spade and strikes deep into the mound. His body shakes as the red bow loosens and the plastic wrapping falls away. Pushing his foot down hard on its lip he scoops up a heap of petals. The red bow joins the plastic wrapping on the white floor, staining its beautiful perfection. To his astonishment the petals feel heavy. He discards them to the side and plunges the spade in again.

Beads of sweat ooze from his pores diluted by the unrelenting drizzle bombarding his face. Exhausted, he steadies himself in the thick darkness. Time means nothing, expectation is his body fuel. His arms ache, his back twisted in pain. His hands burn as if they have been crushed and set on fire. The weight of the wet mud clings heavy to his shoes and trousers. He kicks down hard, sending an echo around the excavated grave. He wipes his mouth, spitting out the fresh earth, and takes a moment to steady his adrenaline-pumped motivation. Sinking down, he stretches out a hand in the dense blackness and feels the rim of the coffin. Promptly he straightens himself up and jabs the spade with a precise and forceful blow; the sound of splintering wood ricochets off the muddy walls. He pushes down hard on the spade and tucks it into his chest, bringing the full force of his body on its handle and wriggling for leverage to prize open the lid. The packed mud on his shoe's tread makes him slip on the lid like a skater taking to the ice for the first time. He falls hard against the damp wall, exhausted but undeterred. He takes to his feet again, his body pushed on by pure determination. Entwining himself back around the spade he thrusts down with all his might, encouraged by a scream that unites every last drop of energy in his body. The coffin lid breaks.

He stops, catching sight of the slender curve of Helen's cheekbone through the radiant white petals. It leads him down to her mouth. The alluring image of her holds him, locking his joints rigid to the spot. Gently he brushes the petals away; his whole being cries out to touch her. He runs a finger over her skin drawing out her outline, its soft warm smoothness tingling his nerve endings. He comes to her mouth and lifts his fingers, smiling, feeling her breath touch them. Captivated by her, he scrupulously picks the petals away from her eyes. Her eyelids flutter open and she stares at him, her expression lost to a blank canvas. A smile germinates as she awakens. Hazel eyes spring into life, sinking to an enchanting soulful depth, stealing the breath from his lungs.

'I thought I had lost you,' Philip whispers, absorbing every insignificant feature, wanting to hold them in his thoughts and savour them forever.

'No, Philip.' Helen smiles. 'Never.'

Her voice sinks seductively into his eardrums making his want for her rise up to a new level.

She reaches out and strokes his face. 'I knew you'd come,' she says softly.

Philip feels suddenly anxious. 'We haven't much time, they'll be back.'

She ignores him and guides his face to hers, kissing him tenderly on the lips.

Her kiss feeds into him, lubricating his muscles, giving a concoction of both strength and emotional weakness.

She retracts, her chest heaving hard. 'I never left you. You know that don't you?'

Philip turns away uncomfortably. 'Why didn't you want to see me?'

'Don't Philip, I was scared. I was on my own.'

She curls a hand around the back of his head and brings him to her gaze.

'You know what my parents are like.' Her hands cup his face.

Their eyes lock on to one another.

'It's not what you think,' she says.

She sinks deeper into him; he can taste her breath on his lips.

'Is it going to be different this time?' Philip asks.

'You know how I feel. I didn't leave you, you have to believe me.'

He feels himself falling backwards, into the arms of his former self, back to the old Philip. The one who had become a distant memory, a fading image tucked away in one of the family photo albums. He had become an odd glimpse in a daydream when he caught himself reminiscing. Pure joy has taken over his body, warm tears well in his eyes. He looks at her, smiling as she wipes them all away.

Philip slips the gear stick into third, his eyes shut, capturing the delicate touch of Helen's hand on his. He unfastens his grip on the stick letting his hand follow hers to her lap.

'Are you alright?' he asks.

She squeezes his hand tight.

'Why do you ask?'

'You must be cold in that hospital robe. When we get back I'll sort that out, I think I know what might fit you.'

'Why did we have to go?' Helen asks.

He turns back to the road, the car's headlights slicing through the approaching dawn.

'You couldn't stay there, I tried …' Philip dips his lights to an oncoming car. 'I shouldn't have left you there. They stopped me. There was a porter, I was too – I had been to

The Ship, I was scared …' He pauses. 'But not this time. Not this time.'

Helen sits perfectly still as the oncoming headlights illuminate her face. They pass and the inside of the car sinks back to a dreary early morning light, partially lit by the dashboard.

'Where's Mum?' Helen asks. She clenches her stomach. 'I thought she would come.'

'Helen, come on, you couldn't stay in the hospital. I had to get you out of there.'

'But – what …' Helen's hands caress her stomach. 'My baby, my baby!' She looks panic-stricken.

'It must be the drugs wearing off. It took me ages to bring you round. I didn't give up on you, I was determined to get through to you.'

'I don't understand.'

'You went into a coma. Yes – that's …' He pauses. 'That's what happened after you gave birth to Michelle.'

'Michelle.'

'They couldn't wake you.' Philip's hands tighten on the steering wheel. 'The state you were in, no matter how hard they tried.'

She turns away from him.

'Is she …'

'She's home.'

'Home! But –'

'There's nothing to be afraid of, not any more.'

He looks at her, juggling the view of the road and wanting to hold her full attention but she's caught up in a whirlwind of thoughts, collating and trying to make sense of what has happened.

'We can do this together,' Philip says.

He smiles to reassure her but her gaze won't leave the road.

She stressfully touches her head.

'Helen, what is it?'

'I don't know what's going on.'

The road veers to a sharp bend. Philip turns the wheel hard, coasting it away from the fast approaching verge. Flustered, he concentrates on the road, letting his adrenaline steadily defuse. Helen stares dumbfounded out of the window.

'What is all this?' she mutters, shaking her head.

'Everything's going to be alright,' Philip says. 'It's going to be how it should have been.'

She turns to him, her eyes bringing a menace to her face that he thought impossible. 'What about Frances?'

He holds the steering wheel firm until his hands throb in pain, her name echoing in his head. Another pair of headlights speed past.

'She's gone,' Philip says, unable to look at her, his eyes firmly fixed to the small space of road in front of him. 'It's all over, all over.'

It's the first time he's admitted it to himself.

'What do you mean, she's gone?' Helen touches his arm. 'You've told her, haven't you?'

He catches himself in the rear view mirror and swallows deep, but still can't summon the courage to look at her.

'I had to, I had to see you. No matter what the consequences.'

'Where has she gone?'

'It doesn't matter, nothing matters apart from us and Michelle,' Philip says. 'Nothing.'

He pushes his foot harder on the accelerator, slamming through a pothole, jolting the car and sending the captured rainwater flying up in to the air. They hurtle past a parked police car discreetly nestled in a single-track road, its windows dripping with condensation.

PC Collinson bolts up from the backseat of the patrol car, semi-naked and covered in a glistening sweat. His breathing steadies itself, watching and listening to the sound of the car fading into the distance. Sergeant Wilson peers over the back of the driver's seat, a worried expression on his face. His hair, which is usually painstakingly sculpted into place, is now shooting out in a variety of directions as if someone has detonated a cartoon bomb. He wipes the sweat from his brow and attempts to regain some control over his hair by patting it down.

'Jesus, that sounded close,' Wilson says.

Collinson pushes Wilson's hands away from his hair, then forcefully grasps a handful and jerks his head backwards.

'Hey, steady on.' Wilson lets out a feeble squeal that turns to a coaxing groan.

'You love it,' Collinson says from behind him. 'Don't you?'

He leans forward, folding his body over him until he can whisper in his ear.

'That's how you like it. The thought of it. The thought of getting caught.' He chuckles, pulling down at the clump of Sergeant Wilson's hair, forcing his head on the back seat.

'Please, don't do this,' Wilson says in a half-hearted protest, eagerly rubbing his buttocks against Collinson's crotch.

The PC scratches his nails down his back and playfully slaps his arse, making the cheeks quiver. Sergeant Wilson lets out another groan of pleasure, the coldness of the back seat rubbing the side of his face.

'Nancy boy am I?' Collinson says. 'Shit pusher am I?'

He plunges hard and fast from behind.

The taste and smell of the seat swirls in Wilson's mind while his face grates against it.

'Come on, groan, you worthless bitch!' Collinson says, flinging his head back.

'Oh yes, oh yes, oh yes,' Wilson shouts out to each pleasure-induced thrust.

He bites down on the backseat, cool pools of saliva stick to his face but the pleasure is short lived. He thinks of his wife, all the lies he has told her. What has he become? The moment dies. He pushes PC Collinson away, knowing what he truly desires is what he has sacrificed, and is now out of his reach forever.

The sound of the back door slamming echoes through the guesthouse. Neither Mr Cole or Michelle react, Michelle is too enthralled in picking out a dress to wear for the party. She's sat in the middle of the bed in a pool of dresses, lifting one after another and then discarding them to the floor with a sigh. Mr Cole stands in front of the wardrobe's full-length mirror; he catches her in the corner of his eye, and raises an eyebrow – will she ever decide which one to wear?

He takes in his own appearance; the top half of his body is naked. He scrutinises his protruding belly and the way his man breasts slouch in a comment to the passing years. Placing his hands on his hips he breathes in, inflating his chest, creating a more positive look. His fingers awkwardly coast over his white chest hairs. His distaste at them being there moulds his expression and glares back at him. He looks down to his waist and below. His mood lightens, becoming more relaxed. The reflection of him standing there in stockings and suspenders, a thong struggling to keep his genitals in place makes his chest inflate even more, this time with pride.

'It's not fair, these are *all* old and don't fit me,' Michelle says.

Mr Cole doesn't acknowledge her, he's heard it too many times. He lifts his arm up and brings it closer to the mirror.

'Doesn't anybody understand? I'm not a little girl any more!' She discards another dress.

Mr Cole is far too engrossed with examining his armpits to say anything to her.

'It's no good, I'm going to have to wax,' he mutters.

He tugs at the hairs, embarrassed and disgusted at their neglected state. Michelle has to stop herself from giggling at seeing the back of his thong grouting his buttocks. She has been too occupied in her frustrated search and hadn't noticed him getting ready. She flops exhausted on the bed to take in the sight. Mr Cole turns away from the mirror and takes a black skirt from the back of a chair. Gracefully he steps into it and with a discreet wiggle pulls it up snug.

'Now you look like a girl. It's not fair you've got something to wear. Why doesn't anyone listen to me.'

'Stop your whining, Michelle.'

Carefully he brushes down on the skirt, ironing out any wrinkles. He spins round to see how his behind shapes up in the mirror.

'I think this could do the trick. The classic look never goes out of fashion.'

Michelle shrugs her shoulders.

He picks up a small bag from the chair and struts to the bed, his lower body language completely contradicting his stocky build.

'Would you like to do my make-up?'

Michelle beams with joy at the prospect. He sits on the edge of the bed and opens the bag. Eagerly she peers in, sending in a roaming hand.

'No you don't.'

Playfully he slaps the back of her hand and she retracts it with a dramatic yelp. Mr Cole searches deep in the make-up bag deciding what he needs. He takes out a palette of eye shadows and a compact mirror and hands them to Michelle. Enthusiastically she puts them on her lap and extends her hand for more. He then reveals a wand of mascara and two tubes of lipstick and gives them to her. She hoards them in her lap. He stops; Michelle watches him, eager to know what he has found. Jubilantly he pulls out a pair of eyelash curlers. Michelle looks puzzled at the bag and then to the growing pile of make-up, wondering how it all fitted. He hands it to her and she rotates it in her hand, examining it from all different angles.

The door opens behind them. Mr Cole glances up and sees Philip with Helen cautiously hovering in the doorway. He turns, blanking both of them, his contempt expelled in an exaggerated sigh. He reaches over to Michelle's lap and plucks out the mirror and a lipstick. Michelle inquisitively looks at Helen, tilting her head as if she is trying to find the flaw in what she is seeing. Mr Cole crosses his legs, flips open the mirror and applies the lipstick to his top lip, as if he did this chore at least two or three times a day. Michelle clenches his arm, uncomfortable at the situation.

'What are you doing?' Philip asks, standing over Mr Cole in disbelief.

Mr Cole doesn't waver, but carries on applying the lipstick now to his bottom lip in a defiant silence.

'Why are you dressed like that?' Philip snaps, 'and stop doing that!'

He takes hold of Mr Cole's arm, making the lipstick quiver in the boundary of his bottom lip.

Helen looks at Michelle. 'Is that you?' she whispers. 'No it can't be.'

Michelle trembles in fear as she approaches. Mr Cole calmly unclasps Philip's hand from his arm.

'You were never like this with your father.' Mr Cole's voice has changed pitch, slipping into his mother's tones.

He meticulously checks his lips for any smudges, snarls and carefully runs a finger along his teeth, removing any trace of lipstick.

'What did Dad do to deserved this?' Philip asks.

'We are who we are,' his mother replies. 'Have to face facts.'

Disapprovingly he turns to Helen, who, to his surprise, is touching Michelle's hair.

'You've always been an ungrateful little sod,' his mother says.

'How can you say that?'

'Don't start whining. If you don't get your own way that's all you do.'

'At least Dad didn't –'

'Stop bringing him in to it, the things I've done for you. Have you any idea the sacrifices I've made for you? For this family.'

'No, you can't say that,' Philip says.

Mr Cole stares at him with his mother's frown stuck on his forehead.

'No you don't, I put everything on the line for you,' the shrill voice continues. 'I have needs as well. It's always the same, you never give in do you.' Mr Cole springs to his feet and takes a shirt from the back of the chair. He spots a splattering of oil on it.

'How does your father get so filthy?' He pushes past Philip.

'I mean it.' Philip's nails imbed into the palms of his hands. 'You're not supposed to act like this!'

'You sound just like your father.'

Mr Cole casts a discerning look at Helen and leaves the room.

Philip stands there, powerless. He wrings his hands in frustration, muttering.

'She'll ruin it like she always does. Don't let her, Dad. Please don't let her, Dad – please,' he pleads.

'I can't believe it …' Helen's sits down next to Michelle, gazing at her, trying to take in every detail of her.

She nudges her body closer, wanting to say more but finding it difficult to work through what she's witnessing.

'I don't want to know!' Michelle snaps at her. 'Leave me alone.'

'No, please, don't,' Helen says, 'I didn't realise it's been so long. Is this really what happened?'

Michelle shakes her head. 'No, no!'

'I'm your mother, Michelle. I've come back to you.'

She touches Michelle's hand but she pulls it away from her.

'No you're not. You can't be.' She looks for reassurance at her sandwich box perched on the dresser.

The party is in full swing. Guests are eating and drinking, scattered around the room in small groups. Along the main wall tables have been parked up, cloaked in table cloths with prints of balloons and banners on them. There are paper plates corresponding to the same brightly coloured party theme piled high with a selection of sandwiches and rolls, all contenders in this popularity contest. The salmon are in the lead closely followed by the chicken, then tuna – each partnered to slices of cucumber and deep red tomatoes. And of course, if anyone wants to dice with their flatulent output, the egg rolls nestle together like some exotic fruit inciting those who dare. There are pizza slices, cold and wanting to be chewed. Plastic bowls of nibbles, a miss-match of colours, filled with a wide range of crisps and nuts. Iced fairy and butterfly cakes stand firm like a military blockade while they're picked off one by one, their paper cases discarded to one side.

The rest of the dining room tables have been stacked up by the bay window, the chairs pushed tightly against the walls. A compilation of party anthems shout out from the stereo on the sideboard. A small group of guests dance like seaweed in a strong current in the middle of the room, with coloured party hats perched at peculiar angles. They bellow out the familiar lines of the song and then retract back to a drunken mumble. Helen is chatting to Mr and Mrs Sullivan. Michelle is on the armchair pretending to watch the TV; it's on but the sound has been turned right down. At every opportunity she secretly pulls herself up to peer over to Helen, drawn by her every move, taking in her every gesture. She wants to hate her but something is stopping her. There's something strange about her. But what is it? She can't figure it out. She looks different without her hospital robe; the dress suits her but it has to be more than that. Mr Cole sits legs apart, his back to the party, sunk in the large sofa next to Mr Pritchard. His tight fitting skirt has ridden up and is snared on his bulky thighs, revealing the tops of his stockings. Mr Pritchard slides his body closer, drowning out the music and the joyful shrieks from the guests.

'The things you say, Mr Pritchard!' Mr Cole's voice is coy in a feminine tone.

Mr Pritchard places his hand on the inside of Mr Cole's leg and caresses his thigh.

'Well it's all relevant.' Mr Pritchard's eyes are half closed, vaguely listening, in full predator mode.

'I'm impressed … to have ambition like that.'

'You've got to try these things. That's what life's all about,' Mr Pritchard purrs in Mr Cole's ear. 'Nothing ventured nothing gained.'

Philip wanders past the sofa, stops and looks down discreetly at the two of them. He shakes his head, sighs and walks away.

'I know.' Mr Cole runs his fingers through his hair, wanting to discard his worries.

'You alright?' Mr Pritchard asks.

Mr Cole reaches over to the coffee table and picks up his wine glass by its stem. 'You understand, don't you. If only my husband was more like you. *Mr Play It Safe*, that's him. It makes so much of a difference.' He downs the wine in one swift gulp, Mr Pritchard touches his hand and moves his other closer to his crotch.

'Stop that, I'm married!' Mr Cole places a hand on top of Mr Pritchard's, bringing the surge along his inner thigh to a halt.

Mr Pritchard leans back, letting his head roll on the back of the sofa. 'I know, I know.'

Philip can't help but glance back to the sofa. He can see the tops of their heads almost touching. Helen rubs the side of his arm, attempting to calm him down.

'Don't, Philip. What else did you expect?' Her voice has a soothing pitch.

'Not this.' Philip's venom spits through his clenched teeth.

'I don't want you to make a scene.' She glances around to see if any of the guests have noticed that he's upset.

'I thought she was going to be different. She broke him, I saw it. The way Dad was after it all. He never got over the affair. Mum didn't care, she never cared. How could she do that?'

'Don't, Philip.'

'Tell me how could she?' The cheerful music turns on him, mocking him, making him more depressed. 'It was our neighbour last time. Our neighbour! They say, *"Don't shit on your own doorstep."* How could he get over that?'

'She's still your mother.'

'Of course she is, left us high and dry. But she's still my mother, mustn't forget that. How can I?'

Philip tugs his arm away from Helen's gentle caress and heads out of the dining room. She follows him closely. He stops in the hall, his heart pounding in his chest. Helen shuts the door behind them and waits for him to get his breath back.

The dining room lights fade, turning to an orange glow that pierces through the closed curtains of the large bay window.

The CD player sits lonely in the corner playing *Celebrate Good Times* by Kool and the Gang, stale food is haphazardly scattered over the tables spilling from paper plates and plastic bowls. The hazy orange streetlight exposes the indiscriminate features and silhouettes of the guests. A group are piled in a circle in the middle of the room, legs collapsing in on one another like puppets cut from their strings. Michelle sits slumped on one of the armchairs, eyes staring blankly, forced into a party frock with the TV trying to get through to her. The rest of the guests are slouched on chairs, party plates precariously balancing on their laps, food smeared around their faces or stuck hanging from their clothes.

Outside the dining room Philip paces the hall, muffled music and voices radiate from the party.

'He couldn't cope without Mum.'

'Philip, calm down will you.'

'He was never good enough for her. And nor was I, or else she would have stayed.' Philip's pacing stops. 'I had to go, he couldn't cope. I didn't want to. But they made me.'

She tenderly reaches out, attempting to defuse his tormented state. 'It doesn't matter any more. You have to let go.'

'How can you say that?'

She doesn't respond, her expressions are caught, wanting to retract what she has said.

Defeated, he turns away, shaking his head. 'I never saw Dad again. Yet I always see him standing there waving, smiling at me. He's always at our old front door, just like when they took me away.'

'Don't, Philip.' Helen's fingers stroke his face. She kisses him. 'Don't say any more.' She holds his face firmly in her hands. 'Please Philip, please.'

'It wasn't going to be for long. That's what he told me. Just till he got himself sorted.'

'Don't do this.' She steps back, her hand slides, cupping around his fingers.

He attempts to speak but she places a finger on his lips. 'Come on.' Helen nods to the stairs.

He smiles and then looks, unsure, at the dining room door. 'What about the party?'

'Come on.'

'But –'

Helen pulls at his hand. 'Let's find a spare room, like old times,' she whispers and guides him to the stairs.

15

Her head drops, fingers scrape at the duvet as she gyrates her pelvis with more ferocity, making her breasts sway at every driving plunge. He squints hard, sensing he's slipping inevitably nearer and nearer to the brink of climax. He wishes he could stop, to hold and savour the physical and mental connection between them, but he can't, it's no use. He lets out a faint murmur.

'I think you've been waiting for that,' Helen whispers, but she has a strange worried expression that disappears from her face as quickly as it arrived. She tilts her head to one side letting her hair fall away from her face as she runs a hand over Philip's pounding chest, appreciating his wasted state.

'Do you think so?' Philip tries to sedate his breathing, shaken by the look she gave him.

'Certainly do.' Helen leans forward.

He watches her reach under the pillow.

She pulls out a strip of toilet paper.

'You're prepared,' Philip says.

She smiles, rips off a couple of sheets and dangles them in front of him.

'Need some?'

Philip playfully snatches them away.

'You were never this feisty,' he says.

'Seem to know a lot about me.' Helen giggles. 'What are you thinking?'

'Nothing.' Philip's breath finds a steady pace.

She snuggles up next to him. 'You can't be thinking nothing.'

'Why not?'

'You can't.' Helen watches him clean himself up, then discard the tissue to the floor.

'What about you? And you can't say nothing.' Philip leans back into the pillow, exhausted.

'That's not fair. I asked you first.'

'So you're thinking nothing as well?'

'No.'

He reaches out and strokes her stomach.

'I know what you're thinking.' Helen cradles his hand.

'How can you?'

'I just do.'

'That's impossible.'

'Why is it impossible?'

'Because I'm not thinking of anything, that's why.' Philip lets out an awkward laugh.

'I bet you I can.'

'Let's talk about something else.'

'You know I can.'

'Helen, come on.'

'You can see them, can't you?'

'The bright lights,' he mumbles, unaware he has said the words.

His eyes slip over the slender curves of Helen's naked body, wanting to capture and store her beautiful uniqueness.

'Sorry?' he asks.

'I told you, you're thinking about bright lights.' Helen's eyes widen.

'Is this some sort of joke? I don't know what you are talking about.'

'You are, I know you are.' Helen strokes his chest with a smirk that's impossible to eradicate from her face.

He shakes his head.

'You're thinking about that night. Come on Philip. You remember don't you? You can't forget. When we were going to meet … the Ferris wheel. Don't tease, Philip.'

He wants to pull away from her but there's nowhere for him to go, he's trapped.

'I – erm. Didn't –' he mumbles.

'It doesn't matter.' Helen runs a finger over his shoulder and along his arm.

'But –'

'No more buts, there doesn't have to be any more,' Helen says. 'We can put this right, can't you see?'

She smiles at him but it's a smile that gives him no room to manoeuvre. An unannounced fear fills him, yet he's more afraid of the consequences if he opts out.

'We can do it, Philip. We can do it again, put it right. It's all going to be different this time. You believe it and so do I. Admit it.'

Philip hurries along the hall, aspirations flying high on a swell of invincibility that washes through him. He rushes into the kitchen making his way to the back door. Something shifts in the office, making him stop suddenly. He turns to the office and then to the back door weighing up what to do next. He steps towards the back door and hears a groan. It's no use, he'll have to investigate. He isn't brushing things aside any more, convincing himself that it hasn't got anything to do with him. It's time to start taking responsibility, this is the start of a new beginning. He walks over to the office and clasps the handle. He can sense whoever is in the office is aware he's outside the door. He bites down hard on his optimism and flings the door open.

261

Adrian's at the computer, his back to him. He stretches out his arms, his body unbuckling to a yawn.

'Doing well,' Adrian says cheerfully.

Philip's unsure of what to say.

Adrian doesn't look away from the computer. 'Lost a bit on the party, good morale boost though. They're almost eating out of your hand.'

Philip moves forward.

Adrian's body tenses.

'Thanks.' Everything in the office is neatly in its place. The old unused graphs and charts have been replaced on the walls with new dynamic ones.

'If you do it right you should have a great little business here. I've contacted a mate of mine through work. Sounded a bit stressed on the phone but anyway, I think we can put a website together, capture a bigger audience.'

Philip stares awkwardly at the back of Adrian's head.

He taps on the computer keys. 'The accumulated profit from the evening meals will pay for it. Let's face it, there's no reason why it shouldn't pay for itself when it's up and running. If we had all the rooms filled ...' He pauses. 'It's just the way the market place is changing, booking on line and catering for short breaks, it's the way it's going at the moment.'

'Do you think so?'

'Well it all indicates to that direction.' Adrian points to one of the graphs on the wall.

Philip tightens his grip on the door handle.

'You've got to look at the bigger picture, see the potential in things.'

Philip gradually closes the door, for once not wanting to argue with him. His voice is bathed in reassurance and a confidence that binds them together.

Philip makes his way along the garden path focusing on the back gate. He can hear it swaying to a sea breeze. It's a clear warm summer's night with the moon on full beam, showing off all its pitted craters. It's one of those nights that allows every star in the universe to come out and look down on the Earth. A rustling sound comes from the bushes opposite him. Philip looks over, rapidly collating any evidence to see what or who is there, but he's met by silence. He turns back to the guesthouse; it draws him, beckoning to him. A few lights are on and a silhouette ripples over the closed curtain of room 2. He isn't sure if it's Mr or Mrs Reynolds. His attention reverts to the gate but he's startled to find Michelle standing right beside him holding her sandwich box. She smiles at his stunned astonishment.

'What are you doing Michelle?'

'Where are you going?'

'I haven't got time for this.' He attempts to sidestep her but she's suddenly in his way again. 'Michelle, please go back to the house.'

She shrugs her shoulders and stands there stubbornly. He tries again but she blocks him, mimicking him like a reflection in a mirror.

'It's not right,' Michelle says, looking at the ground.

'Don't you dare say that. And what are you doing with that sandwich box?'

'I don't know.'

Another rustle comes from the bushes. This time a head pops up obscured by shadows, then another. Philip and Michelle stand still as two figures untangle themselves from the branches and wander, oblivious, towards them. Michelle squints, trying to see who they are. The two figures emerge out the shadows and step into the moonlight; it's Mr and Mrs Pritchard. They leisurely brush down their clothes. Mr Pritchard tucks in his shirt while Mrs Pritchard makes a final adjustment to her blouse. They stop simultaneously, uncomfortable at seeing Philip and Michelle staring at them. Defiantly they link arms in a united front, turn their backs on them and stroll off to the guesthouse as if nothing has happened.

'What were they doing?' Michelle notices the back of Mrs Pritchard's skirt is caught up in her knickers.

Philip looks on, bewildered.

Another rustle comes from the bushes and someone else stumbles out and strides from the darkness. Michelle instantly recognises Mr Cole strutting unevenly like an alley cat who's had a depraved night on the town. He tries to iron out some of the creases from his shirt, his legs bow and with a swift thrust he shoves a hand up his skirt to rearrange his genitals.

'Err!' Michelle screws up her face.

Mr Cole yanks his hand from out of his skirt, now aware he has an audience. 'Ah, Michelle, Philip.' He nods. 'What a pleasant surprise.' He walks over to them with a slight limp, trying to compensate for wearing a heavy-duty boot on one foot and a stiletto shoe on the other.

'What are you doing?' Philip looks down at the boot. 'Dad!'

'Don't be so ridiculous,' his mother's tones bark back, 'look at me.'

He shakes his head in confusion. 'You're drunk. You make me sick,' Philip spits.

Michelle stamps her foot hard on the ground. 'But why can't I come to the fair?'

'How did you know about —' Philip's stunned at Michelle's insight.

'Fair?' Mr Cole raises his voice. His mother's influence slips away but the anger still remains. 'I told you, it's no good! What is the matter with you?'

'Don't lecture me,' Philip says. 'Look at the state of you! You don't change, do you? It's always about you, never think about anybody else.'

Mr Cole ignores him, frantically scouring the garden as if he's dropped a winning lottery ticket. 'Where is she?' He peers over Philip's shoulder, following the pathway to the back gate.

'I don't know what you mean.' Philip's caught off guard sensing his own vulnerability.

'I might have known she'd have something to do with all this,' Mr Cole says, desperately wanting to fire his aggression at Helen. 'Where is she then? It's lucky we're going with you. Did you find a dress to fit her? Scrawny thing, isn't she? I like my women with a bit more meat on them.'

Philip shakes his head. 'You're not coming, none of you.' He backs away from them.

'So why haven't you gone?' Mr Cole's eyes shine with a knowing glint.

'What are you talking about?'

'Couldn't face being with her by yourself. That's right isn't it?' He turns to the back gate. 'She's in the car isn't she?'

'Yeah – but …'

'That's why *you're* in the garden, waiting for us. Poor little Philip. You have to go with the majority in a democracy, or you at least have to take the majority along with you. You've learnt something at least.'

'Please, you can't come.' Philip's tone is defeated and feeble.

'Gratitude.' Mr Cole unexpectedly farts. 'Oh, excuse me.'

'That's awful!' Michelle says, with a cruel grin.

Mr Cole takes in a deep sniff. 'That *is* bad.' The stench hits his lungs hard. 'And awful, I'll go along with that.'

Philip rolls his eyes to the heavens. 'Did you hear me?'

Mr Cole ignores him, takes hold of Michelle's hand and leads her to the gate, her sandwich box swinging in her hand.

Philip drives along the esplanade's colourful light show stretching out either side of the road. Bars and restaurants are closing, tables and chairs being packed away and escorted inside. Neon signs flicker and fade to the shadows. The nightlife is gradually winding down, settling to a peaceful sleep. Small groups of teenagers weave enthusiastically in and out of the amusement arcades, desperate to drain every last drop of entertainment from the day. A few couples stroll along the strip finding comfort in the warm holiday air. Scattered silhouettes of people can be seen on the beach. The sun eventually broke through in the evening, making up for the rest of the dismal day, and they're all reluctant to let it go.

They approach the painted roundabout where the main road swings to the right, channelling the traffic away from the esplanade and towards the railway station. Helen touches Philip's hand as he changes down a gear. They slip past the roundabout and head straight on towards the pier and harbour. Mr Cole lets out a heavy sigh from the back seat, giving them both another distasteful glare, and settles down for a much wanted booze nap. Michelle's next to Mr Cole, snuggled by the rear window, staring at all the coloured lights flicking by, letting her imagination run free.

They drive past the Crown Tearooms, past the Palace Theatre on the New Pier advertising *Aladdin* with Bradley Walsh and that guy who used to play Steve's brother in *Coronation Street*, or was it *EastEnders*? They turn into the harbour area and follow the circular road running along side The Ship, and the Seven Seas fish and chip shop that's tucked away in a back street. A trail of plastic fish and chip cartons and wooden forks lead the way. The crowds have long gone, having spent their time in the fine art of watching the day roll by and aimlessly wandering. Discovering a peace in observing the harbour's fishing boats coming in from a hard day, parking themselves next to the shimmering leisure yachts. Then watching the lorries loading up at twilight, being packed with ice trays of sea fish and crustaceans.

It had been an evening when the boundaries of the bars spilled out onto the narrow streets, the smell of alcohol and after-sun lotion mixing in the sea air. The slamming of fish and chip shop tills singing out across the harbour. While the lucky few sat comfortably on benches, the rest of the holidaymakers packed along the harbour wall opposite The Royal Oak and The Ship, eating their fish and chips and sipping their drinks. The new arrivals always easy to spot with their skin glowing pink and raw.

They head down the single lane towards the Town Bridge. A deserted reveller haggard by a night of drinking swaggers on the edge of a curb; they pass by and Michelle waves to him. He stops swaying, his eyes strain to decipher what he's seeing. He stands glued to the spot, his jaw slowly dropping as the car passes and heads to the bridge. Michelle turns back, uneasy as he stands perplexed on the curb. They drive on over the Town Bridge. In front of them is the Holy Trinity Church. The road swings to the right running along to where the harbour forms a marina, where row upon row of stripped down masts make the boats look like speared party food. Philip turns left on to the pedestrian friendly cobbles that connect them to the coastal road. They keep driving along the old unlit road until the lights of the town dissolve into the night.

Eventually they turn into a lay-by. The steering wheel trembles under the loose gravel.

'This is it, I know it!' Helen gleefully stares out of the window, her hands impatiently clench the door handle wanting to take flight.

The car comes to a halt, the engine dying and being replaced by the sound of Mr Cole snoring in the back, Michelle gives him a hard poke in the ribs. He grunts and shifts over; she grins with a sinister menace.

267

Mr Cole mutters under his breath, 'Factory! My husband doesn't work in a factory, you must have me confused with someone else. He works in an office, an office I tell you!' His fingers caress the white collar of his shirt.

'It's going to be alright. I know it is.' Helen's face beams at Philip, bright and alluring. He opens the car door and the sound of the ocean hitting the shoreline below rushes at him. He steps out and the sea air fills his lungs. The moon is perfectly formed in the sky, its enchanting light shimmering on the ripples out on the horizon. The passenger door clicks open, he sees Helen standing there, the sea breeze pulling her dress tight.

'Come on,' she laughs. 'It's just down on the beach.' Moonlight moisturises her face, giving it a sleek shine. She turns away from him and hurries over to the cliff path. Philip cautiously follows her.

He picks up his pace, rushing over to the edge of the cliff, seeing Helen disappearing in front of him. Stopping at the cliff's ragged edge, a gust of wind punches him, almost sending him to the ground. He peers over the edge, following its clinging winding pathway, aided by a sturdy metal railing negotiating the cliff's drop. He watches Helen descend the path; she stops and glances up at him, the wind vacuum-packing her dress to the slender curves of her body. She waves and carries on. Another blast turns his clothes to sails and delivers her voice to him. 'Philip,' it calls to him, but is abruptly whipped away.

He turns back to the car, the passenger door is wide-open letting in the moonlight. He can make out a commotion on the back seat as Michelle forces her way past Mr Cole.

'Hey!' Mr Cole says, wanting to curb Michelle's eagerness. He looks around. 'We're here then?'

In pure frustration Michelle clambers towards the gap between the front seats, nearly tripping over the handbrake and managing to rip a hole in Mr Cole's tights.

He pulls at the expanding hole. 'Look at what you have done, child. What has got into you?'

She ignores him. 'Wait!' Michelle shouts out to Philip.

She jumps free of the car, runs over to him and stands there, unflustered.

Mr Cole bellows at them. 'I can't see the point of all this, it's not going to work. We should've had a vote on it! Dragging us along like this.'

'You're not going without us, are you?' Michelle asks.

'Of course I wouldn't,' Philip says, encouraged by her concern. He smiles at her.

She doesn't respond but this doesn't stop him holding out a hand to her. Michelle declines the offer, she can't help but feel he has somehow tricked her.

She scoots past him and peers down the cliff face. Philip follows her lead, all the time wanting to hold her hand or take her arm to make sure she's safe. The closer she ventures to the edge the more his heart lurches. They see Helen waving with encouragement but she stops and withdraws her hand sheepishly when she realises Michelle is there. She turns and carries on towards the moonlit beach. A thud from behind makes them both jump. They turn around and see Mr Cole has fallen out of the car.

They all make their way down the weather-worn cliff path. Philip's attention flickers from assessing the way, to Helen who's made it to the beach. She isn't waving back to him any more; ever since she left the path she hasn't acknowledged him at all. It's as if something has captured her attention, whispering to her across the shore. He had cried out to her but she never responded, she just kept walking sombrely to the shoreline until she stopped in the middle of the beach.

Philip looks back, Michelle follows with Mr Cole clinging on to her tightly; he's having difficulty negotiating the path's steps in his one high heel and one heavy workman boot. Frustrated, Philip glares at them but they're too busy to notice.

'Philip, please wait up!' Mr Cole shouts.

Philip shakes his head, wishing they could move more quickly.

'I don't understand. Why are you taking us here?' Mr Cole asks. 'Why wouldn't you let me in? I warned you about secrets, Philip.'

Philip ignores him, turning his back on him.

'We all have a stake in this,' Mr Cole says. 'What I've done for you was for the good of us all and look how you repay me.' He turns to Michelle for some moral as well as physical support. She nods in agreement.

Philip strides on.

'I'm the one who has been guiding you. I know you better than you know yourself. I'm telling you this is not where your true interest lies. Listen to me, Philip.' Mr Cole leans on the cold railings to steady his breath and his building anger.

Philip stops. He clenches his fists, fingernails digging into his palms, his body rigid.

'You know, don't you Philip … don't you?' Mr Cole asks, mocking him.

Philip walks on, leaving Mr Cole resting against the railing, giving his feet a moment's welcome relief.

By the time they reach the bottom, Helen has been standing staring out at the sea for a long time, almost becoming part of the beach. A strange lonely statue protruding from the sand with a slender shadow trailing behind, her dress a discarded piece of fabric caught up in and being played with by the wind. She has become as familiar and robust as one of the rocks at the far end of the beach. The moon is crystal clear in the sky, its light extending out, highlighting everything in its magical

270

glow. Philip walks across the sand, exhausted. Even his arms ache, his muscles strained, but he can't understand why.

'Helen, are you –' Philip walks around to face her, his voice springing her to life.

'I can see it.' Helen beams. 'I told you, didn't I? I told you.'

Philip looks out across the cove, the waves surging from the horizon.

'It's been a long time,' Helen whispers.

'What do you mean?' Philip asks. 'I can't see –'

'Look Philip, it's here,' Helen says gleefully.

Philip turns back to the ocean but this time with a growing uncertainty.

Mr Cole sits down on a rock at the bottom of the steps to get his breath back, holding Michelle's arm for support.

'Look at the state of this shirt. I'm getting too old for this kind of thing, carrying on like a teenager.' Mr Cole looks up to Michelle. 'What's happening?'

He stops, noticing something on her cheek. He squints at a pool of sparkling colours dancing and playing on her glistening skin.

'Michelle,' Mr Cole says, but she doesn't respond as the colours gradually increase in size.

'No, he can't be doing this. Not this!' Mr Cole shakes his head in dismay.

The rippling light is now swirling over the liquid films of her eyes.

'We could have had it all, Philip. A new start for both of us,' Mr Cole says softly to himself, reluctantly turning towards Philip and Helen on the beach.

Out of the clear night sky clusters of stars are breaking into a kaleidoscope of magical dust, falling into the sea making it swirl and fizz. Mr Cole pulls Michelle close; she doesn't flinch, caught up in a trance-like state. Her hand tightly squeezes the handle of her sandwich box, her gaze transfixed to the unravelling spectacle. The sea is coming alive to vibrant colours, communicating with one another, driving each other like an enormous shoal of focused fish heading towards the beach. Mr Cole turns to Michelle, seeing her face about to explode with excitement. Frantically he gets to his feet.

'You don't want this, this is not it,' he mutters under his breath as to his amazement an immense funfair begins to rise out of the sea. Helen holds Philip's hand, pulling him closer. It's a swirling mass of colours as though it's been carved from the skins of cuttlefish, their aquatic pulses rewired to a funfair blueprint. Effortlessly it maroons itself on the shore at the far end of the beach. The colours make the creatures in the nearby rock pools swim and crawl in pure hypnotic excitement. Helen's hand grips Philip's tighter as they see this whole wonder is breathing in the cool air.

They walk across the beach. The sound of the sea is drowned out by the music and people's voices en masse, suffocating the cries from Mr Cole who's being helped along the beach by Michelle. Philip and Helen come to the edge of the funfair. Philip can feel its wall of sound bearing heavily on his chest. It's a hive of activity – rides are racing through the air to cries of hysteria and laughter, voices ricochet from all directions. The merry-go-rounds, helter-skelter, galloping horses, the coconut stand – everything is translucent with pulses of colour rushing through them at tremendous speeds.

And yet he can't see a single person.

Nobody serving the candyfloss, nobody taking the money for the umbrella ride or the bumper cars. No groups of teenagers hanging in clusters like boulders in a stream. But Philip can hear children giggling, feel the body mass of people rushing past him, their footsteps disrupting the sand. They meander past the *Win a goldfish* stand. Water-filled plastic bags hang displaying wriggling shavings of gold. Darts bounce as if they're attached to invisible springs then shoot through the air hitting the dartboard. Two deep sighs are heard at the poor score. They walk on carefully, passing *Jan's Funfair Food* van, dodging hovering pink swirls of candy-floss, burgers dripping fat into the sand and sticky toffee apples being bitten into.

'It must be over here! I'm sure it is.' Helen pulls at Philip's hand, weaving though the unseen people, bouncing balloons, bracelets and accessories made from luminous strips of neon, all moving in surges of organic traffic. At last they reach a barren area in the middle of the fair.

'No Helen.' Philip pulls at her hand but her strength and determination are too strong to argue against.

A glowing light fills the fair. Helen looks up and gasps, seeing the moon descending from the sky. Philip squints, standing in pure disbelief. Michelle and Mr Cole catch them up.

'Stop this!' Mr Cole says. 'Look around you, you know you want to. You're not committed, you're only half thinking about it.' Someone knocks into him, shoving him out of the way.

Philip doesn't hear him. He stares, captivated as the core of the moon shatters into tiny pieces revealing spokes leading to a central hub. The fragmented pieces drift effortlessly away, arranging themselves into stars in the thick black night sky.

'No Philip!' Mr Cole shrieks as someone else knocks into him. 'Listen to me.'

Michelle protectively stands by him trying to anticipate where the next aggressive person is about to come from.

'Sorry,' says a woman's voice, but she still bumps into him again.

The moon-wheel settles on the ground with a shudder, its rim breaking up into individual carriages. They rock gently, filling the vacant space perfectly. Helen lets go of Philip's hand and steps forward marvelling at the spectacle of the Ferris wheel, creating the fair's crowning glory.

'Come on Philip.'

All Philip can do is stand there, caught between hope and fear.

Helen takes hold of his hand and pulls.

'No!' Mr Cole shouts out again, colliding into someone else. Philip's always so tantalisingly close but so far away.

'Watch it mate,' the voice snaps, giving no clue if it's male or female.

Confused, Mr Cole spins around then surges forward again, hitting into another unseen human wall.

'Is there something wrong with you?' says a deep threatening voice.

Mr Cole spots Michelle making her way through the crowd. He looks over to Philip. His head spins at how far away he is from him. He surges towards Michelle, thrown in every direction but at least he's able to gain some headway. Hostile voices crackle and spit at him but he manages to reach her. He snuggles behind her using her like a protective shield.

She ignores him.

'He's fit,' Michelle says, wanting to catch the attention of a passing boy.

Mr Cole shakes his head, he still can't make anybody out.

Michelle wanders over to a candyfloss stand.

'Michelle!' Mr Cole tugs at her dress to get her attention. People's voices hurry by, their odours filling his nostrils, sand erupting all around him like miniature explosions.

'Could I have that one?' Michelle points to a bag of bright pink candyfloss.

'Michelle, we haven't got time for this.'

'Yes we have.' Michelle's voice sounds deeper as if she's got a sore throat. The candyfloss floats down to her and she places some money on the counter.

'Michelle, I'm talking to you. Don't be like this with me.'

'Like what?'

'Thanks,' says a woman's voice. The money disappears.

Mr Cole leans against the counter, exhausted.

She opens out her hand and catches her change.

'There ya go love.'

'We need to get to Philip,' Mr Cole says.

Michelle turns to him. 'What for?'

Mr Cole's baffled at her response.

She opens the bag of candyfloss. 'I said what for?'

'He's your father.' Mr Cole shakes his head in frustration.

Michelle stuffs the candyfloss into her mouth. 'Mmm, yummy. So why did he trick me? I want to be with Mum at the guesthouse. He knows she's there. But he won't bring her here, doesn't want her to spoil it. He *always* spoils it. But we know that don't we?' She turns her back on him and walks away, not letting Mr Cole reply.

Philip and Helen wait in line at the Ferris wheel. The queue is getting shorter quickly. Helen steps forward, Philip reluctantly in tow as the queue disperses.

'Hey, hold on,' Philip says.

'Don't be frightened,' Helen says soothingly.

The carriage radiates as its door swings open, letting a giggling couple off.

'Can you remember how this goes?' Helen asks, scrutinising him, her face in full beam, lit perfectly by the wheel.

He shakes his head, wanting to hide his anxiety.

'What is it?' Helen asks.

'Nothing.' Philip watches the carriage drawing nearer.

He stops, jolting back Helen's eager stride.

He sees it all opening out perfectly in front of him, everything set to a precise motion like the intricate movements of a Victorian pocket watch. Each event, no matter how insignificant, reacting to one another in perfect harmony. He can visualise the two of them being lifted up in the carriage, rising into this perfect night sky away from everybody, out of sight of people's prying opinions and the beliefs they cling to. Do the right thing, that's what you've got to do, that's what he did. He saved his marriage but he sacrificed what really mattered to him. Destroyed the one thing that filled his life with any meaning and made each day different from all the rest. He swallows hard, he could be back there at that precise moment in time, where he had calculated it all went wrong.

He could make amends, say what he should have said. What his heart cried out to say, standing firm to the consequences he knew would follow. He'll be reborn, shedding the years like an old skin, letting the night sky focus everything into perspective, unplugging the world and all its puzzling contradictions until they are looking into a future they had both been denied.

He could see it so crystal clear, her mouth smoothly moulding around each letter, telling him what he has always wanted to hear. This is it, this is where it could all begin again. He has a second chance and the power of hindsight etched in him like a sixth sense. But something nags at him stirring and growing in his psyche. His thoughts had examined what he's about to tell her, approaching the conversation from every conceivable angle. His senses finely tuned to read every small gesture of her body, the hidden subtext in her voice, the fluctuation of her pupils. Rigorously attempting to excavate and locate any uncertainty she's feeling. But that's the trouble. It hits him head-on.

There's no passion, no spontaneity. His heart should be racing, his palms sweating in anticipation. Yet it's as if he's examining a laboratory mouse injected with a virus. Standing there as a technician, his finger curled around a pen roaming down the page, boxes waiting to be ticked to confirm its reactions. The faint smell of a cigarette wafts under his nose chased by Frances' unmistakable perfume.

'I can't do this, this isn't me. How can I – you know what I'm like,' Philip says.

'You can't say that.' Helen looks at him sadly.

He backs away from her.

'It's no good, can't you see?'

'You can't do this to me!' she cries.

'Please no, I'm sorry Helen, I'm so sorry.'

'What are you doing?'

Philip turns and runs through the invisible crowds, hearing Helen's voice calling after him, sinking into the hustle and bustle of the funfair. He forcefully dodges the interwoven current of people travelling from one amusement to another. The further he runs from the Ferris wheel the heavier his heart grows. He bites on his lip holding back his tears.

The music drops becoming more stifled. People have thinned out, their voices becoming indistinguishable, only small patches of sand move and flicker about underfoot. He has come to the edge of the funfair, where the stalls are more modest in their stature and not so packed, elbowing each other for space.

Philip runs out of the fair, out along the shoreline. The wide open space of the beach lifts his spirit, as a cool breeze from the sea hits him. He carries on, the awkwardness of the sand draining his leg muscles until his unfit state kicks in hard. His shoulder and arm bite at him with a surprising pain. His legs give way and he falls to his knees cradling his lungs, coughing and spluttering. He gasps, quenching his lungs as they cry out for more oxygen. Saliva slips from his mouth and dangles into the sand. Unable to sedate his breathing he rests his forehead against the sand, fingers retracting into a fist, feeling the sand filtering through them. He looks up. His tear-filled eyes take in Helen who's standing in front of him, balancing her emotions between contempt and concern.

'What's wrong with you?'

'It doesn't matter.' Philip bows his head submissively.

'How can you say that! This is our chance to truly start

again, to put everything right. The way it should have been. If you don't –'

'Please, no.' Philip holds a hand up in defeat. His breathing begins to steady itself. 'This isn't right.'

She crouches down in the sand. 'It's going to be different this time.'

'No. No, it can't. I let you down. I've let everyone down. I always do.'

'You can make it right. You know you can.' Her smile pumps full of hope. 'We can go back.' The funfair lights flicker on her face and dance over the wet sand.

'No!' Philip cries out.

The music hits him, he glances over his shoulder. The edge of the funfair is somehow only a couple of feet away. 'I failed you, I failed us.' He looks to the sand, ashamed. 'I failed everyone, that's what I do. Don't you understand?'

Helen gathers him close. 'It's alright, it's going to be alright,' she whispers.

'No, please Helen, I'm afraid.' He pulls back staring straight at her.

'Why are you afraid?'

'I didn't want anything to change. But that's all there is, isn't it?'

Philip looks out over the ocean; it's untouched by the colourful lights of the funfair, the sky clear and calm. From the corner of his eye he can see the lights, sparkling, luring him to look, but he forces himself not to, the artificial spectacle would only spoil the natural view of the sky and the sea linked in peace to one another.

'What happens when there's no more excuses?' Philip asks.

'I don't understand.'

'I thought you might not.'

'Philip, don't waste it.'

'I'm so afraid, I can't even trust my own eyes any more.'

278

Helen pulls him close making a strange rustling sound. He shivers at her icy touch.

'You're so cold.'

'I know. I feel achey.'

He rubs her arms and hands to take away her coldness, but it's no use.

'We're going to have to get you back.' Philip's face is a blank canvass, void of any expression or life.

He turns to the sea, watching the waves break over and over again, nothing hindering their quest.

'I really don't feel very well.' Helen leans her head on his shoulder.

'I know, I know.' Philip looks at her and then to the sea again. This time the artificial light of the fair seeps in and distorts the natural beauty of his view.

Philip parks the car at the back of the guesthouse. He waits for a few moments, caressing the steering wheel and relishing the still silence. Everything has changed, the magical moment has been lost and now lingers like an unobtainable faint echo in the back of his mind. He climbs out of the car, walks around to the passenger door and opens it, all the time cowering away from the guesthouse. He can feel it staring at him, criticising his every move. Helen coughs, her face obscured by the shadows of the car. He can feel the guesthouse extending out an invisible arm and resting its bitterly cold hand on his shoulder. He doesn't want to go back there but he knows he has no choice. There's nowhere else for him to go. Movement stirs on the back seat. Reluctantly Philip turns to the guesthouse. The same lights are on as before, but the guesthouse appears to tower up, reaching menacingly to the sky. A shadow casts across the drawn curtains of room 2. A voice shouts out as an argument erupts between Mr and Mrs Reynolds. A light comes on from another window making his gaze leapfrog randomly from window to window. A door slams.

'Philip.' Helen startles him.

Carefully he helps her out of the car, the weight of her body leaning wearily against him. He cradles her around her waist. She coughs deep and sinister, it vibrates in his head.

'I don't know what I was thinking, taking you out there.' His eyes plead for forgiveness.

'Don't be so dramatic,' she says smiling.

He touches her brow. 'You're running a temperature. It was too soon to take you out of the hospital. What was I thinking?'

'Don't fuss, the homecoming party was wonderful. I wasn't expecting that.'

The front seat springs forward like a mantrap. Mr Cole tries to scramble out but gets wedged in between the seat and the door-frame. Michelle slaps him hard on his backside and giggles.

'You should go on a diet!' she says with a mischievous laugh.

'You cheeky little bleeder!'

He steps out of the car avoiding any eye contact with Helen. Michelle coils back into the seat and gathers her sandwich box close.

'Ooh.' Mr Cole rubs his backside attempting to conjure-up a smile. 'That hurt. I'm not joking.'

Philip pops his head in to the car. 'Michelle. Come on out of there.'

From the shadows Michelle throws him a stubborn glare.

'Michelle, I haven't got time for this!'

Her arms tighten around the sandwich box and she bows her head.

'Stay there then.' He shuts the car door.

Philip puts his arm around Helen and brings her close.

'You can't leave her there,' Helen says, looking back.

'She's being a pain – always wanting to get her own way.'

'But she's just a baby. She's not like that.'

He rubs at her arm. 'You're so cold, let's get you inside.'

Michelle clambers onto the front seat and glares out the window at them. Coughs erupt bellowing out of Helen's weakening body.

Mr Cole contemptuously turns away from them and opens the car door.

'It's always about her,' Michelle's voice snarls, her face still hidden by the shadows.

'Come on Michelle.' Mr Cole offers her a hand. 'We can't do anything about it.'

Philip turns back to the car. 'Do as you're told for once.'

'Leave it, Philip!' Mr Cole snaps.

'Stop sticking up for her,' Philip shouts back.

'No, I don't want him touching my baby,' Helen says.

Mr Cole shakes his head, ignoring them, and helps Michelle out of the car, her head bowed in a fixed strop. Another coughing fit takes hold of Helen. She slips from Philip's embrace but he catches her. Its sound is raw and painful. Mr Cole and Michelle stand together silently watching.

Philip turns to them. 'Come on!'

Mr Cole steps forward but Michelle snatches hold of his trousers, stopping him. He crouches to her.

'Michelle, what's got into you?'

Her head is bowed, body hanging, with her curly hair cascading over her face, sandwich box gently swaying in her hand.

'Nothing.' The tone of her voice has dropped deeper.

'Doesn't sound like nothing to me. You haven't caught a cold, have you? Not you as well, what a night!'

Delicately he brushes the obscuring hair away from her face. He stops, feeling her skin; her features are different, swollen. Cautiously he touches her chin, encouraging her to look at him. He wipes her hair back exposing her face. Mr Cole turns to Philip who's escorting Helen through the back gate to the guesthouse. He wants to shout at him, to get him over here to confirm what he's seeing.

But all he can do is stare at Michelle's face in pure disbelief, to confront what he has no way of stopping. Her features have changed, matured in conflict with her flimsy child's body. No longer does she have the face of a young girl. Gone the innocent smile to prise the hardest of hearts wide open. He's now staring into the face of a teenager, enslaved by the power of oestrogen and on the verge of opening its Pandora's box of desires.

16

Philip precariously holds two plates of cooked breakfast. The guests stare in silence, critically scrutinising his every move. One of the plates has a build-up of tomato sauce that's about to dribble and run free to the carpet, while the watery scrambled egg on the other is being soaked up by his sleeve. Nothing has gone right for him all morning. Coupled with the torment of last night, he hasn't slept at all. Helen's health has rapidly deteriorated, her body enslaved in a cold clammy fever.

Mr Cole had taken care of Michelle and had left him to deal with Helen. He'd been so pre-occupied with her he hadn't said goodnight to Michelle; in fact he hadn't said anything to her, too distressed not knowing what to do or where to turn. Helen's coughing fits had escalated until thin traces of blood sprayed her hands and stained the screwed-up toilet paper she held, and there was still that strange rustling sound whenever she moved. It disturbed him although he couldn't put reason to it. She couldn't go back to the hospital, he knew if she did he would lose her again. He didn't know why but he knew this time it would be forever. Eventually, in pure exhaustion, she drifted off to sleep while he sat patiently by her bed, watching her, hearing the rawness of her throat as she slept. Her body was covered in a cold sweat, attempting to wring the sickness from her system. He had lovingly touched her, mopping the sweat from her face, finding a small soothing peace from the rhythm of her breathing. The early hours of the morning laboriously ticked by, with him hearing the guests arguing all around them, even though they were in his bedroom high above the guest rooms. He had held her cold hand, his mind pushing away the shouts and screams – focusing, willing her to find an inner strength and come out fighting.

He walks closer to Mr and Mrs Riley, avoiding any eye contact. His thoughts are leaping everywhere. Helen has to eat or at the very least drink something. He'd made her some toast, spreading the margarine to the corners the way she likes it. His train of thought breaks as he smells cigarettes, but no one is smoking in the dining room. He'd told her he'd be back with a cup of tea later. Tired and desperately wanting to sleep, he'd left her and headed downstairs to wake Mr Cole. He needed help cooking the breakfasts but more importantly he wanted him around, a comrade in the growing hostility. But it was no use, he couldn't wake him no matter how hard he tried. And Michelle was the same.

He stops by Mr and Mrs Riley's table, wrestling with the image of Michelle's face as she slept. How it has changed. The plates nearly slip from his hands. He pictures himself standing, watching over her, seeing adolescent spots emerging on the surface of her skin, turning from a painful red and filling up with pinheads of white pus. He steadies himself, recapturing the moment when he unlocked Michelle's grip that held the sandwich box tight to her small body. He trembled, longing to hold the box close but he didn't want to look inside. No, he can't do that, no matter what.

Carefully he places the breakfasts on the table in front of Mr and Mrs Riley; they stare, unimpressed. Mr Riley takes a knife and jabs at the scrambled egg as if wanting to know if it is alive.

'I can't eat this!' he says.

'It's revolting.' Mrs Riley crosses her arms and sighs with venom.

Philip picks up the plates, splattering some of the tomato sauce on the tablecloth. A fine drizzle hits Mrs Riley.

'For Christ's sake. What's the matter with you?'

'Sorry. I didn't mean —' His body shifts erratically, torn between good manners and wanting to run out of the room.

All eyes are on him, all coiled, activated, like mines in a minefield waiting to explode with contempt at him. Philip nods submissively and re-traces his steps, making a swift exit out of the dining room through a gauntlet of deflating sighs and ringing tuts.

Philip places Mr Cole's breakfast on the table next to the window. Mr Cole is sprawled on the bed, semi-naked and snoring. He opens the curtains letting in the early morning light. The day is overcast and sombre with a strong harsh wind coming in from the sea. He looks out over the bay. The waves are in turmoil hitting the shore. In the distance a small fishing boat sails defiantly out of the harbour into the uncertainty of the ocean.

Mr Cole stirs. Philip steps back from the window, feeling hot as if he's been bathing in rays of sunlight. Mr Cole fidgets, half-consciously adjusts his genitals and falls back to sleep. Philip walks over to him and stands there for a moment, his frustration makes his body quiver. In desperation he pulls him up from the bed and violently shakes him. It's not for the first time this morning.

'Please, wake up. Please you've got to!'

A too familiar groan bellows from Mr Cole as his head rolls from side to side.

'I need you,' Philip says. 'Please I need you. For fuck's sake!'

He lets go, watching Mr Cole fall back on the bed. He slips back into sleep, his snoring increasing in volume at every breath.

Philip picks up Mr Cole's discarded skirt lying next to him and perches on the corner of the bed, letting the fabric slide soothingly through his fingertips. He holds it to his face and inhales deeply. Mr Cole's feet are hanging over the edge of the bed. One is sore and swollen with a muddy stiletto dangling on his toes, the other is snuggled in a hefty muddy boot. He reaches over, unlaces the boot and eases it off his foot. He then wraps the skirt around it and holds them close.

Michelle drops her school uniform in front of Philip. She's still dressed in her pyjamas.

'Where are my clothes? Making me wear this, I don't think so!' Her adolescent features are strong and determined with a voice and attitude to match.

He looks up to her, the boot unravels from the skirt and falls to the floor. The features of her face are held in a strange unbalanced battle against her fragile body.

He turns away. 'Michelle, please don't argue with me.' The volume of his voice is turned down to barely a whisper.

Michelle eyes him suspiciously. 'You can't take her away from me. I know what you're up to.'

'No, I want to –' Philip starts.

'Don't even pretend you care. It's always been about you.'

'Don't you dare say that!' he shouts.

'Can't go to school without my sandwich box,' Michelle says, mocking him. 'Need my case studies as well, but they're all ruined aren't they?'

'Stop it Michelle, you don't know what you're saying.'

'No! You've never liked me working at the school. Being independent … no you don't want that.' She pulls up the sleeves of her pyjamas and shoves her arms at him. 'Look. All bites and bruises.' Philip stares at her arms, they are a deep purple-blue, veins raised to the surface of the skin.

'Stop this, please Michelle.'

Mr Cole unnaturally awakens, bolt upright on the bed, fully conscious.

'Calm down!' Mr Cole shrieks, in his mother's voice.

Philip throws the skirt at him in disgust. 'Always consistent, I'll give you that.'

'Maybe we can compromise,' his mother says, rubbing the smudged lipstick off with a tissue.

'She's a child,' Philip says, picking up Michelle's uniform.

Michelle sighs and rolls her eyes.

'Not from where I'm sat.'

'Put these on now or you're going to be late for school, Michelle.'

Michelle storms off in a strop and sits on a chair.

'Maybe it would be better if she started afresh on Monday,' his mother argues. 'They've got cover for the rest of the week.'

'What are you going on about?' Philip replies. 'You don't really want her around the house do you?'

Michelle looks intensely at Mr Cole, her eyes tightening. 'What does he mean?'

'Philip, not in front of her.' His mother pleads with him.

'No, we can't have that. I always have to be the bad guy.' Philip edges closer to Mr Cole, invading his space. 'What about in front of the next-door neighbours? Another set of rules altogether I suppose. Don't think I didn't know. The whole neighbourhood knew what was going on with you two.'

Philip's slapped across the face, more dramatic than of having any power.

'How dare you,' his mother says.

'That's what I was going to say to you,' Philip spits.

Michelle leaps from the chair and stomps over to them.

'I love her, do you understand?' Michelle says. 'You can't deny me that.'

Stunned, they both turn to her.

'What are you going to do, hit me?' She grins. ' *"Do as you're told, Michelle. Do this, do that Michelle."* ' She wobbles her head, mocking him. 'I'm not scared.' She stops, as if all her energy as been siphoned out, and looks towards the door. 'No, I'll wait for Mum.' She stares back, scrutinising him.

He can feel her contempt embrace him.

A smile flashes at him. 'Yeah, that's right. Going to be all different now. No matter how hard you try you can't deny her. She's coming, isn't she. Mum's coming.' Her stare bores into his eyes. 'You can hit her, can't you? Problem solved, just like before. Easy isn't it?'

He stands, not moving a single muscle.

'But not this time.' Thin layers of tears glaze over Michelle's eyes. 'No, you can't hit her this time.'

The hall telephone rings relentlessly. Philip stares at it, caught in its cry. He manages to drag himself away from its shrieking tones, edging away in between its rings, certain he can hear the caller's voice. He can't fathom out what they're saying but their antagonism makes him tremble. He withdraws into the kitchen. The kettle reaches boiling point and subsides, briefly stifling the ringing phone. Philip walks over to the kettle and stands, subdued for a moment, composing himself.

Next to the kettle in a regimental line is a cup, a teabag, a spoon and a bowl of sugar placed like surgical instruments. He takes a deep breath, jostling everything out of his head, until he visualises himself making a cup of tea in a precise and defined way. He reaches out for the spoon, but a plate slams down by the side of him, breaking the comfort of beginning the process. Mrs Sullivan is standing next to him, displeasure holds her features. The telephone cuts dead.

'Cold, I tell you! It's not good enough.'

Her vice-like grip clamps Philip's hand and plunges it into the breakfast. He can feel his fingertips breaking the cocoon layer of mouldy skin and puncturing the sloppy mess on the plate.

'I've never seen anything so despicable.' Mrs Sullivan's grip loosens.

He snatches his hand away and sees the imprint is deep blue, like a bruise, spun in threads of white mould. The breakfast heals, changing back to the normal inviting colours.

Philip concentrates on the teacup, wanting the ritual to carry him away.

'You haven't heard the last of this.' Mrs Sullivan tuts and wearily saunters away from him.

Philip pours the boiling water into the teacup. The telephone rings again. He wanders over to the office door and opens it. Adrian has his back to him, poised at the computer.

'How much is this all costing?' Philip asks.

Adrian's fingers glide across the keys.

'On the breakfasts you're losing ...' He stops and then giggles. 'It'd be alright if you got it right first time.'

'What did you say?'

Adrian ignores him. 'And on the evening meals ...' His voice crumbles to another giggling fit. 'It's a joke, isn't it?' Adrian points at the monitor. 'Just look how it's all tallying up.'

'I always knew it was wrong to hire you,' Philip says.

Adrian's finger hits the monitor and slides down over the columns of numbers.

Philip slams the office door and returns to the half-full cup. He takes hold of the kettle, the familiarity soothes him. The telephone leaps into life again. Clumsily the kettle slips out of his hand, knocking the cup and sending it smashing to the floor. He sucks in a large breath, stopping himself from bursting into tears. Boiling water floods over the kitchen worktop, draining to the floor. He looks helplessly at the broken cup and the kettle pumping out its water.

Mr Reynolds places his breakfast next to him. Philip stares at the cup and kettle, reaching out to them, wanting nothing else to invade his concentration. But he can feel the annoyed breath of Mr Reynolds on the side of his face.

'Disgusting!' Mr Reynolds snarls. 'What on earth is this?' A light spray of saliva moistens Philip's ear. 'I'm not paying for this, it's a health hazard!'

Philip hears the keys of the computer tapping away followed by another fit of laughter.

Philip sits cupping Helen's hand while she lays tucked up in bed. It seems absurd but it's as if her hand is somehow draining the warmth from him. Mr Cole bites down hard into a thick slice of toast.

'Are you sure you don't want this?' Mr Cole propels crumbs from his mouth.

Helen scrunches up her face, exaggerating her distaste at him being there. Oblivious, Mr Cole takes another slice from the plate on the bedside table and gingerly eyes the cup of tea next to it. Michelle fidgets by them, not wanting to be there.

'You've got to get some rest,' Philip says.

'I'll be fine.' Helen scratches at her legs and stomach giving her momentary relief from the pain.

'She needs to see a doctor.' Mr Cole chews on the piece of toast. 'Take her back to where you found her.'

'Michelle, pass your mother her tea,' Philip says.

Stubbornly Michelle blanks him and walks to the chest of drawers.

'Michelle, please.'

'I'll get it.' Mr Cole butts in to defuse the building tension between them.

He passes the tea while Michelle opens a drawer and pulls out jumpers, trousers and anything else that's in there.

'Michelle! Get away from there.'

Philip grabs her with an alarming force, her shock shoots like a bolt of electricity up his arm. He swings her around to face him. Michelle's startled but still manages to hold her sandwich box.

'What are you doing with that?' Philip asks. 'Do you have to keep carrying it about with you?'

'You had to keep her safe. Never too far away, didn't you?' Helen mumbles to herself, sinking into her own confusion.

Philip stares at the sandwich box. A faint smile illuminates Michelle's face. She lets go of the box and it hits the floor with a thud. Its weak plastic clasps fling open, spewing its contents over the floor. Philip's frozen to the spot as the faint smell of jasmine hits him. Memories swoop down, picking hard at him like vultures on the dry remains of a carcass. There are broken pieces from Frances' musical jewellery box. He can make out part of the black lacquered lid embedded with shells. Its spiked drum turns, springing its comb fingers to life, and it plays. Each note resonates through his body as he stares at the items scattered across the carpet.

There are photographs of Frances and Michelle together, and of his mother and father. Some of Michelle's case studies and a few of the guesthouse work schedules she has drawn on. He can make out the remains of Michelle's broken mobile phone, the neglected Barbie doll with the picture of the soldier stuck to it, the patterned strips of fabric from Frances' dresses. But every single thing has been sliced up and then attempted to be put back together again, only this time with a completely different insight and reasoning. Bits of mobile phone are stuck to photographs that have been ripped up and rearranged with others. The ones of Michelle are woven with strands of Barbie's hair, all looking like an abstract jigsaw puzzle that can only be understood by the person who created it. All linked up with packing tape and splatters of mud.

In amongst all of this is Frances' silver engagement ring. It's untouched, not linked to anything as if it has made it's own space on the floor. It shines out at Philip, blinding his attention to everything else. He had saved hard for it and planned where he would ask her. It had to be out on the small pier at the mouth of the harbour. He thought maybe he should have proposed in Swindon, enforcing his commitment to her, but it felt too rushed. He wanted everything to be just right. He wrestles and pushes away the moment, discarding the cool evening breeze coming off the sea, wanting to erase the taste of happiness and hope fizzing on his tongue, letting him feel connected and at peace with the world. And the view from the pier, the arrangement of colours and patterns of the clouds delicately formed in the sky never to be seen that way again. The moment he saw her face light up like never before. His body trembles.

Helen mutters to herself. 'He said it would be alright.'

She snatches the cup of tea away from Mr Cole, watching Philip's every move. Mr Cole frowns as Helen takes a sip as the music drum begins to run out of steam. Philip kneels down and picks up the ring.

'It's beautiful, don't you think?' Michelle reaches out to touch it.

Her sincerity heightens his emotions.

Philip places the ring in the palm of his hand, noticing there are translucent chrysanthemum petals delicately wrapped around it. Michelle gazes dreamily at it.

'It's so special,' she says.

Philip's thoughts are locked onto the engagement ring. Their wedding had been disappointing, he could see it in Frances' face. She said it didn't matter that her family wasn't there but her sadness peered out between her smiles. He carefully touches it as if reaching out into that evening, when it was just the two of them joining together and making their worlds a different, better place.

'Boys! Mum was right.' Helen shudders as she says the words, the realisation hitting her hard and fast.

Her hand goes limp and the tea slips, washing over the duvet. The cup bounces on the bed and is propelled to the floor. Helen shrieks out in agony, seizing her stomach.

Philip drops the ring as the last strained notes from the drum play out.

'Don't let it go!' Michelle cries.

Torn, Philip rushes back to Helen. In all the commotion Michelle calmly watches the ring hit the short-pile carpet and roll towards the chest of drawers.

'You can't let her go,' Michelle says quietly to herself.

Philip holds Helen's hand, fear and pain are cut deep on her face. Her hand folds over his tightly. Mr Cole stuffs the last piece of toast in his mouth and chews thoughtfully.

'You've got to call Steven but not my parents. Please promise me.' Helen's eyes are wide open, pleading to him. Another pain shoots from her stomach, her face screws up, trying to will the agony away. 'Please, tell him there's no need for him to be afraid.'

A knowing smile scrolls across Mr Cole's face. 'What did I tell you. You wouldn't listen. You can elaborate the past as long as you don't dismiss it. That's when it lays waiting with spite for you, no matter what you do. It's impossible to deny it.'

A dense black liquid spreads across the duvet. Philip snatches his hand away, it throbs at being held so tight. He tries to wrench the duvet from Helen but she grips it hard. He turns to Mr Cole for reassurance, but he shrugs his shoulders, and looks away.

Michelle lays flat on her stomach, body packed against the chest of drawers, reaching out to hook the elusive ring. She stops. She can hear someone, someone familiar. The voice is faint but it still provokes a deep connection to her. Its tone soothes her, calling out to her in her imprisoned state. The veins of the translucent petals around the ring flush with colour and life. She draws her hand from beneath the chest of drawers and listens to the voice coming from beyond the door.

'We've got to go.' Michelle gets to her feet, anxiously wanting Philip to react.

Helen rolls on the bed in a torturous pain that tears at her legs and stomach. Mr Cole sneaks behind Philip, lifts up the duvet and absorbs the image of Helen's smooth, naked legs.

Helen glares at him. 'Get lost!' She snatches the duvet from him, covering herself up.

Philip turns back to the disturbance that has blown up behind him. 'What's the matter with you?' he asks, dragging Mr Cole away from Helen.

'Get him away from me,' Helen shouts.

'Do you really not get it yet?' Mr Cole casts a look of concern to Michelle. 'I can't tell you in front of the girl.'

Philip takes hold of him.

'Please, don't crease the shirt,' Mr Cole says, trying to loosen Philip's grip.

Philip escorts him out of the room. They don't even notice Michelle lingering in tow.

'Don't listen to him,' Helen shouts through the biting pain.

They step into the hall. Mr Cole yanks his arm from Philip's hold. 'Do you mind!' He brushes down his shirt. 'I told you, there's no need for that.'

Helen's cries reach a desperate level. Mr Cole tuts and slams the door on her.

Instant silence follows.

'Doesn't she go on! Right drama queen that one, as if you don't know.'

'What's going on?' Philip asks.

'Suited together, you two,' Mr Cole replies, with a patronising grin.

'What is your problem? What were you doing in there?' Philip views him with suspicion. 'Have you given her something?'

Mr Cole looks down his nose at him as if Philip has toppled off the evolutionary ladder. 'I beg your pardon?'

'I've had enough of this.' Philip turns to go back into the room.

Mr Cole blocks his way. He notices Michelle and feels uneasy at her being there.

'Think, Philip,' Mr Cole whispers, his eyes narrowing.

'Get out of my way, I haven't got time for this.'

'Philip, please.'

Michelle tugs at Philip's shirtsleeve. 'You've got to come.'

Philip snatches it away.

'What the hell's the matter with you two?'

'Please, Philip, listen to me,' Mr Cole says, calculating how low the volume of his voice should be to exclude Michelle.

'No!' Philip says.

A strangled silence wedges itself between them. Philip stares at Mr Cole but his attention is locked on the stairs. He can hear footsteps descending.

'Where's Michelle going?'

'Philip – listen.'

'What is she doing?'

He moves towards the stairs but Mr Cole blocks his way.

'No Philip, don't follow her. I told you not to go after Helen. Begged you. I can't control it any more, it's out of my hands. I was doing it for the good of us all. It's all gone now. You must see that.'

'Stop this!'

295

Philip pushes past him and looks down the short flight of stairs, the fire door at the bottom closes. He takes to the stairs, relieved that Mr Cole is following him closely but afraid at what he has said and at the anxiety etched on his face.

'I don't want you to get hurt.' Mr Cole hovers around him, but Philip isn't listening. 'Philip –'

'Shhh.' Philip's body locks and he holds the fire door open. 'Can you hear that?'

Mr Cole shakes his head.

Philip rushes along the landing and then down the second flight of stairs. Mr Cole pursues him, attempting to keep up, but it's precarious in his choice of footwear. Philip hears voices. He stops, backs up the second flight, crouches down in the shadows and peers through the bars of the banister. A queue of guests are waiting patiently along the landing. Mr Cole catches up and joins him, creating a clumsy spectacle behind him. Philip gives him a stern look but Mr Cole ignores him. He slips the stiletto shoe off and massages his foot. Unimpressed, Philip peers back through the banister. The fire door has been propped open by the guests filing in. Michelle is there, she waves at them both. He feels vulnerable and pulls away.

Mr and Mrs Sullivan stand behind Michelle.

'I bet we've missed it,' Mr Sullivan sighs.

'You can't rush this sort of thing,' Mrs Sullivan says.

Mr Sullivan glances to Michelle. 'Anyway we're not the only ones,' he says, 'look who's in front of us.'

Philip looks uneasy as Michelle disappears through the fire door. It slowly retracts, letting in a silence to the landing. A clammy sweat sticks Philip's palms to the banister. He judges the coast is clear and descends the stairs. Mr Cole puts his stiletto back on and follows him. Philip takes hold of the fire door before it clicks shut. He scans the dimly lit cul-de-sac and is met by an unearthly scream bellowing from one of the rooms. He turns to Mr Cole but his bewildered expression only reflects his own.

Philip and Mr Cole can hear voices coming from room 3. They concentrate hard but can't decipher what anybody is saying. The fire door jolts shut behind them, making them both flinch. Philip turns to Mr Cole, wishing he would put his guide's cap back on and explain everything that's happening. What has he done, is it really his fault? Has it really all gone? What he would give to go back to when Mr Cole made everything so effortless, letting life magically fall into place. But he's met with the same mirrored reflection, this time with a growing fear he thought he could deny in himself.

Carefully he opens the door. The curtains are closed, keeping the overcast day at bay. The guests are standing around the bed obscuring what is happening. Michelle beams out a smile and beckons them over. Mrs Sullivan pulls Michelle close to her. Philip and Mr Cole approach the bed as the guests shuffle out of their way, the human curtain revealing what is enthralling them all.

Lying on the bed is the withered body of Mrs Pritchard. She's slumped, exhausted. Her wrinkled skin covered in sweat, her nightgown sodden and clinging tight to her body. The bed sheets have been stressfully twisted and pulled like chewing gum, the duvet thrown and discarded in a heap on the floor. As they approach they can see smears of blood trailing from her to the far side of the bed. The guests methodically manoeuvre around to see what's there. Mrs Pritchard's grey hair dangles in clumps matted with sweat, nightgown pulled up, exposing her bony knees, her elderly skin raised over the veins of her legs. Her husband Stephen is beside her, tenderly dowsing her brow with a sponge. They try to understand what they're witnessing – it doesn't make sense, she looks like she's recovering from the rigours of childbirth.

Michelle uncouples herself from Mrs Sullivan's embrace and makes her way through the small crowd of guests to the other side of the bed, constantly wanting to run her fingers on the white sheet.

'I think we had better leave,' Mr Cole whispers to Philip.

He ignores him and weaves through the guests, pursuing Michelle.

She pushes her way to the side of the bed and stops, staring down into the narrow space between the bed and the wall.

Mr Cole stands there, frantically muttering to himself.

Philip reaches Michelle's front row position. Everybody is desperate to see what is on the floor. He peers over Michelle to see what all the fuss is about. He's unsure how to comprehend what he sees. It looks like a small skinned seal is lying abandoned on the floor, flinching in its last moments of life. Protectively he touches Michelle on the shoulder.

She turns back to him, her face filled with a heavy helping of hope.

'I can't believe it,' Michelle says. 'You came to see her. Isn't she beautiful.'

She moves forward and his hand slips away from her shoulder. Lovingly she reaches out to touch the blood-covered mound.

'Michelle, what are you doing?' Philip asks.

She stops as a face merges from the form. Philip watches intensely but he can't accept what he's seeing. He bites hard on his lip, tasting blood in his mouth.

'Ouch!' Mr Cole touches his mouth and examines the traces of blood on his finger.

'Frances …' Philip says the name softly, slipping it tightly under his breath but the name rings out inside his head. He feels queasy, it spins him around and around. Mr Cole pushes to the front of the compacted crowd. Frances looks up at him. She swallows, clearing her throat.

'Is this it?' Her emotions slip through, shaking the words like the tremor of a small earthquake. 'Tell me, Philip, is this it?'

He doesn't answer her.

'Is this how you saw me?' Frances asks.

'No, not like this. No this is wrong.' Philip shakes his head.

'No it's not, you still don't see me, do you? After everything, how can you Philip?' Frances' voice is still not able to defuse her trembling. 'You could never see past it. Never see me. Always the cancer, never me.'

'Mum!' Michelle gleefully turns to Philip, wanting him to share in her joy.

'This has gone far enough.' Mr Cole takes off his stiletto shoe and holds it aggressively in his hand.

'No!' Philip tries to stop him but Mr Cole shoves him to one side. He falls backwards, cushioned by some of the guests.

Philip closes his eyes tight, wanting the distorted image of Frances to disappear and for her to be standing there. Her beautiful smile radiating, maturing but never dulling to the years.

'No, please don't!' Frances screams.

Michelle takes hold of Mr Cole's arm and bites deep but he doesn't flinch.

Philip slumps to his knees, holding himself tight, swaying gently. Mr Cole strikes with the pointed heel of the shoe. Frances lets out a frightened shriek and slides effortlessly to one side. He misses and the stiletto heel crunches at the impact.

'That's it, show your true colours,' Frances says. 'When it all gets too much for you, lash out.'

Mr Cole is about to strike again but she sinks into the carpet and disappears.

A stillness holds everyone.

They scan the room, searching for clues to her whereabouts. The whole of the guesthouse shudders like it has been brought back to life from a long suppressive sleep. Michelle closes her eyes, standing there as if she's bathing in the warmth of the sun.

Mr Cole sinks onto all fours, hitting the floor again and again. 'Damn you!' he shouts. 'Damn you!'

Philip reaches out to touch Michelle but she instinctively pulls away, eyes still shut. Mr Sullivan stands protectively in front of her, backed up by Mrs Sullivan.

Michelle turns and faces him. There's a glimmer of concern for him he hasn't seen in a long time. 'You'd better go Dad, please go now.' She skirts around Mr Sullivan.

'I'm not like that, do you hear me?' Mr Cole repetitively hits the floor and tumbles backwards into the crowd.

The guests encircle him. From nowhere a fist strikes him on the side of the face.

'What the –' Mr Cole holds his stinging cheek, cushioning the pain.

Mrs Reynolds lashes out, kicking him hard in the chest. He groans in agony. He looks up at the wall of guests, his eyes glare at them. Philip clenches his stomach in pain, gasping for air. Kicks and punches burst, raining down on Mr Cole. It doesn't matter how psychically fragile the guests look, the precision of each punch, of each calculated strike always has an agonising result.

Pain rips through Philip's body.

'Get away from me!' Mr Cole shouts out, vanishing beneath a blanket of guests all wanting their pound of flesh.

'Arrh!' Mr Cole shrieks. His voice sinks in amongst an incoherent soup of groans and thuds.

Philip struggles to the door, at every step battling against a downpour of malicious blows.

He falls out of the room, coughing and spitting blood onto the floor. The fire door wobbles in front of him as though underwater, the plates of his skull battling to absorb the onslaught. He stumbles into the door and collapses out onto the landing. His body whines, his head echoing the compressed thuds raining down like a tropical storm. He falls against the wall. Bruises blossom on his face. He swallows, tasting blood running freely down the back of his throat. Cradling his stomach, his body feels as if it's on fire, his legs give way, buckling at the relentless attack. The landing moves, circling him like a predator waiting for the right moment to strike. He stumbles and falls down the stairs, every step thrusting out at him like a clenched fist or a vicious kick, until he lands slumped in the hall.

17

The world beyond the front door of the guesthouse beckons Philip, filling him with hope. Somehow he musters up enough energy to get to his feet. Exhausted and bathed in pain, he staggers over to the day door. The streetlight beams through a concoction of blood and tears distorting his view. He tries to open the door but his hand is broken and swollen. Disheartened he watches his hand slide off the handle, propelled by a layer of sweat and blood. His battered body is nearing the point where it's running from moment to moment, each one having to dig deeper to inspire him to carry on.

Feebly he tries the handle again, this time leaning against it. He pushes his battered arm against the door handle and an immense shooting pain fires through his body, the last drops of strength are slipping away. He collapses headfirst against the door, body flinching as more sadistic punches surge at him. Blood races up through his throat violating his taste buds. His mind is close to blacking out, his body crying out for the peaceful serenity of unconsciousness, to be taken into its oasis and to have a chance to regain strength.

Nervously he lets out a breath expecting the onslaught to continue. Someone whispers behind him. He concentrates on the soothing sound. The more he focuses the more the pain falls away from him. He can almost visualise the whisper expanding in the air, revealing more and more voices.

Pain slips away from his body making him feel strangely fresh, awoken as if he has stepped out into a bright cool sunlight after a heavy storm. The voices surround him washing over him and cleansing his body of its assault. He opens his eyes and realises he's lying flat on the floor, caught in a pool of natural light emitting from beneath the dining room door. He touches his face, the swelling and the rawness has gone and to his surprise he can feel he's losing an erection he wasn't aware he had.

Slowly he lifts himself up. The alluring glow is broken by silhouettes of people inside crossing the room. He turns back to the day door. The handle slowly turns, its mechanism ringing out as it casually opens, leading to the front door and to the unseen night. But all he can think of is the clattering of cutlery drawing him to the dining room.

As Philip walks into the dining room he can't believe his eyes. All the guests are happily eating their breakfast as if nothing has happened. The door closes behind him. It's a beautiful morning with sunshine radiating into the room from the bay window. Cautiously he walks amongst them, all merrily eating, but something's not right. He can't put his finger on it. He looks out through the window seeing the bay captured perfectly, the morning light flickering on the sea's surface. He notices a couple strolling hand in hand along the sea front. There's a man walking a dog. Philip tries to hold the image but something still feels wrong.

The couple start arguing. The man pushes the woman then hits her hard in the face, she falls to the floor. The dog turns on its master, biting into his hand. He screams silently in agony, his cries lost to the rising noise of cutlery scraping against plates. Philip turns back to the guests who are devouring their food at an incredible rate, faster and faster. Someone behind him tugs hard on his shirt.

'We want more!' Mr Reynolds points his knife eagerly at his half-devoured plate of food.

His wife shovels food into her mouth yet she has tears running down her cheeks with no sign of them letting up.

'Do you hear me?' Mr Reynolds taps his knife and fork on the table.

Paralysed, Philip stares at the plate. There's a thick expanding pool of blood draining from the sausage, immersing the rest of the breakfast.

'I'll get you a –' Philip begins.

He tries to make sense of it all the way he always does, building an obscure logical explanation he can grasp hold of, hoist up and declare as the truth. But not this time. A drop of blood hits the plate. Mr Reynolds has thin trails of blood oozing from his nose and tear ducts. He stressfully blinks, turning the pupils of his eyes to a deep crimson. Philip backs away.

'If I could just touch her face again.' Mr Reynolds looks mournfully at his wife, his voice quivering as he subdues the emotions that want to burst out of him. Tears stream down his wife's face as she continues to eat at a momentous rate.

'I never had you wrong!' a man's voice says sarcastically from behind him.

Philip turns around, it's Adrian. He's sitting next to Michelle, he hadn't noticed them there before. Michelle stares at him, not moving a muscle. He can almost feel her peering inside of him, shining a light on all his misdemeanours. Her face bursts with change. It's becoming older, connecting with his last memories of her before she died, but still her body remains that of a young girl. Philip's eyes water over. She's a young woman, the way she – the way she was. He repeats it over and over but he won't let himself free from its riddle, he doesn't have the strength to face the answer. He's engulfed by an overwhelming desire to break-down and beg her for forgiveness, but without even knowing what he wants her to forgive him for.

'It doesn't make sense.' Michelle touches her face. 'Why – why be that way with Mum?'

The guests' eating has accelerated to an incredible speed, stuffing food into their mouths until they begin to choke. Their contempt for him shines through their expressions, through their powerless frowns, through the tears blurring their eyes, through their bodies contorted and hunched on the dining room chairs.

'What have you done to her?' Adrian asks. 'Take a look at her!' He grabs hold of Philip's arm to make him face the freak show he has created.

Philip tries to turn away.

'This is unreal! Have you any idea?' Adrian's tone is walking a tightrope of anguish and laughter. 'You know, it's bad enough when someone's careless in a car, a wrong decision, a trivial distraction.' His laughter is empty and shallow. 'Or, maybe …' He claws his fingers across his forehead. 'A misjudgement when crossing the road.' The words stick thick to the back of his throat, making him feel queasy at their acrid taste. 'Even a disease chipping away, at least then you can scrape together some hope, define it to a greater plan. But …' He pauses. 'I can't understand this. Not this. How could you? What right do you have?' Pure hatred radiates from his eyes. 'Tell me, you fucker, tell me!' He bares his teeth, lips quivering uncontrollably.

Philip shudders as Adrian's repulsion for him clambers over his body, raking through his flesh making it crawl on the bone. The sound of knives and forks scraping over empty plates heightens the sensation.

'Poor, poor Philip,' Michelle taunts. 'Does it make you feel better seeing me like this?' She pulls at her dress, getting lost in its pattern. 'Was it easier then? Is that what you think?'

Philip wipes a hand on his trousers, the material soaks up his sweat.

'Shout at me, order me about. All nice and simple then wasn't it? No answering back,' she says. 'I wanted you to let me grow up and not resent me for it.' She looks up at him. 'It was all I wanted from you.' Her expressions become difficult to read. Her lips squeeze in tight.

'I don't know what you mean,' Philip replies.

Adrian notices blood dripping onto his shirt. He touches his face and examines the blood on his fingers.

'Working me to the bone,' he laughs nervously. 'You'll have to put my money up. I'm not cheap, not cheap at all.'

Philip falls back into one of the tables. Its contents hurtle at him like a mudslide while Mr and Mrs Reynolds sit either side of the chaos still vigorously eating.

Then instantly the charade of the dining room vanishes.

Daylight switches to night as if someone has thrown a switch. The guests' features remould into their last moments of life, their final desperate gasp captured on their faces. Their muscles relax, blood dries and flakes surrendering to their decomposing state. One of the table legs gives way from underneath him and Philip tumbles onto the floor.

Plates of decaying food, stained cutlery and cups of tea cultivating mould all slide and crash onto the floor. A weight falls on Philip's chest followed by a stench that rolls and curls around his lungs. Frantically he lifts the overbearing weight of Mrs Reynolds from him. Her head sways, hair hanging in bloodied clumps. Terrified, he pushes her away. His eyes adjust, sieving through the dark. Her dead state makes him tremble in a bitter disgust. He scrambles to his feet, staring at the bodies scattered and slouched on chairs around the room. The sight of them hits him hard almost knocking him back to the floor.

Philip hears a snuffling sound and looks around the room but nothing moves.

'You can't leave me. Not here,' Michelle says, 'not like this.'

Michelle retracts her hand from Adrian who is face-down at the table. Stirring whispers dart from body to body. She slides off the chair and approaches Philip. The whispers turn to a thick vocal fog, layers of groaning and spiteful tones.

'Come on Michelle.' Philip attempts to grab her arm but she briskly pulls it away. 'What are you doing?' he asks.

'Are you sure you really want me?'

'Stop this, Michelle.'

She feels a strange frenzy of needle-like jabs over her arm and rubs at it, trying to eradicate the pain.

'Are you sure?' she asks. 'Is this what you really want?'

He shakes his head, denying what she is saying and picks her up. Putting all his focus on the dining room door, blanking out everything else in the room, but he's taken aback at how bulky and awkward she is in contrast to how she appears. He approaches the door, wrestling with the stench that hangs in the room, feeling the different textures his feet step into. He carries her out and stops in the hall. The orange glow of the streetlight floods in through the front door. Michelle fidgets in his arms. The hatred from the guests is alive and clambering over him, staring out at him from the thick darkness of the dining room. He turns to the kitchen at the end of the hall and walks on, noticing Michelle's protests begin to subside the closer they get to the kitchen door.

In the silent gloom of the kitchen Michelle peers worriedly over Philip's shoulder. He puts her down and closes the door.

'This can't go on any more,' Michelle says softly.

'What do you want from me, Michelle?' he snaps.

'I want Mum back. The way she really was, not the way you saw her.' She caresses her arm.

Philip can just make out her awkward expression in the hazy light.

'Please don't Michelle.'

'I'm waiting for you, you've got to let her in. You know you have to.' She rubs harder at her arm. 'I've seen you, you always want her approval to say you're doing the right thing.'

'No, I can't. Don't make me Michelle.'

'I can't make you. You know that.'

He walks away from her and switches the kitchen light on. Immediately Mr Cole bangs on the back door frantically, trying to get out. Fear radiates from him, his face swollen, covered in cuts and bruises. Michelle sinks to the floor, muttering to herself.

'We've got to get out of here. It doesn't matter what they do to us, we can cope. We can get through this together.' Mr Cole's eyes plead for reassurance. 'It's our only chance.'

'I don't know what to do.' Philip glances back to Michelle.

'For fuck's sake, Philip, what's the matter with you? Make a decision for once. That's all I'm asking!'

Mr Cole strides to the kitchen table and picks up one of the chairs. Philip stands in the way of the door.

'It's no use.'

'Have you got a better idea?' Mr Cole's grip loosens letting a chair leg rest on the floor.

'I can't leave.'

Mr Cole shakes his head. 'Get out of my way,' he growls, lifting the chair up.

'I can't go. They can't do anything to me – the police, the courts. What do they know? Imprison me? That's a joke, look at me. Where do you think I already am?'

'You stupid piece of shit!' Mr Cole spits. 'They're our tickets out of this mess, can't you see.' Enraged, he throws the chair across the floor and takes hold of Michelle.

'Don't,' Michelle says faintly. 'Please just leave me.' She tries to kick out but her leg drags lifelessly down his shinbone.

'You know what I could do to her …' Mr Cole's eyes flicker between hate and desperation.

'Please don't hurt her.'

Philip raises his hands, begging with every molecule of his body.

'That's a bit rich coming from you. I should drop the caring father routine, it doesn't sit well.'

'How can you say that?'

'How quick you forget.'

Philip shakes his head. 'Leave her.'

He tries to uncouple Mr Cole's welded hold on Michelle.

Mr Cole unleashes a precise and accurate head butt, hitting Philip straight between the eyes. He staggers back, dazed, holding his face. Mr Cole shoves him out of the way, dragging Michelle to the back door. She doesn't react to him, lost, muttering to herself in a trance-like state.

'I'm not like that, do you hear me? I'm not like that,' Philip cries. The kitchen spins round and around. He turns to the wooden block of kitchen knives.

Mr Coles shoves his face right next to Michelle's. 'That's it, no point in struggling. You know what you'll get, don't you young lady!'

She closes her eyes. His stale alcohol breath makes her bladder go weak. She lets out a defeated murmur.

'There's no running to Mummy now,' Mr Cole says.

Michelle goes limp.

'It's over,' Philip says. 'It ends here, right here!'

He stands at the worktop with his back to them.

'Give in to it, Philip.' Mr Cole lifts Michelle up by the scruff of her neck like a dead animal and kicks at the door. 'Accept it and give in to the consequences.'

Philip turns to them, a knife poised over his wrist. The artificial light bounces off its enchanting surface. The banging against the back door fades from him. He pushes the blade down, watching it sink beneath his skin. A burning pain runs up his arm but to his surprise it has an addictive taste to it. He drives the knife across his wrist, cutting into the network system of his veins. Mr Cole screams out in agony. He lets go of Michelle and she hits the floor.

Mr Cole cradles his forearm. 'What are you doing?'

Philip peacefully stares at the blood draining out of his body. Mr Cole snatches the knife from him and throws it across the floor. He yanks a tea towel hanging on a hook and wraps it around his open wound. Philip sees his own wound pull itself together.

'It's not going to end like this,' Mr Cole says.

'It's over, it's already over.' Philip sighs.

'Please, Philip. We can get through this. We can. There's always another way.'

'Stop it. Please, stop it!' Michelle begs, covering her ears with her hands, her bottom lip quivering as she suppresses her tears.

'Are you in there?' Philip stares deep into Mr Cole's eyes.

Mr Cole doesn't say anything. Briefly his eyes change, warmth bathes them as forgiveness washes over him. His question is answered.

'That's it, Mum, don't stand in his way,' Philip whispers. He tenderly touches Mr Cole's hand. A smile holds his own. He sees the essence of his dad breaking the surface of Mr Cole's face. 'I – I – l-love …' Philip stutters.

His surging thoughts create a bottleneck in his throat. There's so much he wants to say, to sit down with him and talk about. He longs to put every clock away, hide the sun and ignore the moon. Hear the tone of his voice, savour the way he would laugh, give him a fatherly wink, comrades trying to keep the family together. He'd even love to hear the big band music cutting out a swing number, even though that was always put on whenever his parents were rowing in a futile attempt to keep it from the neighbours. His mother didn't need much of an excuse to leave the house, day or night. He never thought he could get rid of his frustration at the way his dad never stuck up for himself, but now the feeling is draining from him.

He's staring deep into his own bitterness, the part of himself he never wanted to recognise, always trying to avoid. He used it as a crutch through his father's death, whenever life turned on him, it never left him. He hid it deep, never letting it dull over the years, leaking like a dumped barrel of toxic waste contaminating his pool of life, changing its ecology. The abnormal became the normal, the bitterness became the sweet.

He turns away, embarrassed. If only he had the courage to hold his dad, to hear him breathe, recapture the way his presence used to make him feel safe and secure, just one last time, but he can't.

'I don't blame you.' The words tremble from Philip's lips. 'I just had to say …'

The veil of his dad slips away, and again he's staring at Mr Cole. A solitary tear ambles down his cheek and hangs there.

Michelle opens her eyes, the floor throbbing beneath her. A beat radiates through Philip's feet. He turns to Michelle. The vibration soothes her body. She places a hand on the floor stroking its rhythmic comfort, gathering her legs into a foetal position. Philip approaches her. The chequered green and white tea towel around his wrist is saturated in blood and is now dripping onto the floor. Michelle nuzzles her ear to the ground hearing the magical sound of a heartbeat.

Tentatively Philip looks down at her.

'Mum's worried about you,' Michelle says.

'Never thinking about herself. Always everybody else,' Philip says, blood dripping onto the floor and quivering in pools with each pulse.

Mr Cole stands by the worktop arguing with himself. Philip notices the cabinets are beginning to corrode, rust bursts spreading, devouring anything in its way, like the way the cancer ruthlessly attacked Frances.

'Why did you go? Was it me? Was I never good enough for you?' Mr Cole's expressions and body language hold Philip's father's perfectly.

'Stop going on about the same thing every time. We just changed, we both wanted different things.' Mr Cole is encased in a perfect impression of his mother, even getting the slight rocking of her head when her defences were up.

'No, you changed. You had it too good, that's your problem.' The nervousness in his father's voice makes it tremble. He always hated confrontation.

Screws and brackets snap, devoured by rust, sending cabinets sliding off the walls, crashing down with tremendous scrapes and bangs. Cupboards and drawers spew their contents over the floor, plates and bowls smash, splintering into unrecognisable pieces. The proud set of wine glasses for those special occasions Frances had on display, and the hidden-away mismatched collection accumulated over the years. All broken, covering the floor, but coming to a halt around Michelle and Philip like an island in an ocean of debris. He crouches next to her.

'What have I done?' Philip whispers.

Michelle tries to snuggle closer to the floor. He reaches out to touch her but his fingertips stop short. The kitchen table collapses with a damp crack, the legs rotten to the core. He looks up to see the oven standing in amongst the untouched kitchen units on the far wall. Its worn shabby appearance has been replaced by a gleaming surface as if straight off a production line.

Philip approaches it, debris crunching underfoot, mould igniting like fire spreading over the kitchen table. The corrosion follows him, flanking him. Running his fingers along the oven he's entranced by its gleaming freshness. He turns the oven on but it jerks back, switching itself off.

'Please Frances,' Philip says softly, his fingertips skating over its curves. 'I never deserved you. Never.' He lowers his head subserviently. 'Please.' His voice drops to a whisper.

The oven turns itself back on, hissing like a slashed tyre. Mr Cole rushes over, pushes him out of the way and tries to switch the gas off. 'No, God damn it, no!' he shrieks.

Michelle smiles and nods, encouraging Philip who calmly places a hand on Mr Cole's back. He jolts around and faces him.

'Philip, don't,' Mr Cole says, his voice panic-stricken.

'It's going to be alright.'

'What have I done?' Mr Cole asks, scouring the room. 'All I wanted was the family.' His breathing is sporadic but he perseveres. 'All for the family. You've got to believe me!'

Mould spreads over the worktop. Philip opens the cutlery drawer, its sides decaying at a rapid speed. He spots the lighter and takes hold of it, the drawer and the rest of its contents corrode and fall to the floor. In his hand the lighter shines at him as if he's connected to another soul, and finally found what he's been searching for. Mr Cole falls to his knees and sobs uncontrollably. Philip touches the back of his head, his other hand feeling a soothing peace draining from the lighter. He watches Mr Cole trembling and repetitively hitting at his leg. Philip sits down next to him, kisses him on the head and cradles him the way a loving mother would. He glances back to Michelle; her expressions are empty and lost but there are no questions left, no stones left to turn over, no more fumbling around in the dark anticipating what he should be looking for, what he should be doing.

Everything in his mind has come to an abrupt halt. The whole of his being is centred on the lighter, its robust shape releasing a comfort in him. Gone are the confused ideas to mull over what life is about like a series of boxes to tick, a list of proposed things he must do before he reached thirty, fourty or fifty. If he could manage to tick them all, only then could he look back and reflect with a triumphant smile and justify every choice with a knowing nod. Then he hadn't somehow failed. All that time considering and rigorously measuring what he had lost as if it was some sort of divine code. Crack it and everything would fall into place, and he'd be able to see everything for what it truly was. Then he would know why his future had been robbed from him. But this has all gone from him, every last energy-sapping drop. All he wants now is to feel his thumb pushing down, catching the rugged groves of the lighter. To smell its fumes bellowing out of its concealed chamber and catch a glimmer of its destructive aroma in his nostrils. He pushes his thumb down hard. The flame roars, thrusting up like a genie rushing out of its bottle. He throws the lighter into the oven, the hissing gas swirls in his ears.

The explosion throws him across the floor, broken crockery and glass slicing into his face and arms. The kitchen windows shatter, flames screaming out into the night. The blaze rages, consuming the air, igniting and incinerating anything in its path. Michelle lies on the floor, tranquil and untouched by the flames, watching them dance and play to an unheard magical piece of music. The blast retracts, losing its momentum, revealing its destructive embrace. The kitchen is charred, coated in a deep matt black. Random pockets of flames are dotted around the room. Objects implode, still smouldering in the intense heat.

Philip coughs and splutters, breaking the surface of consciousness. Michelle's hand brushes the thin layer of debris away from him. He squints, attempting to drive his vision through the swirling smoke that is rapidly becoming denser. Her hand touches his face and she comes into focus, giving the impression of her floating above him. He blinks, keeping the stinging smoke at bay. Lifting himself up, he wrestles with the pain ripping and slicing at every adjustment his body makes. The left-hand side of his face is unrecognisable, burnt to a deep charred crimson. His breathing is uneven, battling to gain a steady airflow. Michelle helps him to his feet. He glances back to the oven. It's been ripped apart, flames roaring uncontrollably from its exposed gas pipes. She pulls at his arm but he's reluctant to follow. Something is burning even brighter and more furious than the gas pipes. Philip watches as Mr Cole is consumed by flames.

It's only now Philip realises the blast has blown him far across the room. Mr Cole's voice cuts through the roar of the unrelenting flames, through the splintering of cupboard doors and shelves rotting and igniting.

'Always good for a drink, weren't ya?' Mr Cole says, the menace in his voice unrecognisable.

He calmly stands there, looking at Philip.

'Remember me, eh?' Mr Cole asks, his stance unfamiliar.

Philip's head is spinning, shifting through his memories, a sombre smell from room 8 coats his nostrils. The loneliness barks at him. Frances' death, a sickness rises from his gut, a patchwork of images weave themselves in no connecting logic.

Or do they?

Drinking at The Ship – the man at the bar. He was the image of Mr Cole. He doesn't know his name or where he came from, how he managed to be in that bar on that particular night. But he didn't care, all Philip knew was that he listened; nobody else did any more. Sheila the barmaid didn't listen; even Mike and Don, moulded into The Ship like the timeless beams and the solid oak bar. And Frank – he just nodded, his head buried analysing the racing forms.

This small stocky man was gone by the morning. He could see him leaving room 8, everything swaying. He had seen him ruthlessly going through his belongings, taking his money from his wallet. Drunkenly he'd tried to pull himself up from the bed, but the man had turned on him, hitting him again and again until he blanked out.

Days passed in the room. He'd waited like a dog expecting his master to return. He didn't want to think, he wanted to be guided and told what to do. He would snack when he couldn't stand the cries of hunger any more, his toilet routine depended on how necessary he thought it was. Sometimes he didn't bother, his tracksuit bottoms would eventually dry out. That's how he had lived his life, always waiting for something to happen, to put the ownership on someone else, never his fault, that would never do. Couldn't have that. He'd sat at the small table by the window and watched the sea hour after hour. Leaving Ian and Katie to sort out the breakfasts and evening meals. Ian virtually running the guesthouse.

The sea had always been a pleasant backdrop. He had never been enthusiastic about it, the way Frances had. There was no question in her mind when he asked her where they should start afresh. It felt like she had planned it all along. This part of the coast was like a magnet for her, the memory of happy childhood holidays ran deep. As he sat there looking out across the bay he began to understand the attraction. It opened up a sedating peace in him, calming his thoughts, its rhythmic charms never letting him down. Then the waves began to whisper to him, comforting him. He wasn't alone any more; he had found what he had been searching for. He had found the voice of Mr Cole.

Michelle helps him across the debris, manoeuvring him around the spreading flames. Every step gores at his nerve endings, but his stare never breaks from Mr Cole. He stands there lit in silence, captivated by Philip's every move as he disappears out of the kitchen. Michelle manages to lead him along the smoked-filled hall, the wallpaper bubbling and blistering at the intense heat. Unearthly moans holler from the dining room. They come to the bottom of the stairs. Philip momentarily glances to the outside world; it looks back, brooding and foreboding.

'Upstairs.' Michelle tugs at him. 'It's up the stairs.'

Exhausted, he turns to her, his skin hanging flimsily, crisp and burnt off one side of his face.

'What is it?' Philip asks. He notices one of her arms is out of proportion to the rest of her body. It dangles lifelessly by her side, swollen to a deep dark blue.

'You know. What you have been after.'

'I – I don't understand.' Philip can't help but stare at her arm.

She pulls it to her, not ashamed but annoyed at its interference.

'It's hidden in everything you do.'

He falls against the wall, his body shaking at his scolding burns.

'I can't do this.'

Michelle seizes his shirt and yanks it. His body winces at the uncaring force she unleashes.

'You need to see. You have to see, it's what you want. What you've always wanted.'

'I can't go on.' He gulps, thick tasteless blood coating his throat.

'There's no other way, you have to see it all. Only then you'll know.'

Every move his body makes, even the feeblest stretch of a muscle, is met by a ferocious slashing agony. It's left to pure determination to enable him to battle on. He feels he has been

317

stripped naked, his charred burns vulnerable and exposed while being dragged shackled through a dense thicket of barbed thorns. Somehow, with Michelle's help and guidance, he reaches the top of the stairs. He coughs a mixture of saliva and blood. Everything shimmers, viewing the world through a layer of suppressed tears. Glancing back down the mouth of the stairs, flames leap from the climbing smoke. His heart sinks as Michelle eagerly jerks at his arm to carry on. He turns to the third flight of stairs, his mind wanting to erase the previous journey and not compare it to what is waiting for him.

He doesn't know how long it's taken him to climb the stairs and struggle along the landing. How he managed to summon the strength to go through the fire door and face the flight of stairs leading to the top floor. The whole journey is now lost, taken away from him by an unscrupulous pain that reaches out and attacks him at every angle. He can still feel the heat of the flames alive and burning on his back. His body shakes out of control, not in pain but with fear. He watches Michelle's body move awkwardly as she guides him up the stairs, breaking down to a hobble as one of her legs expands and emulates her lifeless arm. She carries on, determined not to give up, letting him be encouraged by her purpose.

Philip looks at his bedroom door and hesitates. Suddenly the door dissolves. He can see the funfair in front of him, but he didn't have to travel out of town, following the coastal road. There's no dramatic windswept cliff path to venture down. He can see it where it always has been, in the bay near the pier where the pebbles stop and give way to sand. But it doesn't look right, none of it does. It's so small, the rides are all for children.

They're riding on the merry-go-rounds, beeping horns on cars that are linked to one another, parents hovering, enthusiastically waving and calling to them. A young girl looks up at him. She's holding a colourful windmill. It spins hypnotically in her hand. He feels a sickening revulsion washing over his body, like his whole world is being spun around and is trying not to topple over. The windmill draws him closer and closer, its pointed edges blur into a bright glowing sphere. He wants to push everything away, not wanting to get lost in it. But it's no use.

He hears Helen's voice.

'Listen to me, Philip,' Helen whispers. 'You know what I'm here for. You've got to help me. I need money.'

The windmill spins faster and faster. He reaches out to stop it turning and hears the door open. The funfair disappears and he realises he's in the bedroom. Michelle shuts the door behind them, not noticing the smoke has followed them into the room and is swirling around. Helen is sprawled peacefully asleep but she sits upright, afraid and trapped on her bed.

'Don't listen to him!' she cries.

She takes in Philip's punished body – the burnt disfigured face, his skin hanging, crisped and cracked, saturated in congealed blood. And Michelle by his side, holding him upright with every ounce of strength she can conjure-up, as she leads his frail body to the bed. He can sense he's at the brink of collapsing. But somehow he reaches the bed, riding high above the pain, not looking down into its void, not wanting to know what he would face if he falls.

He can't take it any more; his legs give way. His blood-stained hands smear the duvet but he still manages to call upon the last dregs of energy to get close to Helen. Michelle cautiously steps back, not wanting to get too near.

'I knew you wouldn't let me down.' Helen looks calmly at him.

He coughs deep and hard and turns to Michelle. 'What are you doing?' he asks.

She doesn't acknowledge him.

Helen's arms entwine over him, pulling him close. He hears that rustling sound again, mocking him, but this time

319

he can see the strips of packing tape wrapped tightly around Helen's dress.

'I don't know her,' Michelle replies.

'She's your mother.' He coughs hard.

'No, she's not.' Michelle looks at the floor. 'Tell me she's not.'

Smoke pumps under the door, building more and more. He coughs again, this time blood splatters his hand.

'Michelle, no,' Philip says.

'Tell me.' Her whole existence stretches out and pleads to him. 'I can't play in the garden any more.' She shakes her head. 'There's no more games to hide in.'

'Michelle.' Philip wants to hold her but he hasn't the strength. 'Come here.'

'I can't. It's not right,' she says.

'Leave her,' Helen snaps, to his surprise.

'It could have *all* been so perfect,' Philip sighs.

'No, you can't say that,' Michelle says. 'You can't deny how you feel about Mum. You've come this far.' Her eyes glisten, holding back her tears. 'Let her in, please let Mum in.'

'No – no, Michelle.' Blood spills from his clenched teeth as he fights his inner battle.

'What are you trying to do to us all?' Helen asks, glaring at Michelle.

'You've got to,' Michelle pleads. Philip looks at Michelle as the tears break free and roll down her face.

'Frances, she's – she – she's your mother.' Philip's salty tears sting at his exposed flesh.

'How can you!' Helen spits.

Michelle smiles, triggering blemishes that burst over her skin, changing its youthful glow to a cold lifeless pale blue, partnered in places with spectrums of purple.

Ashamed, Philip turns away from them both, wishing he could lose himself deep in the fabric of the duvet.

'She was always there for you,' Philip says. 'When it mattered, she never stopped loving you, she'll always be your mother.'

'What are you saying?' Helen shrieks. 'I loved her, I was just a kid, just a stupid kid. I wanted to do the right thing by her. I couldn't have brought a baby up, not by myself. Adoption would have been the best solution for everybody –'

Helen's rant thaws away.

Philip turns to Michelle, she's still smiling at him. It's as radiant as a summer's day even with her bitterly cold complexion. He can't remember the last time she smiled at him like this. Its sincerity warms him. Peacefully she wraps her small arm around her body as if a sharp chill has entered the room. Her neck muscles unshackle their support and her head rolls free.

She collapses to the floor in a strange distorted heap.

He sees her now as an adult, dead and decaying. Tears surge with a momentum leaking and biting at his face. He stares helplessly at her. The argument races at him. The disgusted look she gave him when he hit her, the struggle. Then when he fell on her, the groaning and cracking of her bones shrieking out at him followed by the silence. That awful endless silence.

'Don't look.' Helen's arms coil round his neck, adjusting his attention to her. 'Come on, Philip.'

He wants to turn back to Michelle but Helen holds his gaze.

That pure dense helplessness smothers him again. His fingertips running through Michelle's hair, questions coming out of nowhere as he crouched next to her. What have I done? What should I do? My God, is she dead? Is she really dead?

'Shhh.' Helen kisses him, her hold tightening.

Smoke piles up, erasing the pattern of the carpet and filling the room. The bedroom door gives way to the pillaging flames.

She pulls him to her. 'You're getting too close,' Helen taunts. 'You shouldn't have let Frances in. But you couldn't help yourself, could you? I'm in her clothes, aren't I? Wrapped up nice and tight so I won't fall apart.'

She holds his stare, the tone of her voice void of any emotion.

Philip's body shudders. 'How can I? She's always here.'

'Facing facts are we now. You've left it long enough, haven't you?' Helen whispers to him.

The wallpaper blisters and sags at the scorching heat.

'No, not like this.' His mouth is brittle and dry, cracking every time he speaks.

'Close your eyes, Philip. Close them.'

He can't fight it, he has no choice. He shuts his eyes puncturing the film of tears. Frightened, he tries to struggle from her embrace but he's too weak.

'No, please Helen.'

'Can you see all those pretty lights?' Helen asks. 'You can see them, can't you? Remember, Philip. The lights at the fair.'

'No – no,' Philip says with a muffled groan. 'You can't do this.'

'It's at the fair, isn't it Philip,' Helen mocks. 'That's where it all falls into place.' Her breath is hot and smells like a putrid drain.

Flames roar, ripping into the ceiling. It splutters and spews, igniting patches of the carpet.

'It was all different when we lived abroad. You know the place, don't you Philip?'

He opens his eyes; she stares back at him with utter contempt.

'You know where I mean,' Helen says. 'The hotel in Spain. Good old Mr Cole – enjoy the therapy did you?'

Part of the ceiling collapses, the noise temporarily deadens the roar of the flames.

'Poor Becky, in a car accident. Did it help you, make you feel better? A nice and tidy fantasy with plenty of self-pity. The plain pitiful truth was you couldn't stand Michelle not being here; she had her own life to lead. Have to be careful what you wish for, Philip. Just look, look at her lying on the floor next to us.'

Her embrace tightens.

'But where am I, do you know, Philip? Am I still in the hospital? Did you bring me flowers?' Helen giggles. 'Different ones this time, they're not even my favourite. Chrysanthemums were Frances' flowers remember? Of course you do. You had to bring her, didn't you. You couldn't help it, she's always there, isn't she? You can never get away from Frances, but then you never wanted to.'

He opens his mouth, gargling on a mouthful of blood. He swallows and the foul smell of damp decay pours into his nostrils and settles in his lungs, making him want to vomit. She puts her ear to his mouth to hear his response but he can't summon any more words. His body slouches to a defeated silence as he loses consciousness.

18

Philip tastes salt water rinsing through his mouth; he coughs. His wet clothes cling to him, draining his body heat, making him shiver. He can hear people's voices and the sound of waves breaking behind him. The smell of seaweed swelling in his lungs. He doesn't want to open his eyes in case the illusion is taken away from him. Pebbles nudge him. His body aches – not from the explosion, not from climbing the stairs, not from … He tries to grapple with what follows but it eludes him. No matter how hard he tries he can't remember anything else. He shifts, assessing his body; it feels like he's been lying face down on the beach for a long time.

Sluggishly he lifts himself up onto his knees. He can see the Old Pier. Teenagers are hanging around the arcade while the Chinese restaurant stacked and sticking out on top is getting ready for the lunchtime rush. A seagull calls, startling him. He looks in its direction but he can't see it, only a couple of terns squabbling over the remains of a crab on the shoreline. Rising to his feet he stands directly in line with the guesthouse. He doesn't move for a moment, letting the view soak in, making sure he's registering what he's seeing. The esplanade is awash with people taking in the summer sun. The Bay View glows, shining proudly alongside the others. There's not a single cloud in the sky. He's never seen such a vibrant uplifting blue before. His clothes are dry. He runs his fingers through his hair, feeling the seawater evaporate leaving fine traces of sand on his scalp and underneath his fingernails. The white bathing huts on the edge of the beach shimmer in the heat of the sun.

The air is full of people's voices scattered with bursts of laughter. He slips through one of the gaps in between the bathing huts and onto the esplanade. The guesthouse beams, immaculate, not a trace of imperfection. Gone is the worn blue of the front door, the neglected white window frames, the precarious broken guttering about to give way to the smallest of downpours; even the roof tiles shine like a set of well maintained teeth. He sniffs in the air, expecting to find paint fumes in amongst the smell of the sea, but instead he's hit by a wall of pollen.

Philip weaves through the people milling along like insects caught in a stream. Flowerbeds are in full glory stretching out either side of him. Families and couples spill out of the guesthouses, supplies held in inadequate bags, towels slung under arms, making a beeline for the beach. But no one is coming out of the Bay View. A few people are sitting on the blue and white benches marvelling at the sea. On one of them a small stocky man in a large overcoat is curled up in a foetal position shivering. Mr and Mrs White jog past him; they nod and carry on. He's about to turn back to the man on the bench when a seagull's cry startles him again. This time it's deeper and more sinister than before. He spins around and comes face to face with the gull perched on one of the bathing huts. It tilts its head to one side, giving him a menacing stare. An icy chill crosses his body. For a moment he hesitates, but he's compelled to venture on towards the guesthouse.

He reaches the front door, his hands cold and clammy. It opens, welcoming him into the tiled entrance hall. As he's about to step inside a shuffling sound comes from behind him, making goose bumps hoist up the hairs on the back of his neck. A harrowing cry almost stops his heart from beating. He looks down and is met by two seagulls simultaneously tilting their heads at him, taking in his reaction at their presence. They rear up, extend their wings and screech at him. Philip backs into the guesthouse and slams the door shut, barricading it with his body. An unsettling silence greets him. He takes a deep breath but he can't hear a sound, the outside world has been switched off. Not even the waves of the ocean breaking in the bay can be heard.

Philip finds the day door unlocked and walks into the hall. The interior is spotless with a wonderful smell of lavender caressing the air. It's decked out in old beige and brown wallpaper, a collision between the avant-garde and trying to be conservative in the seventies. He'd forgotten how awful it looked but it makes him smile. An old mahogany table stands in the far corner with a vase of dry grasses spilling out. He steps into the dining room and almost breaks down and cries at the sight of the tablecloths with their embroidered blue trim. They'd had them their first season at the guesthouse, but it didn't take long before they became tattered and had to be thrown away. The old cups and saucers are out. Frances had brought them at the same time. They ended up broken or discarded to the back of the cupboard until Frances reluctantly threw them away. She could find sentimental value in virtually anything. Yet here they are, back in their former glory, brilliant white with gold lines running around the rim. They're laid out with their cutlery to complete the set, not a stain or scratch on them. A framed print of one of Monet's paintings hangs on the wall; he never knew what it was called but it was one of Frances' favourites. There's a mother and child in the foreground making their way through a poppy field. In the background another mother and child are tucked away on a hill to the left. He's sure the picture ended up in the loft, frame broken, its colours faded by the sun. He can't believe he's looking at it. It seems lonely and lost on the wall as if waiting for all the other photographs and prints to come and join it.

A couple of PVC-covered chairs are huddled round an old-style TV set, designed in broad lines and protruding Dalek dials. He shakes his head, they're the chairs from Frances' flat. What happened to those chairs? He knew he didn't really care. They became a pet hate of his. Didn't matter what the weather was, they were awful. If they found naked flesh in the summer, they stuck to it like a limpet, scorching hot. And in the winter you might as well sit on the pavement outside and wait for the piles to congregate. He never thought he would admit it but to see them again chokes him. The whole dining room is the way it was when they first opened, Frances at the helm, enthusiasm running high. He can't help but think she might walk in at any moment. The embossed Victorian-style wallpaper, that was a real bastard to line up. His wandering thoughts break as he hears someone speak and the scraping of a kitchen chair. His body locks, focusing on the voice, but it turns to a faint laugh.

Making his way back into the hall, Philip lets his hand run over everything to clarify it's real, while a gathering expectation pumps through his veins like pure oxygen, heightening his senses. He opens the kitchen door and squints, his eyes adjusting from the soft light of the hall. The kitchen's spotless but it's different to the dining room and hall. This isn't the way the kitchen used to be; this is a different time, years later. Things had changed but there were still some original good old dependable features, the fridge-freezer, the whistling kettle and the knife rack on the old worktop all battling on. Sunlight breaks through the window bathing a segment of the kitchen where the table stands.

He hadn't noticed before but there's a woman sitting at the table with her back to him. She has shoulder-length hair wanting to be washed. He approaches her, trying to anticipate who she is.

Helen. For some reason her name sticks fast in his head.

'Is that you?' Philip asks. 'Is that you, Helen?'

She doesn't answer.

He walks around the table invading her space and stops. It is Helen, but she looks so different. She glances up at him, poised, as if she's about to say something, then looks disheartened and turns away. It's not just the cut of her hair that's different or the use of her make-up, it's also her facial expressions and her body language. She takes a drag from her dwindling cigarette, lighting up its end. He hears the faint tapping of fingers on a keyboard but they're not coming from the office, they're coming from the moving ash glowing from the cigarette's core. It radiates out an unsettling heat. She gestures to an empty chair that's been pulled out from the table.

'Helen,' he says, sitting down slowly.

Still she doesn't answer but takes another deep drag. The tapping escalates and subsides as she blows smoke into the air. Philip feels an overwhelming stinging heat on his face. She watches the smoke rise and fall, then stubs it out on the table by the side of an ashtray, next to another cigarette that's been snubbed out, its filter tip snapped to a ninety degree angle.

Philip turns away from her, his attention drawn to a splinter on the edge of the kitchen table.

'What's going on?' he asks, quietly.

'You tell me.' There's no hiding the bitterness in her voice but she still looks at him with a void expression.

'This isn't you.' He wedges a fingernail into the crevice of the splinter, not wanting to be drawn into her stare.

'Don't you think you've found me?' She watches the last strains of smoke dispersing.

'You toyed with me, didn't you?' Philip's voice quivers as he pushes harder with his fingernail. 'It's not a game. You can't make it into a game.'

'Why not?'

His lips tremble, his focus becoming lost to the protruding splinter. 'I thought I – I ...' The sentence buckles; he can sense an emotional tide is about to engulf him and drag him out into its vastness where he has no choice but to drown.

'I know, but whoever gets what they deserve?' Helen says blankly.

'So it was all just an act.'

'No. I thought you were ... well, kind of sweet, at first anyway. But love?' She shakes her head.

He surges harder in the crevice, desperate to tease the splinter out.

'Why did you do this to me?' Philip spits, his heart pounding as a sickness roams uncomfortably in his body.

'Come on Philip. You knew what I was up against. Don't be so naive about it.'

'That makes it alright, does it?'

'Stop trying to make me feel bad. You're pathetic sometimes. I was seventeen and pregnant. If it wasn't for Frances –'

'And look how you treated her!'

She grins.

'What's so funny?'

'Could be the only thing we have in common.'

'Don't compare me with you.' The moment he says it, he instantly regrets it.

'Oh no, I wouldn't want to do that, that would be a mistake.' Helen mocks him.

The splinter breaks away from the table and hangs precariously.

'I always disappointed Mum and Dad.' She looks impatiently at him. 'They were always too weak with me. I knew where I was with Aunty Frances.' She slips back in her chair. 'I had to come here. I needed time to think, decide what I was going to do with my life.' She pauses. 'And to work out how I really felt about Steve.'

'It wasn't like that.' Philip rips the splinter from the table, his eyes narrow, intensifying his glare. 'Why did you sleep with me, lead me on? Eh? You tell me that.'

'I didn't. That was a mistake, I've told you again and again. I was lonely and …' She points a trembling finger straight at him. 'And you took advantage of me. That's what happened.'

His hand tightens on the splinter, feeling it spearing into his skin.

'I wanted to call Steve, tell him about the baby but I couldn't. I didn't know how he felt about me.' Her teeth clench, reining in her frustration.

'You made me risk everything for you,' Philip shouts.

'Made you! Yes, that was it, you were the victim, always the victim.' She takes a deep breath. 'Found me drunk downstairs late at night, upset because of the mess I had made of everything. Of course it was me who led you on, wanting to drink more to take the pain away. Got you to help me upstairs to bed. Yes that was it. And while Frances was sleeping in the next room, I thought it was a good idea to have sex with you.' Helen turns away. 'I could barely walk. But what the hell. You didn't care!'

Philip slams his fist on the table. 'NO!'

' *"Risk everything!"* You wanted to, you were so embarrassing flirting with me in front of Frances like that.' She shakes her head. 'Why did you think I left? I couldn't take it any more. You made me sick.'

Philip screws his face up.

'It wasn't like that. You left because of Frances, not me!' Tears sprint freely over his flushed cheeks. 'Not me, not me.' He looks at her, eyes pleading. 'Why meet up with me then? Why call me? Explain that one.'

330

'I was desperate, what else could I do? There was no one else to turn to, it was that bad.' Her annoyance towards him still rides high. 'I picked the kids' funfair because I knew it would be a hard place for you to cause a scene, that's why. What were you thinking? Started talking about being a family like everyone else around us, wanted to make a fresh start. You didn't get it, what's wrong with you?'

'I – I …' His thoughts slip away from him. He slams a fist on the table feeling the sting of the splinter. He opens up his hand but the splinter has gone, replaced by a dried out chrysanthemum. He stares at it, shocked.

'I wanted money, I was broke. But no, you turned up drunk saying you loved me.' Helen shakes, recollecting the scene. 'You had to keep putting your arm around me.' She brushes at her shoulders, recapturing the moment. 'You made me feel –'

Philip erupts to his feet. His chair squeals, the chrysanthemum falls from his hand and lands on the edge of the table, disintegrating into a black ash.

'Fuck you! Do you hear me? Fuck you!' he shouts.

Helen watches his every move.

He backs away from the table, drawn to the sound of laughter coming from the garden. He turns away and approaches the kitchen window, feeling her animosity boring into the back of his head. Holding the rim of the kitchen sink he steadies himself for a moment.

'What are you waiting for?' Helen asks.

Philip's legs feel like jelly as he peers out the window, seeing Michelle as an eight-year-old, playing catch with a young military man adorned in metals.

Helen sighs. 'Philip, come on. Steve was an average solider, no war hero. Stop exaggerating everything. Five years and then he was out of there.' She opens her packet of cigarettes and takes out another. 'Mind you, still more than *your* father,' she mutters under her breath.

'That was different, he was too old.' Philip's unable to take his eyes away from Michelle. 'Besides the aluminium factory was important in the war effort, everyone had to do their bit.'

Helen places the cigarette in her mouth. 'I know about your father's breakdown when your mother left. Then you were taken into care, fostered out, one family after another.' A satisfying smirk holds her face. 'Thought he would come for you.' The cigarette lights up, unaided. She sucks back its toxic vapour, thick and menacing. 'Even thought your mother would come back didn't you?'

Philip keeps his back to her, not wanting her to see his anger.

'Seems a good man, Michelle's dad. Three kids, still married, a self-employed chippy.' She mulls over what she has said. 'His eldest lad married a few months ago. I could go on but you know all this, don't you? Every bit of information you've collected and kept.'

Philip wants to run out into the garden and hold Michelle but suddenly she stops playing. Her smile broadens, not at her father but to someone else in the garden, but he can't quite see them from the kitchen window. Precariously he leans over the kitchen sink placing his head against the window to get a better look, but then he pulls back, ashamed at his obsessive prying.

'What were you trying to find out? How to be a good dad?'

He glances to Helen, his top lip curled to a snarl, but her cold blankness defuses his anger. He turns to the garden again. Michelle's dad has gone and now Frances is kneeling down by her, spitting onto a tissue and rubbing dirt away from her hands. They sense they're being watched and turn to him. Philip pulls away from the window. They smile and wave to him in perfect harmony; awkwardly he lifts up a hand. He'd forgotten how beautiful Frances could look. The back door is only a few feet away, his body fills to the brim with adrenaline and the warm comfort of hope. He takes his first step in its direction but is stopped by a loud unearthly screech from the back garden.

He looks back out at Michelle and Frances. A seagull has perched on top of the swing. The gull stretches out his wings and positions itself more comfortably. It tips the angle of its head for a better look at them. Frances is talking to Michelle and they both seem oblivious of the seagull's presence. The gull slowly turns its head to Philip. Another gull descends, this time landing on the fence and is joined by another. His stomach turns over as dread fills his body. He moves away from the window and the gulls throw their heads back, beaks wide, but not a sound comes out.

'Don't be afraid,' Helen's voice is strangely serene. 'You could have escaped so many times, but you didn't want to.'

'What are you talking about?'

A wall of seagull cries erupts at a deafening volume. They flap their wings and take flight.

'Don't rush it.'

'Rush what?' Philip asks.

'You've felt it, haven't you? How pain can come with pleasure? You never truly understood it at the time.' She looks uneasily at him.

Philip sits back down at the kitchen table, mesmerised by Helen.

'I – I didn't want to sit,' Philip says.

He looks up at the kitchen ceiling. He can hear the seagulls landing and clambering on the roof tiles, but it sounds as if they're directly above him.

'Now try and move.' For the first time there's a glimmer of compassion from her but it soon disappears.

He tries but he can't. No matter how hard he focuses on his limbs they won't respond.

'You saw what you could have been through the people around you. A father, a husband, a business man.' She looks at the end of her cigarette, its ash eating up the tightly wrapped white paper, making it bubble and blister.

Philip coughs hard, spluttering on the smoke fumes.

'Things always have a nasty habit of never working out the way we plan them. Or do they? You have to wonder.' She scrutinises him. 'Frances stood by you. That's when you were free, when you were truly free. She just wanted you, nothing more, nothing else.'

The cries and the clambering of the gulls is metamorphosing into the sound of the guests shuffling around in their rooms, banging and moaning, their animosity oozing through the ceiling.

'That's what you're after, isn't it?'

Philip's own tortured anxiety is mimicked on Helen's face, but her voice carries no emotion.

'This is what it's all about.'

He swallows hard.

'The way you treated her. Think about it, Philip.'

'Please no.' He hangs his head low and sobs. The tears flow from him with such power and ferocity it takes him by surprise.

Helen looks up to the ceiling.

'They're coming for you, Philip.'

She extinguishes her cigarette, stubbing it in the middle of the ashtray, all black and brittle. He notices the other cigarette butts are all put into pairs. He counts them, eight all together. Helen grinds the last cigarette on the mound of ash. A fowl mixture of burning fumes and the putrid stench of decay hits Philip, making him want to gag. He chokes, feeling as though she's putting the cigarette out on the back of his throat. He splutters and spits the hot revolting taste onto the table. Through a watery mirage he sees thick black soot encased in saliva.

Doors are creaking opening above him, voices rising in volume as the guests' footsteps meet on the landing. A building rage unifies them, transforming them into an angry mob. Philip's throat dries, realising their footsteps are descending the stairs.

'Don't fight it. This is what you want, Philip.'

He can't move, can't turn away from her. Unable to even close his eyes.

'You thought you could control everything, a life that simple, that uncomplicated. Have you any idea of the consequences of your actions? The anguish you have sentenced their families, their friends to?'

His body has turned to stone.

'This is what you've been after all along. Isn't it Philip?'

Helen's face crunches and twists but her body stays serene and sedated.

'Stephen and Vivian Pritchard.' Her voice pounds in his head as her face morphs into the pained expressions they held before they died. The way their eyes pleaded for him to stop, reaching out in a frantic attempt to find his humanity and beg him to show them mercy.

He has to watch the tortuous sights, his eyelids locked open.

'Mike and Sally Reynolds.'

Her emotionless voice echoes in his head.

'Eddie and Cheryl Sullivan.'

He can hear the guests congregating outside the kitchen door. Momentarily he sees Helen's face, smiling at him as it continues to change.

'You don't have to worry,' Helen says. 'David and Amanda Riley...' The role call interrupts her sentence. 'They're not coming in.'

She leans forward.

'There are no doors, Philip. There are no more places you can hide any more.'

She snatches his hand, squeezing it tight.

He can feel his bowels churning over.

Leaning in closer to him, she whispers in his ear.

'They're already here, Philip. They're already here.'

The words race in a hyper frenzy through his body. He can feel the guests' breaths stuffing his lungs with their odours. The warm sensation of excrement fills his trousers. Incoherent whispers swirl around him like smoke filling up a room. They approach, getting closer and closer, until he can feel their hot breath on his face. His heart holds a beat, tears swamp his eyes, fear raising his body temperature.

'Don't be silly, Philip. They're not in the room. You know that don't you? You've always known that,' Helen says.

Something lurches and shuffles inside of him, his shirt bubbles like the cigarette end.

'They're a part of you. Can you feel them? I bet you can.'

An agonising pain spreads through his body, gnawing at his nerve endings, ripping and sabotaging his organs so they can barely function.

'You like it, don't you? That's what you've been seeking all this time. This is what it is all about. Not about me, not about us and the life we could have had, might have had if you could have sanitised it, planned it all out to a family blueprint. It's about the way you see everything, the bitterness that you won't let go of. The feeling of being cheated out of a life you thought you had a right to. You had to blame someone. Can't you blame Frances? You wish you could, don't you? It would make it easy to make sense of everything, but you can't.' She coughs, throwing thick black smoke from her mouth. 'The awful way you treated her. The one person who really loved you, believed in you. And what did you do? When she truly needed you, you let her down. Can't break the habit of a lifetime.'

Pain rages on, smashing through the metaphysical doors in his mind like an unstoppable furious mob.

'She needed you to stand by her the way she did for you. She wanted reassurance, to know she didn't have to face the cancer alone. For you to at least visit her in the hospice. She was strong, but then she never had a choice, she had to be. All she was ever worried about was how you and Michelle were coping.'

Philip feels pain in places he never knew existed. Helen's voice fades along with the room; it all smudges together stretching out in every direction. Out into infinity, yet at the same time there is an overwhelming sense of intimacy. His subconscious is being unravelled in all its intricate complex details, the same way the body can be surgically taken apart. His soul, the intangible essence that can make a stand and shout out, *This is me, this is me!* now has nowhere left to hide. His self-loathing attacks it, consuming it like acid, eating into everything he ever knew, ever felt, ever touched.

The kitchen's gone from his memory. The guesthouse, the esplanade, the beach, even the bay itself has been dissolved into nothingness. There are no more memories of Frances, no snippets of her voice, the scent of her body when she was close, her smile that could put him at ease when things got to him – they've all gone. Memories of Michelle, her childhood, his hopes and fears pinned on her youth and adulthood are no more. His past is dissolving – his mum, dad, the foster homes, all taken from him.

He's unable to see where his life began any more, how it went wrong, how he could fix it. There are no more *if onlys* or *what ifs* to contend with. No more attempts at breaking the code of life's bigger picture, deciphering setbacks as hidden allies to find a comfort in the set plan of fate. He stares into his unstoppable self-loathing. He can feel it holding every fibre, every molecule of his body, poised, about to unleash its unrepentant bitterness on him. He can see it in all its powerful glory. All the years he has fed, sheltered and kept it safe from misinterpretation. He stares in awe of its presence, as its sheer scale towers over him.

But all he can do is smile.

Calmly smile.

THE END

Forthcoming novel

SHINE

M J Freegard

Daniel's life is changing, opportunities are coming his way. His one-man-band graphic design agency is being sub-contracted to do a brand refresh for one of the UK's biggest supermarkets, Essentials. He'll be working for his old university friend Ed, who runs a high profile marketing consultancy. But why him? Why did Ed refuse to take *no* for an answer? Is this what's troubling him, or is there something else? Perhaps he still feels guilty about the affair he had with Ed's wife Jen, back when they were dating at university. What if seeing her again stirs up feelings he never really laid to rest?

As the team arrives for the marketing meeting, none of them could have ever imagined that the next forty-eight hours will push them to their psychological limits. That the building will be cordoned off by armed police with orders to shoot to kill anyone who tries to leave. They'll have to watch as one by one they fall victim to an illness that holds them in a tormented coma as their bodies hurtle towards self-destruction. In the paranoid intensity they will be faced with the question, can one man change the course of humanity, offering new hope and an insight into the eternal mystery, is there life after death?

And to their amazement, Daniel's presence will have the ability to provide the answer…